SHEET MUSIC

By M. J. Rose

Fiction
In Fidelity
Lip Service
Flesh Tones

Nonfiction
How to Publish and Promote Online
(with Angela Adair-Hoy)
Buzz Your Book
(with Doug Clegg)

SHEET MUSIC

M.J. Rose

BALLANTINE BOOKS • NEW YORK

A Ballantine Book
Published by The Random House Ballantine Publishing Group
Copyright © 2003 by Melisse Shapiro

Grateful acknowledgment is made to HarperCollins Publishers Inc. and Jane Hirshfield for permission to reprint "For Horses, Horseflies" from *Given Sugar, Given Salt* by Jane Hirshfield. Copyright © 2001 by Jane Hirshfield. Reprinted by permission of HarperCollins Publishers Inc. and Jane Hirshfield.

www.ballantinebooks.com

Library of Congress Cataloging-in-Publication Data

Rose, M. J., 1953–
Sheet music / M.J. Rose.— 1st ed.
p. cm.
1. Women journalists—Fiction. 2. Women composers—Fiction. 3. Missing persons—Fiction. I. Title.

PS3568.O76386 S48 2003
813'.54—dc21
2002034470

ISBN 0-345-45106-6

Book design by Jaime Putorti

Manufactured in the United States of America

First Edition: May 2003

10 9 8 7 6 5 4 3 2 1

In memory of my mother.
And for my sister.

FOR HORSES, HORSEFLIES

We know nothing of the lives of others.
Under the surface, what strange desires,
what rages, weaknesses, fears.

Sometimes it breaks into the daily papers
and we shake our heads in wonder—
"Who would behave in such a way?" we ask.

Unspoken the thought, "Let me not be tested."
Unspoken the thought, "Let me not be known."

Under the surface, something that whispers,
"Anything can be done."

For horses, horseflies. For humans, shame.

   —JANE HIRSHFIELD, FROM *GIVEN SUGAR, GIVEN SALT*

PART I

Biography, usually so false to its office, does here for once perform for us some of the work of fiction, reminding us, that is, of the truly mingled tissue of man's nature, and how huge faults and shining virtues cohabit and persevere in the same character.

—George H. Lewes, *Life of Goethe*

ONE

HE IS ADDICTED TO a certain look of pleasure I bestow upon him when he brings me treats. And so he makes an effort with our postcoital feasts. He knows I am always hungry. He doesn't know that, no matter what I eat, I am never full.

Tonight after we make love he brings out a china white plate of thin slices of apple and a pot of honey from Provence.

Apples remind me of home, a place that exists nowhere but in memory. Closing my eyes, I get closer to the reminiscences: to see and feel, smell and taste that past.

He thinks my contented sigh is for him.

Doesn't he know it's dangerous to make assumptions?

IN THE FALL, MY MOTHER would take me upstate to an orchard to get *real* apples—not the mealy substitutes sold in the supermarkets. Those, she explained, were only good for applesauce. "Eating bad fruit is a sin, a waste of a meal. And there are too many wonderful meals to waste even one. Only fresh food, and only in its season," she advised.

Together we baked apple pies, apple turnovers, tartes tatins, apple cobblers, and my favorite—Pauline Pagett's own invention— Apple Humpty Dumplings.

For weeks after visiting the orchard, our Greenwich Village apartment was redolent with the scent of the fruit.

I'd play a game with Maddy, my older sister, who didn't cook back then, making her sniff the air and guess, based on the cinnamon and nutmeg, or the vanilla and butter, what dessert we would be having that night . . .

"JUSTINE?"

He pulls me back. To Paris. To the night. To his bed. I watch him slather another slice of apple with honey, and instead of handing it to me, he holds it to my mouth.

It is easier to be in this present than in that past.

My lips close over the firm flesh. I bite down. Smell lavender. Feel sunshine. Taste a combination of tart and sweet. Hear the crisp snap. I try to forget about remembering.

He offers more fruit.

The shining look of thanks I fix on him draws him nearer. He is unaware that he is moving closer, as close as he can get.

I chew.

He listens. "I love the sounds you make when you eat my food."

Taking another bite, I lean closer to his ear.

He smiles and licks his own lips.

I feel the rush of power. When did I learn that the easiest way to be in control is to give it up? It doesn't matter. All that is important is how well my pretense of submission manages to get me what I need. With people I interview. With editors I work for. With lovers. Though I seem to give up control and let the others set the course, I can still navigate.

From the bedside table he lifts the balloon of Calvados, swirls the liquid, takes a sip, and then holds the glass out for me to drink. The scent floats up and, for a moment, that is all there is. The aroma of apples, the sting of brandy, the burn at the back of my throat.

Leaning forward, he licks my lips, tasting them.

I shut my eyes.

This is how he seduces me—with food and drink—with tastes and with tasting. And my gift back is to try to show him how I delight in him. Knowing this makes him appreciate himself even more.

Our bond is not one of emotion but of common need. This tremulous, fleeting feeling is why we are willing to go through these charades. We manipulate and call it romance. We lust and call it love and then pretend it will save the world.

I am not going to call anyone's bluff; I know better. Romantic love doesn't rescue, it doesn't resolve. At best it's a buffer between levels of loneliness. Oh, I suppose it's better to have than to have not, but as an eternal quest? Not worth my time.

I've seen the remnants of those searches and the residue of that kind of love when, as it must, it cools and calms.

Henri refills his glass with two more inches of Calvados, drinks from it, and then holds it again to my lips. This time he tips it too far: a trickle of the brandy slides down my chin. He grins, suggesting he's done this on purpose so that he can do what he does next—follow the path of the liquor with his tongue as it runs down my neck and onto my breast.

My head falls back against the pillow; his head falls forward against my chest. My fingers play with the blond curls that tickle my skin.

Suddenly the sharp smell of cocoa beans wafts in on the air.

"Stay there. When I tell you, close your eyes and open your mouth. I want you to taste it before you see it," he says as he gets up.

Grabbing the glass of brandy, he takes it with him as he pads toward the kitchen, leaving his robe on the end of the bed.

He is modest when he's sober, but after a few glasses of wine or a few inches of brandy, he relaxes into his nakedness. In this gap—between who he is and who he becomes—an *other* emerges who keeps me interested.

IN MY WORK, AS A journalist, I have permission to search for these hidden souls, and it is my conceit that I am good at finding and exposing them. Certainly I am dogged in the pursuit. Strip away the careful constructions and mythology we each create out of pride or delusion or even hope and there is the *other*, ready to either ruin, illuminate, or enrich the public façade.

This secret self is often the key to how someone lives, explains what choices they make, what drives them out into the world or away from engaging in it. And if I do my job well and with passion, when you read my profiles you will make discoveries. Sweet or foul, the *other* fascinates me. By uncovering what individuates us, we grope toward an understanding of those we know and, ultimately, ourselves.

I'm not sure it's always a good thing, but understanding that people have *others* secreted away keeps me from trusting my first impressions of anyone. And not just first impressions. I have to know someone for a long time before I take any personal chances. *Others* can destroy relationships or build them, ruin friendships or cement them, separate fathers and daughters, bring mothers and sons together.

Others do damage or make repairs. Define our humanity. Or inhumanity.

As for Henri, he has hidden his *other* self from me longer than most and the search is what has kept me here. And that he feeds me.

Usually I find my own stories and choose the people I want to profile. But I first met Henri because Kurt Davis—my editor at the foreign office of the American magazine I have been writing features for since I moved to Paris—had suggested I interview Henri St. Pierre to ascertain if he was a candidate for a story about chefs who might qualify for the title—"Les Enfants Terribles of Post-Nouvelle Cuisine."

Henri St. Pierre had come out of his restaurant's kitchen that first afternoon holding a bottle of cold wine and two glasses in one hand and a plate of *pomme frites* in the other. To his offerings on the table, I added my notebook and pen.

"*Mais non.* You have to eat these while they are hot," he said, pushing away the work supplies and offering me a sizzling potato with his fingers.

I took it, ate it. Smiled. And before I could tell him how good it was, he was offering me another.

He poured us wine. Took a potato for himself, scarfed it down. Lifted one more and put it between my lips.

A bond—intimate and immediate—was forged.

A few days later I was more than a little relieved to tell Kurt that St. Pierre wasn't the right chef for the article—there wasn't a story. He was fair to his staff and welcoming to his guests.

I moved on to other interviewees, and Henri and I moved toward each other.

"You understand people who cook for a living and who live to cook," he told me one night, while offering bite-size pieces of freshly baked brioche and sections of mandarin oranges soaked in cognac.

Afterward he licked the buttery flakes from my fingers. His recipe for good sex always includes amazing food and, after a month of spending a few nights a week with him, I am now five pounds heavier, rubbed raw and satiated from the way he devours me in bed. There is no part of my body that he has not licked or tasted and no food that he has offered that has not been delicious. And yet despite that, he doesn't fill me up.

He compares the color of my hair to espresso and my skin to clotted cream. He roasts chestnuts to show me the exact shade of my eyes. And he buys different berry jams until he finds a raspberry preserve that matches my lips. He charms me, cooks for me, makes me laugh with the stories about life in a French kitchen, and treats me like a piece of ripe fruit.

In return I take him in my hand or in my mouth or inside my body and tell him how his pleasure pleasures me. I say it in the dark but with my eyes open, looking far into him, as if penetrating his soul with my eyes. He bows his head as if hearing gospel.

"Justine, close your eyes."

We have moved away from the apples and are on to the next delicacy of the night. My mouth is filled with something hot, moist, and intensely chocolate. Not a soufflé. There is more crunch to this dessert, and the center is creamy rather than breadlike.

I stick out my tongue to lick my lips, but his tongue gets there first. We kiss, chocolate flavoring the embrace.

"Umm. More," I say.

Another spoonful for me and then more brandy for him.

"I stole the recipe," he whispers as if it is a serious secret. "From André," he names his mentor and one of Paris's gastronomic treasures.

I open my mouth again, knowing how much he wants to feed me.

"I stole all his recipes," he says with a pinch of bravado as he offers another spoon of melting chocolate.

I swallow. Licking my lips. "I'm glad."

He proffers more. My lips clamp down and I suck the spoon clean.

"Smart thief," I say, watching him become erect. Again. So soon. I lean in so my thigh presses against him. It is all the encouragement he needs.

"Actually, I stole more than recipes from André."

My slow, warm sexual glow dissolves and is replaced with an adrenaline rush. This isn't the way I usually react in a man's bed, but the way I feel when I am following the trail of a story.

The fear hits. I don't want Henri to be a story. I like this man: I don't want to investigate him. Or worse, expose him.

But I can't help wanting to know more. I'm a reporter and my career has been standing still for awhile. It could benefit from a breaking story.

I don't like myself for how I'm reacting. I do not alert Henri that his lover might be leaving and a journalist rushing in. But it isn't criminal for me to listen to his bedtime confession—it can only be wrong if I take advantage of this *après-sex* repast.

I should remind him that I am a potential traitor, but I don't. I continue treading this dangerous ground. And then I feel a flutter of fear behind my chest, a familiar sensation my mother used to call *trapped butterflies.* The anxious foreboding that lodges behind your heart, warning you that there is reason to be afraid.

Despite the trapped butterflies, I don't remind Henri that I am not just a woman in his bed, but a member of the press. I can't—I am already imagining this story with my byline on it.

Keeping my voice husky, as if still under his sensual spell, I encourage him. "What else? What else did you steal?"

And as if it is just another component of the evening's seduction, he feeds me the story of how he cheated his mentor by making deals behind his back with both the food and wine purveyors, building up a fat bank account and then using it to open his own restaurant.

"First I stole his recipes, then his money, and then all his clients," the *other* in him boasts.

It has been said that journalists are immoral because they win over their subjects and then betray them. But I didn't intend or even expect this to happen. Henri St. Pierre has not been my subject for the last eight weeks. He has been my lover.

And he trusts me.

Except now he turns out to be exactly what my editor had hoped for: a bad boy.

I should be horrified by what Henri did. This new information should make me question my relationship with him. I should be leaving him because he is a thief. I should be shocked—how could he have done something so awful?—and this should lead to an argument that ends with me walking out.

But I am thirty years old and my career can use a boost. I am a good journalist, but I've never been a star reporter. People read my articles without noticing my byline. This story might change that.

So instead of disgust, I show curiosity and express admiration for his brazen ambition.

"You did that? He never knew? How clever," I say in French.

He tells me more, sharing his recipe for thievery. What it felt like, how long it took, how many hundreds of thousands of francs he accumulated.

It disturbs me that my lover is a thief, but what leaves the sour taste in my mouth is his pride in it. However, what I feel no longer matters. Before I can walk out on this man, I have to get the rest of the story.

"And André never knew, never suspected?"

Henri shakes his head. He smiles.

THE FIRST LINE OF THE story gets typed out in my mind. The lead and then the beginning paragraph. I imagine going to Kurt's office and handing him the article. I'll lean with my elbows on his desk while he reads it, nodding, smiling, excited at the coup. "Yes," he will say, "this is excellent. You've nailed it." He will rub his chin with his right hand, thinking and planning. The story will make the magazine cover, with my byline beneath it.

TWO

I WAKE UP HUNGRY. I've been dreaming about French toast—not anything I have eaten in Paris, but my mother's thickly sliced, egg-soaked challah: buttery and sweet, faintly dusted with cocoa powder. Even though I can cook, I haven't done more than boil water for the last three years, and so the recalled taste of that crisped bread is just one more poignant reminder of missing my mother.

This missing—an almost physical ache—recedes at times, but when it reappears, it is always as fresh as when first experienced. How can this be?

A year, people said, you will mourn for a year and then you'll see, it will become tolerable. They were wrong. That softening of the sadness like butter melting in a hot pan has not happened. My mourning is still rock hard, solid and cold.

Missing, the word itself lasts so long when you say it. The *s*'s do not come to a hard stop but just fade out. The word itself longs for an end.

Besides my mother, I miss the excitement of sharing secrets in the dark with my sister when we were young, and the comfort of coming home from school and finding my father singing in the kitchen when he cooked dinner on Mondays—the one night his restaurant was closed.

But things have changed. I haven't spoken to my sister or my father for three years. The most I've done is exchange basic E-mail with my sister about my apartment, which she sublet when I moved to Paris and she moved back to New York from the West Coast.

Our estrangement began the morning after the night my mother died.

WHEN I'D LEFT MY PARENTS' apartment the night before, at eleven PM, my mother was in the same half-sleep half-coma she'd been in for forty-eight hours. I had walked home to my apartment and fallen asleep, with all my clothes on, on top of the covers.

At six AM, just as I was waking up, my phone rang. At this hour? I thought, but only for a moment, and then I knew: it was going to be my father calling to tell me my mother had died.

It was. While he was sleeping on a cot beside her and my sister was sleeping in our old room down the hall and the night nurse was napping in the living room, my mother had indeed passed away between midnight and two AM.

I reached their apartment by seven and the first thing I did was head toward their bedroom. I had to see my mother one last time. To say good-bye. Or at least try to.

"Justine, she's gone," my father said in a worn voice. I stopped a few feet from the door to their room and turned to him.

"I know, Daddy." I felt sorry for him then. Despite how much I thought he'd let my mother down, his saying this had touched me.

But he wasn't lamenting her death. He was telling me that her body was gone. My mother was no longer there. The mortuary had already taken her body away. And plans had already been made to have her cremated later that morning.

"No . . . You can't . . ." My outburst brought my sister running from the living room. "You can't do that to her."

"She wanted it, Justine." My father has a strong voice and is usually talkative. And if he isn't talking, he's humming. In the restaurant kitchen he shouts orders above the noise and then walks out where the diners are and greets the regulars, regaling them with just enough lively conversation.

But that morning he barely finished his sentences and didn't speak above a whisper. He leaned against the doorway for support.

He—who always seemed so robust—seemed enfeebled by my mother's death.

"You liar," I shouted, and struck out at the air with my fists. "She never would have wanted to go without me saying good-bye."

"Justine . . . She wanted . . ." My sister's voice was solicitous.

I turned on her. "Leave me alone. Leave me alone. You stayed away so long it was embarrassing. Don't tell me what Mommy would have wanted!"

Maddy had seen her that one last time. *She and my father* had been able to say good-bye and at least begin the process that leads to letting go. *Maddy* had been there when my mother's body had been taken away

But I hadn't.

I couldn't touch my mother's hand ever again or look at her face one last time. I couldn't kiss her soft cheek or whisper to her that I loved her more than anyone I'd ever known and pretend to myself that she could still hear me.

I went into the bedroom and climbed onto their bed, which had been remade by someone—the nurse? my father? I buried my face in what would have been her pillows and I cried. I cried for so long and so hard that my father finally gave me some of the tranquilizers he had been taking for years to combat anxiety. And after a time, I fell asleep, there on the bed where my mother had been lying just hours before.

WHAT FOLLOWED WAS A two-month-long haze of pills, appointments with a therapist for grief counseling, and long bouts of weeping. During all that time, my sister—who had decided to move back to New York and was living in my parents' apartment— helped my father make so many decisions. All without my input.

When the fog finally began to lift, I discovered that, in her passive-aggressive way, Maddy had taken advantage of my mourning. Waiting for me was a pile of my mother's clothes that Maddy had decided I would want after going through them and taking her share first.

The rest had been given to charity.

And there was a box of jewelry waiting for me. A half-dozen pieces that Maddy had chosen to give me after, of course, taking her share first.

She kept using that word.

"This is your *share*, Justine. Dad and I thought you'd like her engagement ring. Grandma's engagement ring was in my share."

They were just things. They couldn't make me feel any better. But what made me feel worse was the way it had been done. Behind my back, without waiting for me, or taking me into consideration, Maddy had taken charge, done what she wanted, and my father had aided and abetted her.

I was angry with my sister. But I was furious with my father for allowing it. He should not have favored one of his daughters over the other in the aftermath of our mother's death.

Not only had he sanctioned Maddy's actions, but the last afternoon I had seen him and tried to discuss it with him, he had justified his own.

"You always had more of her, Justine. Let Maddy be. Think about what it's like for her. She's had so many more problems than you have."

"Maddy wasn't even here all this time. She was in LA. She didn't care about Mommy when she was well. She barely even made it back when Mommy got sick." The tears wet my cheeks.

My father offered outstretched arms, but I wouldn't go to him. I didn't want him to hold me.

"You are not yourself," he said.

No. Without my mother, I was not myself. And sometimes I think I am still not myself.

At that moment, I glared at my father. Immobilized on the

couch, yet wanting to flee, I wanted to leave this apartment that no longer smelled of chocolate or butter or baking. All I could feel was an awful missing. I missed having my mother by my side to fight *him*. And that missing became greater than my anger.

I didn't argue or fight with my father or sister. What good would that have done? My mother was gone. Her perfume bottles were no longer on the dresser. Her closets were empty. The herbs in the window boxes hadn't been watered; they'd shriveled and died along with her.

But she had to be somewhere, didn't she? Her soul? Her spirit?

I left New York to chase her ghost, to find her again. Or at least to find a place where I could be with my memories of her. And so twelve weeks after my mother died I moved to Paris. I have not been back to New York since. And I don't miss it.

There are, however, things I do miss . . . some that I've never even had. Like the look couples exchange when they are so in tune that they know what each other is thinking without needing words to explain. Just being held and knowing that nothing more is required—no groping or gasping or surging of sexual needs—but an embrace that is enough in itself, because the two people are in concert with each other, a commingling of something other than bodily fluids and shared yet still selfish releases.

LAST NIGHT WITH HENRI, my last night with him, was distasteful. I am a reporter, not a whore. But I came back to gather up the last crumbs of his story and brought a fine red Bordeaux and an expensive bottle of port.

He'd drunk enough of the wine while cooking to be flattered by, instead of suspicious of, my questions. He had not noticed I'd been unable to eat his food. The port went down smoothly during dessert, and when it was time to go to bed, I avoided having sex by staying just a little too long in the bathroom. he fell asleep while waiting for me.

Now, without looking at him sleeping beside me, I carefully push back the wrinkled sheets and steal into the bathroom on bare feet. Gently, I close the door. There is no need to be this quiet: he is such a heavy sleeper not even the phone disturbs him. But I don't take any chances, do not want to invite any delays. This early-morning exodus has been planned for days, and I intend to execute it with exactitude.

Turning to collect my things, I am confronted with my reflection in the mirror above the sink. On my cheek is a bright red mark—an almost perfect circle. Touching the depression with my forefinger I wonder not what has caused it (because I know it's an impression left from the ring I always wear) but at how insistent the mark is.

For the last three years I have worn my mother's engagement ring on my left middle finger but always spun around so I will never look down and see her hand instead of my own. It's enough to see the platinum band and feel the edges of the stone pressing into the flesh of my palm.

Turning from the mirror as silently as I can, I collect my makeup, a flacon of perfume, and some small bottles of other toiletries and begin to put them into my cosmetic case. One bottle falls onto the vanity and cracks open, spilling astringent on the marble countertop. The sharp, clean smell reminds me of starting over.

Picking up the pieces of glass, a shard slices my forefinger. For a moment there is nothing, then a spurt of blood. But no pain—not yet. For a few seconds there is only the shock and the sight, then the dull throb starts. Wrapping a washcloth tightly around my finger, I hold it there. For days, every time I move my finger I will feel the twinge and recall this smell in this bathroom on this morning. The blood soaks through, bright and insistent against the white cotton. It will probably leave a scar, like the crescent-shaped white mark on my right thumb—the result of an accident with a bread knife when I was eleven.

Looking for a box of bandages in the medicine cabinet, I push aside a myriad of pill bottles. Some of the labels are old and faded. People keep pills long after they expire, just as they keep spices in the rack long past when they have lost their flavor. I think of my parents' medicine cabinet. My father's pills for anxiety, bottles of them, lined up like soldiers. Protecting his equilibrium. Some—long since expired—saved, just in case.

I cover the cut. My mother always put star-studded Band-Aids on my childhood wounds. Sometimes there would be two or three on one hand, because no matter how careful I was, I was always slicing something too quickly, grabbing a pot without a pot holder, or spilling hot melted chocolate on my skin.

"Justine," she would say, "you are too impatient. You can't just grab for what you want without thinking."

BACK AND FORTH, I MOVE from the bathroom, and then from the bedroom to the living room, with the toiletries and the few items of clothing that have accumulated here in a month: a sweater, some leggings, socks, a pair of ballet slippers.

When I have my things gathered, I go to the hall closet and retrieve the shopping bag I stashed there the evening before. By now the cut is throbbing and I try to ignore it. Inside the Galeries Lafayette bag is a black nylon square. Unfolding it, I shake out the duffel to its full size, and as I do, something falls out. I need only one glimpse of the oh, so familiar pink, gold, white, and black silk to instantly travel back in time.

MY MOTHER AND I WERE in France to shoot photographs for the sixth in the series of cookbooks that chronicled our mother-and-daughter escapades in the kitchen.

When I was only six, my mother began teaching me how to cook. The lessons, recipes, and delightful little anecdotes became a book entitled *Justine Cooks*. The success of that book led to an entire series, which included *Justine Cooks Dinner*, *Justine Cooks Dessert*, *Justine Cooks French*, and *Justine Cooks Italian*. Each one was illustrated with photographs of mother and daughter buying ingredients, doing the prep work, and cooking.

In Paris to shoot *Justine Cooks French*, we had taken the day off and had been window-shopping on the Rue du Faubourg Saint

Honoré when a display of colorful Hermès silks enticed her inside
the store.

"Oh, Mommy, you have to buy it—it looks so beautiful," I said
after she had picked out one to try on.

"It's ridiculously expensive," my mother said, but she was smiling at herself in the mirror, her eyes on this scarf tied in a chic knot
around her neck.

IT PAINS ME, LOOKING AT us across the span of years,
to see us living out that afternoon and all the days after that. We had
such a wonderful trip. She was so young and beautiful, successful,
and delighted with the series. Her editor was with us, each night
taking us out to inspired restaurants, where he and my mother
would talk to the chef. I'd sip my glass of wine, even though I was
only twelve—we were in Paris—and feel so grown-up. I can see her
happiness, her delight at dinner that night with the scarf around her
neck, laughing over something. She has no idea of the future. Of
how truncated her life will be. How we will be rent apart just days
before I turn twenty-seven and she is not even fifty.

How long has her scarf been in this bag? Probably since I left
New York. Lifting the silk square to my face, I inhale and my
mother is breathed back to life.

Dreaming about her French toast and now discovering her scarf
seem portentous. Wrapping it around my neck, feeling the silk
under my chin and on the back of my neck, is like receiving a comforting embrace.

Thinking about my mother reminds me of some books I have
here at Henri's, and it is while I am standing in front of his bookshelves, checking for those that belong to me, that I hear his footsteps.

This is not how I planned it. I wanted to be all packed and ready
to go by the time Henri woke up. Just explain it simply, leave as
quickly as I can, and avoid a scene at all costs. Get out and go home
and write up the article.

"Justine?"

I turn.

His face is puffy from sleep and he's frowning as he takes it all in: my clothes piled on the couch, the books in my arms, the open duffel bag on the floor. He is a handsome man, but this morning his features are indistinct.

"*Qu'est-ce que c'est?*" He switches from his native French to slightly stilted English. "What is this all? You are . . . Are you leaving me?"

"Yes."

"Just like this? Between going to sleep last night and waking up this day, I have lost you?" He hits his head with the palm of his hand as if he is trying to smack his brain into comprehending.

"I never meant for this to happen . . ." I say, knowing I'm not really explaining anything.

"We have been good together. Why now? It is the hours I spend at the restaurant, yes?"

"Of course not. My father owns a restaurant. I understand the hours."

"Then why? Have you met someone else?"

The hardest answers fall in the gray areas between truth and lies. He will not understand if I tell him, no, but I finally know him and don't like him.

Nor will he understand if I tell him, yes, there is always someone else, even if I have yet to meet him.

"You have never acted crazy, but how can it be that I wake up one day and suddenly do not know you? Who is this person who can just walk out?"

"It's just . . . just the right time to go," I say softly as I put the books in the duffel bag.

"You must give me a reason. It is only just."

I fold my nightgown, and then hold it against my chest. A dog barks outside the window.

"*Pourquoi?*"

While I try to come up with something to say, he asks, "What about the way we are in bed together?"

I wince. This is not the first time a man has assumed that the quality of our sex life would prohibit me from breaking off the relationship.

But he does not wait for my response. "I do not understand. If nothing wrong has happened between us, then why are you leaving?"

There is nothing I can tell him without endangering the story that Kurt is already waiting for. Salivating over.

My hand shakes as I zip the duffel bag. The metal meshing sets him off and his confusion turns to angry indignation. I have to get out of here.

As I lift the bag, he throws words at me.

"This is another side to you. An ugly side." His ire escorts me to the entryway. "Yesterday one way, and today . . . today . . . I want to know why."

Yes I admit I haven't been honest with this man, and that bothers me, but not enough to stop and explain. What he has done is far worse.

I open the door to the courtyard, startling a pigeon into taking flight. The late November air is crisp. Like apples.

Henri's attack follows me as I rush toward the street exit. "How did you become such a . . . a . . ." He searches for the right word as I open the door. Just as I am about to step over the threshold, he shouts out over the drone of the traffic: "How did you become such a heartless bitch?"

It is a phrase from an American movie we had rented the week before.

The answer: I watched my mother when I was growing up. I watched her love someone too much and never complain when she got so little back. I learned not to be like her.

THREE

M Y   M O T H E R   A L W A Y S   told me not to run so fast. Usually I do race up the stairs to my apartment, but saddled with the duffel bag I move slowly this morning. The bag, filled with the detritus of this last aborted love affair, bangs against my shin and strains my arm.

I climb to the rhythm of the syllables of the curse that Henri threw at me.

Am I unfeeling?

Well, I am thirty years old and have never known unrequited love.

My fingers cramp.

And I have never wanted a man more than he has wanted me. What does that say about me?

My left ankle throbs from being hit by the bag.

All I know of passion is a sudden slickness and deep clenching between my legs. The ache of lust is as familiar as heartache is foreign, and while I have cried out in the throes of an orgasm, I have never cried myself to sleep over a man.

Climbing higher, I wonder—and it seems as if it is the first time I have ever wondered it—if there is something monstrous about me: I have never seriously fallen in love and it has never mattered to me. In fact, I've been anti-love and claimed it was for philosophical reasons.

And when someone I might have cared about—a musician I

knew for a while before my mother died—did offer a real relation-ship, I chose instead to run away. It was easier to leave him than to chance connecting.

But can it be that I have not connected or ever really loved a man because I am without heart?

It is not the question that stops me and takes my breath away—but the answer I want to give.

Until now, standing here on the worn stone steps, I'd always thought it was a blessing that I'd never longed for any man the way my mother longed for my father.

A sheen coats my face. My hair hits just below my chin but is long enough in the back to stick to my neck. If my hands were free, I would lift my hair up so the air might cool my skin.

With every step I search for another word to describe what it is I feel: sorrow? grief?

This is my game—playing thesaurus with my feelings—and by doing so dissipating their power.

Loneliness?

All these have become familiar to me since my mother died, but today I feel they are more acute. If there is an escape, I have not even come close to finding it.

Isolation?

I WAS EIGHT THE SUMMER I invented the game. We had been visiting friends in the country and were driving home. The air-conditioning was broken, and the inside of the car was sti-fling, despite the open windows. A breeze, smelling faintly of gaso-line, didn't offer relief.

Small dark curls—the same deep auburn as mine—stuck to my mother's damp skin, and my father's wrinkled shirt collar was wet with perspiration. My older sister, Maddy, slumped on the backseat beside me, asleep.

That afternoon in the car my fingers were sticky from the caramel-coated popcorn I'd been eating, and one by one I licked each finger and then wiped them off on my skirt.

My mother had not spoken to my father for what seemed a long time. For a while he had continued to try to cajole her into talking, but finally had given up, and now their silence hung heavy as the humidity in the air. It was not the first time I'd had to listen to my mother's silence. It was also how she punished me when she was angry.

I examined my hands, turning them palm side up and then down. My fingers were still sticky. Spreading them wide apart and slowly closing them, watching the V disappear, I promised myself that as soon as all my fingers were touching, my parents would be talking again and the awful silence would end.

I was trying to think of something—anything—except how the quiet made the butterfly flutter behind my heart. I wanted to tell my mother how the feeling was back and how bad it felt inside when they were so quiet with each other. But what was the right word to describe it? I tried one after another, like choosing which blouse to wear.

The process of thinking about what word described my feeling took my mind off the feeling.

After that I played the game all the time. As my vocabulary improved, my teachers and mother praised me. I wasn't sure my father noticed until he came home one night with an unexpected gift.

The box was so big and heavy I couldn't even lift it without him helping, but I managed to rip off the paper by myself.

It was a book—but not like any other book I'd ever had.

The dictionary was leather bound with gold embossed letters on the cover, and inside my father had written:

To my little wordsmith—
With Love,
Daddy

I was fairly sure I knew what the word meant, but "wordsmith" was still the first entry I looked up, and when I read the definition I felt so proud.

Words would give me power—they were going to save me.

And so far they had. But not now. Not today. Not the words Henri had said or the ones I had yet to write.

REACHING THE THIRD-FLOOR LANDING, I hear my cell phone ring. The display shows my friend Fiona's number.

Putting down the bag, I sit on a cold step and take the call. A hand finally free, I brush off the hair plastered to the back of my neck. The air feels cool.

"Did Henri go mad? Are you all right? Are you home?"

"Yes and yes. Well, mostly yes. I'm not completely home—I'm on the steps."

"Call me back when you get inside."

"No, this bag is so heavy. I don't mind sitting here a minute. I still have two flights to go."

"You should have let me come and help you."

"I'm fine."

"So how did he take it?" Fiona asks.

"How did he take it? He didn't understand."

"Can you blame him?"

"No, of course not. Especially since I couldn't explain why I was leaving."

"No, it certainly wouldn't do for you to have told him you were leaving him and going home, sitting down at your computer, and writing up his crime."

"No."

"But even if you hadn't found his dirty little secret, you still would have left him eventually. I've watched you for the last three years. You get to a point with every man when you trade him in. You come right up to the moment you might actually find some real intimacy, and then you run." Fiona states all this matter-of-factly in her very proper British accent.

"I would like nothing more than to find someone I don't have to run from—or trade in, as you so brutally put it. Don't you think I envy you and Kurt?"

"I'm not so sure. You don't trust love at all. Be honest, you think all marriages are doomed."

"Not yours."

"Knew you'd say that. So do you want to meet me for lunch?" Fiona asks.

"Can't. I have an appointment with Vincent Bruzio."

"Ah, yes . . . the Italian screenwriter." Fiona laughs. "Not wasting any time, are you?"

"And you are who? Certainly not my friend with a comment like that."

"Just because I'm your chum doesn't mean I'm blind to your— what shall we call them?—habits. Justine, you mine your assignments looking for assignations."

"How can you say that? What if Kurt heard you?"

"I'm by myself in the car."

"But what if you were home?"

"If I were home, I wouldn't have said it."

"Sometimes, Fiona, I wish you weren't married to my editor. You know, it's his fault that I even met Henri. And I never would have gone out with him if there was any chance there was a story. But there wasn't a story. I'm sorry it turned out like this . . ."

"You do sound a bit mournful. But not to worry. You are a dandelion. A light wind, some rain, a half hour of sun, and you take root somewhere else. You thrive on it. You don't mind moving on. Not with men—or the stories you cover."

I hear the echo of Henri calling out his indictment again.

"But you're good at what you do because you don't mind sticking with something," I tell Fiona.

"Do you mean my marriage, or the Ladies?"

"I guess both—but right now I'm more impressed that you have been able to spend the last three years researching and writing a book about three Victorian writers."

"That's because you need to be able to talk to the people you write about. You need to look at them and get inside their heads and undress them. You can't do that with someone long dead." Fiona pauses. "Oh, no," she adds.

"What?"

"I think I just said there's something you can't do. Now you'll feel compelled to prove you can."

"That's what my mother used to say." I touch the scarf around my neck. "Listen, these stairs are getting cold. I'll call you later."

ON THE FIFTH AND FINAL landing, I let the bag down and look out the stairwell window. The glass is old and wavy, and the paint on the trim has long since chipped off the frame. Leaning on the sill, I look out at the vista.

This is a ritual I perform every day when I come home. In a life with few constants, the smallest ones provide a sense of harmony.

I like this view better than the one from inside the apartment. Glancing over the rooftops from here—where pigeons roost—I see all the way to the river. Now, watching a lone tourist boat heading east on the Seine beneath a sky that is all rain clouds, the tears start.

No, it's not about leaving Henri or the lack of love in my life, but about those wide-eyed visitors watching the city pass by as they listen to "La Vie en Rose" on the boat's loudspeaker.

Tourists come to Paris expecting so much. To be delighted and entertained and charmed—if not with their traveling companion or a stranger they will meet at a café, then at least with the city itself: the ancient buildings, the graceful bridges, the church spires.

Their innocence makes me weep. Each one of them is a child the way I was when I saw these sights the first time with my mother, eighteen years ago. The two of us hung on the boat's railing, listened to the lilting music, and ingested the city, gulping it in. Wetting our parched souls with it.

I have never attempted to settle down with a man, but I have settled down with Paris.

The boat disappears from view.

Since moving here, I have not strayed from this city. Not even been tempted. I have been more faithful to cold stone architecture, tree-lined streets, bread and cheese and wine, churches and gardens and markets than to any man.

FOUR

O N   T H E   F L O O R by Kurt's desk is a large stack of magazines with Henri St. Pierre's photo on the cover: the last face I want to see. He wears a toque and chef's coat and is standing by the entrance to his restaurant: a portrait of a criminal who does not yet know he has been found out.

My name is also on the cover of the magazine, the byline I've been chasing so long. It makes me smile, despite the sour taste I get looking upon Henri's face.

Kurt leans against the window ledge, finishing a phone call. Though I try to look elsewhere, my eyes return to St. Pierre. And then my name.

Fiona has told me that the article has been getting a lot of buzz.

I have not told her—or anyone else—about the late-night hang-ups I've been getting on my phone since the story broke or the threatening E-mail St. Pierre sent. Or the anxiety that burns in me after I hear from him.

You really are a heartless bitch, aren't you? Well, I can be just as heartless, *ma chérie*. This is something you will soon have the pleasure of discovering.

I picture him, late at night, an almost empty bottle of red wine by his elbow, pecking out the letters on his keyboard as he composes the warning.

Kurt hangs up the phone, startling me. I'm expecting my editor has summoned me to give me the go-ahead on a new assignment I pitched a few days ago, perhaps even to offer more compliments on the St. Pierre story. But he is frowning.

"Did you hear André Mann filed a lawsuit against St. Pierre three days ago?"

I nod.

"The wine merchants and wholesalers named in your story are all being investigated. And we are getting all the credit for breaking the story."

Considering what he is telling me, Kurt should look pleased, but he doesn't. He speaks slowly, softly, making a concerted effort at control. A butterfly takes wing inside my rib cage. "That's all good, isn't it?" I stammer.

"Yes, that is all good. Less than good, however, is that the magazine—and you—have also been named in a lawsuit: Henri St. Pierre is suing us."

The morning sun shines through the window right into my eyes. I blink. It is cold outside—and here in the office too—but in this spot of sun there is a bit more warmth. My anxiety bubbles up to the surface. "What do you mean suing us? Me? I've never been sued. Nothing was incorrectly reported."

"St. Pierre isn't suing for defamation." Kurt thrusts a sheaf of papers at me. I look at them, but the words are blurry after looking into the sun. When the letters finally come into focus and make words, they don't make sense.

"Invasion of privacy?"

"It's not what you wrote he is questioning, but your right to write it. He's claiming it was all off the record."

My words fly. "St. Pierre's the thief. How dare he accuse me? No. No. Nothing was off the record." The E-mail threat. Payback time. The anxiety starts to boil.

"That's what I expected you to say," Kurt says, sounding, at last, relieved.

"Nothing was off the record." I may sound confident, but I'm shivering. Can Kurt see my hands trembling? Involuntarily, I glance again at the magazine cover at my feet. I want to kick the stack and see St. Pierre fall. Instead I recall him naked on the edge of the bed, late at night, feeding me slices of crisp apple dipped in honey washed down by sips of Calvados.

"He's got balls," Kurt says. "André Mann is one of France's most beloved chefs. What did St. Pierre expect to happen once everyone discovered how he'd cheated his own mentor? We can't be held responsible because his business is down or that his future business will suffer. This is the last act of a desperate man. He knows what it's going to be like from now on. He's been exposed. What he did was criminal. A story like this lingers."

Like the stench of rancid oil.

Through the window behind Kurt the sky is clear. No relief from the brightness. The clouds inside me roll in. A pigeon sweeps past. In the far distance is the top of the ubiquitous Eiffel Tower. We will be finished talking in a few minutes, and then I will be able to get up and go downstairs and out of the building and feel the cold air on my face. I'll drink huge gulps of it—like ice water—and I will walk. I will walk all the way home, across the bridge, over the Seine, into the heart of St. Germain, where I will stop at the corner café and order some espresso. No one there will pay any special attention to me; they will not know that I was walking on a tightrope, from which I have slipped.

Kurt clears his throat. The skin is tight around his eyes. He looks as if he has eaten something that does not agree with him. "There is one last charming bit," he says.

"Yes?"

"In the suit, St. Pierre claims you seduced him to get the story. Desperate, deplorable man."

I try not to move. I cannot afford to react. I know from being on

the other side how reporters pick up on the slightest signs and signals, and I can't give Kurt any clues.

Smile—lie—and leave.

So I blurred the lines. We all blur lines when we are following
stories. But I have a good reputation. I have won awards. It will be
St. Pierre's word against mine. And he is a criminal. I know I did not
seduce him to get the story, and he knew all along that I was a reporter. He handed it to me—another *amuse-bouche* offered in the
ongoing affair.

"You need to make an appointment with our attorneys," Kurt
says. "They want you to bring your notes, your datebook, and any
tapes you made of your conversations with him."

Holding on to my mother-of-pearl pen, I screw and unscrew the
cap. The nacre is cool and my skin is slightly damp and the cap
slips out of my fingers, falls on the floor, rolls under Kurt's desk, and
disappears. I fight to stay in control, holding back my panic better
than I held on to the pen. I know how to do this, I tell myself, how
to swallow what I'm feeling and hide it from Kurt so he won't
know—so no one will know.

I get down on the floor. The magazines are in my way. I push
them aside, and St. Pierre—multiple images of him—finally spills
across the floor. "My pen . . . it's just under your desk." Damn, my
voice is breaking.

Cap in hand I get up and face Kurt.

I have worked for him for three years. He knows me. Knows my
writing and how to edit it and what matters to me. He's fought to
keep my stories in the magazine when there were budget cuts because he believes in my portraits and says I expose moments that
matter, of insight, or grace, or a fall from grace. I am his wife's closest friend. I have gone on trips with them, he has seen me too late
at night, too early in the morning. Kurt is also an excellent inves-
tigative reporter. He can read my face.

And sadly, I can read his.

"My very first editor told me if you want to cover the circus,
don't fuck the elephants," he says.

What can I say? There are rules and I have broken one. Even though I did not set out to steal St. Pierre's story out from under him, that is what I did. Even though it was backward of how Kurt thinks it happened, I fucked the elephant and now there will be hell to pay.

FIVE

I T I S L I G H T L Y snowing. Inside Café de
Flore, Fiona and I are upstairs sitting in a booth.
She orders espressos while I trace a crease in the
worn leather seat with my forefinger. It's cold, even for February.
Even with the heat on in here, there's a chill. I've kept my coat
around my shoulders and now I smell the damp wool. Rubbing my
hands together, I think about putting my gloves back on.

"The coffee will warm you," Fiona says.

I nod.

"How long has it been since you've left your apartment?"

I shrug.

But she knows that in the last five weeks since the St. Pierre
story broke, there were more days I stayed in bed than got out of it.
Too many times she has called and woken me late in the afternoon.

"How long since you've eaten a whole meal?"

"I've eaten, Fiona. Do I look like I'm starving?"

"I asked when was the last time you had a 'whole meal.' Not
snacks. Not wine. Not oranges and cheese and bread with butter."

An hour ago, Fiona—tired of not being able to get me on the
phone—had just shown up, knocked on the door and insisted I let
her in.

"When you were showering—for what, the first time in a

week?—I inspected your refrigerator and the cabinets. I know what you are living on. I'm worried about you."

She is looking at me as if I am a Dresden figurine that needs to be dusted . . . but is too fragile to be touched.

The waiter arrives with a tray and puts down the two small cups of coffee and two glasses of water.

"You can't hide. What you did isn't half as bad as what Henri St. Pierre did. No one cares that you slept with him—you are *Le Journaliste Le Hot* at the moment."

"No one cares?"

"Well . . . other than a few people at the magazine, no. No one cares."

"Great—that makes me what? The most successful failure I know?" I laugh as if all this really is fine and that it will pass. I cannot even tell her how bad it is: how I can't get any work at all, how I haven't for weeks. I don't want Kurt to hear I'm desperate.

Fiona pulls a pack of Gauloises from her coat pocket, shakes one out, and lights it. I usually don't smoke, but I hold out my hand.

She offers the pack and the lighter. I light a cigarette and inhale. The harsh smoke is delicious. I inhale again rather than speak, swallowing words with the smoke. I do not want to tell her that between legal fees and my rent, I've used up more than half my savings. Or that her husband will not take my phone calls. That he has his assistant give me pathetic blurbs to write—front-of-the-book pieces that any kid right out of J school could handle. And that my rate per word has been reduced from dollars to cents.

If Kurt wants to tell her, that is one thing, but I will not offer up any of these things because no matter how good a friend she is, my editor is her husband. I want neither to invite her sympathy nor to ask her to take sides.

"I've tried to pull some strings, even offered Kurt bribes." Fiona stubs out one cigarette, reaches for another.

"I hope you two have not fought over me."

"I know: you think fighting is bad. But I would guess you're secretly hoping I'm withholding food and sex and wine until he relents."

We both force laughs, and then as the hollow sound dissipates, she leans forward and puts her hand on my arm. "I'm worried about you," she repeats.

This old café—mentioned in Hemingway's *A Moveable Feast*—is still frequented by writers and publishers who work in the neighborhood, like Fiona's book editor, who now stops by our table to say hello.

"Zeline, this is Justine Pagett."

Zeline tilts her head just slightly as she stares a bit too intently at me. And then there is a look of recognition. That "Ah, yes." Until recently the French never looked at me that way because the *Justine Cooks* series was never sold here. But back in America, all too often, when I was introduced to a woman near my age, there would be that hesitation, and tilt of her head. My name rang a bell. I looked vaguely familiar. Could I be the little girl from the cookbooks?

One of the nicer things about living in Paris for the last three years has been that few people recognize my name when they hear it. No one recounts her fond memories about the Elephant Cookies (peanut butter) that she baked with her mother from our book. And no tells me how delicious Justine's Favorite Chocolate Soup is. Or how they, too, made Academy Award Candy the afternoon of the Oscars.

But since the St. Pierre story broke, the few times I have gone out I have been seeing the look again. Except now it means: Ah, yes, I've heard about you. You seduced Henri St. Pierre to get his story and wrote about it, didn't you?

As curious as people are about celebrities' secrets, they are also uncomfortable when confronted with such irrefutable proof of the *other* self: the criminal, the liar, the psychotic personality that had them fooled.

As much as they lose respect for the person being written about, in this case St. Pierre, the author is tainted too. As if by being able to unearth the concealed offenses, we also must be suspect.

It takes one to know one, doesn't it?

Zeline goes back to her own table.

"I'm sorry. Does everyone look at you like that now?" Fiona asks. I nod.

"People will forget about it just as soon as there's something else to—"

"But will Kurt forget about it?" I let it slip out.

Fiona plays with her spoon and catches the overhead light in the silver oval. I don't like being her focus or the object of her sympathy. "Fiona, please. Don't worry about me. I'll find another great story. I'll bring someone back from the dead if that's what it takes to get an exclusive lined up."

Outside it has begun to snow more heavily and a corps of colorful umbrellas pops open. "Picasso. Or Monroe. No. I know. John Lennon. That should get Kurt—or any other editor—to take my call."

Fiona laughs, and I with her, a little less forced this time. Beneath my laugh is the first flicker of an idea, like an umbrella suddenly popping open.

"If I *could* get a significant exclusive . . . Kurt would have no choice, would he?"

Fiona nods.

"Who would be big enough?" I ask.

"We are about to engage in an orgy of networking," she declares.

I frown. "Considering the situation, can't you use a different word?"

Around us tables empty and fill up again, but the list we are working on never grows past three names. And it is the last name on the list—the composer and conductor Sophie DeLyon—that Fiona says will interest Kurt the most.

"I think either of the other two are more likely," I insist.

"Why are you resisting DeLyon? I really think she's the one to tempt Kurt."

"It's a mistake. I shouldn't have suggested her."

"But you said you know her son-in-law?"

"I knew her *ex*-son-in-law. He was also her protégé. His name is Austen Bell. He's a musician in New York, or at least he was . . ." I sip my second espresso, but by now it's cold and I push the cup and saucer away.

"What is it?"

I shake my head as if this will stop her. But of course it doesn't, and I'm sorry I even have brought up his name.

"What *is* it?" she repeats. "You know I'll get it out of you eventually, so save yourself the fight."

"All right. He reminds me of a time I don't want to remember, that's all. I met him a few months before I found out my mother was sick and knew him the whole time she was dying.

"He was kind to me, but . . . even saying his name brings back that last spring and summer. My sister was acting out and drinking and living in LA, almost never home. My father was   It doesn't matter now."

"Did you date Austen Bell?"

I nod.

WE ARE IN BED.

A concerto he has written and performed plays on the stereo. He has not been writing music for the last two years, he says; all his time is taken up with performing. But something in the way he says it—a melancholy lilt to his words—makes me wonder if that's the only reason. And so I have insisted, demanded after his first no, that he let me hear some of his original work.

Austen Bell's compositions—featuring him on the cello—fill his apartment like warm yellow light. The music envelops me. Changes the atmosphere. I keep my arms by my sides, my hands still; I shut my eyes. I want to depress all my other senses so I can absorb the music and take it—like the sun—into my pores.

Now there are two things Austen Bell can offer that allow me to forget about my mother's illness: sex *and* music. And that makes him almost magic. So I crave his bed and beg him to play his compositions over and over.

At first, the time I spent with him was more about where I was not than where I was. I was not at my mother's deathbed.

But that began to change.

Yes, being with Austen was an escape from the illness eating my mother alive. When I was with him, I didn't speak as much as listen. I didn't think in words as much as feel what the music evoked. I didn't eat or drink much except for his body and his touch.

But this has grown into something about the two of us. The way we are with each other: generous, curious. Not lonely.

Austen orchestrates our interludes so that his lovemaking and his music take me on restorative journeys. The music he plays moves us into a world that completes itself. He creates circles, wrapping his arms around his cello and then later around me.

Morning light pours through the wide windows, making his dark eyes glitter. He smiles. There is always music playing in the background. I listen, and he shows his delight that I—who did not hear before—do now.

And then his warm skin and beautiful bones press up against me as he leans in, kissing me behind my ear. It tickles. I laugh.

"You had virgin ears when I met you," he whispers as he moves my hair away from my neck and kisses me more.

"Other men care about how many previous lovers a woman has," I say. "You care that you were the first man to make me really hear music."

"How long did it last? Was it serious?" Fiona asks. When did she order more coffee? When did the waiter bring it and put it down in front of me?

• • •

IT HAS BEEN TWELVE WEEKS since my mother has died.

We have been sitting in a car at the airport for the last twenty minutes. This is one of the few times I have been with Austen when there has not been music playing. Not a cello in sight. Replacing its bulky case on the backseat is my suitcase and computer bag.

"You can't turn your mother into a saint, Justine." His look says more: it says, I know this from experience. There is a long pause. The roar of a jet fills the silence. We have spent so much time in his apartment over the last months that I am used to our days and nights being accompanied by music—not noise. Ugly sounds do not make sense in his presence.

He continues: "I had thought Sophie DeLyon was a saint, and it took me years to—"

"No, it's not the same," I interrupt. "Sophie DeLyon is alive."

His dark eyes narrow, and his eyebrows almost meet. The fair skin on his high cheekbones reddens. And his features—so refined and graceful—pinch in anger and make him look older.

"Damn. Why is it so hard for you to let me help?" he asks.

"You can't help me get over my mother's death."

"How do you know if you won't listen to me, if you won't talk to me about it."

"Just let me go. I have to go and be alone. Be without her and on my own. Just for a while."

His strong fingers grip my wrist so hard it hurts. He is using more strength than when he holds the neck of the cello; I know this because his veins are popping and they don't when he plays.

"Running away won't protect you. What are you so afraid of feeling?"

I pull my hand away. There are red marks from his fingers. "I'm not running away."

Even though he is looking at me with his inscrutable black eyes, I know that he doesn't believe me.

An hour later, flying away in a silver plane, I see the red marks on my wrist have disappeared. For a reason I can't understand, this makes me sad.

I DON'T WANT TO THINK about Austen Bell any more than I want to think about my sister or my father. They are all from a time that I've put away, like the Hermès scarf in the suitcase.

Fiona reads my face. "You don't have to relive all that. Just make one call or write one letter asking him to make an introduction."

SIX

THE ENVELOPE, THE day's lone piece of mail, is embossed on the back. As if it were braille and I were blind, I translate the configurations with the pads of my fingers: the sender is not only wealthy but refined, and protective of his or her identity, for there is no name—only a return address.

The paper is the color of the thick, fresh cream my mother used to whip for the desserts made to tempt her husband. Other women seduce with lingerie and scent—my mother baked.

"This should sweeten up your father," my mother would say prayerfully. But usually the next morning, my sister and I ate our mother's pastry for breakfast.

We did not taste the tears that had slipped into the batter, even if we had seen them fall. We enjoyed the butter and the sugar and licked our lips, not quite sure why, even when we were stuffed, we still wanted more.

While Pauline Pagett sat at the table sipping black coffee and watching her daughters with her sad eyes, we devoured her efforts, leaving no crumbs. Maddy and I were glad our father had not been hungry when he came home: his lack of appetite meant we could play at being princesses. Surely only royalty ate such confections in the morning.

Slitting the envelope's flap, I pull out two thick sheets of stationery folded in three places.

The handwriting is bold and clear. The ink is a curious smoky green and smeared in one or two places, as if the writer had been in a hurry to get all the words down.

Turning to the last page, I read the signature, and my mouth opens in a small O. And then I start at the beginning.

March 10
Euphonia
12 Longneck Road
Greenwich, CT 06830

Dear Justine,

What a clever girl you are! Over the years dozens of journalists have approached me with story and interview requests without success, enabling me to keep the details of my private life private. Not one figured out how to challenge me the way you have. Not one got me thinking about what would happen if I didn't tell my story in my own words and someone else came along and told it for me or fiddled with it to suit their purpose.

As you correctly guessed, the idea of that bothers me.

I don't allow orchestras to perform my symphonies unless I am conducting them, so how can I leave this unfinished one to someone else?

I read the articles you sent. Unlike so much popular culture that only makes an effort to be sensational, the profiles you've written are more than one-dimensional. I know all about the pressure put on a creative person to produce what sells and don't have much sympathy for it. So often these days the trailer is better than the movie. Have you noticed that?

There was, however, something in several of your stories that went past that.

Then I saw some of your stories on-line. Like that one

about Barbara Kellogg. It was even more dimensional with all those links included. As I watched the film clips of her reading her own poetry and listened to some of her lectures, I could imagine a story about me accompanied by my music.

I'd like it to tell my whole story. A full-length profile that includes my music available on the Web and excerpted in your magazine.

We could work on it in May at my music conservatory. There, only two dozen students or so are ever in attendance, and it is quite idyllic. In the meantime, you can reach me through E-mail at sdl@sdl.com. And send me your E-mail address so I can send you notes as I think of them.

This way I won't forget anything.

That is one of the worst things about my age. When I was younger, I kept hundreds of scores in my head and never needed to refer to my sheet music. Now I find myself humming a piece of music that I know as well as my children's faces and find I cannot recall its title.

I'll also pass on names and contact information for people you should interview, although I'm afraid not everyone will be accommodating.

My daughter is concerned that if I tell my story, it will alter my image. My son (and manager) is nervous it will affect my popularity. My grandson is even more protective—though he doesn't know why. He's just reacting to everyone around him. And my oldest friend says she is worried about what will happen when people find out what I'm really like.

What am I like? I'm human, that's all. And you need to write about the things that make me real. The things that will bring me down to size. It is a story right for you, isn't it?

Don't be deterred. Dig as deep as you need in order to get to the truth of this riff that has been my life.

Traveling from concert to concert, books have kept me company on long plane rides and in lonely hotel rooms. In the middle of the night when I can't sleep and notes circle in my head, I find solace in stories well told. My tastes are eclectic and quite often pedestrian. I love nothing better than a good mystery. It is so gratifying at the end when the puzzle is solved and all the pieces fall into place.

Are you up to the task of solving the humble mystery that has been my life?

Fondly,
Sophie DeLyon

SEVEN

ON A WINDY day in the second week of May, I leave Paris for the first time in three and a half years. Chasing a story across the sea, I am unaware of being led into a storm.

Despite the season, it is snowing so heavily in New York that the plane cannot land. For over an hour, we circle above the city. Staring out the window, I try to see something other than my own reflection in the glass, but the snow is too heavy and I turn away. I prefer not looking at myself. Dressing in the morning, I glance only perfunctorily at the mirror. Unlike other women, I don't examine my face too closely, don't stare into my own eyes, for fear I will see my mother's eyes—brimming with longing and disappointment—staring back at me.

The mirror in my pocketbook is cracked. It is a small silver mirror made to be kept in a handbag. Once it belonged to my great-grandmother. Quite lovely, it is shaped like an open blossom, the handle a stem. A scene of two lovers in a garden is raised in repoussé on the back.

I have always liked running my fingers over their smooth forms and finding their small feet and hands and faces. The mirror itself is dotted with mercury. It has been like this since I first found it and appropriated it from my mother's jewel box when I was a teenager.

Using this odd object, I can check that my lipstick is not smeared. Or get an eyelash out of my eye. Or a smudge off my cheek. But because of the cracks, I see my face only in fragments.

There is nothing wrong with my appearance. Men have told me they see something in the cast of my eyes and the direct way I return a glance that excites them. A few have mentioned a coolness that doesn't seem to fit with my dark hair or warm-toned skin. But they forget about that once they get to know me.

Only I know about the wide divide no man has ever been able to traverse. It is my *other* whom I fear shares my mother's suscepti- bilities. I keep her hidden away, shielded and protected.

Most women don't see those same things in me or feel that coolness. Instead they want to share things about themselves with me.

"You look like you'll understand" is something I have heard over and over from female friends.

But since St. Pierre's branding of me, I have taken to wearing sunglasses even when they are not appropriate—like now in the darkened cabin of the plane. It's better to hide my eyes than to risk anyone seeing—what? My coldness? Desperation? Fear?

Fear is a new one for me. And I'm uncomfortable with it. But without a single serious assignment for months, I've gone through most of my savings. I've had to sublet my Paris apartment for the month I will be gone. And now I'm heading back to a city filled with nothing but memories I don't want to remember, people I don't want to see, and a story that has too much riding on it.

Kurt hasn't even agreed to run the DeLyon piece. "Let's see what you come back with," he said coolly. But he did come through with an economy ticket: a small show of faith that mattered to me.

I imagine meeting with Sophie DeLyon in a formal living room, sitting on Louis XIV sofas, our feet resting on Aubusson rugs. DeLyon will lean forward (I've read in the last article written about her in the mid 80s that she does this—leans in, looks at you and connects). When she looks at me, she will feel at ease. In her lap her fingers will relax and stretch out as if she were reaching for the high and low notes of an octave. Her mood will shift from *adagio* to *allegro*. Her wide eyes will sparkle, and the smile she gives me will be inclusive. She will be wearing her signature copper-colored clothes, which match her hair. (The article has thus informed me.) As she moves, her single rope of amber beads—each one with a different prehistoric insect trapped within the resin—will swing to an unheard rhythm.

So, she will say, here is my story.

As long as the rumors about my debacle with St. Pierre have not reached her and killed my chances.

THE LOUDSPEAKER CLICKS ON AND the pilot announces that the flight is being rerouted to Boston, but just as he finishes explaining the arrangements, he interrupts himself to say that conditions have worsened: the East Coast is under siege. The plane will be landing in New York after all.

Landing blind, counting on fallible instruments.

Reaching back into my pocketbook, I pull out my notebook and pen. The silver and mother-of-pearl one my mother gave me to commemorate my first job as a reporter.

I hope wonderful words will flow from this pen.
I love you,
Mommy.

Running my thumb up and down the shaft, feeling the smooth surface, calms me. The pen is my talisman. But there is nothing special about the notebook—it is the kind schoolchildren use. Cardboard, spiral bound, lined paper. I've filled dozens of them with notes on articles, journal entries, and strings of words—not knowing what to do with them, just not wanting to lose them.

Now I write about leaving Paris.

For the next hour it continues to be impossible to see anything out of the window as the plane makes wide sweeping circles in the air: there is no cityscape or afternoon sky to the right or left and no sun above, just the swirling snow.

Suddenly the plane hits a patch of turbulence: glasses slide off tray tables, books fall off laps. A man returning from the bathroom loses his balance, falls, and cuts his chin on someone's carry-on luggage. Another man, who is a doctor, cleans the wound but cannot begin to stitch it while the plane pitches so violently.

All this goes on in front of me.

In my lap, my hand jerks forward, its path charted by the long smooth line of ink that now slants across the whole page.

My seatmate, an elderly woman whose hands are pressed together in a gesture of prayer, makes whimpering sounds.

A stewardess, noticing the woman's agitation, kneels down and, in a reassuring tone, tries to calm her.

"We are not in danger," the stewardess says.

"Do you believe her?" my seatmate whispers to me once the flight attendant has moved on.

"Yes." It is a white lie: the kind that is acceptable to tell.

Like my father telling my mother that he still loves her—to make her happy, to keep her, for just another day, from the inevitable misery that she would one day own. When did he finally tell her? What brought about his confession? I try to pinpoint when I started to see the change in her eyes . . . but I can't.

I'm adept at white lies: my job as a journalist requires it.

"I don't believe her," the woman says. "I think we are in danger."

We are always in danger, I think. Still, I tell her we're fine. To distract her I ask if she was in Paris on vacation and then half listen to her tell me about how wonderful it was.

"And you? Do you live here in New York?" she asks.

"No, I'm here to work."

"What do you do?" The woman seems desperate for conversation.

"I'm going to be spending a few weeks in New York doing research for a article that I'm writing," I answer.

"Oh, you're a writer?" For the first time, the woman seems actually distracted from the storm.

I nod.

"Have I read anything you've written?"

I mention the magazine I write for, and the woman nods vigorously.

"So who are you writing about now?" she asks.

"Sophie DeLyon."

"Oh, I saw her once at Carnegie Hall. She was so impressive, but the people we were with complained that she was conducting just like a man. I wanted to say something, to argue, you know, because what did that mean?"

"Did you?"

"No. I should have, though. Have you met her? I once heard she had an affair with Leonard Bernstein. Or was it John Lennon?"

"Oh, there are lots of rumors about affairs. If they were all true, she never would have had time to write any music—" Before I can finish, the pilot's voice interrupts, announcing that the plane is beginning its descent.

HAVING RETRIEVED MY LUGGAGE AND cleared the long line at customs, I go outside to get a taxi. A blast of freezing air hits and snowflakes pelt my cheeks and catch in my eyelashes.

My first view of New York in three and a half years is blurred.

EIGHT

T HE TAXI THAT is taking me to my apartment—where my sister now lives—moves slowly on the highway. Even after reaching the city, there is no scenery, no cityscape. All the landmarks are hidden by the white blur. Snow even sticks to the street signs. We are moving ahead, but I feel as though I am going backward. Will my sister be there? And if she is, what will we say to each other after all these years of barely talking?

"It's another 1816," the cabdriver says.

"What?"

"1816. That was the year without summer."

From what I can see of him in the mirror, I can tell he's middle-aged, with honey-colored skin. And he's wearing gloves, a baseball cap, and a muffler.

"Really?"

"Everyone thinks this is the worst weather we've ever had. It's not. Almost two hundred years ago there was a year when summer never really came. It snowed all the way into July. Connecticut had what they call a rare summer blizzard. There was snow and sleet in Vermont."

"I didn't know that."

"Yeah. You see the weather different than other people when you drive a cab because you are sort of always in it. Yeah. You are only protected from it to a point. You get a different picture. A bigger picture. You can't hide from the weather."

All I need to do is murmur one yes and then he continues.

"Snow in May. People are saying it's Judgment Day. That's what they thought back in 1816, too, but it wasn't then, and it isn't now."

I murmur again.

"Except it's still very strange to have snow on Mother's Day," he adds.

"Mother's Day?"

"Yeah, did you forget? It's not too late to call. Still a few hours left."

I feel the prick of the tears and blink them back. Of all days to come back to New York, where we were last together.

AFTER A NINETY-MINUTE RIDE that should have taken half that time, the taxi finally reaches Greenwich Village. This is where I'd lived until I ran away to Paris, away from my mother's sudden death, from my own string of unrealized relationships, from my older sister, and from my father.

The cab pulls to a stop. And after I pay the driver, I wait for him to get out of the car and help with my bags. But it is snowing, and this is New York, and I wasn't responsive enough to his tales of weather and woe.

Extricating my bags by myself, I slam the trunk shut. The driver turns around, annoyed. I don't care.

Trudging through ankle-high snowdrifts, I slip but manage to stay upright. On the other side of the glass doors, the building's concierge notices me and quickly glances away. He is not the concierge who was there three and a half years ago, and he does not know me and so has no intention of dealing with such bad weather to aid a stranger.

Once I am inside, though, he is all smiles as he greets me and asks if he can help. Giving him my name, I notice how the silver braid on the man's black uniform gleams as he reaches for my suitcase.

"Oh, yes, Miss Pagett told me you'd be coming. From France, right?" he asks as he hands me a brass ring with two keys on it. The man, who introduces himself as Barry, gallantly carries my bags to the elevator.

Upstairs, I try the wrong key, correct my mistake, then open the front door and step into darkness.

Feeling for the light switch, I find it, turn the light on, and shut the door behind me.

My old apartment doesn't look the same. The small one bedroom in the lovely building on the corner of Fifth Avenue and Ninth Street is overcrowded with things that do not belong to me. Instead of feeling as if I have come home, it's as if I am the stranger here.

And the smells: butter, chocolate, coffee, spices. It reeks of a bazaar, a chef's house—not my house. My own apartment in Paris smells of flowers: of the single spray of lilacs or the three sprigs of freesia, or of the hyacinths I buy from the florist around the corner, next to the *tabac*.

But to live in a place that smells so much of food again?

Making my way to the window, sidestepping several piles of newspapers and magazines, I look out. I miss my walk-up in St. Germain, the florist, and the baker a few doors down who makes the best croissants I have ever tasted. And I miss his large black poodle, who sleeps in the doorway to his shop.

Looking north, up Fifth Avenue, I don't see the city skyline I expect but rather the same vista I saw from the plane: white, empty.

Walking around, I inspect my once pristine kitchen. The countertops are littered with expensive bottles of olive oil, honey, jams, herbs . . . At least there are no liquor bottles.

Turning, I go into what used to be my bedroom, with its eggshell-colored walls, white sheer curtains, and the bleached wooden floors. This room used to be a calm escape, but now there are piles of cooking magazines beside the bed, stacks of milk crates filled with videos blocking the window, and clothes draped over the desk, the chair, and hanging on the back of the door.

I wander like a stranger through my old apartment and wind up in the living room, staring at the wall of books. Mixed in with my books are volumes I've never seen, placed horizontally on top of the others. The shelves are overflowing with hundreds of cookbooks my sister has bought.

The only cookbooks I have ever owned were those written by my mother. All thirteen of them are still on the middle shelf, their spines not even cracked. I have never needed to read them, since I lived them.

I take down *Justine Cooks French* and there we are on the cover. My mother was so young and beautiful: dark hair pulled back off her face, green eyes carefully made up, and that Hermès scarf tied around her neck. Beside her, I am in an overlarge chef's hat and apron.

With my forefinger I reach out and touch my mother's picture—outlining her oval face and tracing her lips—embracing her the only way I still can.

The smell comes unbidden. The vanilla. The flowers. The chocolate. I shut my eyes against the onslaught.

What I wouldn't give to just be able to talk to her, to tell her what a mess I've made of everything, and hear her laugh, and have her help me figure out how to clean it up. Just to have her reach out, brush the hair off my face, and stroke my cheek. Leaving some dusting of flour or cocoa on my skin.

Wanting to remember and at the same time not sure that I can bear to feel all the pain remembering will bring, I open the book and look at the photographs. It was the last year there were photographs.

Every year, for six years, a new *Justine Cooks* had come out, and with each I endured more and more attention. And eventually embarrassment. I was relieved when, at fourteen, my mother's publisher had the series redesigned. The photos were starting to look dated, so in the new editions they were replaced with drawings of a mother and daughter who only slightly resembled us. There were seven more books after that. My name was still on them, but not my likeness.

NOT ONLY HAVE I NOT cooked since my mother's death, I have not looked at a cookbook.

I replace the book on the shelf and am at a loss as to what to do next. I'm used to living alone in Paris, but I'm not lonely there, it is my home. This is a familiar place, but I am only visiting. Maybe it would be different if Maddy were here to greet me, but it doesn't surprise me that she isn't. My sister is a chef at a restaurant and works nights, and to give me some privacy, while I'm here, she and her fiancé are staying at his apartment, which—she made a point to mention in her E-mail—is much smaller than this one.

Shoving a pile of yet more cooking magazines off the couch, I make space and sit down. Why would my sister, Madeline, suddenly be someone I could count on? Even if it is Mother's Day and would be better if we were together, why should she have changed?

TWO HOURS LATER, I WAKE up with a start. It's half past twelve o'clock. Disoriented. This is New York. Where home used to be. I am here to resurrect my reputation on the wings of one of the most important composers and conductors of the last century.

Out the window, the snow still swirls. The year without summer, the cabdriver had said.

How much can you miss a city? A few square blocks? A walk-up apartment on the Left Bank? Why did I think I would be able to come here and investigate Sophie DeLyon's life and not think at all about my own?

You can't walk away from who you are.

The wind is blowing and the snow still obliterates the view of the skyscrapers.

No matter what you think or block or deny, you still go to sleep at night and dream the dreams that have always haunted you.

If only there was a way to change your dreams. Now, that might make a difference.

NINE

THE ROOM IS DARK.
At home my bedroom faces east and, after only one night away, I long for the soft yellow light of Parisian mornings. At home I'd be out by now, jogging along the river, watching the city wake up.

Only after I have put on my leggings and sweatshirt and sneakers do I remember the snowfall from the day before. Checking out the window, I see that, while the drifts have begun to melt, the streets are still barely passable. Especially in sneakers. Two pigeons sitting on the sill, cooing, look back at me but don't budge. Tapping my fingers against the glass, I try to shoo the dirty birds away. New York pigeons, like their Parisian cousins, are no longer afraid of people. Why don't they fly away, I used to wonder, to somewhere with wide skies and taller trees? Why do they prefer to battle the buses and cars and the fumes of the city?

In the kitchen, I rummage through the refrigerator. There are fresh oranges but no bottled juice. Why isn't there something I can just open and pour? And there is no instant coffee or tea bags. Only beans that need to be ground or tea leaves that need to be strained.

Returning to the window with a glass of water, I look past the birds and watch the snow melting off the tree branches, exposing emerging buds.

This morning the temperature is back to normal for May and the snow doesn't have much of a chance. In a few more days these trees will be filled with magnolia blossoms that will scent the whole apartment. If the late frost hasn't done too much damage.

And then it starts to rain.

Opening my laptop and plugging it in, I check my E-mail—something I do too often, which Fiona and I have talked about at length. Neither of us can remember what it was like before there were laptops and cell phones. Always connected. Always in touch.

Even the phone has taken a backseat to sending E-mail. Especially for those people you don't want to really talk to—or listen to—but need to get in touch with. It is safer and easier electronically, and it keeps the pretense of connection alive without inviting messy confrontations.

For better or worse, both Fiona—who swears by E-mail to work out fights with her husband—and I would be personally and professionally lost without our machines.

Since I last checked E-mail, yesterday at home in Paris, a number of messages have accumulated. First I open a note from Sophie DeLyon who, in the last few weeks, has been regularly sending me names of people I should interview, or posting recollections and stories she wants me to have in her own words.

Dear Justine,

As planned, we are expecting you at Euphonia at the end of May.

I have only one excursion—to conduct a memorial concert—for a dear friend in Chicago but should be back the day before you arrive. If by any chance I am delayed, don't be concerned. I won't leave you there alone for long.

Helena Rath, the director and my oldest friend, knows you are coming and will be here to greet you. We're giving you a room near my suite, which includes the upstairs library, where I'm sure you'll be doing a lot of your work.

I must say it's been a pleasure getting ready for your article. I've been searching through shelves collecting all sorts of books I want you to read to help you with background. I've also pulled out old letters no one else has seen. I'm dusting off the secrets and practicing speaking them out loud.

I feel as if I've already gotten to know you a bit from our exchanges, but I look forward to meeting face-to-face. You'll recognize me because I am the only one at Euphonia with dirt under her fingernails.

Cheers,
Sophie DeLyon

A pianist—a conductor—with dirt under her fingernails?

The next E-mail is from Sophie's son's secretary, acknowledging my request for an interview and offering a phone number to call to set it up. But I'm not overly optimistic—an agreement to meet is not acquiescence to be helpful.

Another confirms an appointment for the day after tomorrow with Brian Beckwith, the film director whose scores Sophie has been writing for decades. When the summer is over, she will begin scoring his new film, based on the fable Pinocchio.

I breeze through a chatty note from Fiona, scan a few journalism digests from Listservs I belong to, and then open the last message, which has an intriguing return address—Pride33@The-LyonsPride.com

Dear Ms. Pagett,

We don't want to cause you any harm. But if you proceed with your intention to work on Sophie DeLyon's biography, we will do whatever we have to, to discourage you.

I reread the address: *Pride33@TheLyonsPride.com.*
The Lyon's Pride.
Is it a group of fans? Students?
Sophie has not mentioned it, and it hasn't turned it up in any of my research.

I resume reading.

Her talent speaks for itself. Her achievements need no words to explain them. Sophie DeLyon stands as a beacon to every artist who has tried to do something no one has done before. She has made sacrifices to do this. She has given her art her all.

And that is all anyone really needs to know about her.

What an artist creates is what matters. Who that artist is outside of her art does nothing but lessen the importance of what she has accomplished.

You must understand this.

We live in a time when heroes are dissected by the media—stripped bare and left exposed, naked and unprotected for all to see.

We put their lives under a microscope. We scandalize them and trivialize what they have done, what they have created.

You know this is true because you have been guilty of it.

Do you need Sophie DeLyon's psychic blood on your hands too?

Fair warning—we don't want you to do to Ms. DeLyon what the press has done to every other great man and woman of the last century.

Signed,
The Lyon's Pride

I type *TheLyonsPride.com* into the browser, and a Web site appears. With all the Internet research I've done on Sophie DeLyon, I either passed over this site for how amateurish it looked, or didn't find it.

It's a simple, homemade site that reads like a virtual shrine, and within its links are music files, published scores of DeLyon's work, some theses on her music, and links to an on-line music store selling her CDs.

The only photographs of Sophie presented on the site are the same half-dozen I've seen over and over. The best known of DeLyon in profile, conducting, arms raised, head thrown back. And the Irving Penn portrait of DeLyon at the piano: her head down, her racing hands a blur over the keyboard.

There are a few candids of DeLyon with the musicians after concerts. Even in these amateur shots, there is an aura of drama around Sophie that separates her from the crowd.

I can still remember the crowds surging around my mother and

me in bookstores those summers that we traveled doing tours for the
Justine Cooks series. When other children were at camp, playing
baseball or swimming in cool blue lakes, I was smiling and signing
autographs for other mothers and daughters and being offered more
Academy Award Candy than I could ever eat.

Finished searching the Lyon's Pride site, I bookmark it even
though there is nothing that distinguishes it from other fan club
sites I've seen. Certainly nothing about it implies that it is being
managed by a group of fanatics.

I've listened to all of DeLyon's music, read reviews of her scores
and symphonies. The woman is considered a modern classical master of form. Her conducting style has been written about, debated,
praised, and chastised by every living music critic.

Sophie DeLyon is tall with a theatrical appearance. She is one
of the very few women who have succeeded in a male-dominated
profession. She is outspoken about her dislike of modern dissonant
music and her adoration of Beethoven. She has had hundreds of
students at Euphonia, many of whom have returned summer after
summer to study under her tutelage. People are loyal to Sophie
DeLyon; many have written to tell me what she has done for them,
how she has helped them, what she has given them.

This is not the kind of woman who needs protection.

I forward the threatening E-mail to Fiona, along with a note
asking what she thinks. Since she checks her mail as often as I do,
there will be an answer soon. As I read the Lyon's Pride E-mail for
the third time, I hear keys in the lock, followed by the sound of
boots stamping.

"Isn't this crazy weather?"

Turning from computer, I face my older sister, framed in the
hallway light, standing by the front door.

I do not get up. Maddy does not walk across the room to embrace me.

"Hi there." I forget for a moment how mad I am about the mess
and the lack of a welcome.

"God, you look just like Mom." Maddy steps inside and shuts the door. "Did you always look this much like her? No, it's the hair-cut, and not seeing you for so long."

As if I were the snow, the compliment melts me. "It's good to see you."

"Is it?" Maddy asks.

There is an all too familiar and unwelcome tone in her voice. I ready myself for the blow.

"How much could you have missed me?" she asks. "You haven't come home for almost four years."

Maddy is the only person I've ever known who has no *other* hiding behind the face she presents to the world. There is nothing hidden. The inside is on the outside. Visible, available and all too often ugly.

"So we're going to do this now, Maddy? Right away? You haven't even taken off your coat."

"We might as well." She takes off her coat, hangs it on a hook, and double-locks the door. "Let's get it out of the way. Or else it's going to be there between us like some smelly piece of cheese."

I laugh, having forgotten how everyone in my family uses food to describe everything.

"I need coffee. Want some?" Maddy calls out as she disappears into the kitchen.

"I looked but didn't find any."

Maddy leans into the pass-through and holds up the bag of beans.

"I was looking for instant."

"You live in Paris and drink instant coffee?"

I join Maddy in the kitchen.

She is wearing a shapeless gray sweater, worn jeans, and thick gray socks. Her hair, the same dark chestnut as mine, is caught up in a ponytail that exaggerates her round face. Her fingernails are short and her hands are rough and red. An engagement ring—a siz-able square stone set in gold—sparkles on her finger as she pours beans into the coffee grinder. My grandmother's ring, now hers. And on her ring finger because she is engaged.

"It's not like we haven't spoken all this time." I'm trying to smooth over the rough start.

"E-mail every other month isn't talking and you know it. Damn you. Oh, no—sorry—last month you E-mailed me twice."

I should have known Maddy would be like this. "It was the best I could do."

"She wasn't just *your* mother." Maddy's voice is pungent. "She was my mother too. You didn't own the grief. God, first you made her a saint, and then after she died, you tried to claim her death. You're still doing it too."

"No, I'm not. I'm just trying to explain. I had to leave. . . . I had to deal with it my way."

"*Your* way. Do you realize how selfish that sounds?"

"Oh, Maddy, I'll admit to being selfish, but I'm hardly the only one. Besides . . . you were . . . you didn't come back until she was too sick to care. And then you didn't even help. You—"

"Still can't say it, huh? I was drunk. I was drinking. I was flat-out plastered. It's okay, Justine. Say it. But don't you dare say I didn't know she was sick. Of course I knew that, damn you. That's why I was drinking. I didn't want to lose her. I barely had her."

I look down at my own hands. Not a chef's hands. Nothing like Maddy's or my father's hands.

There is more between us, but there's no point bringing it up now. She will just deny that she and my father did anything wrong. Coming here was a mistake. I should have gone to a hotel. Why did I think that just because Maddy had stopped drinking, I'd like her any better or find her any easier to deal with?

"Oh, there you go—Daddy always said that when you were faced with the truth, you looked away."

I glare at her. "This isn't about him. This is about you and me. Mom was sick and then she died. You kept drinking. I got an assignment in Paris and I took it. And I stayed there. *Mea culpa*. What was here for me?"

"I was here. Daddy was here."

"You two were there for each other—not for me."

The kettle shrieks. Maddy turns her back on me to turn off the gas. She pours hot water into the French press, and the aroma of the coffee fills the tiny kitchen. Her strident posture sags.

"I just don't understand how you left like that. How you left and never came back." She looks at me with the brown eyes of our father, the color of melted milk chocolate.

"I was running away from the grief." This will be the only overture I make. If Maddy cannot understand this, there's not much reason to make other efforts.

But she does understand. "I shouldn't have started in right away."

"Maybe it's better that you did. You were right, we need to get it out of the way," I say, but I wonder if we really will get past it, if any exchange or explanation can ever mend the cracks in our relationship.

"Do you want an omelet?" Maddy asks.

"Cereal or yogurt would be fine."

"Instant coffee . . . instant food?"

"Yes, instant food." I laugh. "Don't you ever have a meal that doesn't require cooking?"

Madeline looks at me as if I have just uttered blasphemy. "You're still not cooking?"

I shake my head. "You're the chef in the family."

"One of the chefs in the family." Maddy sharply breaks an egg against the rim of a milk-glass bowl.

Yes, I know how to cook as well as any of them, even if I no longer choose to. But that's not what Maddy is referring to—her comment refers to our father.

As she cooks, I set the tiny table at the window end of the long skinny kitchen.

We are acting out the opposite of our childhood roles. Until our mother died, Maddy showed no sign of wanting to be a chef. Growing up, I was the one in the kitchen with our mother. Maddy was out being wild—going to parties and being thrown out of one private school after another.

Over a perfectly browned omelet, toasted baguette, and more coffee, we advance the conversation to the present. "Tell me about Oliver," I say.

And after she has, Maddy asks a question of her own. "Tell me about this trouble you got yourself into."

"Pow! Zero right in."

"Oh, should I have asked about the article you're writing first?"

I put my fork down. "It doesn't matter. Things couldn't really be worse with my job. The magazine settled with St. Pierre, but I've lost the credibility it's taken years to build up. This interview with DeLyon is the way for me to redeem myself. She wants me to write an electronic biography about her—with her music accompanying the story. The magazine excerpt may just be afterthought to her, but it's my first priority."

"Can you do that? Write a whole biography?" she asks in a surprised tone that is not altogether positive.

I stiffen, hoping Maddy notices and stops.

"You're a magazine writer. Why would Sophie DeLyon let you be the one to write a biography of her, even if it is just for the Web?"

"That's very supportive, thank you. I've been writing for almost ten years and my stuff has been pretty well received."

"I just meant that—"

"Forget it." Even though my plate is still half full, I push away the food my sister has prepared.

Maddy glances at the uneaten eggs and toast. She's deliberately and thoughtfully making a decision.

"I didn't mean to imply you're not good. You are. I've read your pieces."

I wonder if my face registers the astonishment I'm feeling.

"Why are you surprised? I'm your sister, after all."

"I don't know. Somehow I never thought of you as being interested in the kind of people I write about. Or in me."

"Is it my imagination, or is that a sugarcoated insult?"

It is a phrase I have not heard or thought of in years.

"Mommy used to laugh when she said it, Maddy."

The moment could go either way. We are stale when it comes to being kind to each other. We only seem to remember how to irk and annoy. I wait. Even though I'm broke, I can figure out some other place to stay in New York—then Maddy laughs.

"Do you remember when she made chocolate replicas of our report cards?" my sister asks.

WE TALK ABOUT OUR MOTHER, remembering the easy things. And then before either of us begins missing her too much, Maddy changes the subject.

"So what are your plans? When are you going to start working? How long do you think you'll be here?"

"Here in New York for just a week, and then I'm going out to Sophie DeLyon's conservatory. I don't know how long I'll be there. That depends on how much time she will be willing to spend with me."

"Well, before you leave again, we should try to spend some time together," Maddy says. "There are things I have to do for the wedding, things I should be doing with Mom. But since she's . . . well . . . I hoped we could go looking at patterns and glasses."

The sadness rocks me. Yes, a bride-to-be should be shopping with her mother to choose the crystal and china and silver for her registry. I bite the inside of my cheek to stop one pain with another. "Of course we can go and pick out all those things. When I get back from Euphonia."

Maddy is about to say something, stops, and then changes her mind. "You know Sophie DeLyon and her family came to the restaurant a few months ago. She was like a magnet—everyone noticed her. The hair certainly helped. Have you ever seen her in person? It's so red—can't be real. I don't even think it's her hair."

"How did DeLyon wind up at Sweet Basil's?" I name the unpretentious restaurant where Maddy has worked for the last few years.

"Not Sweet Basil's . . ." She gets up and clears the table.

"But I thought you said she came to the restaurant."

"I haven't been at Basil's for about a year."

I cock my head to one side and wait. When I hear Maddy sigh, I remember my sister's habit of warning you she's about to say something that will have repercussions.

"What?"

Maddy puts a plate in the dishwasher.

Just because I am ready—or think I am ready—to hear what Maddy has to say doesn't mean my sister is ready to say it.

"I've been working somewhere else . . ." Maddy starts and then stops.

But I already know. Without having to hear the words, I know exactly what she is going to tell me—that she is working with our father in his restaurant. But I still listen and wait for her next words.

They do not come right away. My sister, who so often speaks without thinking, is taking her time. I get up and stand in the kitchen doorway, looking around at what used to be mine. The pots hanging over the stove. The spatulas and wooden spoons. The dirty plates on the counter waiting for the dishwasher.

THESE WERE MY FIRST dishes. My mother had taken me to a small store on lower Broadway and let me pick them out. I'd just graduated from New York University and was already working for one of the city's smaller avant-garde magazines. She'd helped me find the one-bedroom apartment just two blocks from the family's larger apartment and had offered to help with the rent.

I remember my mother saying that it was time I was on my own.

I always wondered if that was the real reason or if it was that she was ready to finally deal with the state of her marriage and didn't want me at home to witness what was to come.

The plates we had bought that day were made of green milk glass. Depression glass from the forties, my mother had explained, plates and glasses so cheap back then they were given away by supermarkets.

But I loved the opaque glass. It was soft and light—the exact color of a white-chocolate–lime mousse that my mother had invented. In addition to the plates, there were mugs and bowls, a set of canisters, and a juicer. "You can make yourself orange juice in the morning," she'd told me, "just the way we like—without straining out any of the pulp." And there in the store, even though I'd been excited at the idea of finally having an apartment to myself, I began to cry.

"I don't want to make my own juice. I want you to make it. This is silly. I think I'm getting homesick."

My mother put her arms around me, hugging me tight. I could feel her shoulder blades and smell her vanilla-and-flower-scented perfume and the heady aroma of the chocolate that always clung to her clothes.

"Oh, Justine," she said, kissing my cheek, "I'm only around the corner. You can come home for breakfast every morning and I'll make your juice and your hot chocolate. It's only like this in the beginning of a change. It seems so lonely to do something different, but then it gets exciting. You're going to love living on your own."

It seemed, looking back, that my mother had understood every nuance of every one of my moods. "We are cut from the same cookie cutter," my mother used to tell me, and the idea of it had always made me happy. "Peanut butter cookies with chocolate chips," she'd say, embellishing the metaphor.

STOPPING THE MEMORIES FOR FEAR of where they will lead, I ask Maddy again where she's working. "For God's sake, Madeline. Just tell me."

"I don't want to hear about it for the next hour. I don't want to fight about it. You haven't given him half a chance, and he misses you like crazy. He wants to see you. He wants to talk to you. He wants to give you—"

I want to leave. Now. Get out. Get away. Paris seems like a far-away promise. I can't believe I have been gone for only one day. I walk to the window and look down on the dirty New York snow. "It's fucking May, for Christ's sake," I say.

I miss my apartment. My furniture. My books. I am missing May in Paris, running alongside the Seine and then going to the

nearby café to reward myself with a café au lait and buttery crois-
sant. I miss watching the poodle bask in the sun on the sidewalk
outside and the students on their bicycles racing to class. I miss the
churchyard garden next to St. Germain des Prés that I pass on my
way home and the retired *gendarme* who is always there with a bag
of stale breadcrumbs for the pigeons.

"I've been working in Dad's restaurant for over a year. And he
wants to see you as soon as possible. He misses you, Justine. There
are two sides to every story, you know?"

"But Mom isn't here to defend herself, Maddy. Of course he
can tell us things to make it seem as if he didn't do anything wrong.
What can she say to defend herself now? I lived there. I saw her suffering. You were gone at its worst. She loved him so much and he
gave so little back to her. He broke her heart. And then she died.
What else is there for him to tell me? Where is your goddamned
loyalty to your mother?"

"Justine, it wasn't like that. I heard her treat him with that awful
silence. She had expectations—"

"This is just what I don't want to do. You won't see it for what it
was. You're rewriting it. And she's not here to defend herself."

Maddy shakes her head. Her ponytail swings back and forth, as
if she is shaking off the truth. "I'm only asking you to give him a
chance, to sit across a table from your father and listen to him."

"Okay, you asked."

"Will you do it?"

"I'll think about it."

"When?"

"Don't push me, Maddy."

"When?"

"If. . . ."

Suddenly the jet lag catches up to me. Sitting down on the
couch, I pull a throw around my legs and lean against the cushion.
I shut my eyes, hoping to shut out the sounds of my sister's words.

Behind my eyes I see the clouds from the plane's window. If I
can't go home, if I can't go back to Paris, at least I can go back to sleep.

TEN

THE FOLLOWING DAY I wake up too early. I went to sleep too late. I'm still tired, but know better than to lie there. I need to run and get my blood moving.

My usual morning ritual is to check E-mail and have a cup of coffee before I go out, but today that can wait. My need to leave the apartment is stronger. And I can get the coffee on my way back.

It is raining lightly. I hold my face so that the fine mist alights on my cheeks and lips. After being inside more than twenty-four hours, the spring rain is welcome.

Washington Square Park hasn't changed. Pigeons roost in the arch at its entrance and joggers loop around the ten-block perimeter. Passing the south entrance, I notice that the playground is empty, but farther west, the dog run is busy. So are the drug dealers on the south side, who, like the joggers, are never deterred by the weather.

This place feels more like home than the apartment that Maddy's made her own.

After doing two miles around the park, I run up Fifth heading toward the bakery on Sixth Avenue and Tenth Street, where I'll pick up coffee and a Danish. Jon Vie is one of the few French bakeries here that my mother agreed was on a par with those in Paris.

At Ninth I go west. The dogwood flowers are starting to brown, and soon they will drop their petals and leaf. But I won't be here then; I'll be at Euphonia with Sophie DeLyon.

I'm almost to the corner of Sixth when, across from an apartment building with a blue awning, I stop.

It's not that I'd forgotten. I knew it would be here, but I didn't expect seeing it would cause the ache or such an acute emptiness in my chest. Leaning a hand on a lamppost, I stare at the building that has been there since before I was born.

Counting up, I look at the windows on the fifth floor that belong to the apartment where I grew up. Those were my family's windows; that was where we lived. As if playing back old family movies, I watch my mother come to the window wearing her robe and a sweet smile.

HER DARK HAIR IS PULLED back in her ever-present chignon, and a small diamond cross on a chain glitters as she leans out the window to blow me a kiss.

I wave, not as the woman I am now, but the child I was then—waiting for the bus, wanting to go to school, and at the same time wishing I could stay home and bake with Mommy.

Wait, sweetheart. Justine, I have something for you.

She disappears for a moment and, when she returns, lowers a bag tied with a long red-and-white baker's string out the window and then drops it. I catch it easily.

Inside, I know, for my mother often does this, are butter cookies with almonds or chocolate chips or raisins baked in. Whoever is lucky enough to sit next to me on the school bus will share the sweets.

THE REMEMBERED SMELL OF THOSE cookies and the image of my mother waving from the window overwhelm me. A low moan escapes my lips, and a man walking a dog stops for one instant to make sure that I am all right. This kindness from a stranger is not what I remember of New York. I nod slightly, say I'm fine, and reassured, he walks on.

I'm not fine. I'm frozen to this spot, not ready to leave the ghost on the fifth floor. Wanting much more from her and from our past.

They aren't there now, but I see and smell the abundance of flowers and herbs spilling out of my mother's window boxes. There is sweet basil, and chervil and chives, pungent rosemary and sage mixed in with the trailing verbena that almost reaches the top of the window below. And I know which herbs go with chicken and fish, and which with meats. Even at seven I know these things because my mother has taught me.

She waves again and then disappears inside the apartment. Perhaps the phone has rung. Or the timer has gone off and whatever else she is baking in the oven is done. I wait for her to come back to the window. That isn't going to happen. Not in real time. Never again.

I cannot return.

While I am in New York, I cannot walk down this street again. My memories are potent enough. For the last few years, I have fought to control them, but to come here is to solicit them and the pain that accompanies them.

I am about to turn back, but that would be giving in. Besides, it's only another half a block to the bakery.

Steaming coffee in one hand, a bag of sticky buns in the other, I am pleased to have carried out the activity with dry eyes. Especially when the owner, an ancient gray-haired woman, comes around from behind the counter to give me a kiss and reminisce about my mother.

Mrs. Tesher refuses to take money for the pastry or the coffee and insists I tell her what I have been cooking. Hearing that I no longer bake or do any cooking, my mother's old friend is disappointed.

"But you can't stop cooking. It's like loving. It's part of life," she says.

LEAVING THE SHOP, ESCAPING INTO the street, I cannot help but see yet another landmark. Across the street is the building where I went to grade school. Through the misty rain I see my mother standing, looking through the chain-link fence into the schoolyard.

She would often stop by mid-morning to bring chocolate toffee kisses wrapped in cellophane as treats for my friends and me, and we would crowd together and reach out through the wire mesh for the chewy candy.

SHE IS SO BEAUTIFUL, I think, looking into her eyes as I take the goodies. She smiles, her face lights up. Her skin is luminous.

Then, like a mirror cracking, that face shatters and is replaced by the other face—the sick face, the bone-thin yellow face with the yellowed, haunted eyes—the face I don't want to see.

At first my mother told me something was wrong but that it wasn't serious. "Some minor liver function problem. Ha! I would have guessed, if anything were wrong with me . . . it would have been my heart that would be bad . . ." She laughed ironically.

"You've been to a specialist, haven't you? There's medicine, isn't there?"

Her lips parted in a sweet smile and she took my hand. "Of course there is medicine."

But not for what she had. She had looked into my eyes and lied, not only about the severity of the illness but also about how long she had been suffering with it. I had not guessed. Not seen the lie at all.

As it turned out there was no medicine for her liver cancer. And there was not much time left either.

Only forty-two days later I was sitting beside my mother's bed, holding her hand and watching her while she slept. She had not eaten or had anything to drink for three days. And she had only woken twice. And then only for a few minutes.

The nurses my father had hired came and went in shifts, bathing her, cleaning her up, straightening the sheets; through it all, my mother slept.

It would all be over soon, my father had said. As if that would bring some kind of relief.

It will not be over soon, I vowed. I will make something she loves to eat. Something that smells good, that is sweet and warm and buttery. That will wake her. The smells she loves will bring her out of this.

I imagined her taking the first bite from the fork as I held it out for her. And I could see that one bite revitalizing her enough that she could reach out for the fork and take another bite. And then another. And then she would sit up and ask for something to drink.

It took an hour to make the Apple Humpty Dumplings dessert my mother had created years before. When the butterscotch-baked apples, wrapped in a flaky pocket, were done, I brought one still steaming into the sickroom.

The nurse, who had been sitting by the bed, left the room as she often did when I was there.

I looked at my mother. Her body so thin she barely made a bulge under the blanket. To the right, through the windows that faced south, the sky seemed normal, the clouds ordinary. How could that be, when something so momentous was going on inside this room?

The fragrance of brown sugar, butter, and apples sweetened the air, and I watched as my mother slowly opened her yellow, sickly eyes.

Her green irises were still the same. She was still there in that green. Deep inside, she was there, and I had to pull her back. I smiled and held out the plate so she could see the dessert.

"Are you hungry? I made Apple Humpty Dumplings. Do you remember how we used to make them every fall when the apples were so crisp?"

If she wants some of the dessert, it will be a sign that she is going to get better, I thought. If she sits up, she will get better. If she speaks to me or smiles, it will be a sign she will be well again. This would happen despite what the doctor had said, and what both my father and sister had repeated. No one could convince me of how ill my mother was. Let them give up, I wouldn't. They didn't have to encourage her, I would. They could accept the doctor's ignorance. I knew better.

And then my mother *was* looking at me. Without blinking, without wavering, she steadily held me with her eyes. And she was smiling. But this effort drained her. Her breath grew labored and her body shook. Finally, after weeks of denial, I understood she was dying.

I put the apple dessert on the floor and sat beside her on the bed, holding her thin hand, the way she had always taken my hand when I had been sick.

"Mommy, are you tired of all this?"

Her eyes flutter—*yes.*

"You must hate . . . being sick like this."

Her eyes flutter again, and there is an imperceptible nod. *Yes.*

From another place—I will never know where—I suddenly knew exactly what to say to the woman in the bed who hung on to a life that no longer had meaning. I knew in that moment between the time my mother's eyes shut and opened once more that she awaited my permission to die.

"You don't have to do this anymore, Mommy. We can leave here—just leave—just get on a plane and go to Paris. We'll do exactly what we did before. We'll stay at the Ritz and buy Hermès scarves and drink wine and eat cheese and walk in the Luxembourg Gardens."

"Oh, yes . . ." she said in a great rush—effortlessly—in her old strong voice without any hint of the aggressive illness.

And then . . . then . . . she closed her eyes and did not open them again.

She died that night in her sleep while my sister slept in our old room down the hall and the night nurse napped in the living room and my father slept on the cot in their bedroom and I lay in my bed listening to Austen's symphony . . . keeping the silence at bay.

I HAVE TO GET OFF this street. Up ahead there are more landmarks that will continue to remind me of places we'd been together. We'd walked each one of these streets, gone into every store on both sides of the avenue. The Eighth Street Bookstore, where my mother had bought me *The Secret Garden*. Sutters, the ice-cream parlor where we'd shared sundaes topped with a high tower of whipped cream and raced to see which one of us could get an ice cream headache first and then held our hands to our heads waiting for the pain to recede.

Even though most of the stores have changed hands and names, this pain will not recede. That's why I must get off this street and not come back. It is bad enough to miss my mother without seeing her at every turn.

I concentrate on putting one foot after the other. As excruciating as it may be, it is also wonderfully indulgent to give in to the agony of missing. Not to fight it or try to block it, not even to try to endure it, but to let it flat-out defeat me.

Whoever I was when I left the apartment this morning is gone. The woman walking back has no energy. All of it has been spent in remembering. I hold my breath and play my game, trying to think of words to distract me. Not revenge, no, it is not revenge that I want over my mother's death. It is something else. What?

ELEVEN

MADDY EYES THE paper cup of coffee. She has come for the second morning in a row to have breakfast with me, has arrived while I was out and let herself in.

"I made coffee," she says.

"I'd love some fresh coffee. This is already cold." I sit down at the table and open the waxy bag from the pastry shop. "Do you want a sticky bun?"

Maddy shakes her head no but brings over a plate and a knife, a mug and the French press. My knife. My plates.

"It's odd to be a guest in my own apartment." I take my first sip of her coffee. "It's delicious, as good as Paris." I grin at her.

In the Pagett family, food is a way of communicating. Both the making of it and the consumption.

"Thanks. Dad's been getting these beans roasted just for the restaurant. I bring some home."

I don't react.

"So what night do you think you can have dinner with Dad, Oliver, and me?" Maddy asks.

I chew my food more slowly, then swallow and then sip my coffee. "When I come back from Euphonia."

Even though Maddy is not the daughter who resembles our

mother, her frown is the same. "When you come back? But you don't even know how long you are going to be there."

"A week or two at the most."

Maddy tries to get to the point. "So Mom and Dad had rough spots in their marriage. It wasn't his entire fault any more than it was all hers. You have to realize that—and as an adult—you can't keep looking at her through rose-colored glasses."

I do not respond, which infuriates Maddy all the more.

"You know how you hated it when Mom pulled the silent treatment. Now you are doing it. What is with you?"

"I'm not going to fight with you. It's how I feel."

Not much has changed since childhood. We are expert at annoying each other.

"Well, despite how you feel—what are you doing later today? If you want, you can come over to the restaurant around four. Dad and I could take a half hour off. He'd love to—"

I interrupt, glad for a real excuse.

"I have some E-mail to catch up on, and then I'm meeting Brian Beckwith. The film director . . ." I look to see if I have to explain, but my sister knows who the award-winning director is. "Sophie DeLyon has scored all his films and is working on his next."

"You can't interview him over the phone and see Dad?"

"No, I can't. It's not just how someone answers a question, not just the words. It's watching them—are they trying to squirm away or are they open and comfortable?"

"If you change your mind or if he cancels, you have the number, right?"

"He has already confirmed."

Grousing as she gathers her things, Maddy leaves me to my laptop.

There is only one piece of E-mail—another message from Pride33@TheLyonsPride.com. And like yesterday's the subject reads FYI—Sophie DeLyon.

But this is not a letter. There are no words.

It is a piece of sheet music.

Scrolling down, looking for the end of the black-and-white configurations, I see only more patterns and shapes. No clues. Just an untitled grouping of staves and notes.

I write Fiona in an E-mail.

> There are no words explaining it, and since I can't read music at all, I can't decipher it. . . ,

She E-mails me back a half-hour later.

> What about Austen Bell? Can't he read music?

I read her note, and this is followed by a sensation: a memory of sound—no, not of sound—but of how the sound of the music that he made affected me.

Until I'd met him, I'd never known that I was capable of responding to music on such a deep level.

ONE NIGHT, AFTER WE'D MADE love, I lay in bed listening, drifting, sailing, on sounds. Finally I rose, following the cello music to the living room, where Austen sat, his back to the windows and the curvaceous golden amber instrument between his knees.

Behind him the city lights twinkled and a slim crescent of moon appeared and disappeared as clouds drifted by in some kind of dance of their own.

I stood naked, arms crossed over my chest, mesmerized by his music. Austen's eyes were closed and his face was suffused with a peaceful expression. He was unaware of anything but the music. Wearing only a pair of pajama bottoms, his chest muscles pulled and released as he played.

I'd never known how physical his playing was. A cellist uses not only his fingers, hands, arms, but also his torso, his neck, his abdomen, and his legs.

I was excited all over again. Not from any touch but from his music. It was inside me, the way he had been high up inside me earlier. As I stood there, leaning against the wall, watching and listening, I began to orgasm.

He looked up. I watched him watch me come.

"I don't think I've ever done anything better with my music," he said.

Three days later I found out how ill my mother was. And when I told him, he played me other music, which made me weep.

"Hello?" Austen answers.

"Hello. Austen. It's Justine."

"Well, hello. So you are back." His voice has the timbre and richness of his own chosen instrument.

I'm surprised at how familiar his voice is. As if the memory of it, like the memory of our lovemaking, were just waiting to be revived.

"Welcome to winter in New York. Charming, isn't it?" he adds.

I laugh.

"Ah, that laugh."

I can hear that he's smiling, and this helps me picture his face: the light dusting of freckles across the wide cheekbones, hair the color of raven's feathers, and slightly hooded dark eyes—the color of licorice. "Why is it that so many people comment about my laugh?" I ask.

"Because men hear something in it. . . ."

I am about to correct him and tell him I had not said "men" but "people," but instead I ask: "And what do they hear?"

"Well, a long time ago I used to think your laugh sounded like an invitation," he says.

There is a beat of silence, which does not seem quite as awkward as it might, considering how personal and perhaps inappropriate this comment is.

"So . . ." he says, pausing again after the single word.

I remember this too, how he uses *so* to start sentences, giving himself one more beat of time to frame his words. I used to think Austen would much rather communicate with people by just playing them a phrase on the cello.

"So . . . is this about doing an interview? Sophie warned me you might be asking."

"Not about an interview. I do want to interview you after I've spent time with Sophie, but I'm calling about something else. Someone has sent me some sheet music. I can't read it and was wondering if you could look. See if you know what it is."

We make plans to meet in two days. I don't mention the threats, even though I can't imagine they could have come from Austen or that he could be involved with the Lyon's Pride. Still, I don't know that for sure. And until I do, I have to be more careful than I have been in the past. There is more at stake now. And that's no one's fault but my own.

TWELVE

ARLY THE NEXT evening, I get out of a
taxi on Eightieth Street between Park and
Madison Avenues. It is raining again, and I
hurry to number 25, a brownstone blocked with wrought-iron gates.
A subtle plaque reads, "Solomon Management." A fingerprint mars
the polished surface.

After pressing the buzzer above a speaker on the inside of the
gate, I wait.

Flanking the front door are topiary swirls of evergreen planted
in stone urns. A tiny last patch of snow partially covers one of the
lower limbs.

A middle-aged woman opens the door and introduces herself
only as "Mr. Solomon's assistant." She ushers me down a somber,
elegant hallway lit with crystal sconces to a dark office lined with
wooden bookshelves.

The room is filled with expensive furnishings and objets d'art,
many of which seem museum quality.

"If you will have a seat, Mr. Solomon is in a meeting and will
join you shortly. Would you like something to drink?"

"No, I'm fine."

After she leaves, I take off my sunglasses, put them in my bag,
and start reading the spines of the books on the shelves. Most are

legal tomes, but there are a few on music theory, the theater, and the cinema. A shelf of biographies. No, not all biographies. There is a book on mental illness and—

"I'm sorry to keep you waiting. I'm Stephen Solomon." Sophie DeLyon's son walks across the room toward me. The expression on his face is all too easy to read; he's looking me over. Showing he's pleased with what he sees, he takes my hand and holds it for too long after shaking it.

He probably tests every woman this way. I meet his glance straight on, giving him no indication of whether I'm aware of his tactics.

Six months ago I might have teased back and even wondered about what it would be like to take him up on his silent invitation. Not anymore. I no longer—as Fiona teased—mine my assignments for assignations.

But what if this isn't how he treats everyone he meets? What if he has heard the story about Henri St. Pierre and thinks he can manipulate me by giving me the opportunity to try to seduce him?

My stomach cramps. How long is my mistake going to eat at me? And if news of the lawsuit has reached the States, have Sophie or her son or Austen heard it?

And if they have, how much damage will it do?

Stephen releases my hand and smiles a little too intimately. I would have bet he'd do that; this predictability makes him unattractive.

We sit down and he asks if I'd like coffee or a drink. Within seconds of my saying yes to the coffee, the same assistant brings in a silver service with china cups.

In the soft light, the precious metal glints, sending reflections onto his hands. Sophie's son is every bit as polished as the silver. From his cuff links to his sleek leather loafers, everything about him shines.

"I appreciate your agreeing to see me and giving me a chance to talk about your mother."

"She made quite a fuss about my seeing you—and sooner rather than later. She's so serious about this project."

"It's a bit more than a project."

"I'm not making light of it." He apologizes with his smile, and I walk the line between being responsive without encouraging him.

"Mr. Solomon—"

"Call me Stephen, please."

"Stephen, I think your mother is amazing, and my goal here isn't to—"

"Yes," he says, interrupting. "She is amazing. All those things you've heard are true. Genius. Innovator. Maestro." He sighs and smiles sadly before continuing.

"But then there's the gossip. And that is what we are concerned about. What you will hear and pay attention to and be swayed by. My sister cringes whenever she hears any of these silly things—such as Sophie stealing all her music from her most talented students. Or how she squashed other students whom she saw as competition. And the sexual innuendos . . ."

He gives me a suggestive look as he hands me a cup of coffee.

"But you know about those," he says.

Does he mean the gossip surrounding my own career or the gossip surrounding Sophie?

"She's done such great things, isn't that enough for everyone?" he asks. Hoping he will continue, I don't answer and, a second later, am rewarded for my silence.

"Few people understand the pressures an artist puts upon herself, that others put upon her. Everyone seems to prefer saying something bad rather than good."

"When people are jealous, they search for flaws," I offer.

His eyes narrow, and he does something with his mouth that makes his two lips disappear into one thin line.

He changes the subject. "I've read a few of your pieces. And I was impressed by your observations on the playwright and theater director Jacob Heinemann."

Of all my interviews, Stephen has mentioned the most difficult and, in the long run, the most rewarding.

Still, I do not trust his flattery. I will mistrust everyone I meet

and everything I'm told about Sophie DeLyon until after I have finished the story. Each person who speaks to me will be suspect.
What they tell me will be informed by their own personal agendas.
Sophie, in several E-mails over the past month, has warned me that
many people—even in her inner circle—have things both to gain
and to lose by having her story told.

AND IT IS OBVIOUS, THIS son does not want his
mother's flaws exposed.

Sophie wrote:

> And I? Even I will lie, making every attempt to present
> myself as the consummate artist and give you only the
> anecdotes that ensure your portrait of me dissuades my
> critics and secures my place in my field.

"What was it you said about Heinemann—that he doesn't so
much direct theater as he orchestrates drama, the greatest being the
one he lived?" Stephen asks.

I listen to the actual words and at the same time try to file away
facts, like the oddity that Stephen never refers to Sophie DeLyon as
his mother. This either has some psychological meaning or is just a
business decision. Since his father, Victor, died four years ago, he
has been both Sophie's manager and her lawyer. Perhaps it would
not be professional to refer to her as his mother in a meeting.

He leans forward slightly and looks directly at me. This man is
studied. He knows how to present himself. If it were a little less
practiced, it would be more successful.

For a few more minutes we talk about the enigmatic playwright.

"How much, do you think, does Heinemann's experience in escaping from a concentration camp have to do with his exuberant
subject matter?" Stephen asks.

"Almost everything. Whenever I asked him a question about
those years, he would change the subject. I think his plays are a re-
taliation for the acts of inhumanity that he witnessed. It is as if every

play he writes and directs proves once again that there is nobility and purpose other than evil."

"My grandmother reacted very similarly," he says.

"Your grandmother was in a concentration camp?"

He nods solemnly.

"Your father's mother?"

"No. Sophie's mother."

My adrenaline surges. There was nothing about this in any of the research I did. "I thought—" I have a photographic memory and can picture the *New York Times* interview with Sophie—one of the few she ever gave. "I thought that her parents emigrated from Europe to Canada in 1937, before the war broke out, and then came to the United States in 1947. Except I couldn't find any paperwork to confirm that."

"You wouldn't be able to. There isn't any."

"I don't understand. Why would Sophie have kept something like that secret?"

He does not speak right away, and I wonder what he is weighing. "Sophie has been truthful only in her music. The rest of her life is as much fiction as it is fact. When she doesn't want to deal with reality, she disappears into sound. When she doesn't like history, she rewrites it. I'm not blaming her. When you think about what she lived through, it makes sense."

"Why would she lie about her mother being in a camp?" I still don't understand.

"She didn't want sympathy to influence critics. She was so young when she was discovered; the last thing she wanted to focus on was the past—not with a whole wonderful future ahead of her. So she and my grandmother concocted a plausible story and never deviated from it."

Stephen gets up. He strides to the bookcase, reaches for a volume, brings it back to the desk. His fingers caress the leather-bound book. They are slender and well-manicured. How spoiled is he? This man has never known obscurity. By the time he was born, his mother was already the most famous female composer and conductor in the world.

Before he has time to open the book, Stephen's office door opens and a woman enters. He smiles. "Justine, I'd like you to meet my wife. Zoë, this is Justine Pagett—the writer Sophie is working with on her biography."

Stephen watches his wife's face as he makes the introductions, and he continues to watch as she crosses the room. She's lithe and moves as if hearing music in her head. She wears a pale yellow cashmere sweater, well-tailored black slacks, a string of pearls, and Gucci loafers. All subtle and expensive clothes. Her gold watch on its black leather strap looks simple, but it's a Piaget, and while the diamond wedding ring is understated, I'm sure the stones are flawless.

I shake her proffered hand. Zoë's skin is cool to the touch.

"You're in for an interesting time," Zoë says in a voice as cultured as her appearance.

"Why is that?"

"Because Sophie is a master at seduction," Zoë says with a laugh both engaging and intimate. "And she is wonderful and entertaining and well worth the effort. I wish you luck."

"I was hoping I might interview you," I say to Zoë. "Not necessarily today, but after I've met with Sophie."

"Of course, but I'm not really very important in the scheme of things."

Before she walked in, I'd never have guessed Stephen was insecure about anything, but he has not taken his eyes from his wife. It's as if his gaze were all that were keeping her from disappearing.

"Stephen, there's been a change of plans. Sophie's not coming into town." Zoë touches a ring on her right hand and lightly spins it. A flash of hammered gold catches the light.

"Did you speak to her?"

"No, Daphne called."

If there is a subtext to this exchange, I have no way of understanding it.

He looks over at me. "Have you met my sister, Daphne, yet?"

"No, not yet."

"Maybe it would be a good idea for you to stay and have dinner with us so Sophie stops badgering us about cooperating with you." He turns to Zoë. "Could you call Daphne and let her know to expect the fourth estate?"

I accept, though I'm more curious than pleased about the invitation. I don't imagine that they will so much offer information as try to get information from me about how much I know and in what directions I'm headed.

After Zoë leaves, the slight scent of lilacs from her perfume still graces the room.

"Your wife is beautiful," I say.

"Yes. She is, isn't she?" He finally looks away from the door. "Where were we . . . ?" He looks down at his desk. "Oh, yes, I was going to show you this."

Like the man and everything in his office, the leather volume bespeaks wealth. On the cover, embossed in gold, are the words *Sophie DeLyon*. As Stephen flips it open, I see that it is a scrapbook. The first picture is black-and-white, one which I have often seen reproduced. A twenty-year-old Sophie DeLyon on the eve of her debut at Carnegie Hall. Standing behind her, beaming, is her mentor, Leonard Bernstein.

Even though the young woman at the piano does not yet resemble the adult she will become—with the kohl-lined eyes, copper hair, and dark lipstick that will become her trademarks—she is already a commanding presence.

"Was this taken after the performance?"

"No, before."

"She doesn't look the slightest bit afraid."

"Afraid?" He laughs. "Sophie? She'd been to hell and back as a child. Playing the piano in front of a few thousand people was hardly anything to be afraid of."

"How did your grandmother survive the camp? How did she protect your mother?"

"Raisa was a violinist and one of the members of an inmates orchestra. Before she was interned, she'd hidden Sophie with her music professor—a Catholic woman—who kept her for the duration of the war and raised her as her own child."

"How extraordinary. And all this time, no one discovered the truth?"

"Sophie didn't want it told."

"It's not easy to control the press."

"Control has never been a problem for Sophie DeLyon," Stephen says. Even though he's using the same tone of voice he has been using all along, I wonder if his mother's control has been an area of conflict for him and if it has caused friction between them.

"Is there anything your mother is afraid of?"

Stephen is about to say something and then changes his mind. "No."

"What about the press?"

"No."

"But she's never given anything but the most perfunctory interviews."

"That started when she was young and didn't want to talk to the press because her English wasn't very good. 'I did not wish to speak the language of the monsters while talking about the songs of the gods' is what she told me."

"Most celebrities would have taken advantage of a past like hers, not kept it so utterly secret."

"Exactly. As I said, Sophie never wanted to get attention for anything but her music. She's obsessed with that. That is why you couldn't find out anything about her childhood in Canada. Not even the name DeLyon is real. At Sophie's urging, my grandmother took that name when they finally came to New York and Sophie began studying at Juilliard. There are no records anywhere with Sophie's real name on them."

"What is your mother's real name?" I ask.

For the first time there appears a minute fissure in his façade. The whole time we've been talking about his mother, he hasn't exhibited any emotion: not pride, or love, or admiration, or even ir-ritation. His veneer—as highly polished and impenetrable as the wood on his desk—had deflected my scrutiny. Until now.

"I don't know the name," he says, then closes the book and puts his hands on top of it, as if he were keeping it from flying open on its own. "My sister and I have agreed to meet with you because So-phie has asked us to. The only reason we didn't refuse is that we don't want you to have to rely on what strangers will tell you."

"Well, thank you, even if it is under duress."

"Sophie told me she was going to tell you about the camp and about being hidden. I wanted to save her from having to. It's painful for her—one of the few things that is." He smiles. "Would you mind if I asked you a question?" He leans forward, trying to pull me in. I know exactly what he is doing, because I have done it. I also know how to resist.

"How will you know which is the real story?" he asks. "Won't you get as many different stories as you will interviews? Doesn't each subject give you only what he or she wants you to know? How do you discern the truth from the lie?"

"It's my job," I say.

Just as it's my job to have noticed there is an absence of Sophie here—as important as if she were a presence. Except for those in the closed scrapbook, there is not a single photograph of his mother in her son's office.

THIRTEEN

"MY FATHER USED to say that my mother has an extended family. It includes every student she's ever taught." Although it is meant to be a compliment, there is a bitter edge to Daphne's statement.

We are at the dinner table—suffering, as far as I'm concerned, through a roasted chicken that is dried-out and flavorless. You have to turn the heat up to four hundred and fifty degrees for the first half hour when you roast. You have to use butter.

The wild rice is undercooked. It's a shame to roast a chicken and not roast potatoes and carrots in the same pan, so that the drippings cook the vegetables.

And the skin of the chicken needs to be crispy and dark brown, not this tan color.

The food is ordinary, which surprises me. Daphne surprises me too. While I listen to what she is saying, I look for the clues to who she is as opposed to who she wants me to think she is. This is difficult because first I have to get over the fact she is the ex-wife of a man I dated for almost six months. Austen Bell didn't speak of her often when we were together, except in reference to their son, but I was conscious of her. They'd been divorced for only two years back then and occasionally I'd sense he was still figuring out how to be on his own.

And now here she was: much harder and not as beautiful as I imagined when I'd heard her voice on Austen's machine, talking about their son.

From her reaction to me, I doubt that he had ever mentioned my name.

Beside Daphne sits Zoë. In reaction to her sister-in-law's comment, she sits straighter, juts out her chin a little, and presses her hands together.

Across the table, Martin, Daphne's husband, guffaws at her wit. He punctuates his laugh with a baroque silver fork upon which a piece of chicken is skewered. "Well, now, that's a positive way to spin it."

Daphne frowns. Everything about her is sophisticated except for her husband. I know, from my research, he is a self-made self-starter who has had a particularly bad run of luck in the market for the last few years. He takes a second too-soft dinner roll from the silver bread basket and slathers it with margarine—I can tell it's not butter by its bright yellow color.

"Justine, more wine?" Daphne asks, ignoring her husband.

"Yes, thank you. Can I ask, though, with the time your mother's taken away from her own career to devote to teaching, why it surprises you that she takes her students so seriously?"

"If she just took them seriously, that would be fine. But it's more than devotion. She's always obsessed with at least one student a semester. Sometimes more than one. She gives to this person beyond reason . . ." Daphne doesn't finish because she's been distracted— as I have—by Zoë, who is suddenly, frantically picking up the crumbs around her bread plate, crumbs none of us can see.

"She's just generous," Stephen finishes.

"But generosity is not always the best trait in someone so unrestrained," Daphne says to him.

"What do you mean?" I ask.

Zoë answers before Daphne can. "Sophie has set up dozens of scholarships. By now, hundreds of people have gone through Juilliard because of her largesse."

"Zoë got one of those scholarships," Daphne offers.

"Oh. I didn't know. What do you play?" I ask.

"Piano. But not professionally. I play *at* the piano now. I didn't like the pressure."

"But if Sophie chose you, you must have extraordinary talent."

"Talent is only one thing you need. I didn't have the other things. I came from a small town in New Hampshire. Before meeting Sophie, I'd never even been in a big city or away from home. And of course I'd never met anyone like Sophie. I wanted to do whatever I had to do to please her. But I couldn't. I didn't have any idea what the pressure was going to be like at Juilliard."

"Was she disappointed?" I ask.

"If she was, she never let me know it. When I had a breakdown, she moved me into her house and took care of me."

It does not escape my notice that Stephen sends a sharp look his wife's way.

"Zoë is now on the board of the New York Philharmonic," he says proudly.

"And she hits me up for donations every year," Martin says. "Big ones. She's got balls." He laughs.

The others laugh with him, but it seems forced.

"Zoë and I are two of my mother's failures," Daphne says, smiling. "Full of desire and talent, but just not tough enough or insane enough to make it."

"Insane enough?" I ask.

"Well, it takes a certain lack of sanity to devote so very much of your life to an inanimate object that consumes you, makes demands on you, and, in so many cases, gives you nothing back. Do you have any idea what percentage of musicians actually make a decent living doing it?"

"But more of Sophie's students go on to succeed than the average," I say.

"She's shrewd enough to pick the ones she thinks are going to make it," Martin says.

Stephen laughs. "Shrewd?"

"You all see her as an artist. Yeah, she's an artist. But it takes one to know one. I keep telling you"—he turns to Daphne and speaks directly to her—"you are missing the boat on her. She is more a—"

"Martin, please." Daphne's voice lashes out. "My mother"—she turns to me—"is brilliant and talented, but she is not shrewd." As she sips her wine, her diamond bracelet clinks against the stem of the glass.

"I suppose everyone you talk to will have a different perception." Daphne fingers the bracelet.

"Yes. People have their own agendas. Axes to grind. Old scores to settle," I say.

"But she's helped far more people than she's hurt," Zoë says.

"You can't judge her by ordinary people's standards. She's a woman who broke through in a man's world—who has had a man's career. And to get those things she's made the kinds of choices men make. She's been driven . . . focused. Too focused sometimes, and people misconstrue that and think she's distracted or confused. This is one of those things we wanted you to hear from us, rather than from someone else, so you could ask us what you need to know about it and not rely on outsiders," Stephen says.

Summoned silently, a maid appears and begins to remove the dinner plates from the table.

Martin shakes his head. "You are all nuts, not her. I'm telling you, Sophie is nobody's fool."

I'VE INTERVIEWED MANY CHILDREN OF famous parents. Certainly some have been in awe of their mother's or father's talents, but they have always spoken of other things too: raved about the way their mother helped them with their homework despite her schedule, or how their fathers told them the worst bedtime stories. Other children—even grown children—remembered family stories.

Sophie DeLyon's children, over the course of this ninety-minute dinner, have not once spoken of her as a parent.

• • •

"WHAT WAS IT LIKE TO have a mother who was so well known?" I ask.

"Not all that unusual. Stephen and I both went to private school. Plenty of the other kids had fathers who were just as famous," Daphne says.

"When you are growing up, *what* your parents do is not that important," Stephen says. "We were lucky. Sophie showed us a world that few children ever get to see, much less live. We were spoiled. We had the best of everything," he adds, not even noticing Daphne's odd comparison.

But you didn't have your mother, I want to say, knowing by then that they did not and wondering what kind of resentments they harbored from their childhoods and how those issues affected them still.

Dessert and espresso are served. The lemon tart is not nearly as good as my mother's. The crust is not flaky enough. The lemon curd's balance of sweet and sour is off.

"There's one last question I do want to ask. . . . Do any of you know anyone who has something to lose by my writing this story? Who might be worried that I'll discover something about them in the process of writing about Sophie?"

"Why?" Stephen asks.

"Because I've gotten E-mail discouraging me from working with your mother."

"Threats?" Stephen leans forward, visibly concerned.

"Well, I suppose you could call—" I start to say.

"Who knows your E-mail address?" Daphne asks, interrupting.

"Just about everyone. The magazine I write for has a site and my address is listed there alongside every article of mine that's online. Plus I've E-mailed well over a hundred people regarding your mother's biography."

"How many messages have there been? How serious are they?" Stephen asks.

I look from him to Zoë to Daphne. "Is there something that I could find out about Sophie that could put me or any of you in danger?"

"Danger? No. What kind of secrets could a composer have?" Daphne asks with an insouciance I don't trust.

"I'm not assuming there are secrets about her career. They could be personal. Any woman could have secrets."

"There are no secrets," Daphne says with certainty.

I'd be just as confident if someone asked me about my mother.

FOURTEEN

T HESE ARE THE things I am doing at once: drinking my third cup of coffee, printing out all of Sophie's E-mail to me, and listening to my taped interview with Brian Beckwith from the day before. In my rush to get to Stephen Solomon's office, I didn't have the time to play it back before now.

Forthcoming and open, Beckwith offered a portrait of a determined artist who cared more about success than any of her relationships. Even on the recording, he sounds impressed with her, a little bitter, still very much in love.

"It's always as if we were creating a life together every time we made a picture. Our collaboration had to wind up in bed—we shared so much of our inner lives in our work. I once thought she would leave her husband for me . . ." He laughs. "But that never happened. And that was probably all for the best. I never would have been as accepting as Victor was."

"Accepting of what? Other men?"

"Sophie and I often talked about her music and where she thought her inspiration came from. Most people stick to a main path. Sophie does everything she can to avoid it. She has some crazy idea that her creativity would wither and die if she didn't give in to her excesses."

He had fallen into the state where talking brings back memories that are so pleasurable all hesitancy is gone. "But nothing has
ever interfered with her work. She goes on binges—spending a
few months at a time traveling, socializing, and partying—
and then goes into hibernation to compose heavenly music.

"We are going to start on another movie in the fall," Beckwith
added, and his eyes sparkled at the thought. "Pinocchio. A serious
film—about manipulation, parental constraints, and lies."

"And your affair, is it over?" I asked, hoping to catch him off guard.
He didn't answer, which means either it isn't or he hopes it isn't.

The tape ends.

I pull the last of Sophie's E-mails out of the printer and read.

When I conducted my first symphony at Carnegie
Hall, twenty people walked out as soon as I reached
the podium. I suppose they hadn't realized I would be
conducting. Sometimes I wonder if I wanted to conduct as much as I wanted to tear down the barriers
that had prevented any woman from rising to the level
of conductor for a major orchestra.

Let me tell you what it was like to take the baton,
to hold it, to raise it in the air and begin that first concert. Nothing compared to that moment, not even
having children. That was something any woman
could do, but this was something no woman had done
in the history of Carnegie Hall.

And they were all there with me that night, all the
long-dead composers and conductors who I feel and
sense around me—who I speak to when I play piano.

What a lovely metaphor, I thought, when I first read those lines.
But in another E-mail Sophie referred to her ghosts again, and I no
longer think it's a metaphor.

Beethoven was here today . . . while I played "Moonlight Sonata." I have been experimenting with different
interpretations because for years I have thought something is wrong with the way everyone else performs this
piece. There's more sadness and frustration in it.

So today I played it that way, and I felt his hand on
my shoulder telling me, with that one touch, that I had
found his interpretation.

My computer chimes, alerting me that I have more E-mail.
The first is a long note from Fiona, alarmed at the threat I for-
warded her. The second is from another address I do not recognize.
It's one line:

Justine, someone has sent you a curse!

Beneath that is a live link that says,

Click here.

Waiting for the Web page to download, I bite my bottom lip.
Wary.
Apprehensive.
No. On alert.
A detailed and dark photograph of a rough-hewn wooden box
fills the screen. With a slow creak, the lid animates open, revealing
a raggedy voodoo doll with pins stuck in her fingers, and then, in a
deranged scrawl, a message appears:

This is your third warning. Back off the DeLyon story.

Even on the computer screen, the doll with its crude features and the menacing note make my skin crawl. Who is this
from?

This is your third warning.

Whoever sent this knows about the other threat made by the Lyon's Pride. But how—why—would one of Sophie's handpicked music prodigies resort to such an artless, childish threat?

This is your third warning.

The Lyon's Pride letter was the first threat. There hasn't been another. Or have I missed one?

Going back through my old mail, I find that original letter, and then, scrolling down the list of mail, find the second letter from the same E-mail address—the one containing the sheet music. Is there some kind of cautionary communication within the music?

A wave of uneasiness goosebumps my skin. Whoever they are, they don't know what my mother knew and what Fiona knows: instead of scaring me away, telling me to back off makes me only more determined to proceed.

FIFTEEN

THE STRAINS OF a Bach cello concerto greet me as I get off the elevator. I follow the music down the hall to the front door. Not wanting to interrupt the music, I wait, absorbing the melancholy strains.

The music ends and I press the buzzer—a grating sound after what I've been listening to, after what he's been playing. I feel a flutter of anticipation before Austen Bell opens the door.

He towers above me. I have forgotten how tall he is and how thin—stretched taut like the strings of his cello. I look at him, into his eyes, and watch a smile rearrange his stone face to the face of an old friend.

He doesn't reach out to kiss me or put his arms around me, but I feel welcomed.

"Come in," he says, and steps back to allow me entry.

Almost four years is not that long, but he has changed. Yes, he looks a little older, but that's not it. He's still sinewy; his hair is just as wavy and as dark and as long as I remember: falling well below the collar of his white shirt.

He is sadder. Something is missing or something has broken in him.

Following him, I'm astonished to see that Austen's apartment is no more finished than when I was last here.

Four years ago he'd already been divorced and living here for two years. Eventually, he'd said, he was going to get someone to help him decorate. But there are still piles of books on the floor and stacks of CDs on the windowsill. Large, black stereo speakers dominate the living room and the only furniture is a black leather couch and matching chair. Framed posters from concerts he has given are stacked and leaning against the wall, waiting to be hung.

The most striking thing about this apartment was—and still is—the floor-to-ceiling windows facing Central Park. Looking out now, I watch as a bird with a wide wingspan soars above the treetops. "Look," I say, alerting him.

"Ah . . . a falcon."

"A falcon? Right there in the middle of the city?"

"More than one. They've been nesting and breeding in the cornice of some building off the park, in the Sixties. I think there are five."

The bird swoops down and disappears. "How can something so wild and primal live in the city?" I ask.

"There's still the same sky above the trees, the same food below them."

I remain at the window, waiting for the falcon to come flying up again. When a few minutes go by without its reappearance, the depth of my disappointment seems illogical.

"So what have you done since you've been in New York?" he asks.

I almost say I've been spending too much time thinking about the past, but catch myself. It's been years since I had a personal relationship with him, and the very last thing I want to do is invoke it now.

"I've interviewed Brian Beckwith, met with Stephen Solomon and then had dinner with him, Zoë, Daphne and her husband."

Austen's eyebrows arch.

"Does that surprise you?" I ask.

"It's out of character for those two to open their doors to questions."

"I didn't get to ask too many questions, and there was a whole lot of subtext running under most of the conversation that I completely missed. I was more manipulated than anything else, I think."

"That sounds like them. My ex-wife . . . she's turned out to be such a warm, happy person," he says sarcastically.

"She wasn't always like that?"

"When she was at school, when we first met . . . she was different."

"And Stephen? Is he always so businesslike about Sophie? If I hadn't known he was related to her, I wouldn't have guessed."

"Well, when you talk about his mother you *are* talking about his business. Solomon Management is Sophie DeLyon." Austen stands. "Do you want something to drink? Wine okay?"

I nod. He walks the few steps to the kitchen and takes glasses out of a cabinet.

"What do you think of Stephen?" I ask.

"He has followed in his father's footsteps and outdone him. If anyone could be slicker than Victor, it is his son."

"What's he like underneath the veneer?"

"I've never gotten past it. Stephen deflects people."

Returning with two glasses of wine, Austen hands me one. Our fingers accidentally touch.

THE MEMORY IS UNINVITED, BUT it flies up and assails me: a long-ago night in this apartment. Music was playing then, too. Wasn't music always playing when I was with him? He cupped my face in his hands, and I could feel the calluses on his fingers—from the cello strings—on my cheeks.

"I HOPE YOU DON'T MIND red wine," he says, summoning me back.

"You only drink red wine," I say now, recalling that, too.

He doesn't react to my reference to our shared past. What is he thinking? I can't read his face—and this is annoying. I can usually intuit unspoken emotions from people's expressions. But Austen's eyes are unfathomable, his expressions enigmatic. This is how he looked when I sat in the audience and watched him perform, with no hint of an *other* self behind his public façade. But when we were alone together, he was not closed off like this.

"Tell me, how is it possible that there has been so little written about Sophie?" I ask.

"So . . ." He thinks for a few moments. "I'm not being interviewed yet, right? You'll tell me when we go on the record? I'm not comfortable with talking to you without knowing when I'm being quoted."

I wince. Does he know? Has he found out about what happened with St. Pierre?

"Justine?"

"Of course. No, we're not on the record. I was just hoping you could help me understand why Stephen and Daphne went out of their way to talk about the lies I was going to hear. Is there some secret about Sophie?"

"Absolutely not," he answers quickly. "She's just a private person. And as celebrities became more accessible in the Seventies and Eighties, Victor used the privacy thing as a way to differentiate her from everyone else. He wanted to create an aura of mystery about her."

"Do you agree with that strategy? Do you think it was the right thing to do?"

"I've never even thought about it."

"In everyone's story there are secrets, though. I bet even you have some. If someone were writing your biography—"

"There's nothing worth writing about me. He plays the cello. He has a son. That would be it."

"Is there something about Sophie that, were it made public, would change what people think of her, either as a composer or a conductor?"

He shakes his head.

"You can't think of any reason someone might threaten me and try to scare me off?"

"Is someone threatening you?"

"I've gotten some odd E-mail. I don't want to say too much."

"Ah, E-mail. I'm afraid I'm a Luddite. The Internet is my son's terrain."

"Charlie, right?" I ask.

"Yes. Charlie."

"I remember him. He was a cute little kid . . ."

"Well, now he makes MP3 files and composes on his computer."

"Has he ever told you about a Web site that's practically a shrine to Sophie, called The Lyon's Pride?"

He stares out the window as if deciding how much to tell me. "So . . . It's what we used to call ourselves—her students. We were the Lyon's Pride. I haven't heard the expression for years."

"Do her students still call themselves that?"

"Years ago, when I was spending summers at Euphonia, I used to hear them joking about it. I told Sophie she should dissuade them from referring to themselves that way. I thought it sounded cultist, but she liked it. You'll have to ask Sophie about it. Or the students."

"I guess it can wait until I get to Euphonia."

Now I can read his expression, and it's nostalgic. "It is an amazing place. I won't even try to describe it to you. I haven't been there since before I met you. Charlie's there now. Sophie pulled some strings and took him out of school a few weeks early. He's spending the summer studying with her."

His eyes move to a grouping of framed photographs on a table against the wall.

"Which isn't what you wanted?" I ask.

"No."

"How old is he now—fourteen?"

"No, just thirteen. . . ."

"That's amazing. Even being Sophie's grandson, isn't the program limited to Juilliard seniors and graduate students?"

"Yes, and that's why I'm against it. He's too young to be there, no matter how gifted."

In the photographs, Charlie goes from being a toddler to a young boy with his father's dark hair and freckles. He looks both too tall and too serious for his age. In several pictures he is seated at the piano. In others he plays the violin. "If you don't approve, why is he there?"

"I can't stop him. He's Sophie DeLyon's grandson."

"He's also Austen Bell's son."

"In this case, it's more germane who his grandmother is than who his father is." There is resignation in his voice. And hostility. And I remember that he used to speak of Sophie like this when I knew him. He was angry with her then, too, but he never explained why.

Another CD starts. Unlike the Bach before, this music is jarring. It's like a splinter . . . but the pain is beautiful. Too quickly, Austen walks to the stereo and pushes the button to advance the next CD.

"Why did you change it? I liked that."

"It was just an old rehearsal tape." He shrugs it off.

"It was your music, wasn't it?" I ask, knowing. I recognize nuances, tones, an intensity to it and a roughness that might have made it unappealing but didn't.

Austen's music is not polished, but chopped out of wood and left rough. That was what had always made it so exciting: the brutality of its beauty. The way a thunderstorm can be stunning or a fire mesmerizing. Austen wrote music that showed he looked at the world and saw its contradictions. The fragile and the brutal were there, equally translated into works for pianos, violins, flutes, drums, and cymbals.

"Have you been listening to Sophie's music in preparation for doing this story?"

"Yes."

"This is one of her early symphonies," he says, and for a few minutes we both listen.

"Why did you stop performing and become a studio musician?" I ask.

"Charlie was getting older. The divorce was tough on him, and it didn't make sense for me to be away as much as touring demanded."

"But you've been composing?"

"I thought you were here to show me something."

Wondering why he has changed the subject, I sip the wine, and my mind zigzags, landing in the past.

AUSTEN WAS ONE OF MY first interviews. I had just graduated from front-of-the-book pieces to features. An editor of a New York arts magazine assigned me a feature on Sophie DeLyon's protégé who had recently broken from her, which was something of a scandal. Sophie's students did not leave her.

After walking into the crowded café near Carnegie Hall, where Austen had suggested we meet, I stood in the doorway and looked around. Right away I knew who he was.

There was stillness and, at the same time, an energy about him that I had never noticed in anyone before. He sat, looking into space, his hands splayed on the tabletop, his long, graceful fingers resting.

In the time it took to walk across the room, I memorized the way he was sitting at the table, the self-contained expression on his face and the satisfied look in his eyes.

I was drawn to him and envied him. As I neared his table, I tried to write the lead to the article in my head, playing with different words to describe him.

Later I'd learn he had been sitting there listening to music in his head. No matter where he went or what happened around him, Austen Bell lived in two worlds: the corporeal one and the one of imagined sound.

As we wound up the interview, he asked if I would like to hear him play the cello, and we went back to his apartment. It had not been an invitation to an assignation, but I'd been slightly breathless coming up the elevator, as if I were being seduced.

Though it was only five in the afternoon, it was already dark outside; the room was suffused in shadow. He turned on a lamp and motioned to the couch for me to sit.

He opened a large black case and withdrew his cello. Larger than I'd pictured, its color was richer. There was a satin sheen on its surface. It gleamed.

Austen sat, positioned the noble instrument between his legs, and gently drew his bow across the strings. From the first notes, I was transfixed.

He played for forty-five minutes, seemingly unaware of me. I wasn't even sure that if I were to leave, he would have noticed. And then I stopped thinking, and became as caught up in the music as he was. I rode the sounds, they took me further and further out to sea. It was the deepest meditation and the purest distraction I'd ever experienced.

When he was done, he stayed seated until the music lingering in the air completely dissipated.

I abruptly left. I had to. There was the story, and I couldn't let anything get in its way. I didn't see him again until after it came out. He called me when the magazine hit the stands and asked me to dinner. Later that evening, he'd brought me back to his apartment, and played me something he'd written in the weeks since we'd met.

Again I was transported. I didn't know what I liked more—this man and his talent or his ability to take me away from myself.

Then we became lovers.

Music always set the tone of our lovemaking. We were romantic with Chopin, violent with Stravinsky and reverential with Beethoven. We translated sound to touch, to physical rhythm. One night Austen played more of the atonal modern symphony that he started writing after we'd met.

It was not just the strange unsympathetic music; I'd had too much wine to drink. The week before I'd found out my mother was sick, and I was desperate to be distracted from what I still refused to believe.

My mother had looked much worse that day and I wanted to force her image to recede. It would take something violent and extreme to stop me from seeing her haunted eyes, her yellowing skin, her listless hands—not chopping or cutting or mixing—lying idle in her lap.

I asked Austen to tie me to the bedposts.

While taking neckties from his closet, he told me he hadn't considered himself naïve until meeting me. Then he was silent, concentrated on wrapping the silk around my feet. I'd held my breath, stared at his naked body, and heard dissonant sounds pounding in my head.

"The *things* you know . . ." Austen said as he stared down at me—imprisoned, unable to move, below him in his bed. He was looking at me from a distance. The space between us was the terrain where our pasts were buried. He stayed, standing above me, peering down.

"I'm trying to understand," he said.

"What?" I asked. "Why I want to do this?"

"That, and why I want to."

"Does it matter?"

"It might," he offered.

"It's just a game. More power for you, loss of power for me."

"How can it be a loss of power for you? You asked for this."

"That's why it is just a game."

"Is it dangerous?" he asked.

I knew he did not mean the silk ties themselves but rather taking the step from sensible sex into the realm of the fetish, the unknown, and the visceral instead of the logical.

"It scares me that you are not even pretending this is about being in love." His voice had dropped into a lower register.

Austen has a lilt to his voice, as if music had been his first language, English his second.

"Surely you have made love without being in love?" I asked, then was sorry I'd said it. I was giving away too much.

"I wish I didn't have to wonder about the man who taught you this," he said.

"So don't."

If he had asked me how I knew these things, I wasn't sure I would have told him the truth. I'd never mentioned much about my sexual history, but neither had I pretended not to have one.

Slowly, Austen lowered himself on top of me. He moved as if caught in a wave about to pull him under.

"YOU MAKE ME THINK ABOUT things other than the cello," he said afterward.

"Why does that upset you?"

"It doesn't."

"You didn't hear the way you said it."

"I worry." His fingers played my spine as if it were the cello's fingerboard. "I worry that I am going to lose myself in you, and that would be bad for my music, for the music I want to write. I have to start writing again. Now that I've broken with Sophie, I have to get back to my own compositions."

SITTING OPPOSITE HIM NOW, I'M bewildered by what I've remembered.

Except Austen is the last person I can wonder about. I am going to be spending the next month writing about this man's mentor, the grandmother of his only son. I cannot blur the lines this time. Not walk any tightropes. Not now.

But what was he to me?

I IMAGINE MY MOTHER'S EYES, sad and wistful. Why now? Why do they look at me again now? But I know. Her eyes warn me not to want anyone the way she wanted my father. Loss, I learned from her, is not tolerable. When someone leaves—even emotionally—they take too much of you with them.

And thanks to her warning, I've never lain in bed at night with a pillow smothering my sobs. My sister and I had heard my mother crying in the dark through our thin apartment walls.

The sounds of my mother weeping had been warning enough about love.

AS IT TURNED OUT, AUSTEN left to go on tour before my mother died.

From every stop he sent CDs. His choices from abroad were mostly romantic, and the message he was giving through the music was not lost on me. Rachmaninoff, Chopin, and Tchaikovsky were wooing me while my mother lingered. And then, while he was in Brazil, when she died, he sent me Mozart's *Requiem,* and I played it over and over, lying on my bed, sedated and sad. My tears, I thought, rolled down my cheeks in time to the music.

He was gone for the rest of the summer and early fall, returning only two days before I left for Paris.

Sick of New York and of grieving, I had taken a job Kurt Davis had offered, and arranged for my sister to live in my apartment while I was gone.

When I told Austen I was leaving he spent our last two days together trying to convince me to stay in New York. He drove me to the airport, still trying, but ultimately failing to convince me not to take the job.

"You are leaving too many things," he said. The therapy I'd started. The unresolved and acrimonious relationships with my father and sister. My grief. But he couldn't change my mind.

"What if I asked you to stay for my sake?" he asked.

"Don't," I told him.

In Paris one of my first assignments was to interview a young director, the most recent winner of the Palme d'Or at the Cannes Film Festival. After my profile about him ran, I took him as a lover.

I TAKE ANOTHER SIP OF wine. When I look, I see Austen staring at me, a frown creasing his forehead.

"What is it?" I ask.

"I was remembering how you do everything with such passion, even drinking a glass of wine. You really taste it, don't you?" He shakes his head, trying to dislodge the thought. "I once wrote you a letter . . . after seeing you in Paris . . . but I never sent it. . . ."

"Tell me," I say.

"I tried to describe it in the letter. 'Passion is the emotional twill of the fabric of your life,' I wrote."

I can't say what I want to say, and so I say the wrong thing. "And that was a problem, wasn't it? You also once said that you were afraid you couldn't keep up with me."

"Oh, Justine." I think there is more coming, but he stops, shakes his head. "It's been almost four years. We've changed. I am not going to be tempted by you this time."

Since any involvement with him could so easily compromise my story, I'm relieved. At the same time, hearing him renounce me makes me want to fight back. "I wouldn't want you to be tempted by me," I answer flippantly. "I'm a heartless bitch."

He bursts out laughing. "What?"

"It's true," I say, and then continue, blurting it out, not wanting to, but not quite knowing how to stop the words from coming. "I am missing something. No matter who I'm with. It's something I've re- alized quite recently. I'm bad at relationships."

"Maybe that's because you don't have them."

"What does that mean?"

"You stay outside. You give—but you only give. You won't take anything."

"How do you know that?"

"I remember."

"What happened with us in Paris was bad," I say.

"What? That you were seeing someone else or that I walked in on you two?"

"That's not fair. We never said anything about seeing only each other."

"I wasn't seeing anyone else. It was serious for me. Anyway, it was a matter of trust that became a matter of mistrust."

"That's terrible. . . ." My voice is small, and he has to lean forward to hear me.

"Well, it's a terrible thing to not be able to trust someone who you thought you could trust completely."

I stand up then. It is time to go home. I get all the way to the door.

"Wait," he says.

I turn.

"What was it you came here to show me? Didn't you say you wanted something about sheet music?"

"No, that's okay. I'll show it to Sophie when I get to Euphonia." I put out my hand to open the door.

"Justine, I didn't mean to upset you. Stay, have dinner with me?"

I have to go. The story is too important and Austen is too important to the story. Right now my father and Maddy are in the restaurant working side by side in the kitchen. Maddy wants me to come down there. I should go, get out of here, get away from Austen, be with them. But I can't.

Not without my mother . . . I can't be *with* them *without* her.

"Dinner? Why does dinner make you cry?" Austen asks so sweetly that my tears come faster.

The sound I make emerges as a sort of sob and hiccup and laugh, all mixed together.

"No, it's just the jet lag . . . and being home . . . and not feeling like I'm home, and it's my mother—I keep thinking of her here . . . more than I do when I'm in Paris . . . even though I thought of her there too. . . . It's different—missing her here is worse."

Austen puts his arms around me, pulling me close and letting his shirt soak up my tears.

This is how it happens, our first touch in almost four years, and it is one of compassion and comfort.

I ask him, "Where are we going to have dinner?"

SIXTEEN

WE DO NOT go out to dinner, after all. Austen opens another bottle of wine. I lean in the kitchen doorway, watching while he puts water on to boil and breaks up a head of soft, buttery Boston lettuce.

The table overlooks the sparkling Manhattan skyline. The salad is fresh with a light dousing of fine extra-virgin olive oil, a squirt of lemon, a twist of the pepper mill, and a pinch of sea salt. The pasta is tossed with nothing more than butter, more of the fresh pepper, and grated Parmesan.

This is the kind of meal you have in Europe: simple ingredients of such quality that it is more delicious than the most complicated concoction.

Even more surprising than how good the food is, though, is what Austen says a few minutes after we begin eating.

"Hearing your voice when you first called threw me. Just hearing you say, 'Hello . . . it's Justine.' I could see your gamine face. . . . I remembered how big your eyes got the first time you stopped hearing the music I played and really started to listen to it. I can't remember if you took any pleasure. But, oh, I remember the pleasure you gave."

I want to ask him if he is talking about music now or how we were in bed. I am afraid because I like hearing this from a man I am not supposed to be thinking of this way.

"One phone message . . . that's all it took. Damn. After so long . . . your voice triggered . . . I remember who I was with you. I liked who I was when we were together."

He drinks more wine and I don't move. I don't know why he is telling me this now after what he said about not trusting me.

"I made some calls and found out about your problems in Paris, Justine."

I put down my fork, push away my plate. Has he told Sophie? I gulp the wine that now has lost its rich body; it tastes almost sour. I don't say anything—using my reporter's trick of silence to induce the other person to feel the need to fill the gap. Usually this works. It docs now.

"I understood why you'd contacted me after so long, asking for a favor. I figured I'd help you out, pass on your request to Sophie, and we'd be even. I'd have repaid my debt to you and that would be that. We could go another three or ten or twenty years without seeing each other again."

"You didn't owe me anything," I say.

I don't know why I'm still sitting here. I don't want to hear his confession. Nothing good can come of it, no matter what direction it takes. And I'm embarrassed that he knows the whole St. Pierre story.

"But I do. After a long year of not writing, I wrote my best music in that short time we were together." He turns from me and stares out the window at the night sky. In profile his features are hard and unyielding, almost cruel.

"But you're still writing now, aren't you?"

He turns and looks at me—not answering, not needing to. His eyes are sad. This is what is missing from him. This is what has changed him. Something has gone terribly wrong with his work.

He shakes his head, doesn't explain. And when he starts talking, it's not about his music but about me. "I can't see you again . . . even if I've never known a woman who was better at giving a man's ego an erection." He drains his glass.

I get up.

He doesn't have to ask; he knows I'm leaving. "Give me two minutes and I'll take you downstairs and put you in a taxi," he says.

"I don't need you to do that."

"It's late and I do."

I sit down.

THE NEXT THING I KNOW is that my legs are cramped and my right arm is numb and I'm not at all sure where I am. It is dark, I have a blanket thrown over me and Austen is sitting opposite me.

"I fell asleep?"

"While you were waiting for me to take you downstairs and put you in a taxi. I left you alone for five minutes and you were out."

"It's still the jet lag. What time is it?"

He looks at his watch. "Almost six in the morning."

"You let me sleep here so long?"

He shrugs.

While I'm in the bathroom, washing my face and freshening up, he makes coffee. As we sip it, I finally I show him the sheet music that brought me back to him.

Looking down at the printout, his expression eludes me, but I see how the tendons on his neck tense.

"What is it?"

"It's from the overture of a film Sophie's scored. This particular sequence is from the scene where Joan of Arc is burned at the stake. It's frightening, the most desolate music she has ever written."

He looks up from the page. "Who sent it to you?"

"I don't know. I've gotten three pieces of E-mail from someone who only identifies himself—or herself—as Lyon's Pride."

"And what do they say?"

"That I shouldn't write about Sophie."

"Why?"

"Because whatever her flaws—they shouldn't be exposed at the expense of her genius. That the media does damage to artists. That we destroy careers rather than bring insight. It's so popular lately to blame the media. Joyce Carol Oates has described it as *Pathography*; she defines it as a mean-spirited trend of emphasizing the sensational underside of a subject's life."

"Was there an overt threat in the letter?"

"Just that they will not let me destroy Sophie."

"Sounds like the kind of thing an obsessed student might say."

"And are there a lot of students obsessed by her?"

"We all are at first. You can't imagine how large she looms. How many legends there are about her."

"When did you first meet her?"

"I was in New York, a sophomore at Juilliard. She had just started Euphonia. My professor suggested I audition for the summer session. I was daunted, trying out for such an elite group. Twenty-two students handpicked by Sophie DeLyon."

"Twenty-two?"

"The minimum needed to make up an orchestra."

"How old were you?"

"Seventeen. I'd started Juilliard at sixteen. Maybe it wasn't a good thing, starting so young." He glances at the photographs of Charlie. "I don't like to compare what he's doing with what I did. But what about you? Was it good for you to miss out on so much?"

"Miss out? By spending my summers on book tours signing autographs and making chocolate soup on TV morning shows?" I laugh. "I have nothing to compare it to."

"I just want Charlie to be a kid. He's got the rest of his life to be a grown-up."

"Except it was what I wanted, Austen. I loved being with my mother." I feel the ache. "That's what matters. If it's what Charlie wants."

Austen gets up to put a new stack of CDs on the player and doesn't say anything until he has finished.

"It's what he thinks he wants. It's what Sophie and Daphne praise him for. It's what gets him attention and makes him special."

Austen remains standing.

"But . . . ?" I ask.

"I'm worried about him. He's not easygoing. He's not happy. You know I try . . . I try to let him know that I will love him whether he is a musician or not. I try, but mine is just one voice. When we spend the weekend together, we don't do anything that has to do with music. He's a natural athlete and we play tennis, ride bikes, and go to baseball games. Sophie taught him to sail and he likes that. But lately he doesn't want to spend time doing anything but play the piano or the violin and sit at the computer and download MP3 files. He's gotten pale and sickly looking, and he's just thirteen. He should be . . . I want to get him away from the rarefied air around Sophie. But I don't know how much impact I can have two days a week. And now this . . . this summer at Euphonia, it's not what he should be doing. He should be having fun."

He returns to the couch and sits down. "What got us started on this?"

"You were telling me about the first time you met Sophie."

"That spring of my sophomore year. Yes, it was at the audition for the summer program. Christ, you'd think after almost two years at Juilliard I would have gotten over stage fright. But sitting in that empty auditorium, with Sophie DeLyon as my only audience, it all came rushing back. I was all nerves."

"But you did all right?"

"It didn't start off well at all. My playing was slow and flat. I was trying not to look at her, to stay with the music, to get inside the music. But I couldn't: she distracted me. Sophie is never just in a room, she owns the space. She filled that empty auditorium.

"When I was only a quarter through, she stood up and started to walk out. It was an amazingly rude thing to do, and I hated her for it. No matter who she was—or how badly I was playing—it wasn't right. Watching her back as she walked to the door, I forgot about how nervous I was. Suddenly I had something to prove. I wanted—more than anything—to make her turn around. To make her apologize and tell me she'd been wrong."

"Did she stop?"

"No. She walked out."

"What did you do?"

Austen smiles. "I kept playing, piece after piece. On and on. I sat there—alone for an hour after she'd left—and I just kept playing. The next week I got a formal letter of invitation to Euphonia."

"Did she ever apologize?"

"Sophie? No, never. That's not something she would do. Years later she told me that she had stood outside the auditorium and listened to my whole performance."

"Did that make you feel any better?"

"By the time she told me about it, it didn't matter." His voice has gone flat.

What has Sophie done to make Austen so angry? There is time to ask him that, I think, afraid that if I push too hard now I'll stop him from talking. "I know. Apologies only soften the edges of anger. They don't file them all the way down. Only time can do that. And only if you are lucky," I say.

"Whoa. Who are you angry at?"

"My sister. My father." I shrug. "Austen, why haven't you been composing?"

"I haven't had time." He says this as if it doesn't matter.

I don't say what I am thinking: that once it was all that mattered.

"More coffee?" he asks.

While he gets it, I watch, appreciating the efficient way he moves: an economy of motion that I've never noticed in anyone else. It is the same way he speaks; rarely saying more than what is necessary. It is the same way with the music he composes.

The right sounds layered on each other creating an exacting but rich, distinct sound. Austen's music is like water dripping into a pool, tumbling over rocks, crashing in waves on the beach. It is like fire leaping up to devour brush in its path or dying down when the destruction is done. It is the water putting out the fire. And the fire starting up again.

Across the room, Austen looks at me. I feel a sudden lurch, an involuntarily intake of breath.

WHEN I WAS SIXTEEN, I WENT sailing with my mother, her editor, and his wife. It was a strange day. My mother was excited and nervous and I didn't know why. She wasn't afraid of the water.

"But I've never gone sailing before. Isn't that crazy? Forty and never been out on a sailboat?" she explained.

It was a calm day with a slight breeze, which made for an easy trip. We dropped anchor, lunched on food my mother had provided, swam in the water, and lay on the deck, tanning. My mother and Paul Enderling talked about books and cooking, and his wife— I don't remember her that well—spent most of her time with their seven-year-old little boy.

On the way back, a sudden wind came up. The sails puffed out to their limit as the jib swung around and the boat took off: speeding through the water, leaping ahead and breaking through waves. The sea spray—salty enough to sting my eyes—flew into my face and wet my clothes.

I felt every thrust of that boat in every muscle of my body.

My mother was afraid and Paul sent her below. But I wasn't. Something was waking up in me. My senses were becoming more attuned. I experienced the boat ride in a way that I had never lived through anything before. I loved it. To live on the edge of the wind like that, to be buffeted and propelled and pushed to my limit without allowing the fear to overwhelm the experience.

I FEEL THAT SAME AWAKENING now, holding Austen's glance. My senses are sharpening. I take deep breaths of air. The atmosphere has changed and I can't get enough oxygen to my lungs. As if he has ordered me to—though he has said nothing—I walk to him in the kitchen area. I go to him and wait inches from his face.

Not him. Not this.

Without taking me in his arms, without touching any part of my body except for my lips—almost as if he is afraid that if he touches me he will not let me go—he kisses me.

It is the need to breathe that finally forces us to separate, to step back. When we do, it is not pleasure that I see on Austen's face.

"It might be that I've been heading toward you a long time and didn't know it. But it's too late, isn't it?"

"How can you take so many chances?" is his odd response.

"What?"

"You ask questions that other people would never dare ask. It must make you a good journalist."

"If I don't ask, no one will tell me."

"But so direct . . ."

"And so few people are?" I finish his thought.

"I'm sure it works for you, at least professionally. I'm sure your questions catch people off guard."

"Not everyone answers me."

"Even if they don't, they're telling you something."

I'm surprised at the insight. "That's true."

"And so, Miss Reporter—" He used to use this endearment with me. "What have I told you with my response?"

"That you, Mr. Bell, have no idea what to do with me now that I am actually here. Perhaps you were even hoping you would hate that kiss because you don't trust me. And if I remember correctly, I am too passionate for you."

"I knew I'd regret saying that."

He's managed to avoid telling me if I am on target with my guess. Slightly angry, I turn my back to him and walk to the living room.

He easily catches up to me. Reaching out, he takes me by the shoulders, turns me to face him and is about to say something. Instead, he kisses me again. Suddenly, this is exactly where I want to be. His mouth is warm and so are his hands through my sweater. Or is this exactly where I don't want to be?

I've always thought of kisses as being of the night, of the darkness. But I glimpse colors moving in time to music when his lips are on me. Lights move inside me, relieving me of gravity. I might lift off into this light.

I pull back, break the connection. I've made a mistake and have to undo it. But how do I explain without insulting him and running the risk of losing his cooperation on my story?

He takes in my hesitation and translates it for himself. "I have no interest in finding out how long it will take you to move on this time, Justine. Interview me over the phone. I'll be happy to answer your questions about Sophie. But this—tonight—what happened just now, it's a mistake."

"I didn't move on," I say.

Why am I arguing? I should just be thankful that he is still willing to give me an interview and get the hell out of here.

"No?"

"Austen, are you still angry at me?"

He doesn't answer, doesn't have to. His face is stony again.

"Why are you angry?" I ask.

"I'm not."

"Of course you are. Why do men hate talking about their feelings so damn much?"

"Oh, Justine . . . a cliché from you?"

"Good diversion, but I'm not taking the bait and getting involved in conversation defending my choice of words. What is so awful that you can't tell me?"

"You did exactly what I expected you would do."

I know I've bullied him into responding, but I don't care. This man, usually so even-keeled, so ephemeral, is talking through clenched teeth.

"You took another lover. What was it, Justine? You need sex that much that you couldn't live without it for a few weeks?"

"That is an awful thing to say."

"But you are not denying that it's the truth."

"It was other things."

"I know." His voice grows weary, as if he has said this often. "Too much of my energy and attention go to my music." His eyes search out and rest on his cello, which stands guard in the corner of the room.

"Ah, your mistress."

"My . . . my what?"

"I know how much your cello means to you. I've seen how you hold her, how you touch her. I know what you can do with her. Sometimes when we used to make love, I thought you fantasized that I was that instrument."

"And . . ."

"And what?"

"And it bothered you. It bored you. It made you jealous. I could go on. Do I need to?"

"No, Austen. It exhilarated me."

He stares at me skeptically.

"You don't believe me?"

"I'm not sure. Even if you mean it, your exhilaration didn't last long."

I say nothing because I don't know what to say. I don't normally feel guilty or regret what I've done, so then why is this conversation so disturbing?

"You think that it's the sex that matters to me. That my passion is so strong that I can't—"

"Why does what I think mean anything to you?" he interrupts. "We knew each other for a short time, a long while ago. We don't know each other anymore."

Music fills the silence. I see myself getting up, sitting next to him, touching his leg with my hand, his neck with my lips. But I don't move. It's too easy. What is harder is to resist, not to give in, not to be filled with sensations. To do the right thing, get the story and go back to Paris.

"Do you want to get something to eat? The Empire Diner. Stays open all night."

We'll be safer there, I think. And he might talk about Sophie. There is no reason not to go.

WE ARE STILL AT THE diner at seven-thirty when Austen's cell phone rings.

"Who could . . . ?" Austen answers the phone quickly, obviously concerned about who would be calling so very early.

"Hello?"

He listens and then: "Charlie, I don't understand. Are you all right?"

Again he listens.

"Earlier this morning or last night? What are you saying?"

There is another pause.

"What time did she leave?" There is more silence and then: "Do you want me to come and pick you up?"

He is frowning, his lips pursed. His fingers grip the cell phone. "I'll be there soon. All right?" Another pause. "Listen, is Helena there? Can I talk to her?"

I mentally run through my notes. Helena Rath is the director of Euphonia, one of Sophie's closest friends.

Austen says good-bye and closes his cell phone.

"Is Charlie all right?" I ask after he motions to the waitress for the check.

"Charlie's fine. He's shook up, but he's fine. It's Sophie." His voice trembles. He seems uncertain and confused.

"What about Sophie?"

"She went sailing last night. Her boat's back—beached. But she's not on it."

PART II

No one can love the country as much as I do. For surely woods, trees, and rocks produce the echo which man most desires to hear.

—LUDWIG VAN BEETHOVEN, IN A LETTER TO BARONESS VON DROSSDICK

SEVENTEEN

WAITRESSES CARRY PLATTERS of eggs and bacon and pour steaming coffee into standard white china mugs. The diner is filling up, and the smells and noise and activity are at odds with the solemnity of our conversation.

"If something has happened to Sophie, Charlie is going to be devastated," he says.

I get up and sit beside him.

"What did he say?"

"Charlie woke up and went down to meet Sophie on the beach. They take a long walk with the dog early every morning. She wasn't there and her boat was beached."

"But Sophie can swim, can't she?"

"Like a fucking fish. She goes swimming almost every day. She's out there no matter what the temperature is."

The waitress still hasn't arrived with the bill and Austen looks around for her—nowhere in sight.

"When did she take the boat out?"

"Charlie doesn't know. After dinner he went to his room to work on a composition and didn't see her after that. This morning when she wasn't on the beach, Charlie went to her room. Her bed hadn't been slept in."

"And nobody realized she was missing till this morning? Why didn't they notice last night?"

"When Sophie's composing, she often goes off by herself in the boat and stays out overnight on a mooring. It's not unheard of for her to stay on board for a few days and nights. The big house can be distracting, especially when all the students are arriving and getting set up. But even when she stays out, she usually docks overnight and comes back to walk with Charlie and have breakfast."

"Charlie must be in a panic. The boat just washed up on shore, empty?"

"I suppose so." The information is starting to sink in. "Charlie said he woke up Helena and she's called the Coast Guard and the police. They're on the way." There is fear in his eyes.

"I'm sorry."

"It will be fine. It will. Sophie's whole life is about overcoming and surviving. And Charlie is there. She couldn't . . . wouldn't do this to him. He is her future the way neither of her own children are."

"What are you talking about?" Suicide, I think, but am afraid to name it.

Nervously, he picks up the salt shaker and spins it on the black glass tabletop. It falls. An abstract swirl of crystals spills out on the table, stark white against the black. Like stars in a dark sky.

Austen looks like a child who has just fallen but does not yet understand what has happened, sitting on the ground in shocked stillness before it hits him that he's hurt.

It is in this moment that for the first time in my adult life I feel the awful pull of wanting to—but not knowing how to—help a man. Only toward my mother have I ever felt anything close to this sudden wrenching.

"So I need . . . to go to Euphonia . . . to be with Charlie."

"If you want, I can come with you."

He looks surprised, then grateful, and then his expression changes again.

"Why, to get a good story?"

I wince. "No, not for the article, but because it's an hour's drive and you shouldn't have to go out there alone."

He straightens up and brushes the salt onto the floor, where it disappears. He clears his throat and makes an unsuccessful effort to appear calm. "It will be fine. Nothing more can happen to Sophie. It's all happened to her already."

He hasn't turned down my offer.

SOPHIE'S SOUNDTRACK TO BECKWITH'S *Saint Joan* fills the car. It is not heroic, not triumphant or spiritual. It is brutal music that weeps and shudders in pain—a precautionary theme that bears witness to a young girl's tragedy. The notes twist and turn in anguish as Joan feels the first licks of the flame.

Listening, I have no doubt someone sent me a considerable warning. And wants me to believe he or she is serious about protecting Sophie.

Austen pushes the pause button.

"Frightening, no?"

"Yes."

Whoever wants to protect her should have been more concerned for the tide and the waves, which have put Sophie in more jeopardy than my proposed article.

Austen hits the play button and the overture begins again.

From my bag, I pull out my pen and notebook. Computer printouts of all Sophie's correspondence are stuffed between the last page and the back cover. But I don't read the notes; I bring the pen up to my face. The chilly metal and shell against my cheek bring back the familiar sense of loss and longing for my mother. I stuff my things back into my bag and sit quietly for the next few miles, listening to the music, trying to ignore the pull and the ache that never seems to abate.

Austen grips the steering wheel tightly. "I can't bear to think what this will do to Charlie."

"Don't. Not yet. Don't die twice."

"What?"

"It's something my mother would say when I'd worry. All the obsessing in the world won't prevent whatever is going to happen or keep you from having to deal with it when it does. Spending time agonizing about it beforehand is just wasting time. If it doesn't happen, you've worried for nothing. And if it does, you've suffered twice."

Austen takes my hand. Half to comfort me, half to be comforted. His skin is so cold and his grip is tight.

This is all right, I tell myself. I am just being compassionate. There is nothing more to this clasping of hands: it is not an embrace. For a moment I sense that surge of power I'm used to feeling when a man is making love to me—when he is lost in the rhythm and the heat, and I am moving him forward. But this—this has nothing to do with sex.

As the minutes pass and the scenery changes from city to country landscape, more of my concentration focuses on our hands and the small point of skin where our wrists are pressed together. I can feel his pulse beating against my skin. I doubt he is even conscious of still holding my hand. Or how much he is hurting me.

But if his fingers are so attuned to nuance—from sliding up and down the strings and stopping on exactly the right spot to make the right sound—maybe he can sense what I am thinking through his skin. Despite myself, my reaction to his touch reaches down between my legs, where it rests—half-formed and niggling. It scares me. I am crossing into dangerous territory. He may need solace now, but he is connected to my story and I have already jeopardized too much of this chance to resuscitate my career.

I remove my hand. Austen replaces his on the wheel and navigates a turn.

Fifteen minutes later, Austen parks on the main street in the town of Greenwich. He's been smoking nonstop during the drive from Manhattan and needs more cigarettes. It is Sophie's disappearance, he says, that has caused him to return to this habit.

Getting out of the car, I look up and down the wide avenue. It's taken only forty minutes to get here, but it feels far away from the city.

One- and two-story buildings and trees dotted with small white and pink flowers line the street. There is a steady stream of traffic, but it is easygoing and not frenetic, like in New York. Here, people stroll. A woman walks by pushing a baby carriage and holding a toddler's hand. As she passes, she smiles.

No, this is not the city. Even the air smells different. There is just a hint of the sea and none of the smog. Across the street is a U-shaped post office. In front of it is a garden of tulips: purple, pink, red, magenta—the wind blows and the flowers bend. Two teenagers sit on one of the wooden benches and drink sodas.

This is obviously a wealthy town. There is no litter on the sidewalks. The windows of the stores are shining clean. Two huge flower baskets hang from each streetlamp all the way up the avenue. Purple verbena, heliotrope, ivy, and pink petunias hang in colorful masses over their moss-filled wire basins.

Luxury cars drive past—most of them gleaming. A woman gets out of a car, the large diamond in her ring sparkling in the sun. Despite the jeans and blazer, the shoes and the bag are expensive brand names.

We walk into a variety store. An entire wall is devoted to magazines and newspapers and the array is almost dizzying. In front of the cash register are shelves of candy. As many kinds, it seems, as there are magazines. A stand holds postcards: glossy pictures of sailboats in Greenwich Harbor, New England whitewashed churches, and picturesque gardens.

One card attracts my attention. It's a black-and-white old-fashioned-looking photograph of a gothic castle rising from a snow-covered forest. It conjures up Wuthering Heights, Xanadu, and Manderley, places that don't exist except in the imagination.

Turning over the card, I read the description of the scene in the left-hand corner.

Euphonia—a music conservatory housed in what once was the Standish Castle. Built by famed architect Anthony Slavin in 1857, Euphonia is part of a 154-acre preserve on the Long Island Sound and is now devoted to the study of

music. Concerts are held at the end of the summer, which
is the only time the grounds are open to the public.

Several people stand in line waiting to buy newspapers, magazines, lottery tickets, candy, or cigarettes. A man in paint-splattered
overalls talks to a woman in tennis clothes.

"Awful about Sophie DeLyon, isn't it? I knew something was
going to happen to somebody last night. Those winds came up so
sudden, and even though they died down right away, for that half
hour it was treacherous out there. And so many people had just put
their boats in the water for the season. . . ."

"I just can't imagine dying that way," says the woman.

Austen, at the head of the line and about to pay for his cigarettes, spins around. Holding a ten-dollar bill, his hand is frozen
midair. "She's not dead," he says to the strangers in a low, measured
voice.

"Well, I sure hope not." The painter shakes his head. "But that
boat was empty and the water is cold. If she fell over—"

"She's a good swimmer. She could have easily gotten to land."
Austen sounds as if he is pleading, even though he is using declar-
ative sentences.

"I heard she was drinking a little and didn't realize a storm was
coming, then got knocked overboard," the woman on the line says.

"I heard the police are considering foul play," a second woman
says.

"You mean they think she was murdered?" the first woman asks.

"Such an amazing woman," the second offers. "We always went
to those concerts. I used to love watching her conduct. All that energy . . . She was unique, wasn't she?"

What a small town this is. A conversation like this between
strangers would never happen in Paris or New York.

"You shouldn't be talking about her as if she's gone. . . ." Austen
is saying. "She swam to shore. And she's at someone's house sleeping off exhaustion. When she wakes up, she'll tell them who she is
and this will all be just a bad dream."

It finally occurs to the shoppers that they might have been talking to someone who actually knows Sophie. They exchange a look and they back up a little—leaving Austen and me alone, giving us room.

"Austen?" I put my hand on his arm.

He drops the ten-dollar bill on the counter and walks out.

Behind us the conversation continues. "Was that one of the musicians who teaches up there?"

"Oh, no, how embarrassing."

"IS IT FAR?" I ASK when we are back in the car.

"No, just another ten minutes."

Shaking a cigarette out of the fresh pack, Austen fumbles with a cheap plastic lighter, lights up, then inhales deeply. The sharp smell of burning tobacco fills the car.

After a few miles he turns down a road that leads into a park. The pine trees here are tall and little sun penetrates the thicket. Everything has taken on a blue-green hue, and the air is at least ten degrees cooler. Austen shuts off the CD player and rolls down the windows. Birdsong fills the air.

For the last few miles, I have been trying to figure out how to ask him if there is anyone who might want Sophie dead, if there really is any possibility that she might have been murdered. But I don't know how to phrase such a question, so I ask nothing.

Austen slows in front of a large iron gate. From inside the stone gatehouse, a guard looks up, and then comes outside.

"I'm glad you're here, Mr. Bell. It's been a long time since we've seen you. Welcome back. I wish it was under different circumstances."

"Thank you, Sam. Is there any news? We've been in the car for a while."

"No, Mr. Bell. We are all praying for Miss DeLyon's safe return."

"Thank you. How are Nancy and the girls?"

"Fine. Thank you for asking. You'll see Nancy. She's still working in the gardens. And the girls are at college, thanks to Miss De-Lyon. They're on their way home . . . too upset to stay away. It will be so hard on them to see police . . . at Euphonia." He shakes his head sadly, and the gate lifts.

Austen drives on. Stone walls, covered with lichen and moss and in many places overgrown with ivy, hug the road and are all that separate it from a forest densely populated by pines. The air is redolent with scent.

Occasionally I glimpse cottages hidden among the trees. Austen explains that these are residences for the staff at Euphonia — the chef, housekeepers, a handyman, several gardeners — the people who keep the place functioning.

Other than the evergreens, there are groupings of birches and oak trees. My eyes are filled with more greens than I can name. Yellow green, reddish green, and then an ashen green. The road twists and climbs, and now mixed in with the scent of pine is the salty air of Long Island Sound.

After Austen takes the next turn, we clear the forest. On top of the next hill is the stone castle from the postcard. The building glows, gold spires on each of the turrets shine, and what seems like hundreds of mullioned windowpanes blaze. Euphonia looks as if it is on fire.

EIGHTEEN

I N F R O N T O F it now, I realize that of course Euphonia is not on fire. It's the sun shining down, reflecting off every surface. Austen stops the car and shuts off the engine. "It hasn't changed at all," he says. The birdsong mixes with sounds of the sea slapping the shore. From inside the castle comes the long, slow, and sorrowful sound of a violin pulling, tugging at me.

Between the driveway and the house is a grassy island where a life-size Pan stands blowing his flute, out of which comes water instead of music. Over the years the sea air and the moisture have dulled the statue except for its shining bronze flute. Nestled in a ring of pansies surrounding the basin of the fountain is a plaque.

In 1853, the composer Hector Berlioz discovered the imaginary land of Euphonia, a small village at the foot of the mountains in Bavaria. There was just one rule in this idyllic town: Every citizen must be involved in the making of music. Members of the orchestra, instrument makers, composers, and students were all welcome, as they, too, are welcome here.

A coin plinks against the metal basin.

"Sophie's tradition," Austen explains. "The first time you return for the season, you symbolically pay your way—throw a coin in the fountain—and then"—he reaches out and touches the flute—"For luck."

Reaching into my bag, I find a quarter, toss it, and I, too, touch the flute, understanding now why it shines.

The violin lament ends. Without the music, not even the birds or the water splashing in the fountain fill the sudden emptiness.

Turning back to the car, Austen retrieves both his suitcase and mine, and together we walk up the stairs toward the front doors. Now, only a few feet away, I realize why the castle glows pink: it's covered with thousands of scallop shells embedded in the façade of the building.

I utter an astonished, "Oh."

"It's amazing, isn't it?"

"Was it always like this?"

"No. When the family gave the estate to Sophie, the castle hadn't been inhabited for over fifty years. The façade was concrete and it—as well as the inside—was falling apart. The grounds were equally unkempt. Sophie spent months finding the right architects and landscapers, and then moved up here full-time to oversee the restoration."

"Whose idea were the shells?"

"Pure Sophie."

Inside, our footsteps echo in the entranceway. I'm not sure where to look first. The walls in this large foyer are covered with botanical prints and oil paintings of the sea and sky, the floors with Oriental carpets. Up above—at least twenty feet up—sky and clouds are visible through a skylight. Hanging down from its center is a long chain and a chandelier made of black, white, and pink glass drops—no, these are shells too.

"Sophie says this is what her music would look like if it were an edifice. She chose every stick of furniture, every towel and sheet and plate and fork in the place."

"How long did it take?"

"Six years."

"The six years she was retired?" I ask.

"Well, she said she was retiring. But when she wasn't working on the renovation, she was writing her *Euphonia Symphony.*"

Mirrors shimmer, lights glow. Large nautilus shells have been turned into wall sconces. On top of side tables are informal arrangements of flowers spilling over their tall vases and scenting the room. Silk shawls in rainbow colors are thrown over chairs and couches. But something is missing,

"Austen, the house is sad."

"You can feel that?"

I nod. "But I don't know why."

"It's the music. The house only comes alive when it is filled with music, and—"

Approaching footsteps interrupt. The woman walking toward us is a study in black, not just her clothes, but her expression. There's no color in her cheeks or her lips. No vibrancy to her except her eyes, which are an extraordinary light blue—the color Renaissance painters used in the Virgin's robes. Bone thin and well-groomed, she is ascetic, but for the luxuriant dark hair that curves around her face like parentheses.

By her side is a cocker spaniel, who ambles over to Austen, sniffing at his feet.

"Hello, Helena," Austen says.

She tries to smile, but it slips, leaving her lips twisted in a tragic curve.

"Austen." Her voice is hoarse and barely above a whisper.

When my mother was dying, it was all I could do to get dressed—and yet this woman's hair is blown-dry, her slacks are sharply creased, and her sweater is knotted just so around her neck.

As if embracing cardboard or ice, Austen takes Helena in his arms. As soon as she is sheltered by him, a sob escapes her throat, as if this one kindness has been too much for her.

"Is there news?" he asks.

"No. Nothing yet. But she'll be back. She has to come back." Helena's voice cracks again. "I'm sorry—I seem to be losing my voice." She telegraphs such extreme despondency that even though I don't know her, I want to say something to soothe her grief.

Austen steps back. "Justine Pagett, this is Helena Rath—the director of Euphonia." We shake hands and I am startled by how cold Helena's hand is, as if there were no blood circulating in her body at all. As my name registers, so does her surprise. "I'm sorry. I seem to have forgotten that you were coming."

"Of course, who could blame you?"

Helena nods, as if bowing her head in prayer. Then she brings her eyes—now full of tears—up to meet mine. "Sophie is looking forward to working with you."

The dog is now sniffing my feet, and, not knowing what else to say to Helena, I bend down and rub him behind the ears and under his chin.

"This is Ludwig," Austen explains. Hearing his name, he wags his tail and continues nuzzling my hand.

"He's Sophie's," Helena says. "He's been moping around all morning, following me as if he knows something is wrong. He'll be fine. We all will as soon as she comes back."

"So . . . where is Charlie? I'd like to see him," Austen says.

Helena takes a deep breath, as if she needs it to propel her ability to speak. "He's fine. He'll be here soon."

Austen tenses. "Fine? Where is he?"

"I couldn't stop him, but he's fine and on his way back." Whatever little control she had regained now disappears. Her hands begin to shake so badly she has to hold them together to stop them.

"Where is he?" Austen repeats.

"He took one of the boats out and went searching for Sophie. He did it without my knowing it, without telling anyone. But I called the Coast Guard and they found him and are bringing him back."

"He went looking for Sophie alone? Is he crazy? He's not old enough to be out there by himself."

"He's a good sailor and it's a clear day. Sophie's been encouraging him to take the boat out by himself. She wants him to be self-sufficient. She'll be proud of him. They are with him and should be back within the half hour."

"You are sure?" Despite her assurances, Austen's voice is strained.

"I just spoke to them fifteen minutes ago. Charlie's fine. At least physically. He's just so distraught that she's missing."

"How could he just take a boat out? Damn her. He shouldn't even be here—pulled out of school early—much less on a boat by himself."

Helena does not answer. She looks from Austen toward me, uncomfortable—at what, though, that Austen is upset? That an outsider is listening to this?

I had imagined coming to Euphonia and meeting Sophie. Sitting down with her in her own house and listening to her explain the way things are. Wrapping myself in Sophie's words, her stories, and her music. But none of what is happening is the way I thought it would be. And it's taking more time than I have to readjust to the idea that I am still here as a reporter. No matter what happens, there will be a story to write.

"So . . . let's get these bags stowed and get down to the beach to wait for him. Where do you want us?" Austen asks.

"Your room is just upstairs," Helena says to me, and then she turns to Austen. "I've put you in the cottage."

"Where is Charlie staying?"

"He's been staying here, but I'm sure now that you're here, he'll move to the cottage with you."

Austen picks up my suitcase and together we all walk toward the stairs. They lead to a landing, then split into an east and a west staircase.

"How many people usually stay here during the summer?" I ask.

"About five faculty members."

"And the students?"

"They live in the cottages on the grounds." She directs the next sentence to Austen. "They're starting to come, even though the session isn't supposed to start for another week. Six students have already arrived and are out walking the shoreline—" Her voice breaks once more, and she halts her ascent for a moment, holds on to the banister, clings to it a few seconds, and then starts up again.

At the first landing is a large window with a complicated design that casts yellow, orange, melon, pink, lavender, purple, and green shadows. Staring at the melody of color, I'm not sure what the window is made of and step closer. Putting out my hand, I run my fingers over the smooth and sharp edges of shells.

Helena has continued on, but Austen pauses beside me, setting down our bags.

"After Sophie gets back, she'll take you on a tour of the house and show you her collection," Austen offers. "She's proud of all the shell work."

"I've never seen anything like this," I say.

He points to the boxed shell mosaics on the wall. "She has the largest collection of 'sailor's valentines' in the world—all from the late 1800s, made in the Caribbean and bought by sailors on leave—given to wives and girlfriends upon their return."

Splashes of color fall across him. His face and hair are tinted orange, his arms and hands awash in violet. I hold out my hands, submerging them in pink light.

He takes a small step toward me, moving past the lavender light and into a pool of pale green. The cool and hot colors move inside me as if seeping through my skin, staining both of us at the same time, connecting us in an inexplicable way that makes me afraid.

We are not touching each other, but the light touches both of us. The color on his hands and lips is on my skin and my mouth, and I can tell from the way his eyes have partially closed that he feels something too.

"I think you'll be comfortable here," says Helena, who has reached the top of the stairs.

Her voice breaks our spell. Austen picks up my bag again, I retrieve my tote, and we hurry to catch up.

Helena is now waiting just inside an open door. The large room is painted robin's egg blue with white trim. There are deep lavender accents in the cushions, on the couch, and in the carpet.

"Sophie had picked out this room for your stay. She thought you'd need some workspace." Helena gestures toward the large desk and chair facing out toward the sea.

"It's wonderful," I offer. I'm not looking at the room. My eyes are fixated on the view. Always having lived in small spaces, always in cities, always having looked at buildings from my windows, I find the infinite vista before me is almost uncomfortable. Might I disappear here—just float out of the window and be swept out to sea?

"Sophie said she wanted you to—" Helena shakes her head as if trying to steel herself, but she can't finish the sentence. She takes a breath. She goes to the desk and opens the drawer. "Here's a booklet"—she points to it—"with all the information you'll need. What time we serve meals, the phone numbers of various rooms and offices, and a map."

It pains me to listen to Helena's voice. I remember what it is like to have to talk to people about mundane things when your mind is panicked with fear and loss.

"Thank you, especially for taking time with me when you must be half crazy with worry."

The amazing blue eyes fill with tears again. She looks toward the window. "That's . . . look . . . I think . . . yes, that's Charlie."

In the distance a boat flying red sails is heading this way. To its right is a Coast Guard cutter.

Austen's neck muscles relax. "Thank goodness."

"I don't think I've ever seen red sails before," I say.

"Sophie's sense of design is quite dramatic. One style juxtaposed against another. The boats are outfitted like gypsy ships. Or else they are modern and sleek. While this house is extravagant, the stone beachfront cottage is monochromatic, soothing and serene."

He leans out the window, pointing a few hundred feet away. "It's just a short walk from here, and—" He breaks off. Following his stare, I see beyond the cottage and to the left where a wooden boat is tipped over on its side on the beach. Its brass fittings gleam in the sun. Yellow police tape attached to poles stuck in the sand cordons off the area where two policemen are working the scene. A group of bystanders stand to the side.

"Helena, what time did Sophie leave yesterday?"

"After dinner sometime. I don't know exactly. I was busy. There's so much to do before a session starts. She took a thermos of coffee and said she was going for a long sail."

"Were there storm warnings?"

Helena doesn't answer. Like Austen, she watches the police climbing on Sophie's boat.

"Helena," Austen asks gently, as if he is bringing her back from out there, "were there storm warnings?"

"I don't think so."

"Why didn't you go with her?"

"She wanted to go alone. That's not unusual." Helena's tone is not defensive, but her words are. And now that she has started talking, she doesn't stop. "And why shouldn't she? Every other day she took Charlie, but yesterday she wanted to go alone. She's working on a new symphony, so of course she'd want to get out on the water by herself. Did I tell you that? A new symphony." This last she offers with a deep pleasurable sigh. And then she shakes her head. "She never would have gone out if she knew there were storm warnings. But I don't think there were any. It was only a half hour—a squall—and then it was gone."

"Well, it doesn't make sense," Austen says.

"What doesn't?"

He doesn't say. Instead he asks another question. "Was she upset about anything?"

"No. She was happy with her music. Of course, she was tired from her tour. She hasn't been sleeping that well, but we were working on that." Helena turns away and fusses with a twisted phone cord on the desk.

"How bad was it?"

"Oh, I don't know, Austen." For the first time she seems annoyed rather than sad, and her tone becomes accusatory. "When was the last time you saw her or talked to her?"

As a reporter, I've learned how to disappear: remaining immobile for minutes at a time. I slow my breathing and become almost invisible, so no one notices my presence.

"How bad was it?" Austen asks again.

"She had only just gotten back a week ago. You know how tough jet lag is after a tour."

"Was she feeling well otherwise? How were her moods?"

Helena's gaze drifts over to me for just a second. It is almost imperceptible, but I can tell she's worried about my hearing this. Except why does it matter if I hear them talk about how Sophie was feeling?

"Other than her problems sleeping, she was fine."

"But sleeping problems can be important. Are you sure?"

"Believe me, if I knew anything, I'd tell you."

"Not necessarily, Helena. Not me or anyone else. You'd lie if Sophie wanted you to."

"Why does it bother all of you that I understand her so well?" she asks in a high-pitched voice.

"It doesn't bother us, Helena." Austen makes an effort to modulate his voice into a smooth river of sound. "We're grateful, all of us. You have been her succor." He speaks slower now, each word like balm, and even I can feel Helena calming. "No one knows how Sophie would have ever managed all these years without you."

Helena crosses her arms, and her hands grip her elbows. More than any words or tears, it is this tight, desperate hug that conveys the depth of her pain.

NINETEEN

AUSTEN, IS HELENA hiding something?"

Still staring out my window, he does not take his eyes off the returning boat. "What is there to hide? It's just the impression she gives. She's been Sophie's shield since before I knew her. They've been together for thirty years. Like all the rest of us, she was once a musician. But somewhere along the line she gave that up to become Sophie's personal assistant. And now she's the director of the school. I've always thought of her as Sophie's watchdog. Fiercely loyal and annoyingly protective."

"Do you trust her?"

"Sophie is her entire life. So . . . yes, I trust her when it comes to doing what is right for Sophie. Is that what you mean?"

"I don't know. Why does she seem so embarrassed by being upset?"

"She's always been the stoic. It's one of the reasons she's lasted with Sophie all these years."

I have more questions, but there is no time to ask them because the two boats are now close enough to shore that Austen can see Charlie at the helm.

• • •

DOWN AT THE BEACH, I hang back as Austen runs forward to meet his son. Charlie, eyes downcast, stops a few feet away.

"Thank God you're safe." Austen scoops his son up in his arms, but it is not a comfortable embrace. Charlie squirms away. "What were you thinking, taking that boat out?"

"It's no big deal. Grandma lets me. And it's no good making them bring me in. I'm just going to go out again. I have to find her."

"That's what the Coast Guard is for."

"But I can look for her too."

"Charlie, you're not supposed to go out on your own."

"Grandma said that's just you and Mom being overly—"

Austen shrugs. "I'm not competing with her—not now—not over this. We've had this conversation already, haven't we? We don't have to have it again."

Now, mimicking Austen, Charlie shrugs. "Guess not."

Father and son look alike. Their coloring is the same, and Charlie is already tall for his age.

"No matter who is in danger or what is going on—you are not to take a boat out by yourself again. You understand?"

"But the Coast Guard are saying that if Grandma fell overboard—if she's in the water—she needs to be found soon. The water's cold."

"Which is why they are searching for her."

"But she's been gone for at least twelve hours. They've been looking for almost half that time." The boy is getting more agitated. "What if they don't find her?" He moves to the edge of hysteria.

Austen puts his arm around Charlie's bony shoulders. "They will find her. That's their job."

"They're talking like she might already be dead."

"No one knows that. It's just their way," Austen explains.

"She's not dead." Blood rushes to his cheeks.

"I know she's not."

"No, you don't." Charlie's on the verge of tears.

"Charlie?" Austen puts both hands on his son's shoulders and turns him so they are face-to-face. He looks him in the eye and says his name once again slowly. "Charlie, the people who know how to do this best are out there looking for her."

"You can't let them give up. Grandma warned me that this might happen. And she said if it did, she'd definitely be coming back."

"What are you talking about?"

"We were working on a Chopin piece, and she was being . . . I don't know . . . sad, I guess. I got upset and told her that when she got like that, it was as if she was missing. The part of her that I know."

He is too young to accommodate this much grief.

" 'Even if it seems like I'm gone, Charlie, I'll always come back . . .' she said. I thought she was talking about being gone like when she was preoccupied . . . but when I was out there looking for her, I was thinking she meant something else."

"I need someone to make an ID," one of the policemen shouts.

Austen freezes. I know what he's thinking and what Charlie is thinking—that they have found Sophie's body.

Austen turns to me. "I'll go. You stay with Charlie." He breaks into a jog.

"No, Dad. I'm coming too." Charlie follows.

"Can one of you help us?" the cop asks.

"I can," Charlie says in a small voice as he steps forward. But Austen steps in front of him, shielding him.

But it's only a red plastic clog.

"Those are Grandma's shoes. . . . She wears them to garden and when she takes walks and to go sailing. Everyone tells her they aren't safe on the boat, but she does what she wants," Charlie finishes.

While the police bag the shoe, Austen questions them. They tell him they've walked Euphonia's shoreline twice, have dozens of searchers on the peninsula checking every dwelling and looking behind every rock, and are checking every house twenty miles up and down the beach.

"We might as well go back," Austen says, but Charlie keeps staring out over the water. "Charlie?" he repeats.

Finally, the boy turns.

While we walk toward the house, Charlie focuses on me. He has the same kind of assurance with grown-ups I had when I was thirteen.

"My grandmother told me you were coming,"

"Yes, to work with her and write her story."

"The truth, though; not the lies," he challenges.

"Hey, Charlie, where'd that come from?" Austen asks.

"I heard Mom arguing with Grandma, saying some people are going to lie in interviews because they are greedy or jealous or— something." And then he forgets about me. "Oh, Dad, I forgot. Mom called and said you have to drive me back, but I don't want to leave here."

"Your mother is right. It would be better for you if—"

"No. I don't want to go. I have to stay here. I can't go anywhere."

"You belong home—with your mother and me in New York."

"No. That's not where I belong. I belong with Grandma, and you have to let me stay."

I look away so that I don't have to see his face—my face in the mirror the day I found out my mother was not going to get better, and my face the day after that. And the day after that.

"I have to be where Grandma is," Charlie repeats.

Austen relents.

TWENTY

I N   M Y   R O O M , I sit down on the bed. Though hungry, I'm also too tired to go downstairs and forage for something to eat.

When I was growing up, snacks were always feasts. Not a bowl of chips or a plate of store-bought cookies, or sticks of carrots and celery, like my friends got. My mother offered fresh figs stuffed with goat cheese, or stewed pears with caramel drizzled over them in a swirl. Or my favorite, a bowl of ripe strawberries sliced and sugared and bathed in fresh heavy cream.

I'm dreaming about food: custard-filled ramekins decorated with swirls of raspberry *coulis*. I have four of them and put one down in front of my mother, who is so pleased that I have made something for her, she smiles up at me.

I know I'm dreaming, but it's so sweet here I slip back.

Taking a spoon, my mother makes a big show of scooping up the custard and tasting it. "Look," she says. "She's here. Sophie's here."

My mother is staring down into the white porcelain dish, and I look, but now the sea is swirling in the bowl. And before I can figure out how to use the spoon to get Sophie out, I wake up. And the first thing I think of is that I want to see my mother. Tell her about the dream. And the second thing I think of—much more awake now—is that she is gone.

It has been almost four years and I still go through this torturous process of forgetting and then remembering, and with the remembering, feeling the ache and the emptiness. And without thinking about whether it makes sense or not, without going through any kind of logical process, I pick up the phone and call my sister's cell phone number. We are two daughters of one mother; maybe I will miss my mother less if I can find something of her in Maddy.

But once I've said hello and explain where I am, I realize that this call is a mistake. There is nothing of our mother's natural curiosity in Maddy's response. My mother would have been interested, wanting to hear all about Euphonia and the mystery of what has happened to Sophie.

"Oh, Justine, how could you just leave? You always do this. I mean I went all the way downtown to have breakfast for you, and you were just gone. Couldn't you have waited till the weekend?" Maddy's voice is stretched tight. "You hardly explained anything in your note. And not only did you stand Oliver and me up tonight—you left without talking to Dad. For Christ's sake, Justine, we haven't been together—the three of us—for so long. Doesn't that matter?"

I sigh. "Maddy, please. It's work."

"Oh, bullshit. You know I'm tired of you putting us off until it's convenient for you."

"That's not what I'm doing." And then I think of Austen—of him reaching out for Charlie, only to have his son turn and run away in the opposite direction, in need of someone else's solace, which he might never find again. I sigh.

Maddy's voice is discordant in my ear: "I just don't know what anyone did to you to make you like this."

This is not the phone call I wanted to have.

"What has anyone done? Well, for one thing Dad just went ahead and had Mom cremated in the goddamned middle of the night without discussing it with me. And you were in the house and you didn't stop him. He . . . he couldn't wait to get rid of her. He didn't think about us and what we wanted for one fucking minute. Talk about which one of us is selfish. For Christ's sake."

"You only see it from your point of view. He didn't talk to us because he'd talked to Mom and it was what she wanted."

"Don't lie in order to defend him. It's been you and him against us forever. Why am I not surprised that that hasn't changed? Why can't just you and I have a relationship?"

"Because sharing a mother is not all that connects us, Justine. We have a father. And he's not dead, even though you've made him dead. And I'm the one who knows how that makes him feel. I'm the one who has seen how it has affected him."

I miss my mother and Maddy is making that missing worse. I want to cry, but instead bite the inside of my mouth and hold back. I do not want her to know how defenseless I am. I take one breath and then another. Maybe if I do what she wants, then I will find some solace with her.

"What day is the restaurant closed?" I ask.

"Tomorrow."

"If it works for you and Dad . . . I could take the train in and we could all talk.

A beat of silence. An intake of breath. On each end of the phone.

"Yes, I'm sure Dad would love to do that."

And now I hear it—what I called for—the sweet tone and the slightly raspy texture—the raspberry jam voice, my mother used to call it.

Maddy has my raspberry jam voice.

Don't I have your voice too, Mommy?

You? No sweetheart, you talk in caramel.

And even though if I were going to eat one or the other, I liked caramel so very much more than raspberry jam, I would be just a little jealous that Maddy had our mother's voice and that my own was different.

A half-hour later, Maddy calls back to say that our father has suggested they drive up to Connecticut instead of me coming into

New York. She gives me the name and address of a restaurant in town owned by one of our father's cronies.

The setting sun colors the clouds and the water. The yellow tape cordoning off the boat flaps in the wind. A clap of thunder in the distance is followed by far-off lightning. Then the downpour starts, and heavy raindrops completely obliterate the beach. From the window I see dozens of policemen running to their cars like insects being chased.

Did the rain come this suddenly the night before? What would it be like out on a boat right now—with no visibility?

Shivering, I pull the drapes closed.

TWENTY·ONE

B Y   T H E   T I M E I arrive downstairs for dinner, the meal has already begun. Music
plays—but not Sophie's. This is baroque, per-
haps Handel, I'm not sure. But it is as rich as the carpets and the
tapestries and the shell chandeliers. Belonging, like the antiques, to
another era.

From the doorway, looking into the candlelit room and glancing quickly down the long mahogany table at all the somber faces,
I see neither Austen nor Charlie.

The smells of the dinner make me realize how hungry I am.
Garlic and butter mix with the scent of fresh baked bread.

If not for those scents, I would consider going back upstairs and
avoiding the somber group of nine—who, judging from the way
they interact, are not strangers. I will be the only one there who is
unknown to them.

It would be a waste of the food, but more important, of the opportunity to meet these people who have assembled here for just
one reason: they are all worried about Sophie and want to help.
Even if all they can do is hold a vigil. Through an open door, I see
into the kitchen, where one of the cooks leans against the stove,
weeping. Another stands beside her, trying to comfort her, but
weeping herself.

As I approach, Helena, seated at the head of the table, nods to me. While the food on her plate is untouched, her wineglass is almost empty.

Helena tells the assembled group who I am and why I'm there, making a point to explain that Sophie invited me. No one makes an effort to acknowledge me. But considering the circumstances, I don't read any meaning into their indifference.

There are only a few empty seats at the table, and I wind up between two Japanese men, neither of whom speaks during the rest of meal, unless it is to directly answer my questions.

When I ask if they are going to be studying with Sophie this summer, Leo, the one on my right, tells me no, he is an ex-student and is here to help find her. When I ask Raymond, on my left, he tries to explain that he, too, was here the summer before, but he is so upset his English becomes confused and Leo finishes for him.

"What instruments do you play?" I ask.

Leo answers again. "We are violinists."

I cut into the grilled garlicky shrimp—charbroiled and sweet—and hold myself back from devouring it in one gulp. Even though I haven't eaten since seven-thirty that morning, I go slowly. Watching and listening as well. Tasting every forkful of gracefully herbed rice and crisp asparagus spear.

While I eat, at one point or another, every one of the people seated around the table eyes me, some covertly, others openly staring. It can't be that they recognize me from the cookbooks; that never causes this kind of discomfort.

At first I assume it's because of who I am—the journalist in their midst ferreting out the story while they deal with personal tragedy. It even occurs to me that some could know the St. Pierre story. But, no, these looks are more horrified and surprised.

And then I become aware of the sound of my silverware on the bone china plate . . . only mine. No one else is eating. Not even making any pretense of it. I alone am not showing signs of being sad and worried. The only one who is neither a student nor a teacher nor a contemporary, the only one who does not know Sophie De-Lyon personally.

I am not a member of the Lyon's Pride. I eat when they cannot. And there's more. I'm preventing them from spilling out their stories and memories. They are not sure they should tell these stories in front of a stranger who is, to make matters worse, the journalist who will be writing this story, no matter what its outcome.

Even though I'm hungry enough to eat more—to take another soft roll from the silver bread basket in front of me and slather it with butter—I don't. I have done enough to insult these mourners.

This tragedy is looming over everyone at the table. Sophie's absence is so great I can only imagine how large her presence would be.

WHEN SHE WAS ONLY thirty-five, my aunt died in a car accident. Everyone had come to our parents' apartment to pay their respects. Uncle Sam, my mother's brother, had lashed out, screaming at his brother-in-law, blaming him for letting Caitlin go out in a rainstorm at all.

My mother had rushed forward, grabbed her brother by the arm, and pulled him out of the room and into the kitchen, where I was making more coffee.

"If anything," my mother said, "in the face of something so sad, we should be all the more kind."

I had not understood, or even remembered, until years later when my mother herself had died and it was I who wanted to lash out at anyone who would listen. But mostly at my father, who would not listen at all.

I tried not to lash out because I remembered what my mother had said that day in the kitchen. Had everything important in my life between my mother and me been said in a kitchen or over a table? Were there any memories of my mother that were not connected to the smell or the taste of food?

THERE ARE TIMES WHEN THE human heart cannot cope with such sadness, when the chest has to be forced to take in air and expel it and then take in more. You do not want to go on breathing when you are not sure you are brave enough to go on living. The diners at Euphonia all suffer like that.

A man named Walter sits at the opposite end of the table from Helena. He has an imperious air and commands attention when he speaks.

"Isn't there a possibility that she's been kidnapped?" he asks.

"She went out sailing," Helena says.

"But what if they took her before she got on her boat and just set the boat loose. What if they had their own boat and transferred her to it and took her away? I know it sounds far-fetched, but she is Sophie DeLyon," he insists.

"But there hasn't been any demand for ransom." Helena pours herself more burgundy. She takes a sip, then sighs. "I'd almost be happy if that were true. It would mean we could just pay whoever it is and get her back."

One person speaking out loud about one worst-case scenario gives the others permission to speak. For the next few minutes, theories are thrown out like pieces of a jigsaw puzzle.

"Did the police say the boat had been tampered with?"

"Could anyone have been hiding on the boat and waiting for her?"

"Yes, like some student who she turned down for the Euphonia program?" Walter asks. "Let's put together a list. Who do we know who is crazy enough to flip out over being rejected?"

Helena's posture, which had been ramrod straight, is like a soufflé falling in on itself. She cannot hold herself up against this onslaught. "Stop, all of you! This is difficult enough. Staying sane while they are searching. Waiting. Holding our breath. The least we can do is not make crazy guesses about what happened. No one hurt Sophie. No one broke in. There was an accident. And she's going to be found. She will be back tomorrow. We are going to get a call. If not tonight, then in the morning."

For a few seconds no one speaks. Helena's poignant hope has silenced them.

By the time dessert is served, I have pieced together that Walter is one of Sophie's most successful students, and that the young woman named Gala sitting next to him is the most promising of Sophie's current students. She's spoken just once, to ask if anyone wanted to rehearse after dinner.

Other than Helena, an elegant black man in his mid-thirties is the most despondent person at dinner. They sit side by side, and several times during the meal they have leaned toward each other to say something. He speaks to no one else, and no one directs anything to him.

Since I cannot just come out and ask if any of them is Pride33@TheLyonsPride or knows who that might be, it seems best to connect to just one of them and start there.

Trying to make myself as inconspicuous as possible, not wanting to inhibit their comments, I continue to listen and say little. As Pride33 said in his or her E-mail, DeLyon is their beacon, and without her light they are adrift.

"If she is gone, Helena, what will happen to the summer session? What will happen to—" Walter asks.

Helena interrupts him. "She is not gone." Her eyes plead with him to stop.

The cook comes out from the kitchen, eyes red, her voice shaky, to ask who wants coffee or tea. She places a plate of miniature tarts—glistening with glazed apples, raspberries, and blueberries—on the table.

I eye the pastry, knowing I cannot ask for it, hoping someone passes it.

"I'm sorry. I must have missed something." Gala looks at me. "Who are you?"

I explain.

"This must be awkward for you then," she responds.

"I'm not sure what you mean." Of course I do, but I want her to explain. I'll learn more that way.

"Having come all the way here and now having to leave . . ."

I mimic Gala's body language to help relax her.

"Well, Sophie invited me and expects me to be here. I don't want to disappoint her when she gets back. I'm staying."

There are reasons I'm staying that I don't admit, like how much I have riding on this. How I have to get this story and bring it back to Kurt to resuscitate my lifeless career.

From the head of the table, Helena stares at me. I feel her eyes on me, and so I look up and meet her gaze. She tries to smile, but it is so subtle, I might have missed it if I weren't paying so much attention. "So many people have already given up." Her voice, like her demeanor, is weak and heartbreaking. "Thank you for not being one of them. We all need her so very much. We'd be lost without her."

Including me.

ABOUT HALF OF THE PEOPLE at dinner are in the living room, tuning up, while the rest have gone to search the beach, despite Helena's explanation that the Coast Guard and the police have been and still are doing that. They go anyway, as if the only way they can accept the reality of Sophie's being missing is to make sure for themselves.

The random sounds end. There is a moment of silence, and then as if trying to breathe life back into the house, the music begins.

Helena and I are the audience. I sit near her, aware of the trouble she's having staying focused on the music, the difficulty she is having breathing. Every few minutes she takes deep gulps of air into her lungs.

And then I focus on the music and the musicians.

Each of these performers is talented and is used to being singled out, but if there is jealousy, the chords of sympathy and comradeship that bind them together are stronger.

Walter plays the piano so sorrowfully that my chest tightens. His eyes are shut, his lips are parted, his head is thrown back, and his hands blur as they move. The music pours forth.

Other instruments enter and exit the dialogue, but there are false notes, tenuous cadences, and cueless entrances. They are off and they know it. They are getting worse. And the worse they get, the more dissonant and disturbing the music becomes.

This is the sound of Sophie's absence.

"Stop, stop," Helena says loudly. And one by one they do. "You can't just play without someone keeping you together. One of you needs to take Sophie's place, and—" Her sentence hangs unfinished.

This will happen now, over and over, for as long as Sophie is missing and longer if she is gone for good. You say things without thinking and shock yourself. Idle words—at other times so innocent—are poisonous and deadly now.

Gala leaves her violin on her chair to come to Helena and embrace her. Then she stands in the center of the semicircle, ready to conduct. "Let's try the *Emperor Concerto*."

She raises her hands and then lowers them back down to her sides. She tries again, and then her arms hang unmoving by her sides. "I can't do this. I don't want to play without her."

TWENTY-TWO

O N   T H E   W A Y back to my room, I stop in the library. There are dozens of shelves and hundreds of books, and I'm not surprised to find the majority of titles are on the theory and history of music. But there are also whole shelves with books on shells, gardening, and women's history, and mysteries.

Pulling down du Maurier's classic, *Rebecca*, I read the first familiar paragraphs and decide to take the book back to my bedroom. But even with the book in hand, I am not ready to leave; this room is too soothing. After another half hour of rooting through more of Sophie's titles, I come across one long shelf that contains two dozen random titles, including books on post–World War II trauma, Holocaust survivor guilt, biographies of Nadia Boulanger and Leonard Bernstein, as well as psychology books including *Manic Depression and Creativity, An Unquiet Mind, The Noonday Demon*, and a book of essays called *Unholy Ghost: Writers on Depression*.

The spines on all these books are cracked, and when I pull one out, I see how many of the page corners are folded down and how much marginalia there is.

Over and over I see the same notation: *Discuss with Dr. Gleckel*.

Sitting in the armchair by the window, forgetting about how

tired I am and how little sleep I've had in the last twenty-four hours, I skim the book that has the most pages turned down. *Touched with Fire* includes analyses of famous artists, writers, and composers who are believed to have suffered with manic depression.

I'm reading a passage on Beethoven when I hear . . . *What is it?* A mournful chord being played on a cello? An animal whining? There are two doors in the room, one leading back out into the hall, but the sound is coming from the other one.

Opening the door, I peer into a bedroom. Even in the low light I can see that everything—the lampshades, the silks on the bed, the rug—is the pale pink color of the inside of the shells studding the house. On the walls are twenty or thirty mirrors—some as small as a light switch—others two or three feet long, each decorated with a shell frame.

And then I notice the woman lying facedown on the bed, her face buried in a pillow, her back shaking with sobs. Everything about her pose bespeaks desolation.

It's as if I am looking at myself four years ago. Crushed by loss. Knowing that the worst part was ahead of me. The endless stretch of days that would go on and on, and no matter how many of them there were, they would all be without my mother.

Zoë Solomon, Stephen's wife, picks up her head and looks at me through tear-filled and red-rimmed eyes.

"Are you all right?" I say.

Zoë doesn't react. Everything is frozen except for the tears running down her cheeks. I should leave, but it's hard to walk away from someone in such obvious pain—pain that I know leaves you weak and incapable of action.

"Can I get you anything? Some tea? A glass of water? I'm sorry to intrude. I didn't know this was your room."

"It's Sophie's room," she says in a voice much younger than the one I remember from a few nights ago.

I look around again. "There are so many mirrors."

"Yes. Aren't there. She once told me seeing her face repeated over and over reminded her of who she was. She was afraid of disappearing. So many images settled her fears . . ." Zoë doesn't end the sentence with any inflection. She simply stops speaking before she completes the thought. A moment goes by. And then she speaks again.

"No one knows I'm here. I shouldn't be here. Stephen said . . . He and Daphne said it doesn't matter where we wait for her. That my being here won't help anyone find her. But I couldn't stay away. If I could, I'd be out there on a boat looking for her. The least I can do is wait here. This is the only place that feels like home now that Sophie is missing. Does that make sense?" She sounds like a child talking about her mother.

"Yes, of course. It helps to be around her things, her smells."

Zoë nods, and her sobbing begins afresh.

"Are you sure I can't get you something?"

"Do you think you could get me an Ativan? I'm pretty sure Sophie has them in with all those other prescriptions." She nods in the direction of the bathroom.

Except there are no amber plastic pill containers at all in the medicine cabinet. No Ativan. Or anything else. Everyone has pills in their medicine cabinets: standing sentry, lined up on the shelves, half of them usually long expired.

"I'm sorry. There aren't any," I tell her.

Zoë looks at me quizzically, gets up off the bed, and goes into the bathroom herself. Opening the mirrored cabinet, she moves makeup remover and moisturizer and deodorant and aspirin bottles around. Her fingers graze a nonprescription bottle of cough medicine. She pushes aside contact lens cleaner and eyedrops.

"Something's wrong . . ." she mutters half to herself.

"What?"

Not answering me, she returns to the bedroom and crawls back into Sophie's bed.

"Do you want me to find Helena and ask her?"

"No. No! Helena doesn't even know I'm here. I sneaked up while everyone was having dinner. Helena won't let me stay in here, in this room. She'll be deferential because I'm Sophie's daughter-in-law, but she doesn't really want anyone here, especially not me. She'd move me to a guest room right away. And I need to be here at least one night."

My questions are like caged birds flying at the bars to escape. But I can't ask Zoë anything now. I don't want to alert her or remind her that she should be more careful of what she says in front of me.

"Do you think you can get me something to drink? Brandy? There's a bar downstairs in the music room."

When I get back, I hand Zoë the tumbler and sit in one of the two slipper chairs by the fireplace.

Thanking me, she gulps the amber liquor and grimaces. I know the burn is a momentary relief from the grief.

"The center isn't going to hold," Zoë says.

"That's from a poem, isn't it?" I ask, knowing full well it is.

"Yes. Yeats. Without Sophie we are all going to lose our center and spin out of control. Everything will change now." She shakes her head and moves to put the glass on an end table. Her hand is shaking, the glass hits the base of a lamp with a crack.

Zoë stares at the broken glass as the liquor spills. She doesn't move. "I gave Sophie this lamp. I found it in an antiques store. She said she loved it and told me that people hardly ever went to so much trouble to find things that she'd like."

I take the shattered glass from her hand and pick up the shards from the tabletop while Zoë continues talking. "It isn't stained glass. Did you think it was?"

"Yes," I say.

"No, they are shells. That's why she loved it so much. More of her beloved shells."

She reaches inside the lamp and pulls the string. A mélange of warm yellows, pinks, and melon colors spills over the tabletop.

"It's beautiful," I say. "No wonder she loved it."

"Opaque until the light shines through. You'd never guess they have this much color, would you, that shells are so translucent? All these beautiful seashells that Sophie collects. Ask any of them why she collects shells. Even the ones who say they love her. Ask them and see how many of them know."

"Do you?" I ask while wiping the liquor from the table.

Zoë nods. "Of course I do. They are protective coverings, the beautiful armor that hides the ugly slug. Excellent hiding places. Everyone says that they love her but don't you think it's strange that her children aren't here, that I'm the only one here?"

Yes, I think it is strange, but I keep it to myself.

TWENTY-THREE

BEFORE SUNRISE, I lie in bed, letting the sound of the waves lull me. I'm not really awake, not really asleep, but breathing in the salty air, feeling it cool my bare arms, drifting on the sound.

I should sort through the information I've collected, but it's Austen's image that floats in my mind and his voice that I hear. I'm seeing his hands holding the steering wheel of the car yesterday, but now his right hand moves past the stick shift and over to my seat, making contact with the fabric of my skirt and my thigh. I shiver as the pressure of his skin on mine intensifies and his hand creeps between my legs. I feel the first kick of anticipation—for that is the only way I have ever been able to describe it—a punch that takes the air out of my lungs and makes my blood rush to my center.

As his fingers continue, I forget the pillow behind my head and the sheets pulled over me. There is only the sensation that he is creating as his fingers push aside the elastic of my underwear, searching and finding—yes there—the wetness that speaks for me.

His fingers make small movements that feel too large to be contained. A throb shoots up, moving and spreading across my stomach, my breasts, my neck, my shoulders, and down my arms. While this is happening, his fingers—which I have forgotten are my own fingers mimicking what I imagine his would be doing—continue moving so very s-l-o-w-l-y until they come to rest on exactly the right spot. Now the gentleness is gone and his fingers—my fingers—rub and flick and squeeze, and the pressure is some pain and some pleasure until a final rush of sensation takes over and I am lost.

Nothing for a few minutes. My breathing eases. The beat of my heart steadies. The urge will be gone now that it has been satiated, quieted. But it isn't.

What is it that I want, to have sex with Austen? Or to know he wants to have sex with me? Usually, I get a kick of power from watching a man give up his control . . . but . . . No . . . I cannot think like this about the father of Sophie DeLyon's grandson, a man who would threaten the work I'm doing here.

In the last few years I haven't wanted much from any man I've been with. Certainly not romance. Not what my mother craved and lost.

It's easier to just concentrate on finding friendship and conversation and the physical release that my body believes is its right.

Other women feel this too, but few are willing to speak of it. Sex disengaged from love is perceived as a male prerogative. Women complain about that in men. Sure, occasionally television, movies, or novels portray a single, working woman who uses sex, but she always sees the light and learns to love in the end.

But why is using sex any worse than using love? Which drug is really more damaging? I saw one wipe out my mother and I'd rather take my chances with the other.

There is no right or wrong about these things, no one kind of sex that leads to love and another kind that leads to hell. There is sex attached to feelings and sex divorced from feelings. It's not that I've wanted only to have sex without whispers of love; that's just how I've had it. I have never minded and I don't mind now.

The sounds of the waves mix with music as Euphonia wakes up. Someone is at the piano. Someone plays a violin. But without Sophie the practice strains and pulls. The off notes are all reminders that a monumental musical legend might be lost.

Might be dead.

Might be dead.

I can hear it in the rhythm of the waves through the open window. Deceptively gentle, this sound is hard to reconcile with the violent ending that Sophie might have met in that water. I have been listening to it without cessation for an hour, and now is the first time I am hearing music in the swells slapping on the shore.

"The very best in music does not equal even what is mediocre in nature. And therein lies my shame as an artist—that I can get just so far—but never quite achieve my goal," Sophie had written to me.

Her *shame* as an artist—how strong a word, how specific and how seemingly inappropriate for a talent like Sophie.

The sun shines directly into the window and onto my face. I feel its warmth.

Despite months of listening to Sophie DeLyon's music and reading her notes and watching a video of her conducting, I did not come close to understanding her at all. But here, at Euphonia, I am at last beginning to.

TWENTY-FOUR

TAKING A PATH made of crushed shells, I walk toward the shore. There were Coast Guard and police here yesterday, crowding around the stranded boat, and they will be here again soon, but it is still early and the beach is empty. I cannot remember being in such a quiet place: I am a child of one city who moved to another.

The tide is low, and large black boulders, shining and slippery with patches of algae, give the shore a primeval look. These are the rocks that Sophie's boat crashed into in the storm.

There are no clouds today, just a light blue sky that meets the horizon in a haze. I'm not sure where one stops and the other begins, so close are they in hue.

Walking, gazing at the water instead of looking down, it is several minutes before I realize that I am following footprints: medium-sized made by either a sneaker or a shoe with treads. And alongside them, paw prints.

The man or the woman and the dog walked forward in a straight line without uncertainty of what direction to take. I follow the trail until it disappears in another cluster of rocks. From here on there is no suggestion of where the walker and the dog went next and there are no returning footprints.

As I head back, I notice the shells—scallops, clams, and mussels—every few feet. It must be a coincidence that they follow the trail of the person and dog.

Looking out across the sound, I wonder how far Sophie De-Lyon was in her sloop when the storm came up. What happened? In the sudden rain—and in those red clogs—did she fall overboard in water that was too choppy and too cold?

The vista stretching before me is as vast as the magnitude of the tragedy. If Sophie is dead, it will be—at least for a time, to her family, her students, her fans, to the music world—a loss of indescribable proportions.

Knowing what a family goes through when someone dies, what a daughter goes through, and what friends and even business associates go through, I shiver. Forcing myself not to think about my mother, I concentrate on Sophie.

On Sophie.

Sophie.

I repeat her name to myself as I take each step. The feel of the sand is so different from that of pavement. It offers less resistance.

AUSTEN AND CHARLIE ARE WALKING down to the beach from their cottage and our paths are about to intersect. I'm afraid of my immediate reaction, of the pleasure I feel seeing him. Rather than allow it to build, I focus on Charlie, kicking sand and sending it spraying with each step.

They are close enough now that I can hear their conversation.

"But she is coming back," Charlie insists.

"I hope so," Austen says.

"No. Not hope. No. You have to know it."

"We can't know it. I want Sophie to be safe as much as you do, but we just can't know."

Without waiting for Austen to finish, Charlie turns and starts to walk away in the opposite direction.

"Charlie—" his father pleads.

He half turns and shouts, "I just want to go practice. She expects me to play at least three hours a day."

"I'm sure Sophie wouldn't mind if you skipped a day," Austen says.

"No, I skipped yesterday. I have to play and be ready for classes when they start. That is what she expects."

Austen shrugs his shoulders in defeat.

Charlie has almost reached the main house when Sophie's cocker spaniel, Ludwig, bounds up and drops a stick at his feet. Charlie doesn't notice. The dog circles him, barking until Charlie finally picks up the stick and throws it.

The dog runs off, retrieves it, and brings it back, dropping it once more, as he's learned to do with his mistress. Something about this breaks him: Charlie crumbles to his feet, burying his head in the dog's neck, his back heaving with sobs.

And it's this fragile shaking of his shoulders that breaks me and makes me turn away, feeling my own tears sting my eyes.

"You should go to him," I tell Austen.

"Do you think I haven't tried? He only wants to know that Sophie is safe and I cannot tell him that."

"But you are his father." I want to make him go to his son and relieve Charlie of some of his pain. Watching this is harder than was standing outside my parents' apartment building and looking up at those windows and seeing the specter of my mother. This—like coming upon Zoë last night—is feeling the pain as if it were fresh. This brings back not only the days when my mother was alive and our bond was vibrant, but the mourning days, the first ones, when I felt like nothing but a shell—functional but not alive.

Austen shrugs. "Maybe your father gave you sustenance and comfort. But even if I offered it, Charlie wouldn't take it from me."

My father? I try to equate the idea of my father with comfort and sustenance, with the idea of seeing him again later today.

Together, Austen and I watch Charlie get up and walk back to the house. He shouldn't be alone but, instead, walking with Austen, sheltered under his father's wing.

Once Charlie is inside the house, we continue on.

Up ahead I see Ludwig run all the way to the rocky outcropping where the beach ends and start to bark.

"Ludwig," Austen calls.

The dog continues barking, just a few yards away from where the boat first hit the rocks, according the Coast Guard. And I'm impressed with his ability to sense this even now with the tide so high.

Austen again calls the dog, and this time he obeys, following us as we walk from the beach. We move up stone steps to a path around a pond. An overplanted bit of an island is in its center. Poking from its treetops is a stone minaret of a bronze angel blowing a trumpet. Her wings catch the light and shine in my eyes.

Following the path, we take a few steps down to where the beach starts again and continue to walk along the shoreline. To the right is dense foliage, tall trees, and the scent of damp earth. To the left is the sea. Egrets stand regally, staring out at the water. Seagulls sweep down and rise up, crying as they soar.

We cross over a wooden bridge and pass a bench, one of many that I have seen, facing the sea. And then we turn right away from the water and go further into woods.

"It's easy to get lost here: You can walk for hours and hours and not see a soul," Austen says.

"Sounds like you've done it often."

"Euphonia is one of the most soothing places I've ever been," he says.

"Why did you stay away so long?"

"It's just as beautiful out there sailing—when it's calm," he says, ignoring my question.

For another quarter of an hour we walk without saying much, but I am never unaware of him, of the sound of his breath, of his feet crunching gravel.

To understand Sophie's love of this place I have to walk its pathways and see its sunsets and its shadows. There is nothing wrong about taking this walk with this man, on this morning.

At a fork in the path, he stops.

"There are dozens of trails off this one, leading to other parts of the preserve. If you do get lost, listen for the sea and go in that direction. Just to orient you, that way is the Holly Grove and that path will take you to the Meditation Garden. Sophie designed it herself. She placed every tree and pathway and created a mandala made of shells."

"She wrote me that while she gardens the music grows in her mind, and when she sits down it just spills out."

Austen nods. He knows.

After ten minutes we cross yet another bridge. "The maze is over there," Austen says, pointing up to the right. "And beyond that, more student residences. The chapel is down there."

"Down by the water?"

"Yes, it's an outdoor chapel. No roof. Just stone pews and a clearing. There are nondenominational services there on Sundays. No preaching, no homilies. Just music, Sophie's preferred form of worship."

There is an edge to this. Rancor? Sarcasm? Anger?

"What is your preferred form of worship?"

"I don't worship anything."

"What about *your* music?"

"You can't worship your own breath, the food you eat, what keeps you alive."

"And why not?"

He answers as if he has thought about this before. "What you worship has to be an ideal to reach toward and so, by virtue of that, it is either unattainable or not worthy if you get close enough to see it clearly."

"Sounds as if you've had the experience?"

"Come this way. I'll show you the maze and the secret garden."

"What is that way?" I'm more curious about the direction Austen does not want to take.

"The boathouse and the docks."

Without waiting for him, I choose the path he wants to avoid.

First, I see the masts of the sailboats bending slightly in the breeze. Then I hear the hollow chime of their fittings clanging.

When the rest of the boats come into view, Austen stops and inhales and then, as if it takes extra effort, continues down to the dock.

The fleet includes two teak motorboats, three fiberglass sailboats, and a rack of canoes and kayaks. Austen heads toward the edge of the dock to an empty slip and sits down, feet dangling off the edge.

Reaching him, I sit too. The smell of the sea is stronger here and the air is cooler. My elbow is slightly touching Austen's arm, and I focus on our point of connection, making an effort not to disturb it. And then, realizing the game I'm playing, pull my arm away.

"I don't want to think so for Charlie's sake, but I can't help feeling that Sophie is gone," Austen says. His voice is hard to hear over the water splashing up and hitting the sides of the boats. He's never spoken this softly: it's almost as if he doesn't want to hear his own words or understand their meaning.

"If she'd swum to shore, she would have contacted someone by now. If she had been found and was in a hospital, we'd know that too. One way or another—if she survived that storm, we would know by now. You can see"—he points to the shoreline stretching out on either side of us—"there just isn't any undeveloped land. There's not a stretch of beach out there without a house on it, except for land that belongs to Euphonia. And they have walked every inch of this place and inspected every building top to bottom. Damn her."

I know that many people are angry when those they love die. I was for weeks after my mother died, until that anger turned into missing her.

"The Coast Guard is still calling it a rescue, but after today they are going to downgrade it to a recovery." He closes his eyes and takes another deep breath. "Can you smell it? The tide is going out. It's such a raw smell, almost unpleasant."

"Not unpleasant, just real," I say. "We are so used to manufactured, sanitized smells."

"No matter what anyone says, Sophie is a great talent," Austen says, not explaining the non sequitur.

"And what do they say about her? What is the secret everyone is so afraid will get out?"

"I don't know what you mean."

"You must. You and Zoë and Helena are all so careful when you talk about her. So protective of her. Why?"

We are interrupted by Helena on her golfcart, beeping the horn and waving with a frantic motion. Tears roll down her cheeks. "The Coast Guard called. They've found some clothes they think belong to Sophie. Charlie listened in on the phone, and now I can't get him to stop playing the same song on the piano over and over and over. I'm scared, Austen. You have to come back. You have to be with him."

TWENTY-FIVE

COMPARED TO EUPHONIA, the town of Greenwich is frenetic. It feels wrong that I'm in an Italian trattoria-style restaurant when I could be waiting with the others. I stand at the door by the front desk and press myself up against the wall more than once as waiters with trays come too close.

The dishes clattering and people chattering sound too loud in the small room. If it is like this to reenter civilization after being at Euphonia for just one day, what is it like to leave there after a summer?

"Justine?"

My father's voice comes from a distance and I think I am remembering it until I feel his hand on my shoulder. Even though I've been waiting for him, I am unprepared for the sound of his deep, rich voice, the sensation of his touch and his smell: herbs and spices.

I'm surprised he's not taller. In my memory, I am always looking up at him. But he is imposing.

Despite myself, the child in me wants to reach out for my father. I resist, keeping my hands by my sides. When I feel his dry lips on my cheek, I think about how long it is since I last kissed him.

My father is seated between me and Maddy. Although she does not drink, he orders white wine, and we make small talk until it comes. The waiter serves it along with a bowl of aromatic olives—jewel-like green and onyx, flecked with herbs and glistening with oil. I take one, sucking on it before biting down, happy to have something in my mouth so that I can't talk. And as soon as I swallow its meat, I reach for my wineglass and concentrate on the smooth slippery way the liquid slides down my throat, like Austen's music slides over my skin.

"I'm so glad you called, Justine," my father says. "I'm tired of missing you. Missing your mother has been bad enough, but you too. And not even really knowing why."

I don't want to see the pain in his eyes, but there it is. A variation of the pain in Charlie's eyes when he was standing on the beach this morning. And the pain in Austen's eyes when he wanted to offer solace but knew he was not the one Charlie wanted.

It's only Sophie who can comfort Charlie. But Sophie is missing and Austen knows that.

Just the same way that it's only my mother who can comfort me. And my father knows that.

"Are you ready to order?" the waiter asks.

As we each tell him what we have chosen, I marvel at the mundane act of placing an order right in the middle of this awkward family reunion. My mother would not have missed the irony that her husband had picked a restaurant—a very public restaurant—to try to seduce his youngest daughter back into the family.

He thinks every kitchen is his own. . . . He can make himself comfortable anywhere there is good food, good wine, and some attractive women around. It's what I fell in love with. I was never that easy about anything. It was your father who taught me to stir slowly: not a bad gift, that.

Where were we when she said that? And was she angry or smiling? I can't remember and it bothers me. How can I have forgotten anything about her? Quickly, to reassure myself, I bring her face to mind. She's smiling. I can even smell her perfume commingled with the scent of chocolate. And then as swiftly as I summoned her, I push her away because as always she is too real and today I need distance between the past and the present.

The waiter brings a basket of fresh hot bread and dipping oil.

Maddy takes a slice of the crusty bread and then obsessively dips it and redips it and then dips it one more time before taking a bite.

We both know the same tricks.

"So tell me about Paris, about the food—" my father is saying.

"You know Paris," I say, "and you know much more about the food in Paris than I ever will."

Maddy shoots me a searing look: *Make an effort*, she mouths, while our father is momentarily distracted by the waiter, who has brought a refill of the olive dish.

"Then tell me about this article, about Sophie DeLyon," he says. "Did you meet her before this accident?"

"You don't really want to talk about any of that."

"Justine!" Maddy says.

"Maddy, relax," my father says, and turns back to me. "You remind me of a very stubborn ten-year-old I used to know."

"Very funny," I say.

"Listen. Justine. I'm not good at this kind of thing."

"What kind of thing?"

Across the table, Maddy gives me yet another pleading look. I ignore her.

My father takes a long drink of the wine. "At figuring out what went wrong. And trying to make it up to you. I don't understand what happened after your mother died that made you run away so fast to France. But can't we move past it? I'm tired of calling you, and the few times a year when you actually take my calls—you're hurrying off. I call to talk to you, not just to find out that you are still alive."

"You didn't make her happy," I say, surprised to hear how accusatory and ugly my voice sounds even in my own ears. I didn't mean to say this. In fact, I had been determined to come to this lunch and be polite and act as if I was just fine and let them go back to the city—to just see him, because it was better than not seeing him.

"At the end, neither of us made the other happy." His voice is sad. The depth of his disconsolation surprises me, but I don't acknowledge it. Instead I say, "And so she died unhappy. That's awful. She died, Daddy, unhappy and miserable."

"No. She died unhappy with me. Not with you. Not with Maddy. Not with her work . . ." His voice drifts off. His eyes look past me to the door to the restaurant. He is weighing something with his hands. Shifting air from the cup of his left hand to the cup of his right hand. His glance returns, first to his oldest daughter and then to me.

His fingers open and the imaginary ingredients fall out of his hands. He puts his palms flat on the table. Whatever he was holding has disappeared.

The food arrives. Maddy has ordered a pizza, and the rich cheese and fresh tomatoes are still bubbling and sizzling. My father's grilled tuna, seared with very even lines crisscrossing its flesh, sits atop a mound of glistening salad. In comparison to their generous lunches, my Caesar salad, with its four grilled shrimp and a dusting of Parmesan cheese, looks meager.

I'm sure the food here is good, but my heart isn't in eating and I didn't want to order something only to have it go to waste.

To Maddy and to our father the food is not an intrusion to the conversation. There is nothing inappropriate in picking up forks and knives and chewing and swallowing while you talk about important things. That's how we grew up. There has never been anything in our lives that was not wrapped up in tastes and smells, sours and sweets. I've become used to this.

Maddy swallows, looking back and forth from me to our father and back to me. "I can't stand this. Whatever it is, can't you just let it go, Justine? Haven't you had enough relationships by now to understand that no one person is ever all right or all wrong? Daddy didn't mean to leave you out when he made all those decisions. And Mom was no saint, for God's sake."

"That's not fair. Mom is not here. She can't defend herself. And some things are wrong."

I look at my father now. Really look at him. His hair has more gray in it than the last time I saw him, but his jawline is still firm and his skin is not heavily lined at all.

Your father is a wonderful chef, but it's how he looks at women that makes the restaurant so successful.

How old was I when my mother told me that? And how did she say it—with longing? With laughter?

No matter where else my father looks, his eyes keep returning to me. He's reeling me in. And I know that if I am susceptible to him, despite how angry and betrayed I feel, it must have been much harder for my mother to resist.

"I'm not going to explain myself, Justine. You can't presume to know what was between your mother and me. And it's wrong to make whatever happened your cause. If you don't want to have me in your life because of some misguided idea that I didn't treat your mother well and you have to defend her, there is no way I will ever win."

He takes another long drink of wine.

"Pauline would not want and does not deserve your turning yourself into a martyr for her. And I can't defend myself against her if you make her—as your sister has said—into a saint. I won't try. The one thing I will do is apologize for that night and what happened. I could have waited. I didn't want to. I wanted the awful part done. And I was wrong."

I don't say anything. My salad has wilted and I push it away. The shrimp were tough and tasteless.

It's Maddy who won't give up, even now that it seems both my father and I have.

"I don't get it, Justine. What good will staying mad do any of us now? I want our family back. Dad wants it back."

"Mom is dead. We can't have our family back."

"No, but we can be together—the three of us. I'm going to get married soon. I'm going to have children. So will you. We can't stay strangers like this because you think you owe it to Mom to stay mad."

M Y M O T H E R S I T S A T T H E table with us. Not the woman she was at the end—jaundiced and only partially alive—but the way she was when I was twelve. She is wearing a turquoise-and-green dress, and her hair is pulled back, and her eyes are sparkling with some kind of surprise. She blows me a kiss.

Guess where I hid it? Guess what it is?

My mother was always buying Maddy and me little gifts, hiding them and making us play a game to find them. A seed pearl bracelet for Maddy. A suede-covered journal for me.

You're getting warmer. Warmer. Cold. Cold. Warm. Oh, you're hot—you found it! Do you like it?

She was good finding new hiding places we couldn't guess. She loved playing all kinds of games with us for hours and helping with our homework for as long as it took, as if she didn't have a job or any deadlines. She'd do her work at night after we were asleep rather than give up spending time with us.

How can someone so beautiful be gone? How is it possible that I can't kiss her soft cheek and inhale her wonderful scent? *Shalimar*. The word itself conjures her. After this lunch I'll find a store and buy some of my mother's perfume. Just open the bottle and sniff the stopper.

And she will be back.

Shalimar is a sexy scent with just enough vanilla to imply some innocence: the perfume of a woman in love, but not a dangerous woman. A woman who can be trusted to pick up her children at school and stand by her husband. But with a look in her eyes that is just a little wistful, that says, yes, there are things I've missed, that I've given up, that I've sacrificed, but that's all right.

Maybe this is something I can do for Charlie to give him some little bit of solace. When I get back, I'll go to Sophie's room, soak one of her scarves with her perfume, and bring it to him.

• • •

"DIDN'T YOU HEAR ME?" Maddy asks.

"No. What?"

"I asked you what you are getting from holding on to all this anger for so long."

I don't know how to explain it. I only know it is my role to take my mother's side against them. And to steer clear of making my mother's mistakes.

"It can't ever be the way it was," my father says.

This last effort is less enthusiastic. And from his monotone it's obvious he's losing hope that he'll get anywhere with me.

Good. Maybe he will give up and leave me alone.

Unless he isn't doing this for himself or for me but for Maddy, who has never been able to relax if anyone around her is bickering.

"Why are you here? Really? What do you want from me?" I ask him.

The question is so direct it stumps him and he takes a sip of wine before he attempts an answer. "I want you to stop being angry about the wrong things. No, no, that's not all of it. . . ." He looks at me, right into my eyes, just the way my mother used to. "I want my daughter back."

Why can't I just give in and make some kind of peace with him?

It is almost as if I hear my mother's voice in my head:

Because you are afraid.

Yes, I am afraid that if I give in, if I open myself up to him, he will make me unhappy, too.

"Would you all like some coffee or dessert?" the waiter asks.

This moment, that shouldn't even be happening in a restaurant in the first place, has been interrupted by a waiter. I am not really surprised when both my sister and my father order coffee and dessert. It underscores the differences between us. After ordering, my father leans toward me.

"We've started," he says. "That's what I came here to do. To get started again." He smiles.

What makes your father so easy to love is his perennial belief in the possibilities of things. I think it's because when you are a chef, what you learn is that if you put in all the right ingredients and bake it for the right amount of time, there's little chance of failure.

Somehow we manage to talk about easy things over the espresso and dessert. Obediently, I begin to eat the half of my father's chocolate mousse he has put in front of me, as if sharing the bittersweet concoction seals an unspoken bargain.

Now that the lunch is almost over, I am finally and perversely hungry.

"I know about Henri St. Pierre," my father says as he puts his credit card down on the bill.

I think that I might be blushing. I'm embarrassed and I'm angry that my father knows about my problems.

As delicious as this dessert is, I push it away, a little too forcefully. My spoon clatters to the floor.

Chocolate was my mother's ingredient. She baked and cooked desserts like this—better than this—and to accept it from my father makes me feel as if I am betraying her.

"Well, I wasn't using Henri St. Pierre to get the story. We were involved. It was a real relationship. What happened is a journalist's nightmare. And it happened to me with a bastard who played dirty. There are reporters who do worse things. They want the story to be about how the movie companies take advantage of the screenwriters, so they only interview the screenwriters who were screwed. They don't lie. They don't fabricate the truth. But they only interview the sources who will feed them the story they want, the juicier story. I didn't do that. What I reported was honest."

"How much trouble are you in?" he asks softly as he puts his hand on mine. His skin is warm and his touch brings a rush of memories.

If it were my mother's hand on me—if she were asking—I would be so grateful for the chance to talk. Instead, I shrug off his hand.

"Other than the damage it's done to your reputation, you aren't in any kind of litigation, are you? Are you all right financially?"

If it were my mother asking, I'd tell her how little money I have left and tell her how much my career really has been hurt. I'd ask for advice and take any help that she offered. I'd even tell her about how Henri called me a heartless bitch and how much it has bothered me. How I don't understand it, even as I'm afraid it might be true.

"I'm okay. I wouldn't be here doing this story if I wasn't," I tell my father with false bravado. I pull the plate toward me, pick up my fork and eat what is left of the mousse, cringing at the sound of the silverware scraping the china.

Outside on the street, my father and Maddy stand side by side facing me. Two of them. One of me. The shadow of my mother by my side. I don't know how to say good-bye. I still haven't really said hello—not in a real way.

After they leave I walk down the avenue looking for a drugstore where I can buy a bottle of my mother's perfume so that I can breathe it in again.

I pass a jewelry store with astonishingly expensive baubles in the window, then a bathing suit shop. Next is a tony real estate office. The lettering on the window boasts branches in New York and London.

A woman steps out just as I am passing by. At first I don't know who she is, but then I recognize her. Stopping a few yards down, in front of a shoe store, I pretend to inspect the merchandise while I listen to Daphne Solomon Sobel talk to a man I realize must be an agent.

"This is all very premature," she says.

"Of course."

"This is a very sad time for my family. We have a lot to get through."

"Of course."

There is something illicit about the way they stand in the shadow of the door and talk. His smile is intimate, hers seductive.

"Please be assured, Mrs. Sobel, we'll be discreet. And we're very sorry about your loss."

"Yes, thank you," she says.

No matter what their words, there is an undercurrent of excitement to their conversation, not sorrow.

TWENTY-SIX

IN A CAR borrowed from Euphonia, I drive down roads I don't know the names of and then turn around and follow the same roads, going the opposite direction. There are exclusive areas of the town where the homes are set hundreds of yards back from the road and mostly hidden by tall trees and stone walls, and there are wide open expanses of rolling hills without a house in sight.

I park on a road ending at a pier jutting into Long Island Sound. A group of men sit in plastic beach chairs fishing. Two gulls swoop down and make passes at the bait. Sun glints off the water. If you took a boat from here and went due south, you'd reach the East River in less than an hour. And from there you could look up and see the apartment building where my mother grew up.

WE ARE STROLLING BY THAT river, just the two of us. I am eighteen and about to go to college. We are going to have lunch with my grandmother in a little while, but first we are taking a walk. My mother is telling me how proud she is. "You are going to own your own mountain one day, Justine." She loops her arm through mine. "Don't wind up with a man who is going to be jealous of that. A man can ruin it."

• • •

WHEN I PULL INTO EUPHONIA, Sam recognizes me and nods a greeting. The gates swing open and I drive through. The forest is empty and quiet, but coming around a bend I have to slam on my brakes to avoid a gardener pruning a dead branch off of a large tree on the edge of the road. The encounter shakes me up, and my hands tremble as I drive the rest of the way to the house and return the car to the garage.

Walking through the front hall, I pass the music room, where tea is laid out in the afternoons. The raised voices are hard to ignore and recognizing Daphne's for the second time that afternoon, I stop to listen.

"Did you check to see if it is all right?" she asks.

"I'm not asking Helena's permission to stay at Sophie's house." Zoë's voice is strained but resolved. "As much as Helena might not want me here, she is not going to throw me out. She is Sophie's puppet—not yours, not Stephen's."

"It doesn't matter how you feel; you have to think about how this looks. You should be by Stephen's side. He needs you with him. Don't you realize how much this is hurting him? It's not bad enough that Sophie is missing and might be dead, but he has to face that alone."

"He's not alone. He has you." Her voice is bitter.

"That's ridiculous. I'm his sister, you are his wife. Now, listen, I want you to come back to New York with me tonight. I'm—" Seeing me walking into the room, Daphne breaks off.

I've heard enough in the hall. I want to see what I can find out in person.

"Oh, I'm sorry. Did I interrupt? I was just going to get some tea."

Daphne is staring, trying to place me. It takes her only a few seconds. "You're the reporter, aren't you?"

"Yes, Justine Pagett." I barely finish my last name when she interrupts.

"Who invited the press?" she asks Zoë. "Do you know about this?"

"I'm so sorry about your mother," I say to Daphne at the same time that Zoë starts to explain to her that Austen brought me up with him and that, yes, even Helena knows I'm here.

Daphne pulls a cigarette out of a pack in her purse, lights it, and takes a deep drag. Zoë puts down her teacup and stands up, using my entrance as an excuse for an exit. At the door she stops. "Daphne, thanks for offering a lift, but I'm staying, for better or worse, till Sophie comes home."

"This is her school. It isn't her home." Daphne sounds petulant. "That's with us, in New York."

"No place is more her home than here," Zoë says sadly, and then walks out, leaving Daphne dragging on her cigarette.

"This is an emotional time for all of us," Daphne says, as if an explanation is needed.

"Of course."

"You aren't going to write about this, are you?" An inch of ash falls from her cigarette to the mosaic floor.

"I don't have any intention of exploiting what you're all going through. I was invited here to write a biography of your mother, and once she is found . . ."

"*If* she's found." Daphne frowns. "She shouldn't have gone out on the boat alone. My mother is in her sixties. She gets distracted, especially when she is obsessed with music." Then she smiles. She's remembering her mother, I think, and I feel for her. "You know she needs help with the most ordinary things. For God's sake, she talks to Beethoven out loud. She disappears into these fugue states. . . ." She takes another drag of the cigarette and looks for an ashtray. "Out in a boat by herself, can you imagine? She's not in her right mind when she starts obsessing over a new work. Anything might have happened."

"What do you think happened?"

"I have no idea. But I love her. And so does my brother."

"Of course you do." I hope I haven't registered any surprise at the out-of-context comment.

Daphne picks up a pale porcelain bowl rimmed in delicate gold leaf and grounds out her cigarette in it.

"I'm sure you understand how hellish it can be between mothers and daughters. Friction is expected. Or are you one of those women who get along perfectly with her mother?" she asks.

I put my hand in my jacket pocket, feel for my pen, and hold on to it tightly.

"I'm sure that your mother will be found. She doesn't sound like someone who gives up easily."

Daphne doesn't notice that I haven't answered the question.

"No, she doesn't, and she never loses. Not even against things that defeat other people. Anyone with her problems would be devastated by them." Daphne doesn't finish the thought because her attention has been distracted by Charlie, walking across the terrace toward us.

Opening the doors, she rushes to him, grabs him, takes him in her arms, and holding him, coos in his ear. Charlie doesn't relax; he is no more comforted by his mother than he was by Austen. He endures the embrace.

I leave, afraid that if I stay any longer, I will break down. When I look at Charlie, I see the part of me that will forever be in mourning.

TWENTY-SEVEN

THERE ARE NO locks on the bedroom doors at Euphonia. Housekeepers make my bed and clean up the bathroom each morning. They leave fresh towels and empty the garbage and straighten up. But it is still unnerving to know that someone has come in while I was in town and left this gift in my room.

It is a glossy white shopping bag with red tissue paper peeking out of the top and a ribbon, in the same red, tying the handles together in a festive bow. It sits in the middle of my bed, waiting for me. How light it is, I think, as I put it on the desk next to my computer.

Somewhere in the house a violinist and pianist play a mournful duet and lose step with each other. The result is jarring. The musicians try again. This time the piano is hesitant and the violin rushes. The house falls silent.

I pull the ribbon. It falls to the floor, a satin snake curling at my feet. Reaching in, I push aside the paper and something sharp sticks my finger. I pull my hand out quickly to find one tiny drop of blood on the fleshy section of my thumb.

More carefully, this time I reach into the bag and lift out a rag doll. A voodoo rag doll identical to the virtual one I received over the Internet a few days ago. Just like the two-dimensional image, this one also has straight pins sticking in each finger except for the thumb.

More disturbing than opening E-mail and seeing this image is holding the doll in my hands. I throw her down to get her away from me, and she lands, legs and arms akimbo, half in and half out of the wastebasket.

I feel sick.

There must be a card, some sort of message. Riffling through the tissue in the shopping bag, I find a sheet of plain white paper. Even the typeface is disturbing, the very slant of the letters and their unevenness is threatening. And although it has been printed and not handwritten, something human and cruel crouches in the spaces between the letters.

This is your fourth warning. Get out of Euphonia and leave Sophie's story alone or you will be sorry.

TWENTY-EIGHT

ACKING AWAY FROM the note and the doll, I flee my room. The beach is the only place I can think of going. I run down the stairs and out of the house onto the wide expanse of sand. Somehow I feel safer in the open.

I don't notice Austen until it is too late for me to turn around. He's sitting on a large rock, looking toward the lighthouse across the sound. I imagine what a relief it will be to tell him about the doll and how scared I am and how soothing his voice will be and how he will know what I should do.

Except I can't tell him what's happened nor ask his advice. I can't involve him in my personal drama. I won't jeopardize this story.

I need to interview him, not weave us closer together.

"The Coast Guard called a half hour ago. They've downgraded it to a search and recovery. That means they think they are looking for a body," he says in a flat, unemotional voice.

"What about the clothes they found this morning?" I ask, forgetting about the doll in the face of this news.

"They weren't Sophie's." He opens his hands and looks down at them as if there were some message written on his palms. "And the police have been questioning all of us."

"Questioning you? Why? Do the police think that someone kid-napped her?" Or murdered her, I think, but do not say.

"I don't think they suspect any foul play. It seemed to me that it was just routine questioning. But Daphne was indignant. She was here. She came up to spend time with Charlie, and never expected to walk into an interrogation."

"Are they done?"

"For now."

He's quiet for a moment.

"You look furious. Did the police do something wrong?"

"No. After they left, Daphne said that she and Stephen are going to start planning a memorial service."

"They are giving up?"

"She is, and Stephen is, but Charlie—who heard everything—keeps insisting that his grandmother isn't dead and that Daphne not do anything yet."

"Is Daphne going to stay here until Sophie's . . . until she's found?" I ask.

"No. She's spending the rest of the afternoon and is going back after she and Charlie have had dinner."

I stare out at the water, sifting sand through my fingers. "What do you think she and Stephen will do with all this . . . if . . . if the worst has happened?"

"You mean with Euphonia?"

I nod.

"They won't do anything with it. Euphonia's been left to Juil-liard, along with an endowment, so that it will stay a school. The only provision is that the stone cottage will belong to Charlie to use and after that for his children, but no one can ever sell it."

"She's leaving all this to strangers?" If I were her daughter, I'd be upset. No, I'd be angry to be cut out of an area of my mother's life that was so important to her. I touch the round diamond on the inside of my finger to my cheek.

"She's given them everything else. They each have huge trusts. So does Charlie," he says.

"I saw him up at the house. I ache for him."

Austen nods. "I know. And when he heard the Coast Guard was downgrading the rescue . . ." His words trail off.

"Have you been able to get him to talk about how he's feeling?"

"He won't talk to me or to Daphne. He's Sophie's child, no matter what the birth certificate says. He's shut himself off and is in denial—insisting over and over that she's coming back.

"He's so connected and attuned to Sophie I'm afraid that if I'm the one who convinces him he has to give up hoping she's found alive, he'll never forgive me. I will always be the one who told him; it will become a wall between us.

"And you know when I look at him, I want to believe she's alive. When I'm talking to him I *want* to believe what he believes. But Justine, she's been missing for more than forty-eight hours. Over twenty-five cutters have been looking for her. Dozens of police have gone house to house all up and down the shoreline. They've walked every inch of the peninsula. There's no sign of her." Austen leans toward me.

I want to meet him halfway, but I don't move.

"Austen, isn't it possible that she made it to shore and someone found her and . . ." My voice drifts off. I don't want Sophie to be dead either. Without her I'm back to where I was before I left Paris. But more than that, I want Sophie to be alive for Charlie's sake. If he loses his grandmother now, it will be like me losing my mother. And he is too young to learn to live with that kind of loss now.

He should be older than this before he has to deal with waking up every day and remembering all over again that it's not a dream but his new reality and that he has to live without her for the rest of his life.

"I'm not sure he'll make it if she's gone," Austen says.

"He will. We do, despite ourselves," I say.

"I don't know."

"He's your son. He has your strength."

"Strength?" He laughs derisively. "I've taken so many easy outs.

Disappointed so many people . . . everyone who ever mattered to me. Except for the one person who disappointed me first. . . ."

I look out at the calm sea and think about what to say. He is alone with something, too, just like Charlie. And I know how difficult that is.

"Sophie?"

He nods.

"What did she do to you?"

"It's another story for another day."

"But you loved her once, didn't you?"

He nods again.

"That's what you have to share with Charlie. You have to be together in how much he loves her and how you once did."

"If only I wasn't so angry with her for what she's done to Charlie. For being stupid and taking that boat out at night. For being so much larger than life. For playing God with us and our careers and pushing us to protect her own—" He stops. For the second time, he's said much more than he intended.

"Austen?"

"You are going to use all of this in the story. . . . I can't talk to you about it."

I sidestep. "I'm not even sure what will happen to the story." He hears what he wants to hear.

"Do you want to come over to the cottage later and have dinner with me? There's enough to cook up something simple. I'll tell you what I can about her."

I know, all too well, you talk about people to try to keep them alive for as long as you can. That was what my father and sister wouldn't do when my mother died. They closed up and shut down. Around them my mother was dead.

In the streets of Paris, watching the tourist boats on the river, walking in the gardens smelling the roses and lilacs, and drinking the wine and eating onion soup and apple tarts, it was easier to keep her alive.

We plan to meet later and Austen goes back to the cottage. Not anxious to return to my room and face the rag doll, I take off, jogging away from the beach into the heavily wooded area beyond the pond. I haven't come this way yet, but if I go straight and keep the sea on my left, I shouldn't get lost.

Except after only five minutes I'm so deep in the woods that the glimmer of the water is no longer visible and I can't hear the surf. When I look down I see I've left the stone path and am running on a forest floor covered with a blanket of pine needles and twigs that snap beneath my feet.

It is cooler in the shadows of the trees, and when I breathe, I not only feel the air, I taste it. There's not much choice; either I go forward or try to find my way back. Ahead is a bridge. I cross it and then follow a path that brings me to a pair of wrought-iron gates, which open into a walled-in garden.

Ivy trails over the brick walls, and moss makes the ground slippery. To the left is a small waterfall, a pond filled with lily pads, and a weeping willow that sways gently over the water. A cutout in the wall opens up to a vista that looks out to the harbor, where a lone sailboat heads toward the late afternoon sun. In the center of the garden is a large mosaic mandala made of white, beige, and black shells. And kneeling beside it, weeding, is a gardener. A russet cocker spaniel, sitting nearby, picks up his head and stares at me, alert and at the ready.

It's Ludwig.

The dog has noticed me, but the gardener hasn't. While I watch, she continues working. Her head is down and her short salt-and-pepper hair falls forward over her face. Her work clothes are stained with grass and dirt.

A trill of birdsong distracts the dog and he runs off, but the gardener doesn't break her rhythm or look up. As with everyone else at Euphonia, there is an aura of grief around her and I back off, not wanting to interrupt.

Leaning against a tree, listening to the waterfall, I watch a tiny bird land on a rock by the edge of the pond. The light here is remarkable: shadows fall in patterns. Everything has been designed for this play of sun. A breeze sways the ornamental grasses; their tips reach down and touch the ground and then slowly rise. Beds of hostas and iris wave in the wind.

There is a lot you can learn from the land, Sophie had written to me. *No man is larger than a tree. No woman is as fecund as the earth. A gardener nurtures. What do I do compared to that? I open my doors and say come here and I will teach you to make music and turn you into stars. That is a lot of power to hold over someone. What humbles me is the land. I look at it. I know its real value. The trees will be here long after we are gone.*

TWENTY-NINE

I LET THE HOT water run while I get undressed. Stepping into the shower, I pull the curtain. Steam surrounds me and pellets of water hit my face, my neck, and my breasts. Reaching for the soap, I lather under my arms, on my neck, across my chest, between my legs.

The oblong violet bar of soap arouses me. Leaning against the wall, with the cold tiles on my back, I put my right foot on the edge of the tub so that my legs are spread wide enough for the water to hit me.

The tiny drops shoot out of the showerhead and I don't have to do anything but imagine someone. I won't let myself see his face, just his body. Water is running in rivulets down his body too, down his neck, his torso, his thighs, his erection. Now his hand is between my legs, rubbing me, and I arch against him, thrusting out my hips. Damn, I can see his face even though I wish I couldn't. I see Austen's eyes watching me, and then—

A sudden sharp pain sears the bottom of my foot. The water runs red. Sitting down on the edge of the tub, I inspect my right sole and find a clean cut an inch across the ball of my foot.

Turning off the shower, I watch the pink water swirl down the drain and look. There on the porcelain are three, no four, slivers of glass.

Naked and wet, with my foot bleeding, I start to shake. There is the possibility that this is an accident. A housekeeper cleaning the tub broke a bottle of some sort of cleaning agent.

But aren't those usually plastic?

I don't want to connect this to the threats. Don't want to believe this is the beginning of the things planned for me if I stay and write Sophie's story. But glass doesn't just appear on shower floors any more than voodoo dolls show up on beds.

The blood stops flowing after a few minutes. I find bandages in the first aid kit under the sink and dress the wound. Tentatively I step on it. Just a twinge. I've cut myself worse. It isn't throbbing, and if I'm careful it will barely affect my walking.

THIRTY

TWO HOURS LATER, on the cottage's
deck, Austen and I sit watching dark clouds
roll in.

"How far away is the storm?" I ask.

"About three miles."

"It looks so beautiful from here."

"Yes, from here. But if you were further out . . . if we were on a boat sitting under those clouds with the rain pouring down on us and the wind tossing us around, you wouldn't think so. Sophie and I got caught in a storm like that once. It was terrifying being buffeted and beat up by the water and the wind. But it was worth going through to have heard it."

"What do you mean?"

"The sound reverberates inside of you." He touches the center of his chest. "The only composer who's even come close to representing it is Beethoven in his Sixth. The *Pastoral* Have you heard it?"

I shake my head.

He goes inside, and seconds later the music pours out of the open door and windows.

There are words to describe it, but they cannot translate the experience of how the individual notes come together to create, not the actual sounds of a storm, but the essence of it.

"There is very little that has been created by any artist that compares to this," he says in a defeated voice.

"Austen, why have you stopped writing music?"

"So . . . I still write. I just keep it to myself and don't have expectations anymore about how it will be received or that it will get played."

"Sophie can't help?"

"Help?" He laughed sardonically. "She stopped championing my music a long time ago." His eyes narrow. I can't tell if his expression is one of anger or disappointment. "She denounced what I wrote." His mellow voice has turned brittle; his eyes spark with anger. "She was the most avant-garde composer of her time, but she couldn't stand it that I was pushing further. She withdrew her support. And without it, I was . . . It doesn't matter anymore."

"Will you play me something?"

"You won't like it. That's the problem."

"Can't I judge for myself?"

"Even to a trained ear, what I write sounds jarring. I've gone even further into twenty-first-century sound than when we knew each other four years ago. Go talk to the musicians in the house, listen to what they are performing. They'd rather play eighteenth- and nine-teenth- and early twentieth-century music. If musicians don't even get it, imagine how audiences respond. Maybe two percent of real aficionados want to hear the kind of music I write. And half of them only because they think it's chic or intellectual. People still walk out on concerts where twenty-first-century compositions are performed.

"And to make it more complicated, the environment has been polluted with a lot of bad new music. It's easy to pretend you know what you are doing with modern harmonies. Who is to judge what's good when no one understands it? You don't have to adhere to the guidelines of having to sound harmonious. So . . . it's just like how people can't tell difference between a Jackson Pollock and a piece of shit."

"But I can."

"Because you've had some training. You haven't with this music, though."

"What makes it sound—what word should I use—wrong?"

"No, not wrong. It's not wrong. The harmonies that we traditionally consider pleasing are the intervals that occur lower in the overtone series. The sound waves in these intervals seem to fit together. But when you get to the uppers—which are the intervals I'm using—the sounds don't seem to fit together. Because they aren't fitting. The sound waves don't hit at the same time but instead hit against and fight each other. That's why the sounds and tensions that come across are dissonant."

"Not to trivialize what you are saying at all, but it sounds like the whole world we're living in."

"Ah. A realist. Yes. Well, any artist worth his salt is translating his world into his medium. Be it paint or stone or words or music. Twenty-first-century harmony reflects twenty-first-century life. We are not living in a serene uncomplicated world that is immediately pleasing. New York City is a complicated place. Not like walking through the Vienna woods. Why should my music go the same place that Beethoven's went?"

"The dissonance reflects the dissonance of modern life?" I ask.

He nods.

"Like our relationships. Our dysfunctional families. My dysfunctional family. We pay lip service to the idea of love when it is only duty or passion we are experiencing," I say.

Neither of us speaks for a few seconds. Inside, the Beethoven is between movements and suddenly, the only sound is that of the lapping against the shore.

"But if you want to create music, new music, what choice do you have?"

He looks at me kindly, but anger flashes in his eyes. "You don't count on your teachers or even your contemporaries. You stop asking anyone to listen. You stop using appreciation or understanding as a benchmark for success. And when the people you respect laugh at what you have done and call it noise, you turn the other cheek and pretend it didn't hurt.

"You explore, but do not expect anyone to be interested in your explorations. My music is not about what sounds right, not about the experience of pleasing tones. Like abstract painting is not about pleasing the eye."

"If every writer or painter or sculptor . . . if every artist sheltered their work like you do . . . think of all we'd miss," I say.

"Oh, don't worry about what I'm depriving the world of," he says without any self-pity and with a definite tinge of humor. "So . . . did you see your father and your sister for lunch?"

"You do that a lot. Just change the subject when you don't want to answer a question."

"Wait a minute—didn't you just do that? I just asked you how lunch was with your father."

I laugh.

"Ah, yes, that laugh. There are bells in it. . . . I've never heard a more beautiful laugh."

"That can't be possible."

"I wouldn't have said it if it weren't true. I don't lie, Justine."

"Everyone lies."

He shakes his head. "No. Not everyone."

"But some lies are necessary."

"You're too smart to base your argument on little white lies—those are simple kindnesses. I'm talking about true falsehoods." He shakes his head.

"What is the worst lie you ever heard?" I ask.

He rubs his forehead with his hand as if it has just begun to ache. He averts his gaze from me, looking instead out at the sea. But his voice gives him away. It is strained, low and measured, as if concentrating on each word and its pronunciation is the only way he can stay in control.

"I was five years old and I remember it was a very warm Sunday. My mother had gotten my sister and me dressed up as if it was an occasion, and we drove to the airport. When we got there, my father bought us presents from one of the stores. I got a toy truck. It was yellow. And a perfect replica. Leslie got a baby doll that cried when you tipped her back and stopped when you put a bottle in her mouth.

"It was just as hot in the airport as it was in the car. I wanted to take off my jacket, but I remember my mother telling me not to.

"There was a constant stream of announcements of flight arrivals and departures, but only one of them got my parents' attention. My father kneeled down and took me in his arms and held me tightly. Then he kissed me on the forehead—and then repeated the sequence with my sister. Finally he stood up and started to walk away, but after taking a few steps he turned around.

"I had never seen him cry and it was very frightening. He was openly sobbing and tears were streaming down his face. He couldn't control himself. My mother pulled both of us close to her. I could feel her legs against my back and her hand gripping one of my shoulders—but I pulled away and ran to him. It was horrible. Fathers—"

Austen's voice cracks. I, who have been riveted by the intimacy of his tone, hold my breath, afraid to break the spell. He clears his throat and continues.

"Fathers are not supposed to cry. They are supposed to comfort you when you cry. I ran to him, I was sobbing too. He hugged me close, and this time I felt his tears. They were hot the way everything was hot that day. 'I will see you very soon. I'm just being silly getting upset like this. I'll see you very soon.'"

The word soon hangs in the air plaintively. I can see the scene in the airport. The tall man—because he had to be tall, since Austen is so tall—and the small boy, both crying while around them passengers taking much-less-emotional leaves are walking by.

"That was the worst lie. He never saw me again. And by the time I was old enough to go and find him and try to understand why and what had happened, he was dead."

"I'm sorry," I say.

He nods. Swallows. And then smiles ruefully. "I have him to

thank for my devotion to music. It filled the gaps his absence created. It was bigger than any one person could ever be. Even him. Even the most important man in my life. Symphonies were bigger, the cello was bigger, all those beautiful and awkward sounds drowned out everything else. And they were mine. No one could take them away."

I'm seeing the small boy watching his father walk away from him.

"Oh, don't. I didn't mean to make you cry," he says to me.

But I can't stop. I know the size and shape of the loss that the man's absence left in Austen's life. And we both know Sophie's disappearance is threatening Charlie's life the same way.

Austen puts his arms around me, leaning his forehead against mine. His hair falls on my face and soaks up my tears. He is comforting me when I am the one who should be comforting him.

I pull back sharply so that we are no longer touching, and he settles back in his chair. "So what happened today? Did you see your father?" he asks.

"One rum straight / One soda back / Light another cigarette from a new pack / You tell me your stories, I'll tell you mine / And we'll swear to each other that tomorrow the sun's gonna shine."

"What is that?" he asks.

"Some song." I'm not comfortable telling him it's something I wrote back when I'd first met him. The woman he knew then was different from who I am now. "I thought I was the only one who couldn't stop missing my mother, that there is something wrong with me because I still think about her every day. My immediate reaction to so many things is: I have to call her and tell her this, and then I remember and have to go through the shock of her being gone all over again.

"But today at lunch, my father talked about how much he still misses her. I don't think Maddy does. Not the way I do. She's been able to move on or maybe she never missed her that much in the first place. But my father is still mourning her, and I didn't expect that. How can he when he never . . ." I don't know how to finish the sentence.

"They were together a long time."

"But they weren't happy. He didn't make her happy. She loved him much more than he ever loved her."

"So . . . that doesn't mean he didn't love her." Austen says this as if he understands something about it that I don't. "You can be furious with someone . . . can stop talking to them and not see them for years . . . but you can still love them for those things about them that were once there."

What is he talking about? His feelings for Sophie?

The fourth movement of Beethoven's symphony builds to its next crescendo.

He's looking at me with such a sincere expression it's as if his empathy itself touches me and encloses me in an embrace. We've crossed a bridge while we have been sitting here, and I am afraid of what is on this side. The only thing I am certain of is that it will damage the story I am here to write.

"What will you do if Sophie doesn't come back?" he asks, as if reading my mind.

I shrug. "Get on a plane and go back to Paris."

For the first time, Paris seems a long way away. A wave of loneliness overwhelms me and I swirl in its current. Two weeks ago I thought I knew exactly who I was and what I wanted. Now I'm not even sure where my home is.

Seeing New York, my old apartment, my sister, and now my father, being here at Euphonia surrounded by so many people who are so sad and worried, being scared myself . . . I am not as tethered to my old address and routines as I was.

"Do you mind me staying here and waiting?" I ask him.

"I'm glad you are here."

"Are you?"

"I told you: I don't lie."

"But I'm the one you can't trust, remember? We'll always have

Paris . . . getting between us." I've made a pathetic joke. He grimaces in response.

"Come on, let's walk."

Slipping off my sandals, I follow him down to the beach. The
sand is cool, but the wave that surges up and washes over my feet is
freezing. And it stings. Leaping back, I come down hard on my bad
foot. Damn, I forgot about the cut and the bandage. With a little
limp, I walk back to the deck.

"What's wrong?" Austen asks, following me.

"It's nothing. Just a cut." Sitting down on the steps, I brush the
sand off the bandage.

"Let me see."

Before I can object, he bends down and inspects my foot.

"There's sand in there. Sit still, I'll be right back."

He is only gone for a minute and comes back with a bowl of
water, some hydrogen peroxide, and a fresh bandage. Sitting beside
me, he cleans the cut. His fingers on my skin make me shiver. I
curse my sensitivity to him.

"How'd you do this?" he asks.

As much as I want to confide in him, I can't. There are too
many conflicts of interest.

"I broke a glass in the bathroom."

A seagull swoops down, landing on the porch railing. The birds
at Euphonia seem not to care anything about the human inhabi-
tants. Ignoring Austen's shooing movements, the bird takes a few
steps closer to the bowl of peanuts on the table, brazenly reaches
out and pinches one in his beak. Austen doesn't bother to scare the
bird away again. Instead, he takes the bowl of nuts and holds it over
the porch railing.

"Watch how fast they know—all of them—that there is food
here. It's almost instantaneous."

He's right. Even as he spills the nuts into the sand, the birds are
gathering, maneuvering. Each one seems to be getting a chance.
Two birds hang back. They are smaller than the others and seem
not quite sure how to compete for their share. Noticing them,

Austen takes a handful of nuts and throws it off to the side in their direction.

"Do you think Daphne and Stephen resent the fact that Sophie is the one who lived and their father is the one who died?" I ask.

"That's an awful question."

"I know, but it's not that uncommon a reaction."

He seems about to say something, but stops himself.

"You were going to ask me if I felt that when my mother died?"

He nods.

"I did," I tell him.

Austen goes inside. Through the window I watch him pick up the bottle of wine, and I also see how he cannot pass his cello without looking at it.

I go to the doorway. "When I first met you, you were playing on a very expensive cello that had been loaned to you by one of your professors. Is this the same one?"

Austen touches the instrument's curved wooden shoulder.

"No, this is a different one, a better one, loaned to me by another one of my professors."

The one he used to have was insured for almost half a million dollars. I don't even guess at what this one might be worth.

The amber instrument, with its graceful lines, closely resembles a woman's torso. At its widest point, it's broader than my hips. Watching him caress the cello's neck, a jolt of jealousy zaps me.

The wine forgotten, he picks up the bow and sits down, taking the cello in his arms. He begins to play. Not his own music, but a piece I recognize as Bach. He is in full control of this inanimate object, bringing it to life, making it sing with his hands.

I want him to touch me like that. To hear what he can coax from my body and see if he can do it so effortlessly and expertly. I listen so intently that even when he is finished, I can hear the reverberations of the strings in the air.

"It's so beautiful. The music. And the cello. Who gave it to you?" I ask again.

"You haven't guessed?"

His question is the only clue I need. "Sophie gave it to you, didn't she?"

"To play, yes, but it doesn't belong to me. If anything happens to me it goes back to her, and after her to Charlie. I tried to return it to her when we became estranged. As much as I didn't want to keep it, I was equally relieved that she wouldn't take it back."

He looks down, inspecting the bow.

"What was she trying to buy by giving you the cello?" I ask. "Was she apologizing?"

His only answer is the first note of the next piece. Mournful, solemn, exquisite; another one of the Bach sonatas that he told me years ago are in every cellist's repertoire.

The music slows. The sound goes deep and dark, like the black water of a nighttime ocean. The cello's sonorous tones in a room this size absorb all the air. The instrument takes it in and expels it out, changed and altered. The atmosphere becomes the music, and it is in every breath I take and let out.

The sound is inside me, so in a way, he is inside me. It is not all that different than if he were making love to me, because what is that but one person reaching inside another, touching them to their core and giving them some moments of ecstasy? What does it matter if he gives those moments to me with his music or with his body?

"What a pleasure it must be to be able to make music. What does it feel like?" I ask after he finishes and lays down the bow and the cello.

Not answering, he gets up, takes me by the hand, and brings me over to a large chair. He sits first and then tells me to sit in front of him. As I do I feel the insides of his legs hugging my hips, his chest up against my back.

He maneuvers the cello into position in front of me and then weaves his arms under mine. He places my hand on the bow and then his hand over mine. With his other hand he depresses my fingers on the strings in the correct position, and then he draws my hand and the bow across the cello.

The music escapes from the fine wooden body in an achingly

long and slow chord. I feel it in my chest, in my lungs, through my arms. The music reverberates against my skin and gets deep into my bones.

This is something that Austen feels every day of his life. I no longer have to wonder how a musician can become so committed to playing. Not composing. Not creating. But just the act of playing. It is one thing to hear music, but another to bring it forth, to release it and take it back in with the air you breathe, in the breath you expel.

Body and cello become one, as if Austen is indeed playing me. Is my blood beating to the beat of the music, has my heart slowed to the tempo of the song, or is that his blood and his heart?

At some point I open my eyes. Through the window, I see that the moon has risen. Its light dances on the surface of the sea. For a moment I fantasize that our music has pulled the white orb into the sky.

Austen continues moving my hand. He is the bow, I am the strings. I allow myself, for just these few minutes, to be in this moment and no other. Not to question, but to connect. Music takes away the images of my mother's sad eyes and all thoughts of her heartbreak. This sound we are making is a greater promise than her loss is a warning.

The phone rings once, then again. And reluctantly, as if being woken from a dream, Austen stops playing and gets up.

"Hello?" His eyes focus on a point in the distance, the line of his mouth relaxes and then hardens again.

"THAT WAS CHARLIE CALLING FROM a restaurant in Greenwich," he says after hanging up. His voice is suddenly tired.

"Daphne is pleading with him to go back to New York with her after dinner, but he wants to come back here and wait for Sophie. I'm going to pick him up in an hour. Damn her."

"Sophie?"

"No, Daphne. She's playing games. She told him he didn't have to call me, that if he was so insistent on coming back here, she'd bring him herself. But he thinks that once he gets in her car, she's going to drive him back to New York regardless of what he wants. She's telling him she needs him with her. He's just a kid. He's not supposed give her support. It's such bullshit. She doesn't need support. She resents the hell out of Sophie. Daphne's capable of using any opportunity to recapture Charlie."

"What do you mean? Sophie's her mother. She must be upset." But even as I say it, I picture Daphne on the street in Greenwich with the real estate broker, Daphne in the study arguing with Zoë. Austen is right.

"So . . . are you hungry?" he asks, looking at his watch. "We have enough time for something quick."

"Yes," I say. "Do you want to drive into town, grab a bite, and then get Charlie?"

"No, let's stay here."

"A sandwich or a salad is fine. Whatever is easier."

"How can I serve a cook a sandwich?"

I laugh. "I'm not a cook. And a sandwich is totally fine."

WE TAKE THE TOMATO, MOZZARELLA, and basil sandwiches and more wine down to the water's edge and sit on a rock, eating quietly. There is more than enough moonlight to see shells and rocks and bits of seaweed in the sand and to illuminate Austen's profile.

I want to lean up against him and know that he wants me there. I want reach out and glide my fingertips across his cheekbones, down his neck, and touch where his skin is warm beneath his shirt. I want to feel his heart beat against the palm of my hand.

I also want my story.

I dig my toes into the sand and fight these conflicting instincts. Six months ago I would have reached out and touched him. Six months ago we would already be locked in an embrace on Austen's bed.

If you want to cover the circus . . .

The sand is cool, and the gritty surface feels smooth and rough at the same time.

He's just another man and there will be other men. Why do I need to put my fingers on the skin beneath the cuff of *his* shirt? To trace *his* veins and feel *his* blood pulse?

A familiar clench throbs between my legs. It has been months since I've had sex and I feel the lack of it—not as an urgent need, but as something missing. It is something new to deny my body the urge to satiate itself, to surrender to the pure feelings of the act and get lost in sensation. I haven't been with anyone since Henri. But I can't connect that easy fucking with Austen.

"What are you thinking?" he asks, turning to face me.

I'm not sure of what to say, certainly not the truth. "Nothing."

He laughs. "Not nothing. I can tell from your face. You are deep in it. Is something wrong?"

"Not wrong. No. Just thinking . . . not understanding something, that's all."

"But you don't want to talk about it?"

"Boy, you ask a lot of questions."

"Not usually."

"Then why now?"

"I'm not sure, but watching you, I wanted to know what you were thinking. . . ." He pauses.

My hands move in small circles on the sand; the grit gets under my fingernails.

"So . . . I suppose I wanted you to tell me you were thinking about me," he says.

"Oh, did you now?" I tease, but his admission makes me nervous.

In the sand I find a piece of glass smoothed by endless washings in the sea. Lifting it to my face, I rub it on my skin. A harmless piece of sea glass, not anything like the glass in my bathtub.

Even though I've made light of his comment, I don't take it lightly. I allow it to sit between us on the beach while I consider it. Trying to ascertain why now, why him, why what he says matters so much. Something between us—despite my efforts to disavow it—is alive and growing.

I tell myself I really can't do this. Cannot complicate or compromise this story. It is my only chance.

And then he reaches out and touches me in the same spot where, a moment before, I'd been rubbing the piece of glass. I inhale his scent: rosin, wood, oranges.

"I hear you thinking. What's wrong?" he asks.

I don't know what to say, so I tell him part of the truth.

"I like it here more than I imagined I would. I've never spent any real time by the water. I've been to Cannes and Nice, but they are cities by the water. Big hotels. Crowded beaches. I've always thought of the sand as hot and burning, not this cool soft surface. I guess I never felt this connection to the water."

What I want to be saying is that I have never quite felt this simple willingness to sit beside a man, never been so reluctant to pursue him. I have always needed to prove that I could seduce a man and have him lust after me. Until right now, sitting here. But I can't say it. I'm embarrassed. And I don't know what it means.

"I'm not ashamed of who I've been with or the way I've lived my life."

"Who said you should be?" he asks, making me realize that I had said that out loud.

"No one. I just . . ." I pick up more sand and let it fall through my fingers. I can't find the right words. I want to separate him from Sophie. From this place. From the story. And I can't.

"Justine, why don't you like looking in the mirror?" he asks suddenly.

"What?"

"I've noticed that whenever we pass a mirror you avert your eyes."

I lift my hands and then let them drop again.

"There's nothing you should be afraid to see," he says.

But there is. I'm afraid to see a reflection of my mother, to see *her* sadness in *my* eyes.

"Have you ever made love looking in a mirror?" he asks.

Involuntarily, I shudder.

He laughs. "So . . . I made Miss Wanton cringe. I used to think there was nothing you wouldn't do in bed. No passion you would see as a perversion. But I've found one, haven't I?"

Before I have a chance to answer, he leans forward and kisses me. Giving in to the pressure of his lips, of his arms around me, I let go and enter that realm where there is only sensation and smell. I feel his rough skin on my cheek and inhale his cotton shirt mixed in with the salty scent of the sea.

Awe at how the roar of the waves orchestrates the second kiss.

Curiosity as the taste of wine and some sweetness I cannot name flavors the third.

By the fourth kiss we have shed our history and begun anew.

I hear his sigh. It touches me as softly as his fingers that are stroking my cheeks, then my neck. I feel myself traveling toward him with an organ of my body I have never felt move before—my heart.

Not now. No.

Not him.

The sixth kiss.

The seventh.

It is not simply the kisses, the touches, tastes, sounds, or scents. Not just the shock of his newness. Or just another connection. It's that I am not showing *a man* what I can do, not impressing *a man* with my passion or proving my prowess. I am—for the first time— allowing someone to give to me without worrying about giving anything back.

What a shame that he cannot know about this most unusual gift, my simple surrender.

This is the one thing I have never given to a man, but I yield now. No, I do not like looking in the mirror, because no matter what I have done or who I have been with, I have never seen any reflection of it in my face and that scared me. I have always remained untouched and unmarked. And I know, from looking at my mother's face, that if you let someone touch you, not with their hands or lips or tongue or legs or fingers or penis, but if you let their essence and emotion touch you, it marks you and leaves you altered.

I wonder if . . . he kisses me again. The tenth kiss.

I wonder, if I looked in the mirror now, would I see him reflected in my eyes, in the set of my mouth?

I am sure that I would.

The eleventh kiss.

This is wrong. I have made this mistake before. But it's worse this time, and I pull back, breaking the embrace like prying open a shell.

"We'll be late," I tell him.

WE WALK BACK TO THE cottage.

Inside, he retrieves his keys and wallet. I have only a few seconds before he comes back, and so I hurry. I have to end what is starting before I do any more damage.

What I am about to do is betray not just him, but myself also. I know I'm taking the coward's way out, but it's the only way I can think of to force this ending and leave no loose ends.

I open my bag, take out my notebook, uncap my fountain pen, and start taking notes on the things Austen has told me in the last few hours about Sophie.

"Do you want to come with me to pick up Charlie?" he is saying as he walks back into the room and over to me. "Or meet me when I come back . . ."

He sees me writing and stops short.

"What are you doing?" he asks.

Pen in hand, notebook open, I look up, then quickly cover the words with my hand.

I try to appear as if I've been caught in the act; I want him to think my expression is one of guilt.

And he does. His initial incredulity turns quickly to disappointment and then finally his face settles into anger.

I force myself not to blurt out an explanation, not to tell him I'm sabotaging our connection on purpose. Something seizes up inside of me, but I feign innocence and answer him.

"I'm just taking some notes. You said some things about Sophie I don't want to forget."

"Fuck me. Here I am, despite myself, opening, while you're playing with me to get what you want for the damn story."

I cannot bear hearing the disgust in his voice even though I've orchestrated it. "I'm a reporter," I say. "What did you expect?"

"Not that you would rush back here and write down what I told you. Not those private things." Austen frowns. "Did you get enough? I sure hope so because you are not getting anything else. Not another word. I'm not going to talk with you about myself or my son or Sophie DeLyon. Stay away from me. Stay up in the house and wait for Sophie if you want; I don't care. Just don't come back here."

He pulls on his jacket, strides to the door, and holds it open for me. I'm too frightened by his tone and tenor to move. I've gone too far. My bravado is gone.

"Austen?" I do not know why I have said his name. It is not my right to say any more. I have forfeited that. I cannot smell the rosin on his fingers anymore. Cannot look into his eyes. Cannot feel his lips.

But I *can* write the story.

I recap the pen, close the notebook, and hold on to both tightly—to stop myself from reaching out as I rush past him and out the door. And then I keep walking away from him, toward the big house, not slowing down, not looking back.

Two words ring in my ears. *Heartless bitch*. But this time, I hear them said in my own voice.

Austen is . . . he is nothing to me. I feel nothing for him. I will not remember kissing him an hour from now.

I stop to listen, but he is not coming after me. He won't, I know. Like he's done with his own music: it's easier for him to deny what he wants than to fight for it. And that's good. It's better. Because I don't need to feel those things that he was making me feel.

They are the emotions my mother used to have for my father, etched into her face not as a smile but as sorrow.

THIRTY-ONE

SLEEP HARDLY SEEMED possible, so I didn't even try. Instead, I read one of Sophie's books about manic depression, *An Unquiet Mind*. And now my own mind is unquiet. Long past midnight, I can no longer see the moon or its reflection in the water. Like the dark, the disease I've been reading about shrouds its sufferers. To live a lighter life, the only choice being to take drugs that too often dull one's capacity for the highs while tempering the lows.

From the desk, looking out the window, I can see the lights are on in the stone cottage and I wonder if Austen is awake. No. I can't think about him anymore. And I'm thankful for that. I am. And for the professional distance between us.

I don't realize I'm biting my lip until the pain hits and I taste the slightly sweet blood. Back to work, I tell myself, and sit down at my computer to read through my notes. But first I check my E-mail.

Scanning a dozen letters I check the senders' names, but there's nothing from the Lyon's Pride. A momentary reprieve from my nemesis.

I read Fiona's first. She's concerned about the threats, especially since I wrote her about the broken glass. She thinks I should go to the police.

Among the remaining is a letter from an address I don't recognize. It has an attachment and is something I'd normally delete were it not for the subject line: "Information for your story."

The message is four lines long and unsigned.

> Not a saint. Not even a sinner, but a sad sick soul. For years, with help, she has hidden her illness behind her symphonies and sonatas. But an insanity like hers should cause you to question her every decision.

I click on *download,* and forty-five seconds later the movie player icon pops up and I hit the play button. A grainy image appears of a woman's naked back slicked with sweat. Long blonde hair. A seductive shoulder.

There is faint music in the background that is tinny on my little laptop but familiar nonetheless. After listening to so much of Sophie's music these last few weeks, I'm sure this is a DeLyon piece under the sounds of two people breathing.

The blonde woman moans slightly. Two hands reach up and grasp her around the waist as if tethering her. The woman starts whispering something over and over, too low to make out over the music. She writhes in pleasure, back and forth, her movements so rhythmic they seem to be choreographed. And then she lets out a sharp cry, arches back, and reveals the other person—who is not a man after all but an older woman.

Her face is hidden, but I can see her lined neck and her slightly sagging breasts.

The blonde puts her hand up to stroke the other woman's face, and as she does a thin band of battered gold shimmers on the ring finger of her right hand.

The sounds of the women's lovemaking are now in counterpoint to the music.

I've never been moved by X-rated videos, but this is different. These women are not acting, there is nothing lurid about this sex— no, not sex, this lovemaking.

The blonde swings forward and the string of pearls around her neck gleams. For the first time the older woman comes into view, and I get a glimpse of dark red hair and lipstick. Reaching up she touches the blonde's lips, outlining them. The younger woman sucks on her fingertips.

And now for the first time I hear the blonde whisper a single word: "*Sophie.*"

The camera pulls back and frames both lovers. The blonde from the back and Sophie from the front: her eyes closed, her lips slightly parted, lost in a dream of her own making.

THIRTY-TWO·

AFTER A LONG night and little sleep, the early sun and the beach are welcome distractions. Mug of coffee in hand, I walk the shoreline and notice the same set of footprints I followed yesterday.

Today they lead even further, to a stretch studded with boulders; here there are more pebbles and broken shells than sand.

There's no way anyone walking here would leave an impression, but I keep going, stepping and then slipping on an algae-covered rock. My mug falls and breaks. Leaving a splatter of red shards that stand out against the rocks, I continue onward, navigating through a bed of reeds.

My sneakers squish in the muddy water. When I turn, I see my footprints are already filled in, but I keep going.

Around the next bend, a cliff juts out and casts shadows over the beach. Walking under its shelf, looking up, I try to figure out where on the peninsula I am, but I don't know the topography of the area well enough.

And then I see the caves, alcoves cut in the rocky outcropping. The first depression is about ten feet deep. The second one is no deeper. Emerging from the reeds, I step in water. The tide is coming in.

There is a third cave, but I can't get to it now with the tide coming in.

Turning around, I'm startled to see Ludwig. The cocker spaniel barks as I approach.

"It's okay, boy."

He runs to my side. Agitated and disturbed, he barks again. I pet his soft fur and whisper to him. "It's all right. Let's go back." Together, we turn and walk back to the house.

A FEW HOURS LATER, I am on the opposite side of the peninsula sitting in the audience at the outdoor chapel. Facing us, instead of a minister, there are six musicians. A cellist, two violinists, two flautists, and a harpist are tuning up.

The Sunday morning service is crowded with all the students, friends, and associates holding vigil at Euphonia. I listen in on the conversations around me; not surprisingly, they all relate to Sophie.

"She told me to stop stringing notes together to make music," a woman behind me is saying. "It made me furious."

"But you didn't stop trying, did you? Her criticism always made me work harder. I wanted to write just one thing that she'd accept," another woman responds.

"Her music bypassed words and dealt directly with people's feelings—but what I write? It's just sound," a man to my right says.

"I know. She's more manipulative than someone using words to confuse. You are just sitting there listening, and tears are pouring down your face and you don't know why." This, from the first woman.

"You know, and I can picture her conducting—using her hands to urge the right expression from us. But I can't hear her voice. It's driving me crazy. I can't hear her voice," her companion responds.

Panic overtakes you when the memory of someone you love begins to erode. At first you can see her face and hear her voice just by thinking of her. You don't notice when the picture first begins to fade or the sound gets muffled, until one day you think of her and it's a thought—not an image anymore. You have to pull out photographs to see her exact expression. You have to remember one specific conversation and replay it—concentrating hard—and even then you can't quite hear her inflection.

Worrying about this softening of memory works temporarily to stop the process, because it forces you to keep the images close at hand—to work at hearing words that have evaporated into the air.

The dead control the living if you let them.

Sophie controls everyone here: obsesses them all. She has spent her life controlling them. And if she has done this with her students and her orchestra in the classroom and on the stage . . . then, away from school and off the stage, she must do the same thing.

Sophie must have been an expert at pulling strings and coaxing what she wanted from those around her. This clue to her character may solve the mystery surrounding her accident.

The music begins and attention is drawn to the stone altar. There are no denominations here—music is the universal faith they share, and Sophie DeLyon's is the only composer's work performed.

But the musicians don't play the piece all the way through. After a false start, they try again. And after a few minutes of tentative playing they stop, put down their instruments one after the other and give up.

In the silence that follows the failure, I hear crying. Shifting slightly, I look around and am not surprised to see tears coursing down Helena's cheeks. Walter, sitting beside her, is also weeping, even though his sorrow is incompatible with his stern expression. Behind them, Zoë, too, is crying, but it's Charlie, sitting between his aunt and his father, who is the most distraught. Despite Austen's arm encircling his shoulder, the boy can barely control his sobs.

Leaning over, Austen whispers something in Charlie's ear, but this appears only to upset the boy more because he shrugs his father's arm away.

Even with his own family around him, the boy's isolation is so clear it defines him. Yes, I know what this is like. To be your own solitude. To live in the chasm it creates.

The open-air concert is over only a few minutes after it begins. Everyone stands and walks out of the pews, but no one seems to want to leave the area. As much as I hope to avoid Austen, I am drawn to Charlie's side. Seeing me, Austen's expression turns cold. It chills me, but it's satisfying the way pain can be, because now there is no fear of the pain to come. What caused the anxiety has come to pass, and its reality—as unbearable as it had seemed—is more tolerable when you are right in it.

Being at Euphonia now has nothing to do with this man and me. Even though he is not a main character in Sophie's story, he has a minor role, and recasting him in another will only get in my way. I can concentrate wholly on how each and every person at Euphonia is reacting to Sophie's absence.

Charlie is using his foot as a shovel, digging the ground, creating a crater with the toe of his sneaker. And when the hole is deep enough, he breaks off a branch of a nearby tree, strips it of its leaves—ripping them into smaller and smaller pieces—and then drops them into the shallow grave.

"I'm sorry about last night," I tell Austen, "but my priority is being a reporter."

"Fine," he says, without glancing away from Charlie.

I look down at the hole in the ground and then at the boy busily ripping up another branch.

"Hey, Charlie, let's go . . ." Austen puts his hand on his son's shoulder.

Charlie doesn't respond.

I recognize the vacant look in his eyes—these are the eyes I see in the mirror. When the one person you want is gone, it doesn't matter who else offers time and company. And other people, a father or a sister, who try to make it better, actually make it worse.

For me, it has been easier to tolerate my grief in private. And perhaps for Charlie, too. As I start to walk away, I can still hear Austen trying to engage him.

"How about lunch . . . we can go to the diner? You still like it there, don't you?"

"No."

"I know you're upset, but we have to eat. Your grandmother wouldn't want you to—"

"You do not know what she would or wouldn't want," the boy shouts out.

A moment later, Charlie is running past me, panting and crying again.

Austen sprints after him, but Charlie is fast and Austen gives up, stopping beside me.

"Damn it, no matter what I say, it's wrong. He just won't let me anywhere near him." For the moment, his frustration with his son is greater than his anger at me.

"Let me go. I can talk to him. I was like that when my mother died."

And then, before Austen can explain why he doesn't want me to, I take off in Charlie's direction.

I SPOT CHARLIE ABOUT THIRTY yards away, sitting on the deck of one of the sailboats. I stay where I am, just watching him. His head is down on his knees, his back heaving. After a few minutes his sobs abate. He lifts up his head and stares out at the water.

As I walk toward the dock, he doesn't seem aware of my approach. Rather than startle him, I say his name as quietly as I can. The wind picks up the two soft syllables, and he does not hear them.

"Charlie?" I repeat more loudly.

Now he does turn but says nothing.

"Do you mind if I sit with you a while?"

"Why?"

"Sometimes it's better to talk about the person you miss."

"Yeah, right . . . as if you mean that. I know you just want me to say yes so you can ask me questions about my grandmother."

"No, that's not why. I may be one of the few people around here who knows how you feel."

"You'd like me to think that . . . but it's a trick."

"That's not true."

His face—so much like Austen's—becomes contemptuous. "Whatever." He shrugs.

"Well, it's *not* true. Yes, I'm at Euphonia because your grandmother asked me to come here and write about her life. She invited me. I didn't just barge in. But that's not why I'm down here—I'm *here* to talk to you because I know how much it hurts to worry this much about someone you love."

I take his unresponsiveness as a positive sign. "Mind if I . . . There's a word for it, isn't there? A word that explains getting on a boat?"

"It's called coming aboard."

"Right. I don't know much about boats, but I like them." And with that I awkwardly step off the dock.

But the current is rocking both the dock and the boat, and it's difficult traversing the suddenly wide span between them. Jumping just in time, I manage to make it and avoid landing in the water.

Charlie eyes me as if my unfamiliarity with the sea and nautical terms are character flaws.

Sitting there, trying to figure out just what to say to him, I become aware of the warmth of the sun and the breeze. Wide sea and wider sky. Blues, grays, greens. No jarring colors, noises, or sights. The waves pitch the boat to and fro, and the constancy of motion becomes soothing. I can understand why of all the places he might go to find comfort, Charlie has come here.

In the silence—his and mine—the sounds of the gulls and water lapping against the side of the boat offer their own melody. It is not that different from the music we were listening to only a half hour ago.

Being at Euphonia even for just a few days has made me more

sensitive to sound: to the tone of someone's whispered voice, the tune of birdsong, even the sonority of the air. Loath to interrupt the peaceful sounds, I hold back.

And then thirty or forty feet out, a motorboat screams by—not only destroying the tranquility but also rocking our boat violently. Lurching forward with the sudden violence, I lose my balance and put my hands out to steady myself. In doing this, I touch the boy's arm and he flinches.

"Sorry," I say.

He doesn't respond.

The waves settle down. The boat stops rocking.

"When you are worried about someone you love—it seems as if everyone who can behave normally is being blasphemous, doesn't it?"

I continue. "For me it was all those everyday things that people do that were so hard to reconcile. Like your father saying you should go have lunch. I could never understand how people could still get hungry or how they could still tell jokes and laugh. When I lost my mom, I wanted everyone in the world to stop what they were doing and just sit still and mourn. The way I was mourning."

He nods his head. Not vehemently, but enough so I know I'm reaching him. But I also know he's still suspicious of me. And I don't blame him.

"Did you sail with her often?" I ask.

"Yeah."

"Did she teach you how to sail or did your dad?"

"Sophie did. She taught me everything. She's the best teacher. Has anyone talked to you about that? If you are going to write about her, that's what you should say."

"I'd like to write about that aspect of her life, but so far no one has talked to me much at all about anything. That's okay though. I haven't wanted to bug anyone or intrude."

He nods again.

"But from listening to the music before, it's easy to imagine how good a teacher she is."

"Do you know she's had over three hundred students?" He's enthused now: this is an aspect of his grandmother that he is proud of, and despite being suspicious of me, he wants to talk about her because talking about the one you love who is lost to you brings her back and makes her real again.

Even if only for a few minutes.

He continues. "And almost all of them have become well-known. And it's because of her. Because of what she does for them and how she pushes them and promotes them. She can work with someone for just a few weeks and know what their strengths are and what they should pursue. Colin James thought he wanted to just be a violinist, but Grandma told him he'd be a really good conductor. And he wound up being the youngest one the New York Philharmonic's ever had."

"That's amazing. Did she tell your dad he should be a cellist?"

"I don't know."

"How does she know what someone will be best at?"

"She just does. I don't know how. I never asked. But it's a good question. Maybe you can ask her when she—" He breaks off at the thought of Sophie returning or not returning.

"And what does she think you should do?" I ask quickly, getting Charlie to refocus.

"Well, for right now she says she wants me to master the piano. And then the violin."

"Right, your dad told me. That's what you are doing here this summer, isn't it, working on the piano?"

He nods his head.

"It's wonderful that you're spending the summer here with her and all the other talented students. Your dad also told me that you're the youngest student ever here."

"Yeah, I guess."

"It's not easy though, is it?"

"What?"

"Being professional all the time. Being with adults nonstop. I had to do it. My mom put me in a sort of spotlight from the time I was six. There were parts of it that were wonderful, but other parts were horrible."

"Like what?"

"I didn't get to do a lot of the things my friends were doing."

"But what other kids do is just a waste of time."

"You miss out on stuff."

"Sophie made sure I didn't. We don't just work. She's been teaching me all about sailing. That's fun. And when I was little, she played games with me all the time."

"What was your favorite?"

"Hide-and-seek," he says without having to think.

"Was she good at finding you?"

He shakes his head. "I was never the one who got to hide. She was. She loved to hide. I got to find her. But it was hard because there are so many places here to hide."

"It sounds like fun," I say. "But playing with other kids is fun, too. Hanging out with other kids, being like other kids, isn't always bad."

Charlie shakes his head vehemently. "If you are going to be a real artist, you have to devote yourself to your art and make sacrifices. That's all there is to it."

"Sophie said that?"

"Yes."

"You two are really close, aren't you?"

"Yes. She is depending on me to become a great musician."

"That's wonderful. But it must be hard, too. I mean, to always be there for her and know she expects so much of you."

I know before he says a word that I've gone too far. Suggesting Sophie has put too big a burden on him was a mistake.

"You tricked me," he snarls.

"What do you mean?"

"You were talking about how you felt just to get me to talk about her. It's just like they said: you are here to dig up dirt on her and make her look bad. I bet your mother isn't even dead. I bet you made that up. I bet it's your father who died. I bet you don't have a father, but your mother is just fine."

It's like a slap across the cheek, sharp and stinging, and I'm shocked at the intensity of Charlie's words and my reaction to them. The way I've lived my life—I don't have either of them anymore. My mother is dead and my father might as well be.

"No. My father's alive, Charlie."

"Then why didn't *he* make you feel better when your mother died?"

"Because . . ." I came down here to offer him some comfort, not to emotionally capsize again. "Because I did what you are doing. I shut him out. I thought I had to miss my mother by myself. That no one could understand how I felt about her." And now I begin to cry, softly, quietly.

This finally seems to touch Charlie.

"When did she die?"

"Almost four years ago."

"Four years? And you're still crying?"

"I still miss her. You know, she taught me a lot, too, like Sophie taught you. She taught me how to cook. She was a chef."

He doesn't say anything.

"And she was wonderful at it. Everything about her was wonderful."

"If that's true, about her teaching you, then what can you make? What can you cook that she could cook?"

"I don't know. A ton of things. What's your favorite food? Desserts? Breakfast? Dinner?"

"Desserts, I guess."

"Well, I can make chocolate soup. Did you ever hear of it? My mother made up the recipe."

"I've had it." He's looking at me intently now, watching for one expression that looks fake, listening for a word that rings a false note.

"One night I'll make it for you. I'll have to go into town and get the right ingredients. I haven't cooked anything in a while, so I may screw it up. But I'll try."

"What do you mean, you haven't cooked in a long time? If that's what she taught you, how could you stop?"

He is suspicious again. Or shocked that someone could cut the ties that bound them to the person who was gone.

"Well, I just stopped cooking when my mother died."

I've never said it out loud before—to hear the words gives them another tenor.

Charlie sits Buddha-like, watching me and waiting for more of an explanation.

"I just couldn't cook anymore after she died."

"Well, that's not what I would do. That's crazy. If Sophie died, I'd never stop playing piano. Not for days."

And then his face closes up. "It's just like she said. You really are manipulative. You just pretended to understand what I'm feeling. If you understood, you wouldn't be talking about this at all. What are you trying to do? Why do you want to hurt my grandmother?"

"She? Who said that? I don't. Hurting Sophie is the very last thing—"

"I heard Helena telling my father that the reason Sophie is even missing is because of you. That she was so worried you were coming up here that she wasn't thinking straight and that's why she took the boat out when a storm was coming. My father tried to argue with her, but he doesn't know. I saw her—I was here—and it's true. She was sadder than I've ever seen her. Sadder than she has ever been."

"Charlie, your grandmother invited me here. I have her E-mail in my computer if you want to see it. She's been writing me for weeks telling me all about her life and this place and you. If she hadn't wanted me here, I never would have come."

"Well, she's not here now. So just go away. Go away from Euphonia. Leave us alone."

THIRTY-THREE

GREENWICH'S POLICE STATION is a three-story art deco building on a wide street lined with quince and apple trees. Unlike any police station in either Paris or Manhattan, this one, like the rest of the town, is quiet and genteel. From my research I know there has only been one murder here in the last five years and that when one of the ten jewelry stores in the tiny shopping area was robbed, it was front-page news.

Just as the station house is so different from those in big cities, so is the detective sitting opposite me. He's neither haggard nor rushed. And while there are papers on his desk, it is not an unholy mess.

"There's not much I can tell the press, Miss Pagett."

"I understand that, Detective Lavettry. Can you at least define the case for me? Is the DeLyon case a murder investigation?"

While he thinks about this question, he presses his lips together and sucks them in—he is physically closemouthed.

"Maybe you can just confirm that it isn't a murder investigation. As far as I've been able to tell, Sophie was well loved and respected and very unselfish. Her children are already wealthy on their own. Plus, she's set up trust funds for all of them."

He's nodding, but I can't read his expression. I have no idea if, in fact, the police suspect anyone of wrongdoing.

"The most valuable thing she owns is Euphonia, but she's left it to the Juilliard School. Intact and endowed."

At the mention of the school, something in the detective relaxes; his face softens.

"It's an amazing piece of land, isn't it?" I say.

"Yes. Yes, it is. Every summer my wife and I go to the concerts there at the Point. For the last ten years. Nice nights."

"They're open-air concerts, aren't they?"

"On the beach. A full orchestra on the beach." He smiles. "My wife plays piano herself. She really appreciates what Miss DeLyon does up there."

"Everyone seems to feel the same way about her. I guess it can be that way with artists. When most of what they do is bring beauty to the world, it's easy to love them."

I pause, to allow him to respond. But he's smart. "You don't think I'm going to fall for that, do you? I should be annoyed that you're even trying."

Smiling, I apologize. "It's just that she seems such an unlikely target."

Lavettry leans forward. "Listen, Miss Pagett, it's not a big secret. We think it was an accident. And, no, so far we haven't come up with any motive for anything else. I can tell you we considered kidnapping, but there hasn't been any ransom request." He shakes his head. "And of course we thought all that waterfront property could be a motive. But like you said, that land has been left to the music school in New York."

He rubs his beard. "If it hadn't been, the land would be motive enough. Around here, just one acre on the water—even without a house on it—can go for a million plus. There's over one hundred fifty acres out there on that point."

MY NEXT STOP IS ONE of the town's two bookstores, Diane's Books, around the corner from the movie theater. Inside, books are piled high on every conceivable surface, inviting you to linger a long time and make discoveries on your own.

I head for the nonfiction area in the back room and search through the titles on mental illness: specifically manic depression and its treatment. Many of the books on Sophie's shelf are here, as well as some others.

No one bothers me, and after a half hour of skimming several volumes, I decide to buy the one that explains the most about various drug treatments and their side effects.

"Will that be it?" the tall white-haired woman at the register asks.

"Yes."

While I wait for my credit card to go through, I spy a small rack of postcards. Among the pretty pictures of the town and the shore are several postcards of Euphonia. Pulling out one of each, I hand them to the woman.

"If the charge has already gone through, I can pay for these in cash."

She takes the cards and looks down at them. "It's so sad."

"About Sophie DeLyon? Yes. Did you know her?"

"Of course. She bought all her books here. She's such an avid reader."

"Mysteries, right?"

"Mysteries, yes. She'd show up with her tote bag and just say, 'Diane—fill 'er up.' I have special clients like Sophie, and when a book comes in that I think they'll like, I put one aside for them." She glances over to a corner behind the register.

"Do you have books waiting for her now?"

"Yes. I've been thinking I shouldn't keep putting more books there—just more for me to reshelve later. But there's still a chance, they say."

"Can I see them?"

Diane thinks about this. "I suppose so. They're all mysteries. Miss DeLyon especially loved the ones with psychiatrists in them."

"Did she buy a lot of psychology books, too?"

"No. Just fiction."

Bending down, I inspect the shelf.

FIFTEEN MINUTES LATER, I'M AT the top of the avenue on the cross street at another bookstore. Just Books is smaller than Diane's, but there is the same sense of welcome and invitation. Taking off my sunglasses, I put them on top of my head.

This store is long and narrow, and as I make my way toward the back, I glance at the books on either side of the aisle.

A man sitting at a desk, surrounded by books and working on a computer, looks up. "May I help you?"

"Yes, I was wondering if you have any books on manic depression."

He gets up and walks me to a shelf near the front of the store. "Is there anything special you're looking for? I can always order it if I don't have it."

"Yes. I'm staying at Euphonia and there are quite a few books on the subject in the library there. I found Kay Redfield Jamison's book *An Unquiet Mind* really interesting and wanted to see if you had anything else she'd written."

"We do." He pulls another Jamison title off the shelf, one I haven't seen in Sophie's library.

"Great. I'll take that."

I follow him to the desk, where he takes my card.

"It's quite a library at Euphonia. I thought this book was there, though. I sold it to Miss DeLyon myself when it came out."

"Oh. Maybe it's been misshelved. I didn't know she shopped here," I say. More than the missing volume has me confused: Diane said Sophie bought all her books there.

"Yes. She was a faithful customer."

"Mysteries, right?"

He looks momentarily confused. "Mysteries? No. Only nonfiction. Music. Art. Psychology."

"Mental illness?"

The man is about to hand me the receipt to sign but pauses. He scrutinizes me, suddenly cautious. My question was too abrupt, too interrogatory.

"I don't feel comfortable discussing my clients' book purchases, Miss . . ." He looks down at the card. "Miss Pagett."

One store where she bought only fiction. The other store where she bought only facts.

Leaving Just Books, I walk down the avenue to the real estate office where I saw Daphne two days ago. There's a thrill to chasing a story, and it's easier to feel it here—away from the sad eyes and haunting music back at the school.

Inside the entrance is a large map of the town, which I inspect while the man I want to talk to—the one who had been talking to Daphne—is on the phone.

After he hangs up I introduce myself as Jane Chatterley—a name I sometimes use—and tell him I'm the personal assistant of a couple who are looking for a waterfront home and that I'm doing the preliminary legwork.

"It's not really a question of money," I say. "Not if it's the right piece of land."

He describes three estates and I take notes.

"Can you show them to me on the map?"

He points them out.

"And what's this area? It looks like it has more beachfront—and that's one of the things my boss really wants."

"Standish Point." He nods and purses his lips together. "Well, that is all privately held land. It belongs to the conductor Sophie DeLyon. There is a school there now."

"Sophie . . . DeLyon? The woman who is missing?"

"Yes. It's really a tragedy. I know her family, lovely people."

"Does that mean that it will be for sale?—gee—I'm sorry. I guess that's gruesome of me to ask."

"No, totally understandable. After all, you don't know her. It's really too early to talk about it—but I have heard there is a possibility it will be going on the market. All very premature. I really wouldn't want anyone to know."

It takes all my effort to hide my surprise. "The last thing we'd do is tell anyone and risk losing a chance at it."

Going into the real estate office wasn't a long shot, but walking into the local drugstore is. Taking off my sunglasses again, I head toward the prescription counter. It's busy, which is good—too busy for the pharmacist to remember many faces.

"I want to refill a prescription for my mother," I offer when my turn comes. "She told me it is on file."

"Name?" the pharmacist asks.

"DeLyon." I wonder if everyone in this town knows who Sophie is and if this woman will know I am not Sophie's daughter.

But without hesitating she types the name into her computer. And then looks up. "I have quite a number of her prescriptions. What does she need?"

"Lithium."

My heart is beating hard. I know enough from my reading to know that the medications have to be changed and altered all the time. That patients' levels and moods require new cocktails. And that when one stops working, the patient is in danger—can go on manic highs or crash into deep depressions. Too many of which wind up in suicide.

"I'm sorry, there's no prescription for lithium."

"No? Wait, let me check what I wrote down." I make a show of opening my notebook. "I'm sorry, it's Elavil."

The druggist looks down at the computer and back at me.

"I'm sorry. There is no prescription for Elavil either. Just painkillers, several antibiotics, and cough medicine on file with us."

No, of course not. One bookstore where she buys mysteries. Another where she slips in books on mental illness mixed with purchases of music and art volumes. If Sophie DeLyon takes antidepressants and it is a secret—if it is worth keeping hidden—then the prescriptions would never be in her own name where a pharmacist could stumble upon them looking up *Dellinger* or *Dellon*.

THIRTY-FOUR

I F I W E R E in Paris I would be sitting at Les
Deux Magots with Fiona having coffee and croissants and gossiping about other journalists. But
here, I'm isolated. And having family so close only reminds me of
the problems I have with them.

I picture the street I live on and smell the bakery's goods. I see
the poodle sleeping in the doorway. The sky is cerulean blue, and
CoCo is standing in front of her flower shop arranging summer
blooms in aluminum containers that glint in the sun. I stop to buy
fresh hyacinths. And one dark red rose. CoCo has forgotten to cut
the thorns, and one pricks my finger and draws a drop of blood.

Shaking myself out of the reverie, I look down to see I am holding my pen and gripping it so tightly my fingernails have made in-
dentations in the flesh of my palm. I touch one of the half-moons.
And then I put the pen down on the desk next to my computer and
beside the books I bought in town. Without overthinking it, I pick
up the phone and dial.

"Hello," he answers on the second ring.

"Hi."

"Hi, sweetheart," my father says after hearing my voice.

I feel better and worse all at once. A knot of pleasure coming
undone in my chest at hearing his voice, so familiar and comfort-

ing, and a spike of annoyance, because I suddenly see my mother's sad eyes. Damn, why can't I talk to him without thinking about her?

"How is it going?" he asks.

"Not good. Sophie's still missing. I'm getting all kinds of mixed signals. She was—is—a very complicated woman."

"We all are. Each of us is a different person with everyone we know."

"You always have been able to do that. Maddy too. You just get right to the basics of a thing," I say.

"It comes from reading too many recipes. The same simple in-gredients. Eggs, flour, sugar, butter. Think of the thousands of desserts you can create, but they all start with those four ingredients, and then just by adding some vanilla or almonds or extra egg whites, you have a meringue or a butter cookie or brownie."

"I never thought about it that way."

"And with bread, even if you use the exact same ingredients, the water alone—French water versus water from Maine—the loaf is just that little bit unique."

I smile, realize he can't see me, and say, "I like that way of de-scribing it."

"Your mother used to be fascinated with the subtle differences in chocolate. No matter where we were in Europe, she would buy what was made locally. She got so good at detecting subtleties I could cut a piece off any bar and she always knew where it had come from and who had made it."

Her smells—Shalimar and chocolate. More than any other food, it was the rich, pungent, dark-cocoa scent that permeated the kitchen and her clothes.

"Well . . ." I don't know what to say.

"I don't want to lose you too, Justine."

"You only lost her because you let her go."

"You can't be so sure about what happened between us. It was a marriage, Justine. There were *two* people who didn't make it work."

"But I know what she felt."

He sighs and hesitates. I hear him about to say something and then stop himself. And then begin again. Only to change his mind.

"What?" I ask.

"I don't like the phone—"

"Well, then, I'll let you go," I interrupt.

"I didn't say I didn't want to talk to you. I just said I don't like the phone. We need to talk. To keep talking. Will you meet me tomorrow if I drive up?"

"But what about the restaurant?"

"Maddy can handle it."

"Are you doing this for her?"

"That question doesn't make any sense. Everything I do is for both of you. You are being too hard on her. Your sister had a serious drinking problem and a bad drug problem in LA. For the last three years she's worked very hard to stay straight. You breezing in and treating her as if she is the enemy isn't easy on her."

"So this is about Maddy needing me to be overly sensitive so she doesn't start drinking again."

"I think if you could hear your own voice, you'd be upset. I know your mother would be."

"Oh, please, don't presume to tell me about what Mom would or wouldn't do or think."

"I don't have any right to do that?"

"You don't. You didn't understand her. You didn't make her happy. And Maddy didn't either."

Out the window I see Charlie walking alone again on the beach with Sophie's dog trotting beside him. He looks so much like a younger version of his father. But Charlie's by himself out there. Something in me pulls apart and aches.

"Maddy and I—you and I—your mother and you—your mother and Maddy—you keep linking us or separating us from each other. You're making alliances, assuming there were enemies. There weren't."

I want to argue and explain that there were and there still are. The righteous anger pumps my blood faster, but he doesn't give me a chance.

"What time should I pick you up?"

On the beach, Charlie sits down and puts both arms around his own knees. Hugging himself.

And I feel that awful pull again—to go to him, to ask if there is something I can do, to help him.

"How about noon?" I answer.

THIRTY-FIVE

I STAY IN MY room through dinner and read over the books on manic depression. At ten o'clock I go downstairs to find something to eat.

I'm in the kitchen, cutting a granny apple into quarters, when Helena comes in, weary and worn.

"Oh, you surprised me," she says. "I was going to make some tea. Would you like some?"

"Yes, thanks."

She notices the apple. "You weren't at dinner, were you? It was a mess. There are too many people here, and there's not enough room. I need more help in the kitchen—the cook wasn't prepared for this kind of crowd."

As the days have passed, the circles under Helena's eyes have deepened and darkened and her skin has grown paler. She is still carefully dressed, but her fingernail polish is chipped.

"No, I was reading . . . trying to do some work."

"It is too quiet here. Everyone is losing hope. Sitting around staring at their music. Not playing. Drinking too much. Too much coffee all day and too much wine at night. Including me."

"Including you? You're losing hope?"

Helena is confused. "No. Sophie will be home . . . maybe

tonight. Maybe tomorrow. I know that. I just meant I've been drinking too much coffee and too much wine. I'm still hopeful."

"You and Charlie."

Holding the bag of loose leaves in one hand, Helena uses a
measuring spoon to put tea in a pot. "When you meet her . . . when
you get to know her, you will understand why we know she can't be
gone. Someone as important as Sophie . . . no, she will be back.
Maybe tonight."

"I wanted to ask you about her illness."

"What illness?" Helena turns around and faces me.

"Her manic depression."

Helena shakes her head back and forth. "No. Not Sophie."

"What I don't understand is why everyone is so determined to
keep it a secret."

Helena takes china cups and saucers out of the cabinet. "There
isn't a secret. She wasn't depressed, just tired. She'd made an appointment to see the doctor because she thought she needed some
vitamins, but she canceled it in the morning and said a long sail
would do her more good. She didn't want to go into Manhattan.
She'd been in Europe too long and missed the water."

Helena puts the cups back in the cabinet. And now withdraws
two mugs. Then she puts the mugs back and takes out the cups
again.

"I'm assuming, every few years she's had to have her medication
adjusted. And that it was time she needed another adjustment but
didn't get it."

The kettle whistles. It is a harsh sound, off-key and unsophisti-
cated compared to sounds one usually hears in this house.

An insistent stream of steam escapes into the air, and when
Helena pours the water into the teapot, some splashes out. "Damn
it," she says, shaking her hand where the water's burned her flesh.

"I found books on her bookshelf with notations in the margins.
And it tracks with things people have said. Brian Beckwith. Austen.
Even Charlie. But no one will admit it. What did you do—hide all
the drugs that were in her medicine cabinet sometime after she

went missing? Why? Was she depressed again? Do you feel it's your fault that she didn't get to the doctor?"

"Sophie wasn't depressed. She wasn't manic. Sophie wasn't the one with the disease. She's fine. And she certainly didn't kill herself."

"How do you know?"

Helena looks up. Her left hand is clamped over the burn spot on her right. Clutching her hand at an awkward angle, she nurses the burn, and the light glints off a thin band of hammered gold on Helena's right ring finger. In the middle is a round signet. Looking more closely I can make out an etched figure—Pan with his flute—like the fountain outside the entrance to Euphonia.

"Because I know," she says.

THIRTY-SIX

I N MY HALF-AWAKE state, with no sense of
time, I hear the surf and try to let the waves lull
me back to sleep.

Floating on the sound, I drift off.

I'm standing in a room that is all windows looking out on a
rough sea. All the danger is outside. Which is where I want to go,
because I have the sense that if I go and swim in that water, it will
calm down, that somehow I have the ability to soothe the sea. But
something is stopping me.

Then I realize I am naked and wonder if this is why I can't go
outside. But I have always gone out naked before. What is different
about this time?

The rules, I think. Yes, that is what's different. This time there
are rules.

But you made them, I say to myself, you can break them.

And then I am aware that while I understood what I just said—
understood it as words—it was music. I was not speaking syllables
and vowels but notes and chords.

Astonished by this I say more words—*sky* and *mother*—each
one is another musical phrase.

There is some kind of rightness about this transformation. It
should scare me, that I cannot speak anymore—but it doesn't.

Why doesn't it?

This wanting becomes physical.

And then behind me, a door opens.

It is cold, there is a draft on my skin.

I'm scared. The danger from the outside has come in. I want to cover myself with a blanket. If I don't I might die. Disappear. Crumble. This makes no sense, but I feel it anyway.

Now his fingers are on my naked back and the cold is gone and my blood starts to warm me. Smelling him, I relax. There is danger, yes, there are eyes out there in the rough curl of the waves and they are looking at me, but it doesn't matter anymore. Because he is here now.

I want to drop to my knees and take him in my mouth. So badly do I want to do this that my mouth opens of its own accord. I want to bury my face between his legs and feel him throb and shudder because of what I can do to him. I want to smell the woods and the earth and taste that first sweet, salty drop of him.

But I don't move. He has told me—even though I have not heard him say a word—he has told me not to touch him.

"Not yet, Justine, not yet. First this . . ."

I hear it inside of me but not with my ears. In my blood, my lungs, in my stomach. And so I ignore the wetness between my own legs and the urgency to touch him and feel him and what that will do to me. I stand still and let the sensations wash over me the way the waves are washing over the sand. Retreating and returning.

Just looking at him and knowing he wants me that much might make me come, but this is not allowed either.

He moves his hands. One lifts the bow—which he must have had all along—and the other goes to my back. And where my spine is, Austen finds the cello strings. With a nod of his head he places the bow and with his other hand he manipulates the strings. Music pours out of me and fills the room. It soars up and out through the windows and soothes the sea.

He plays to calm the waters. And to inflame me.

The bow sails across my back, his fingers move up and down, I feel the calluses and the softness and the horsehair bow at the same time as I feel the music coming out of me. In the window, hovering, floating in the darkness is the specter of Sophie conducting this song with her baton.

No—Austen says to Sophie without using words—this is not your orchestra. She disappears and now there is nothing outside but the dark night and the darker water, which is still calm. Everything is calm now except for the sounds: building and intensifying. The notes lift up and up and crash down, swirl even lower and encircle us as they grow louder and then louder and while he is still facing me and still playing me, Austen is also inside of me. I arch and the music spills out of me. I moan but the sound is of one long note straining to hold, hold, hold . . . until it passes from an active sound to the slow dissolution of sound and as it dissipates in the air Austen lets the bow drop but holds on to me as he shudders.

And I wake up.

The intensity of my orgasm has left me out of breath. My heart races and my skin is damp. My hair is pasted to the back of my neck. I have never dreamt love with a man like this.

A half hour later, still awake, restless and unable to fall asleep again, I get out of bed, pull back the heavy drapes, and look at the night—black sea, black sky, and the soft rain.

Wrapping my arms around my chest I press my forehead up to the glass and shut my eyes. The long dark hair, the proud features, the sadness in his eyes. I want—more than anything right now, more than I want to be in his bed in his arms—to talk to him and find out what has made him so unhappy and why he really has stopped writing his music. These are not the thoughts of a heartless bitch. But am I thinking like this because he is a challenge? Or because his playing moves me and his dedication inspires me?

No. It is because he is the one man I should be staying away from.

Turning from the window, I pick up yet another book on manic depression and start to read.

After a few pages I become aware of a scent emanating from the pages and inhale. It is flowery, but not in a sweet way. These are night-blooming bloodred flowers with thorns and oversize velvet petals that tempt and trap the insects that come too close.

Putting on my robe, I pad barefoot out of my room and down the hall to Sophie's suite.

I mean to find the scent, spill a few drops on a handkerchief or scarf of Sophie's, and then to bring it to the cottage in the morning and give it to Charlie.

The lights are on, the bed is turned down, and there are fresh lilacs in a silver vase above the fireplace, as if Sophie were expected to come to bed any minute.

I'm invading her sanctuary and I know I should leave, but now that I've stepped inside I'm curious. There are more clues to Sophie here: secrets I am desperate to discover.

Sitting on the dresser, nestled in between dozens of photographs in silver and enamel frames, are several perfume bottles. Sniffing each, I find the one that matches the scent in the book. It is spicy and floral and dark.

But I need something to put the perfume on, so I open the first drawer in the dresser. I'm only looking for a handkerchief or a scarf—but the innocent effort mutates into a real search.

Carefully, I lift up silk underwear, feeling the fine fabric against my skin. I push tortoiseshell barrettes and suede headbands apart. Drawer after drawer is filled with accessories. Socks. Hairbrushes. Slips. Bras. Hosiery. Underpants.

I've never gone through anyone's personal things before, never searched there for anyone's secrets: not those of any man I've gone out with, not those of my parents or my sister. I've never intruded on anyone's physical privacy.

Until now it has always been enough to invade the environs of their minds, but I don't have access to Sophie's thoughts and recollections—only to the objects of her life.

But there is nothing.

No notes, no empty leather jewel boxes, no old leather wallets filled with receipts. There is only information about sizes and color

preferences: peach underwear, reddish brown suede hair accessories, and scarves in dark browns and oranges. But doesn't everyone have secrets in their rooms to the parts of their lives other
people cannot even guess at?

Walking away from the dresser, I go to the closet and open the
door.

Pushing apart the hangers of russet- and cream- and brown- and
camel-colored skirts and blouses and dresses and capes and caftans,
I look for some one thing that does not belong. On the floor I move
the shoes to see if anything else is shelved there. No half-empty
shoe boxes with hidden letters or diaries or journals. None of her
children's baby clothes.

But when I turn around, I'm caught by surprise.

There on a shelf are six styrofoam wig stands, all wearing wigs.
Sophie's bronze-colored hair framing faceless dummies.

Outside the wind picks up, and branches hit the windows, tapping their fingers as if they, too, want to come inside and aid me in
the search.

OLLIE, OLLIE, OUT AND FREE.

I'm ten, and my mother and I are playing hide-and-seek in the
Metropolitan Museum of Art's Egyptian wing. My mother has been
hiding, and I've been looking for her for over a half hour. Finally by
getting down on the ground and searching for my mother's feet, I spy
her hiding behind a wide-standing sarcophagus of an Egyptian queen.

After I find her, we go to the dining room. While my mother
sips an espresso, I eat a dish of vanilla ice cream with chocolate
sauce served in a silver dish. On the wall are large painted mirrors
rescued from the art deco cruise ship the *Normandy*. And there, reflected in the glass, are images of the young beautiful mother and
her daughter laughing together.

THERE ARE NO ANSWERS IN Sophie's bedroom
or bathroom. All that is left to do is what I came here for—soak one
of Sophie's scarves with her perfume and bring it to Charlie.

The green crystal flacon is next to a photograph of Sophie with Stephen and Daphne as children. Next to that is one of Charlie with Austen on the deck of a sailboat. Then another of Sophie with her husband and children at Christmas. On the other side is a shot of Sophie with Helena, arms around each other, sitting at an outdoor café in what looks like the south of France. Then one of Helena alone, eyes shining, years younger, wearing a pale blue evening dress at a chic restaurant. The table is set for two. A bottle of champagne is in a silver bucket by her elbow. She is wearing a necklace of faceted stones the same color as her eyes.

In a red enamel frame, Stephen stands with Zoë at their wedding. It's a close-up, and Zoë is laughing and feeding Stephen a forkful of wedding cake.

Her hair is blonder—and longer—and falling over her eyes, her dress is cut low, and the string of pearls around her neck gleams.

I stare at Zoë's blonde hair.

"What are you doing in here?"

Zoë is standing in the door. Her eyes are rimmed red. The pearls, ever present, are around her neck even though she is in her robe and it's three o'clock in the morning.

There is no need for me to look back at the photograph of her when she was younger, or at the film clip in my computer again. Why didn't I realize it before?

I hold up the scarf and explain what I wanted to do for Charlie.

"That's kind," she says, and holds out her hand. I hand her the scarf and she holds it up to her face and buries her face in it.

"I can't stand to be in that room Helena gave me at the opposite end of the house. It's as if she's trying to keep me as far away from Sophie as she can."

"You miss her so much, don't you? I'm so sorry."

Zoë sits on the bed, taking one of the pillows and hugging it to her chest as if it might give her some ballast.

"There were things Sophie was planning to tell you about . . . that you should know," Zoë says. "Some of them are going to be harder to tell you than others. But I really think it's what Sophie would want."

"You don't have to—"

"I want to talk about her. She's more real when I do."

I nod. I know.

"I started Juilliard when I was just sixteen. My mother wanted it. No, that's not fair. I wanted it too. I lived for the piano. For music. I wanted to be there. Sophie heard my audition and helped me get a scholarship. She took me under her wing, and I was one of her star pupils."

Zoë fidgets while she talks. Pulling off and putting back on the ring on her right hand.

"I went on tour right out of school, but I just wasn't . . . I didn't have something that I needed. After the nervous breakdown, Sophie took over and was like my mother. Well, not like my mother—who was just disgusted that after all that work I couldn't perform. But the way you want a mother to be. There was no judgment. No anger that all the years she'd helped me were for nothing. She didn't blame me."

She puts the ring back on and turns it around and around.

"Sophie moved me here to live with her. Took me to wonderful doctors. She gave me myself back. Encouraged me to see men. And when Stephen met me and became interested in me, Sophie wanted it to happen. She wanted me to have all the things she had—children, a home. She was so unselfish. And it was so wonderful—to have her be my family." She breaks off, and I wait.

Zoë involuntarily glances at the pictures on Sophie's dresser, but she doesn't say anything.

Scanning the photographs, I try to read the faces as if they were short stories. Who are these other people? How many of them are friends? How many are more than that? What information is hidden in the smiles and gestures?

It's time for me to take a chance. I need someone to open up to me about this enigmatic woman.

"You and Sophie were once lovers, weren't you?"

She doesn't seem surprised or annoyed that I've guessed, but seems incredibly relieved. "We weren't together as lovers till I was twenty-two. Two years after I graduated. After the breakdown. When I was living here. But she really did want me to marry Stephen. It was hard at first to give up wanting to be with her that other way . . . until she made me understand that this way we'd always be together as family. And it was better because I knew she needed other lovers. The reality of it was that she always moved on. And she didn't want to hurt me that way."

"So others came after you?"

She nods.

"Zoë, would you be upset if anyone found out?"

"About Sophie and me being lovers?"

"Yes. Who wouldn't want that information to get out?"

"I don't know."

"Stephen?"

"No." Zoë smiles sadly. "Stephen and Daphne know."

"Does Stephen care?"

"You have to understand. Sophie is larger than life. Not just to her students but to her family too. I think—I don't know—I love Stephen, but I think he and Daphne enjoy what's different about Sophie. In an odd way, it makes her more human. They need her foibles. Her eccentricities. They almost collect them. I've heard them talking about how forgetful she's become, or how much she depends on Helena, almost as if her problems are evidence of something they need to prove."

She turns the ring around and the light spins off its surface of battered gold. Leaning forward, I examine it and find the small insignia of the faun.

"Your ring . . . is it the same one Helena wears?"

She nods. "A few of us have one. Like a sisterhood." She smiles ruefully, looks down at her ring and touches it gently—as if she is connecting to Sophie. "And no, not everyone who has one is one of

Sophie's lovers. You were going to ask me that, weren't you? But Daphne has one too. And others who I know weren't in Sophie's other life."

Zoë presses the ring to her lips. Her eyes are haunted. "I just can't believe that's she gone. What will we do without her?"

PART III

Failing to fetch me at first keep encouraged,
Missing me one place, search another,
I stop somewhere waiting for you.

—WALT WHITMAN, "SONG OF MYSELF"

THIRTY-SEVEN

USING AN INSTANT Messenger program, I'm writing in real time with Fiona, filling her in and getting her advice.

FionaDavis: Why don't you just call me?
JustP#1: Someone might overhear.
FionaDavis: You are joking? Is it that bad?

I explain what's happened and what I've found out in the last twenty-four hours. All the disparate and confusing parts of it. The threats. The duplicity with the bookstores. Daphne and the real estate issue. The X-rated film clip sent by—whom? Not the same person who sent the E-mail threats or planted the voodoo doll in my room; that person wants me to find out less, not reveal more. I tell her about Zoë's sexual revelations. The subtle references all around—but especially from Daphne about Sophie's mental health.

FionaDavis: All right, then work from this premise: two different camps. Those who are threatening you on one side. Those who are feeding you information on the other. What do they each have to gain or to lose? What's at stake? What impression have they given you of Sophie?

My fingers pause over the keyboard. I look out at the sea. What impression have they given me?

JustP#1: Yes, right. Thinking of them as two sides might make some sense of it. If I start with the threats—they're clear. Someone or a group of people don't want me to tell this story because they think I will find something that will threaten Sophie's legendary status.

FionaDavis: Okay. But Sophie hasn't done anything criminal, has she? I mean what have you found out? That she's probably a manic-depressive and is bisexual. Hardly destructive information.

JustP#1: No. But that's all I have. There must be something else I don't know yet.

FionaDavis: Okay, let's look at the other side. Someone is also sending you information. Someone who wants her to be brought down a notch?

JustP#1: But who? Why?

I think of how Sophie betrayed Austen and hurt his career. Was it really because she thought it best for him? Or because she was jealous? And if she did it to him—are there others she treated similarly? I start to type out Austen's name—about to tell Fiona—and then I erase the letters. Her next message comes through.

FionaDavis: You've met all of them by now—who acts threatened by you other than Charlie? And who doesn't seem to mind you being there?

JustP#1: Okay—other than Charlie, no one in the family is upset that I'm here. If anything, Daphne has been the most forthcoming—along with her brother—about Sophie, practically coming right out and telling me she's a little crazy.

FionaDavis: Crazy like most celebs are crazy?

JustP#1: No. Crazy, as in disturbed or maybe manic-depressive.

FionaDavis: And what would her children gain by having you think that?

The tide is low and the expanse of beach stretches for a mile. It amazes me how beautiful it is here.

FionaDavis: Justine?

JustP#1: How does this sound? Daphne and Stephen want the story to come out about Sophie's manic depression and her bisexuality so that she will be exposed.

FionaDavis: Right . . . but . . . why?

JustP#1: Because if I paint a portrait of a woman who is mentally ill, who seduces her past students, who goes against the grain, then maybe Stephen—who is a lawyer— can nullify her will? Fiona, this place is worth hundreds of millions of dollars and it's left to Juilliard. Maybe Sophie's children have figured out a way to keep it in the family.

FionaDavis: And where does the boat accident come in? Do you still think it's an accident?

JustP#1: Yes. I think they're capable of stealing her money but not killing her.

FionaDavis: If you're right about this, you can't say anything to anyone. Not even Austen. Just pack up and get out of there.

JustP#1: I can't walk away now.

FionaDavis: Won't. You can, but you won't. You are in danger. The story is not worth that much.

I spend the next hour on the Net, researching real estate sites that include Greenwich properties.

If a developer were to break Euphonia down into five-acre lots, there could be as many as thirty homes on the island. Each one large enough to command at least five million dollars.

Next I check a legal site to see what kind of effort it would take and what kind of evidence one would need—a son would need— to have his mother declared mentally incompetent.

And then I write Fiona back.

JustP#1: You still there, Fi?

FionaDavis: Yes.

JustP#1: Let's say her kids are doing this, why now?

FionaDavis: What might have kept them from action before now? Maybe they were waiting for someone like you to show up. From what you've said, they're very much the children of a world-famous conductor and composer who've lived off her fame their whole lives. As much as they might want to pull her down, they don't want to lose their own status in the process. They want the millions Euphonia would be worth on the open mar- ket but not if it means they will become social outcasts.

JustP#1: Of course. They couldn't be the ones to an- nounce to the world that their mother is crazy. They need a disinterested third party to do that.

FionaDavis: They need you.

JustP#1: And if Sophie had any idea that they were planning this, it would be enough to send her into a deep depression. Except, Fiona, why didn't she just hire a lawyer? Tell someone? Go to the press?

FionaDavis: Justine?

JustP#1: Yeah?

FionaDavis: You are the press. Maybe she expected you to expose them. And maybe they expect you to ex- pose her.

JustP#1: Then they are both playing me.

I'm surprised that my reaction isn't one of elation at a discovery but rather a wave of sadness. I can accept that Stephen and Daphne are trying to use me. But not that Sophie is. Or was.

THIRTY-EIGHT

HERE ARE A dozen people having breakfast. Students at one end of the table and Charlie and Austen at the other. I wanted to arrive before all of them, but I was out walking on the beach again . . . caught up in following the footsteps and the now familiar shells past the cliff and toward the caves. Again today, the tide was too high for me to do any more exploring. And then on the way in, I ran into Zoë, who was going back to New York.

"I'd rather stay here, but Stephen really does need me back home. At least Helena will have one less thing to worry about," she said.

"Have you given up thinking Sophie might come back?"

Her eyes were bright with unshed tears. "It seems impossible that she could really be gone."

But she hadn't really answered my question.

Helena comes out of the kitchen with a fresh pot of coffee. She looks even more haggard than the day before and more scattered. Her eyes roam — checking to see who is eating, checking the sideboard to be sure there's enough food. It's probably not necessary for her to be worrying about this. There is a cook and she has help. But preoccupation is an antidote to panic.

Some of the students start complaining to her that two classes

Sophie had on the syllabus are missing and another two required classes are scheduled at the same time. They've barely finished explaining the problem when the cook comes out of the kitchen to report to Helena that the menu for the next two days is missing and she needs it before she goes to the market.

Helena looks from the cook to the students, down at her silverware, over at Charlie, and then at the dog lying by his feet on the floor—as if none of it is familiar to her at all, as if she doesn't know what she is supposed to do. Her eyes fill with tears, and pushing her chair back, scraping its legs on the floor, she just walks away. On her way out, blinded by the tears, she bumps into the edge of the table. It shakes. Someone's juice glass falls and cracks on a plate. Helena breaks into a run, leaving the dining room but none of her problems behind.

Pouring a glass of orange juice, I drink it standing right there by the sideboard. And after the first glass I pour another. I've wanted this juice for hours, and it tastes fresher and colder than it did in my imagination. Tart and sweet, fresh-squeezed, the way my mother made it. The way she and I liked it, but not the way my father or my sister preferred. For them, she would strain it, and their juice looked so much thinner in their tumblers. As if they were drinking an entirely different beverage.

When breakfast was done, my mother and I would scoop up the pulp that was left over in the strainer, each spooning up the soft fruit until the wire mesh was scraped clean. And then we'd lick the spoons clean.

It's just one more memory, but the emotion it evokes makes me want to weep.

Divestiture.

Deprivation.

Dispossession.

None of the words makes the feeling any less intense.

I'm hungry for the creamy scrambled eggs my mother made and an English muffin, lightly buttered before it's toasted—so it's a little bit soft and salty.

I settle for dry rye toast and overcooked eggs and sit down on the other side of the table from Charlie and Austen. I don't look at either of them while I eat, but I listen to what they are saying, trying to block out the other conversations going on around me.

"It doesn't matter how many classes your grandmother said you could take. She's not here." Austen's voice is patient and calm. "I am. And four hours a day is enough."

"It's not enough. You don't know how I feel."

"No. That's true. But I do know what's too much for you and what you can handle."

"You think you do, but Grandma said no one really understands artists. She said people think we're crazy to care so much about our music and that they think we are insane to want to play six or seven hours a day. But that's what I want to do. It's what I need to do."

I drink more juice.

"I don't think you are crazy, Charlie. Just trying to do too much. And I don't think your grandmother is crazy either."

Is this another veiled allusion to Sophie's illness? Does this mean that Austen knows? Well, if Daphne and Stephen know, Austen must know. Does Charlie know?

I run my tongue on the lip of the glass. It's crystal, too fine for juice. My mother used thick, heavy and inexpensive glasses. They kept it cold. They felt like something in your hand. Their weight matched the intensity of the juice.

My mother collected glasses, and we played a game that involved pouring different kinds of liquids into various glasses and deciding which made which beverage taste the best.

Which size was best for tomato juice?

For water?

For Coca-Cola?

Milk in crystal was perfect if you were having it with dessert. But if you were dipping Chocolate Bricks (Pauline's version of chocolate chip cookies), wide-mouthed jelly jars were best.

"Why do you want me to be miserable?" Charlie asks. "All I have is the music. Now that she's gone. That's all I have."

"I don't want you to be miserable." Austen looks at his son. "And that's not all you have: you have me. And your mother."

I can't help but respond to the frustration and sadness in Austen's voice and, for just a few seconds, let my eyes rest on him. It's a relief to look at his face. He doesn't notice; he's focused on his son.

"Mom doesn't even act like she misses her."

"But I do, Charlie," he says.

"But you never even saw her anymore."

"That's between your grandmother and me."

Charlie's right hand is playing across the stem of his fork as if it is a keyboard.

"No. Nothing is *just* between you and Grandma. Just like nothing is just between Mom and Grandma. We are all the same family. Even if we weren't related by blood, we'd be related by music. We have that. All of us. You have it for the cello. And Grandma and I have it for the piano and the violin. And that's important. You know it is. Why are you trying to take that away from me, too?"

"You are too smart for your own good," Austen says.

"You are too smart for your own good. How dare you get yourself a diaphragm? You are only sixteen years old." My mother is standing in my bedroom and she is shaking.

"What's so awful? I went to a doctor and got a diaphragm. Would it have been better if I was stupid and got pregnant?"

"But you are sixteen."

"And?"

"You don't even love Ronnie. He's just a guy you are seeing. That's what you told me. That's what you've been saying for the last five weeks."

"Right, but that doesn't mean I can't want to sleep with him. Besides, what's so great about loving someone?"

"What do you mean?" my mother asks.

"Love screws up things. Look at how you are with Dad—you

are way too in love with him, and he doesn't love you back the way you want."

In slow motion my mother's hand comes toward me. I don't step back or duck to get out of the way. In my memory I hear the sound of flesh slapping flesh before I feel the sting, but I will never be sure because my mother had never hit me before. Would never hit me again.

Even though she is not the one who has been hit and whose face smarts, my mother starts to cry.

"I don't want you to be afraid of loving someone."

It's not me who needs comforting, but my mother, and I put my arms around her.

"Don't. Mom, please. Be happy for me that I'm not going to ever get hurt. I'm the one in control. I won't let anyone matter to me so much that they can hurt me."

I remember the expression of despair that came over her face. At the time, I didn't understand her reaction. But watching Austen with his son, I finally grasp some of what she must have been feeling that day. And seeing Charlie's contempt, I recognize that stage you go through as a teenager when it is inconceivable that anyone knows more than you do. Especially either of your parents.

It is almost as if you have to be this sure of yourself at this difficult age or you would give up. You would be defeated by the steep incline of road ahead if you understood it.

"WHEN GRANDMA COMES BACK, she'll tell you I can play six hours a day."

"It's too much pressure, Charlie. You need some release. And Sophie would tell you that, too. She's pushed herself too hard and paid a big price. She can't want you to suffer as much as she has."

"Yes, she does. She says that you have to hurt sometimes if you want to get to the real center of the music."

"That's what Sophie has to do. It's not what you have to do. You are her grandson, but you aren't her."

"Mom says that too all the time. Why? What would be so awful if I was just like her?"

Austen shakes his head.

Charlie, like me, senses that Austen is holding something back.

"What are you all afraid of? Is there something wrong? I want to know," he says.

Austen's eyes sweep the table. "Let's talk about it later."

Charlie follows Austen's glance and looks right at me. "Do you know? Do *you know* what would be so bad—what's wrong with my grandmother?"

I shake my head. So he doesn't know.

"But there is something, isn't there?" he asks.

"I don't know," I say.

"Why don't you? Isn't that what you are here to do?"

"Yes."

"Charlie, stop badgering her. I told you we'd talk about this later."

But Charlie has found an outlet for all his pent-up frustration and fears. "What do you know that you are going to use? Are you going to make a fool out of her?" he asks me.

"No, of course not."

Austen puts his hand on his son's arm. "Why would anyone want to make a fool out of Sophie? Why would you say that?"

"Because that's what Mom said Justine is going to do. She said that when it's all over—no one will take Grandma seriously. And she acted like that was okay."

"What are you talking about?" Austen asks.

"What do you care?" Charlie bites his bottom lip and chews on it for a moment. Making up his mind about something, he turns back to me. "I don't want you to do it. Don't write about her. Don't tell her secrets. No one will think of her the same. She's so big, and if you write about her you'll make her small—like everyone else— and all fucked up."

So he knows—unconsciously he knows—even if he doesn't want to acknowledge it.

"Your grandmother invited me here so that she could tell me her story. And that's all I'm here to do."

Charlie looks at me skeptically.

"I'm going to practice now." Without giving Austen a chance to respond, he gets up and leaves.

By now all the other students have left the table and the two of us are the only ones in the room. I take a last sip of the orange juice and then I leave, too.

THIRTY-NINE

I PASS THE MIRROR quickly, avoiding a glance; afraid, as always, to see the flash of another's face, the glint of her eyes in my own. I'm halfway to the desk when I hear the sound of rustling paper. I look over just in time to see a note being pushed under my door.

Instead of taking time to pick it up or look at it, I rush over and fling open the door and look down the hall, but it is empty and silent. Not even a distant piano or violin disturbs the quiet. And that's wrong too. Why aren't there classes going on? Why isn't Charlie practicing?

I feel it first as a vibration in the doorknob and then through the reverberation of the floorboards. The music starts up again. It was only an odd coincidence of silence. The house breathes a sigh of relief.

Picking up the envelope, I examine the front and the back. There is nothing there. Damn, I'm getting tired of the drama. I've never worked on a story where people sent me covert messages in E-mail or slipped letters under the door.

I would like to talk to you about Sophie DeLyon. Can you meet me in the maze at 10 tomorrow morning? It is better if no one sees us talking.

To find the center—once you walk into the maze—take your first right. Then a left. Two rights. And the next two lefts. There is a stone bench at the center and I'll wait for you there.

I run my finger over the type, but there's nothing to feel. I sniff but it has no scent. Just an ordinary sheet of paper printed out on a computer, folded, and put in a plain envelope. More than curious, I'm suspicious.

Then, leaving the room, I close the door behind me, wondering why I've bothered.

FORTY

E ARE CIVILIZED. Anyone looking at this father and daughter walking down the main avenue would not guess at the currents roiling beneath our words. Stopping at a gourmet coffee shop, we each get espressos and carry them to a table by the window.

The shell-studded house seems unreal now. An imaginary place filled with ghosts and promises, threats and music.

The café is so noisy and I have become oversensitive to sound.

"Be angry at me. But not your sister. She needs you to forgive her," my father is saying.

"Why do I have to be the one to forgive her?"

"Because you are the stronger one. Because you do not have an addiction that demands almost all your energy just to keep it under control."

"You don't know that."

He looks at me the same way Austen looked at Charlie this morning: with concern, empathy, gentleness. All things I do not want to see on my father's face.

This is because of Austen—this, too, is because of Austen.

It is only when I unclench my teeth that I realize that I have clamped my jaw shut.

This man is *my father.* He is not just my mother's husband, but my own father, and I can't remember when I last acknowledged that.

He is searching my face now, smiling.

"What is it?" I ask.

"Sometimes you look so much like your mother it stuns me. I wonder how much like her you really are."

"Not that much."

"You said that as if you are glad of it."

"I am. I have fashioned my life to avoid all her mistakes." This comes out harsher than intended, but there is no way to take it back.

"You don't understand what you are saying."

"How do you know that?"

"Because you only know one side of Pauline Pagett. A mother doesn't show her children all of herself. You don't know the girl-friend she was, or the wife, or the lover. You don't know the daughter she was.

"When we have children, we do them a disservice. Because we think we need to *become* a mother or a father. We don't understand, until it is too late, we don't need to force ourselves into that role; it will come of its own accord. But we do this filtering thing. Or else, we wonder, how can we be examples—how can we guide and nurture our children if we burden them with our flawed personalities?

"But I think it's a mistake. It's like serving only the main course. There are appetizers, soups, desserts."

"Then tell me about her. Tell me about my mother." It comes out as a challenge.

Reacting to the tone of my voice, he leans back and away from me. "When you really want to know, I will tell you."

"You are talking to me like I am thirteen."

"You are acting even younger than you did when you were thirteen." He drinks some coffee, trying *not* to say something. But he fails. "Especially where Maddy is concerned. She has worked so hard staying sober. And now she's met Oliver and they are going to get married. But she's got this obsession about you—and your distance. Not just the physical one. She needs to understand why you left. Why you won't forgive her. Why you are so uninterested in her life. She misses you, Justine." He drinks more coffee. "She does. And I do too," he says.

And that is when I notice he is still wearing his wedding band, worn and rubbed, on the ring finger of his left hand.

He sees where my eyes are.

"When did you start wearing that again?" I ask.

"It's been there since your mother placed it there, thirty-five years ago."

They weren't happy—the last eight or ten or twelve years they were together. He wasn't in love with her anymore. They were sullen with each other. At family dinners, he kept his eyes off her face. She picked at the food he cooked, the worst insult she could inflict upon him. But she devoured her own desserts. Ate all the sweet sugary last courses and threw coq au vin and risotto Milanese away—scraped every bite into the garbage and then slammed the lid shut on the untouched food.

"What would it take for you to forgive Maddy?"

"I'm not mad at her."

"Then what is it?"

"I don't know."

"Yes, you do. You are smart. You write stories. You follow leads. What is standing between you and your sister?"

"I can't forget what it was like. How awful it was. Mom was . . . she was . . . so . . . I was all alone with her so much of the time. Just me and those nurses. I know you were there every morning and every night once the restaurant closed. But those afternoons were so long. And Maddy never helped. She never did. She disappeared."

"I'm not excusing her, but she was sick too."

"No, she was drunk."

"It's an illness, Justine. And it was worse than ever when your mother was sick. Maddy couldn't deal with what was happening.

She felt left out of your grief. You and your mother were so close. Your sister didn't know how to get in there."

"That's ridiculous."

"No, it's not. Pauline loved you both the same, but she liked you better. You were more hers. Maddy knew it. I think it's the reason she's had so many problems. She was the only child until she was five, and then you came along and she wound up in second place."

"But she had you." I haven't touched the marble cake I ordered with my coffee. Now I take a forkful but it tastes dry.

"She could have had ten fathers, but I could not make up for what she did not have with her mother. You were the one that Pauline picked. She became famous with *Justine Cooks*—not *Madeline Cooks*.

"Why did she pick you to do the series with? Just you? Did you ever wonder?" he asks.

"No." Not until this minute, but now I do. "Do you know why?"

"I have my ideas. But only now, in retrospect. No reason to bring them up when we can't be sure of them."

"I'd like to know what you think."

He sighs, looks at me, and then looks away. He is trying to figure out how to say this. I know that is what he is doing because I do this too when I am talking to people.

"You were younger. More innocent. You wouldn't fight or argue or question anything asked of you."

Is it relief I see on his face? Yes, he's pleased he figured out what to say. To tell without telling. I know this too because I recognize it as something else I have done—with friends, with lovers, in interviews—he has found that area between the truth and the lie.

"What aren't you saying?" I ask.

Annoyance flickers in his eyes. "Why do you think there is more?"

"Because I do that; what you just did. I know how to twist the words around and say just enough without saying too much."

"My little wordsmith." He smiles now—not only with his mouth but also with his eyes. His heartfelt genuineness softens me.

I forget about what he's told me because I have thought of the thing I have been longing to ask someone, anyone, who might know. And it occurs to me now that he might. He is my father, after all. Fathers are supposed to know such things.

"Daddy . . ." I do not even realize at first that I have used my childhood name for him. "When will I stop missing her?"

But he has heard it, and he leans forward to be closer to me so that when he tells me, I will really hear his answer.

"When you can finally see her."

"You mean when I die?"

"No." He laughs. "Goodness, no. I mean when you finally allow yourself to see her for all of her strengths and all of her faults. When you see the truth of her."

"I see her that way now."

He does not argue the point, but I know that he doesn't agree with me. And so I am left to wonder, what truth is there that I do not see? Or worse, what lies?

As we leave the restaurant, I think that I have not been as exhausted by this meeting as I was with our first lunch three days ago. That encounter felt like work. Well, I was angrier then and holding on to my anger. That requires effort.

No, that wasn't it. Holding on to my mother's anger requires work.

We walk back up the avenue and stop at my dad's car. He opens the trunk and pulls out a white box.

"I never knew about this—until I moved out of the Ninth Street apartment last year. It was in the corner of a closet. I don't know how long it was sitting there. For years, probably." He is staring at it. "I thought about sending it to you in Paris . . . and kept meaning to, and then Maddy said you were coming home. I don't know if I should have brought it up here . . . but . . ."

On the top, in my mother's all too familiar handwriting:

Cookbook notes—mine and Justine's.

The tears escape even though I wish I could stop them. I don't want to cry here on a street in Greenwich with my father watching me.

"We figured they belong to you. But it didn't occur to me until just now that you might not want this up here. I can take it back to the city and—"

"No, I want it . . ." I say, my words half sobs.

My father rests the box on the edge of the trunk, reaches into his pocket, pulls out a white linen handkerchief, and hands it to me.

THERE USED TO BE DOZENS of these handkerchiefs in my father's bureau drawer. My mother would iron them and stack them in a perfect pile. And when I was young, whenever I cried, he'd pull one out of his pants pocket and use it to wipe my cheeks. He'd also give them to me as talismans when I was scared and didn't want him to leave me alone in the dark, or didn't want him to go to work. He'd hand me one of these white squares, and I would hold it for hours, smelling it, stroking my cheek with it, a way to keep him close. A way to keep me safe.

Another memory: My mother pretending to be horrified while my father uses one of his handkerchiefs to sop up a mess in the kitchen when he couldn't find a towel.

TAKING IT FROM HIM, I wipe my eyes, and I can't help but smell that familiar scent: not my mother's, but my father's—full of spices and herbs from the kitchen. How many hundreds of times, when I was little, did these handkerchiefs offer me comfort and blot my tears?

And my mother's, too.

•   •   •

WE ARE ALL AT A MOVIE, and tears are streaming down my mother's cheeks—cheeks bathed in Technicolor tears from the film's reflection. My father hands her his handkerchief—it's not white anymore, but blue and green—and then as the scene changes, it is red and then brown. He leans over, whispers something in my mother's ear, and she smiles at him. Sitting on his other side, I see the look on her face, the naked need she has for him, all of her vulnerability.

THE MEMORY MAKES ME CRY harder, with childlike heaving. My father puts the box down on the sidewalk and takes me in his arms.

"I miss her, too," he says softly into my ear. "I still do, despite everything, damn it. I miss her."

And it's this that I cannot forget as I drive back to Euphonia. It's not the notes in the box I'm thinking about but my father's words that repeat over and over like the words of an old song you just can't get out of your head.

Despite everything, damn it. I miss her.

BACK IN MY ROOM AT Euphonia, I put the box on the desk to deal with later, when I'm ready to confront the rush of memories that surely will leap out and assault me from its depths.

On the table it seems even bigger now than it did in the car, and I imagine—even though I know it is not true—that if I were to try to pick it up, I would no longer be able to. What will happen to my carefully constructed mechanisms for dealing with the loss if I open up that box and really do find my mother there? Or worse, much worse, what if I cannot find her there?

The minutes pass slowly. The box on the desk seems to be making time run at different speeds.

Memories speed by while the moment here takes forever to pass.

Why did my father bring it with him?

To offer me something so that I would forgive him? Or just to get rid of it himself?

FORTY-ONE

T HE SKY IS CLOUDY. It looks as if there
is another rainstorm coming this way. Hoping
I can make the meeting in the maze and get
back before the downpour, I jog along the beach. One foot down in
the sand. Pushing the grains forward. The next foot down.

Who am I meeting? Which one of them? And what is it that he or
she has to tell me that must be heard in secret in boxwood hallways?

I put my hand in my pocket and feel the outline of the Swiss
Army knife I've brought with me—a pathetic weapon if I really
need one, but all that I could find. After the glass in the tub, I don't
want to be caught completely off guard.

The line of dark clouds moves in fast. The horizon is already
gone. There is a bevy of gulls up ahead and beyond them fog. One
foot down and then the next. I've reached the birds. The gulls are
not shy around me, and even my running through them barely disturbs them.

Only one bird gets out of the way. There is no hesitation to his
flight. No question about where he is going or what his mission is.
In one motion, he dives into the water and comes up just as fast,
with a fat black mussel in his beak. He flies in the direction I am
running and then drops it on an outcropping of rocks just ahead of
me. Swooping down, he retrieves it and drops it again.

This time it breaks, and when he comes back up, flying past me, his beak is empty. He dives back into the water and comes up with another oblong black shell in his beak.

If only it were as easy to find answers.

At the end of the beach, I turn right and take the path through the woods. It is darker here. The maze looms up ahead. Slowing down, I approach the long wall of solid green. I've read that people have died of exposure in mazes.

I hesitate at the entrance and listen to the far-off sound of thunder. The wind has picked up. Tree branches sway, but the hedges are so thick nothing moves.

Inside the maze I am immediately enclosed within the evergreen puzzle. From a few feet away I didn't realize how high the walls were, but now I can see they are at least seven feet tall. Even standing on my toes, I cannot see over them.

Following instructions, I walk down the first main corridor. There is no relief from the sameness of it all. The maze is so well pruned not a twig or a leaf mars the perfection. I take my first right, then a left. And then I make the other turns as I have been instructed, but I don't reach the center. So I go backward and try again. In one of the rooms there are three exits. Which one did I use? There is no way to know because there is nothing to distinguish one from the other.

"Hello? Hello?" I call out.

The living walls seem to absorb the sound of my voice. Hearing a rustle, I look around. A rabbit is staring at me. There is so much green—the verdant grass below my feet, the bluish boxwood walls surrounding me. Damn—somewhere I must have made a wrong turn, and now I can't find my way either to the middle or back to the entrance.

Backtracking once more, I reach a dead end. Where am I?

Breaking off some branches, stripping them of their leaves, I snap their lengths into short sticks and begin to mark a path. And after what seems like a half hour I come back full circle, still not having found the center.

"Hello? Is someone here? Hello?"

No answer.

"Hello? I'm lost. Is anyone here?"

Still, there is no response.

The panic starts in my mouth. The dryness, the chalky taste. And I'm sweating—not the way I do when I run, which is a clean, hot feeling. This is clammy and disturbing, as if fear itself is coming out of my pores. I stop walking. There has to be some logical way out of here. A person cannot get lost inside a maze anymore.

No. If the worst happens, if no one comes along, if the person who was supposed to meet me does not arrive, if I can't find a way out, I will just rip apart the boxwood, break the branches apart with the knife, push my way through and escape.

But how can I destroy this carefully grown and groomed architectural conundrum?

I take out the Swiss Army knife and pull out one instrument after another until I find the small but sharp blade. I will give it a few more minutes and then start to cut.

"Is anyone there?" I am surprised to hear how tight and frightened my voice sounds in my own ears. But the only other option, besides trying to cut my way out and tear the walls down, is to call out and hope that someone responds.

A light rain begins, and at first it's just a mist. But the clouds are still rolling in. In no time it is going to pour, and then there won't be any chance that anyone will be walking by and hear me calling.

"Hello?"

I begin to cut through boxwood hedge, surprised at how dense it is and how long it takes me to cut even a few inches. Frustrated, annoyed, I grab at the slit I've made and try to rip it open further, managing to cut my hands in the process. I come away with long scratches and handfuls of tiny leaves.

"Helloooooo?"

My fingers dig deeper into the hedge, break through another few inches of the thicket. Broken branches scratch the scratches. My hands sting.

"Helloooooooooo?"

"Who is there?" The voice that calls out is accented.

"I'm lost."

"Stay there, yes?" the woman calls.

"Yes."

"Keep talking, all right?"

"Yes. Yes. I will. Can you hear me?"

"Yes." It is a deep voice with a strong European accent.

The light rain has changed into a heavy downpour. Within seconds I'm soaked through and the water is dripping into my eyes. But even through the sheets of water, I can make out the approaching figure—someone shrouded in a hooded yellow slicker.

"How long have you been lost in here?" she asks.

"Almost an hour."

"Come."

Each turn leads to another identical hallway, but we keep moving, not hitting any dead ends.

"If you hadn't come along, I might have been in here for hours."

"Yes," she says.

We walk quickly, the large raindrops soaking into my clothes. Rolling off the woman's slicker.

"I'm lucky you found me. I was starting to panic. I don't think I've ever been lost before."

"You are lucky then. Most people are lost at some point or another."

A few more turns and we reach the exit and walk outside the maze.

"You shouldn't go in there without a map," the woman says.

She looks familiar. "I had one—" As I pull the instructions out of my pocket, my pen falls to the ground, and before I have a chance to, the woman picks it up. I hand her the instructions and when she takes them, I notice that she has the hands of someone who works hard for a living. Scratches. Dirt under the nails. Torn cuticles.

Now I know where I've seen her before. She is the gardener I saw in the meditation garden the other day.

"These instructions are not right."

"Well, it doesn't matter now," I say.

The sound of a motor approaches. In the distance I can just make out Helena's golf cart.

"Do you know how to get back?" the gardener asks. Is she suddenly in a hurry or is that my imagination? Maybe she just wants to get out of the rain. "That way." I point.

"No." The woman points in the opposite direction.

I look that way, and when I turn back, she's already started to walk away.

"Thank you," I call out, but I don't know if she can hear me over the sound of the rain and Helena's golf cart.

"WHAT ARE YOU DOING OUT here?" Helena asks when she finally sees me walking toward her in the fog. I don't answer, I'm not sure what I should say about what happened. But she doesn't seem to notice. "Get on—I'll take you back to the house. You are soaked."

The rain is coming down harder. I can see only two or three feet ahead. Why was Helena out in the rain? Did she send me the note? Was she on her way to meet me in the maze?

"I'm lucky you were driving by," I say.

She nods. "I was down by the beach. I was waiting for Sophie."

There is no doubt in her voice that Sophie is coming back. No lessening of the certainty I heard the first day I arrived. It doesn't matter to her that the Coast Guard has downgraded the search, or that Sophie's own children are already planning a memorial. She remains steadfast in her conviction that Sophie DeLyon will be coming home.

FORTY-TWO

TRIPPING OFF MY soggy running clothes, I'm still trying to figure out who invited me to the maze and why he or she didn't show up. Wrapped in a towel, I sit down in the chaise by the desk overlooking the window. The rain has momentarily stopped, but more storm clouds are moving in. And then I notice—not what is here, but what is missing.

My computer isn't on top of the desk where I left it.

My eyes dart around the room, taking in the bed and the chair. Not there. I jerk open all the drawers in the armoire, although I'm sure I didn't put it there. A housekeeper cleans these rooms daily; perhaps she put the computer away. I scramble down on my knees and look under the bed, under the desk. No, not there.

The closet? I swing the doors open and shove the shoes away, clearing the floor. No. Not in the closet. Not anywhere.

My head starts to ache.

Not my computer.

Quickly, I pull on a pair of jeans, a T-shirt, and some shoes and, without bothering to dry my hair, run downstairs to ask anyone I can find if they have seen it. But no one's around. There is music coming from classrooms, but I can't just walk in and interrupt to ask if anyone has seen my laptop.

I don't think about what I do next, don't rationalize it, or worry about it. I'm scared and I've been threatened too many times. I've been cut, and now I've been led to the center of a maze to give a thief time to go to my room and take my computer. I am sure of it. That's the ultimate prize for whoever Pride33 is—isn't it? My notes? The information others have given me about Sophie?

I knock on the cottage door. There is no answer, but I hear music that is loud enough to mask my knocking if Austen is inside. The door isn't locked.

The living room is empty.

I follow the strains of the symphony down a hallway.

Tracking the music, I reach a second door, which is open just enough for me to look inside. Charlie's head is bent over; he's reading. And listening to one of Sophie's strong, vibrant symphonies.

A movement ends, and in the few seconds of silence before the next movement starts, I hear the familiar click of a computer file being opened. I take a step inside his room.

Charlie is sitting on his bed with my laptop open in front of him.

I do not think I have made a sound except to breathe, but perhaps that one breath I took was too loud, because he looks up now and he sees me. Instinctively he clutches the laptop to his chest.

"You can't write all this about my grandmother. She's not crazy. She's not . . . what do you call it? . . . manic-depressive. That's not what's wrong with her."

"Charlie, you shouldn't be reading my notes. And you shouldn't have tricked me. You sent me into the maze, didn't you? You gave me the wrong directions on purpose." And what else did he do: leave the glass in my tub, arrange for the voodoo doll, send me the sheet music . . . did Charlie orchestrate all that to protect his grandmother?

"My mother would never have Grandma declared incompetent just to take this place away—it would kill her."

"They are just notes, Charlie. Guesses. I have no proof of anything; it's just what I'm thinking."

"If this stuff shows up in some magazine, it will change how everyone thinks about my grandmother. It will make her look . . ." He gropes for the word. "It will make everyone think about *her* instead of her music. This stuff is no one's business."

He stands up, the computer still tightly clamped to his body. His cheeks are red, and he blinks back tears. He's seen his grandmother through my eyes, and he now knows what he has to protect her from.

"Charlie, give me my computer back."

He doesn't move.

I inch toward him, my hands outstretched, fingers ready to grab at the machine and wrest it back. But he outmaneuvers me, running around and past me before I have a chance to react.

He's out the door and down the hallway before I take off after him, and when he flings open the front door, it slams back and shuts in my face, so that I am forced to waste even more time getting it open again.

The blur of the beach.

The cool air of the woods.

The rise of the bridge.

I push myself to run faster. He not only has a head start but he is younger, faster, and knows the terrain.

Damn, it's started to rain again. Heavy drops hit my face. Strong wind blows my hair across my eyes.

Not rain. Not water on the computer. Everything—years of notes, not just about Sophie, but from all my stories and my journal—could be ruined.

I follow him across another bridge. My throat stings and my lungs hurt as I gulp for breath. His lead increases by so much that I lose sight of him. But only for a few hundred yards.

I come around a bend and see him running toward the outdoor chapel. Where is he going?

And just how much of what I wrote did he read? Worse, what did he see?

Everything about his grandmother and her lovers and her children who may be out to take everything away from her? One of her children is his mother. How will he be able to process what his mother is doing to his grandmother? What his uncle is doing?

Did he see the video?

I lose sight of him again but keep going. Uphill until I get to the path that leads down to the dock. And there he is, boarding one of the sailboats, untying the knots.

I won't be able to reach him in time.

"Noooooooooo . . ." I call out, but he does not look up.

The roar of the motor sounds like more thunder. As the boat moves away from the dock out into the cove, he unfurls the sails. By the time I reach the dock, he is heading into the storm. Can't he see that? But he knows how to sail, doesn't he? I think about going back to the house to call the Coast Guard. To find Austen. I can't just stand here and watch the figure on the boat get smaller and smaller.

And then the wind whips up, the sail comes about, and Charlie isn't standing anymore.

I don't know anything about boats. I've never taken one out on my own, but I can't worry about that now. Charlie's boat is getting farther and farther away, pitching and listing from side to side.

And still he does not rise.

Four sailboats and one motorboat are tied up at the dock. Jumping into the motorboat, I struggle with ropes, trying to untie them, until I've finally freed the boat. Now to start it. I've seen this done a hundred times. You start the motor by pulling on something. There is rain in my eyes. What should I pull?

Charlie's boat is drifting farther away.

I get it on the third try and quickly endeavor to grasp the key elements of steering. The boat lurches and crashes into one of the sailboats. I jerk on the wheel, awkwardly pull away, and finally navigate the boat away from the dock area and into the open water.

The waves batter the boat and lift me in the air. Water splashes in my face, stinging my eyes. Almost by accident, I deduce that I have to ride to the side of the wave.

Charlie's boat is drifting farther off. I'm not going fast enough, and it takes precious minutes to understand how to give the boat more power. Finally I surge ahead and start making headway. I push the boat and feel it straining against the rough water. The wind blows in the wrong direction, but the motor is powerful. Endless rain runs down my face, but that doesn't matter. I'm getting closer—close enough to call out. "Charlie?"

No answer.

I've reached the sailboat and manage to come up beside it.

"Charlie?"

My boat swipes his and bounces off. I try the approach again and come back more slowly this time, sidling up to Charlie's boat.

Quickly, putting my boat in idle, I reach out and try to grab hold of the edge of his. My hands slip, but I manage to grab hold of a rope and pull. My shoes skid on the slick surface of the boat—I'm going to lose him. I kick them off and pull harder. The two boats smash together again. My left hand is caught between them, but I don't pay attention to the flash of pain. I get one end of the rope tied around one cleat. And then another.

Finally, I climb on board his sailboat.

Charlie is facedown, awake, but in obvious pain.

"What is it?"

"My leg," he groans.

I crawl to him. The boat is still pitching, and twice I slide away before reaching him. I see my computer sloshing in the foot of water on the floor of the boat. Useless. Fried. Nothing that was written there exists anymore.

"Charlie, I need you to tell me what to do. I don't know how to get us back to shore."

FORTY-THREE

BEFORE WE REACH land, a Coast Guard cutter pulls alongside us, and one of the officers hops on board to bring us in. I hold Charlie's hand and feel him wince every time we hit a wave, but he never cries out.

When we pull into the dock, an ambulance is waiting—along with Austen, Helena, and several of Sophie's students. Medics rush on board and lift Charlie off and onto a stretcher.

While I wait for him to be taken off the boat, my eyes sweep the shore and notice the gardener who found me in the maze. She's up higher on the hill, behind everyone who has come to watch our rescue, but she's visible to me because I'm facing the land. She's still wearing the yellow slicker and, like everyone else, has water dripping down her face, except I can't help thinking that on her face the rain looks like tears. As soon as our eyes meet, she turns and leaves.

"I'm fine," Charlie is saying to the paramedics with the same bravado he showed on the boat.

"Your son's leg appears to be broken, Mr. Bell."

The medics take his vital signs. Helena hovers by his side, watching with wide, worried eyes.

"Anything else bother you, son?" one asks him.

"No, just my leg."

"That's how it looks to us, too, so let's get you off to the hospital now."

Carrying my waterlogged laptop, I follow behind Austen and Charlie the few yards to the waiting ambulance, and as the paramedics put Charlie on board, Austen turns to me.

"Thank you. For following him. For saving his life."

I nod. He doesn't know that I chased Charlie because he'd stolen my computer—*my computer, my notes.* Now that we are safely back on land, the idea of what I have lost begins to overwhelm me.

Austen is talking, but I haven't heard what he's said.

"What?"

"I asked if you are all right. Do you need to come to the hospital with us?"

"No. I banged my hand, but it's just bruised. I'm okay." And then something occurs to me. "Austen, how did you know we were out there?"

"I didn't. Someone called the Coast Guard, and they had the police call us."

"Who called the Coast Guard?"

"There is some confusion about that. They said the woman either used the name Sophie DeLyon or said she was calling from Sophie DeLyon's place."

Charlie, who is being lifted into the ambulance, has heard this. "Maybe it really was her."

"Yes, yes. It must have been." This from Helena, who suddenly has come to life.

"After we get you to the hospital and check out that leg, we can talk about it." Austen shoots Helena a warning look.

Helena ignores his silent message. "I know it was her." And then she puts her hand on my shoulder. "I wanted to tell you . . . Sophie will tell you when she gets back, but she's very grateful for what you did, for going out there after Charlie. He is Sophie's future. More her child than either Stephen or Daphne are," Helena says. "He has a gift. Sophie's gift."

FORTY-FOUR

ONCE THE AMBULANCE takes off, with Helena and Austen accompanying Charlie, I trudge back to Euphonia. I'm exhausted and uncomfortable in my soaking clothes—wet for the second time today—and miserable over what I've lost. My hands, which were already scratched up from the maze, are now banged up and sore. And I'm so cold, I'm starting to shake.

Back at the house, I turn on the bathwater in my room and sit on the bed waiting for the hot water to fill up. I lean back on the comfortable pillows, the soft sheets. Oh, to crawl inside and sleep. To just sleep one night all the way through. And then I see the empty desk.

Without my computer.

Over a hundred pages of interviews and notes about Sophie were in that computer. And my E-mail address book with years of contacts in it: all things I won't be able to replace easily. Ideas for other stories.

But it can't all be gone. It isn't all gone. Most of the time I remember to E-mail myself transcripts of what I'm working on and don't open them. It's an easy way of backing up. There must be dozens of those copies in my E-mail still. But how many? How much did I back up?

Suddenly this becomes the only thing that matters to me: to find out how much of the work I've done for the last month on this story still exists, even in note form. It becomes imperative for me to get on-line and see what is still there.

I have to find a computer. My bath can wait.

I go down the hall to the opposite side of the building. I've only been in Helena's office once, but I remember seeing a computer on her desk.

The large airy room is painted a soothing light green, and the walls are covered with mementos of Sophie's career. The desk faces the window.

I have a new-found respect and amazement for the sea and for anyone who dares to harness the wind and ride those waves and currents. If the storm had been worse, if I had fallen, too, I might be out there still. Might have died out there along with Sophie—if indeed she is dead.

A beep alerts me that the computer is still connected to the Internet and E-mail has come through for Helena. She must have been on-line when the police called about the accident on the boat.

I sit down at the desk. Damn, it's a PC and I use a Mac. Plus this computer has a mouse and I have always used a track pad. It's not that I can't work here; it's just going to be awkward.

Like wearing your shoes on the wrong feet.

Ineptly, I move the mouse, and the pointer on the screen slides all the way into the upper right-hand corner.

I bring it back. My damp hair is sticking to my forehead. I brush it away. I'm tired. My arms hurt and my head aches. I type in my browser's address and wait. This is an old computer and it's on a telephone modem, not a cable line. The browser takes its time.

It is dusk, and the light on the beach reflecting off the water reminds me of a Monet painting in the Musée d'Orsay. At home. Or where home was. But is it really home? Or just the place where I have put my life on hold for a time? I am too tired to think this through now. My eyelids are heavy; I could fall asleep just sitting here.

And then I'm watching Charlie's sailboat in the distance and trying to get to him, but the current is so strong. The rain soaks my shirt and my jeans and blinds me. It's almost impossible to stay on course, but I'm getting closer. Finally, I reach the boat and struggle with the ropes.

Charlie is lying on the floor of the boat, in pain. My computer is not far from him, sitting in the water that has sloshed into the corner. I reach for it and hear it humming, not a mechanical sound, but the way someone in the kitchen would be humming while she mixed batter for pancakes.

Turning it on, I press the E-mail icon and look at the list. The E-mail is from my mother. The rain doesn't matter; the waves don't scare me anymore. None of that is important in the face of the unopened E-mail. I reach out to move the cursor and the Internet connection breaks.

I jerk awake. How long have I been sleeping here in the chair in front of the window in Helena's office? I check the computer screen. That was a dream too. The connection is still live.

I'm still thinking about how I felt seeing E-mail from my mother: the elation of that, and then the letdown once I woke up. This awful missing that makes me feel hollow and hungry takes over.

I don't have the energy to fight the sadness now.

Think of a word, I command myself, but my brain is too tired. A beep alerts me that another E-mail has come in. I am so tired. I click on the mail icon. Of course I have mail. I always do. There are ten letters, but I don't recognize the sender's addresses on any of them. And I don't see any of the backup E-mail I have sent myself.

Confused, I click on the mail-sent icon.

A long list of letters appear. I scroll this list, but none of these look familiar either. What has happened to my mail?

And then at last I do see my own E-mail address. One of the letters I sent myself with my notes. Which notes, though, how complete are they? I click on the first letter: "Justine, someone has sent you a curse!" Beneath that is the live link that says, "Click here."

But how can this be in my sent-mail file? I never sent a copy of that to myself. Checking more and more E-mail, I realize that I never connected to my own account.

I'm in Helena's account.

Wide awake, heart pounding, I start opening more and more of Helena's sent E-mail. I find each of the threats I received, plus her receipt for the E-mail voodoo doll.

It wasn't Charlie who was threatening me. Running down the beach, following him onto the dock, I'd become convinced it had been him. No. All Charlie did was lure me to the maze so he could get to my laptop and find out what I was writing about his grandmother.

I try to remember what Fiona asked me the night before. And I ask that question now, but fill in a name: why would Helena be desperate for me to abandon Sophie's story? Why would she care? What does she have to lose if the truth of Sophie's illness or bisexuality were revealed?

And if she sent the threats and left me the voodoo doll, did she also put the glass in my shower? And if she did that, what else is she capable of?

"What are you doing?"

I jerk my head up and look at Helena in the doorway. Before she can reach my side, I quit the E-mail program and shut off the whole system. Then I realize that I haven't covered my tracks at all. When she signs back on again, she will be able to figure out I have accessed her E-mail and read the letters that are now in the old-mail file.

"I was hoping I could use your computer. I lost everything." My voice sounds strained, and I can tell I'm talking too quickly. In an effort not to alert her to what I've found out, I try to slow down. "But I usually back up most of my notes in E-mail. I was waiting for you, hoping you'd let me check. Can I log on through your system and see what I saved?"

Is she looking at me suspiciously? I should get off the subject of the computer.

"How is Charlie?" I have to make an effort not to stare at her, looking for a physical sign of the *other* inside of her.

"It was a clean break. And he asked me if you would come down and see him. I think he wants to apologize."

"Is he back already? Are they at the cottage?"

"Yes."

"Sure."

I get up and start toward the door and then I stop and turn around. She is watching. Has she looked at the computer and noticed it is off? Does she remember that she left it on?

"I want to thank you for your hospitality and tell you that I'll be leaving tomorrow. It just seems pointless to stay here and be in everyone's way. There's just nothing to write about without Sophie."

Her eyes drop and rest on her own hands, on the gold ring glimmering in the light. "Sophie is coming back." Now she's angry with me for being a nonbeliever.

A photograph on the wall of a much younger Helena and middle-aged Sophie attracts my attention. "You two have known each other a long time, haven't you?" I ask.

"Thirty years. She was my teacher at Juilliard."

"What did you study?"

"Composition. I was good, but I just didn't have the stamina." Her voice has lifted—there is no rancor, no disappointment. She's happy about this.

"How did you realize that?"

"I watched Sophie. What it took, what she gave. I didn't have it." She's elated.

"Are you sorry?"

"That I gave it up?" Helena looks surprised, then smiles, and her beautiful blue eyes shine.

"Yes, are you sorry you gave up composition?"

She laughs a young girl's joyful laughter. "I gave up being a second- or third-rate composer to spend my life with one of the really great composers and conductors of our time. To be the one she relied on . . . who she depended on. To be the one who protected her, whatever the cost, from the vultures. I was the one who made sure her reputation was never tarnished. Without me, they would have destroyed her, eaten her up alive. I would do anything for her. You don't second-guess decisions you make out of love." Her voice breaks.

I am afraid to say anything.

To someone who didn't know, everything she's just said is perfectly innocent, said by one friend about another, said by a loyal employee about an ideal employer.

But to someone who knows, as I do now, it is an admission that she would do whatever it took to make sure no one ever found out that Sophie—to whom Helena had devoted her life—had chosen other lovers over her.

Like my mother, Helena is another of love's victims. And realizing this makes me, more than anything else, feel sympathy for her.

Why is it that women take whatever they get and accept it with a martyr's masochistic pleasure? No matter how charismatic Sophie was, no matter what kind of genius she was, Helena's life was not worth this.

"What will you do now?" I ask.

"What do you mean?" Helena opens her hands by her sides. "I'll continue doing what I've always done. Keep the session going so that when Sophie comes back, she can pick up without skipping a beat. It's what I've been doing the last thirty years."

"But what if she doesn't come back?"

"That's not a possibility."

"Do you know what plans Sophie made for you if anything were to happen to her?"

"Yes, of course," Helena says without any emotion, as if she is reciting directions. "Nothing will change. Just some papers will change hands and Euphonia will belong to Juilliard. If I survive her, I will stay on as director."

"I don't think you will."

"What?" She's confused.

"I think Daphne and Stephen are going to try to have Sophie declared legally insane and contest her will so they can take control of Euphonia in order to sell it."

Helena shakes her head. "That could never happen. Sophie told me she was going to make sure that couldn't happen. That's part of what you were going to expose. Because she doesn't want to—" She stops, realizing she's said far too much.

"So she *did* think they were going to try?" I ask. Of course Sophie had an agenda. I was naïve to think otherwise.

Helena nods. Suddenly she needs to be reassured more than keep the confidences entrusted to her. "She doesn't delude herself about who her children are or what they are capable of. Daphne had let Sophie down. Disappointed her. Stephen too—but then she'd never expected as much from him. He was like his father." Helena's face puckers as if she's just tasted a lemon. "He even had cameras hidden here. He filmed her and she found out about it. It was terrible.

"Daphne is awful to her, too. Watching and waiting for every opportunity to offer up pathetic complaints about how absent Sophie had been as a mother, how many times she'd needed her but she'd been away . . . how much she missed her." Helena rocks back and forth as if the momentum is all that is keeping her from dissolving. "Easy to miss, too. The attention of her eyes on you, the energy focused on you, the touch of her hand on your shoulder, your cheek . . . you can't imagine . . . when Sophie fixes her gaze on you, it is as if you are being given a great gift. But when she pulls away—sinks into herself, disappears, focuses on someone else— you've never felt so alone."

I murmur compassionately, tilt my head, try to give Helena support . . . whatever it takes . . . just to keep her talking.

"Is that why Charlie is so important to her? She is going to be a better grandmother to him than she had been a mother to Daphne and Stephen?" I keep Sophie alive and in the present tense the way she does.

Helena starts to cry softly. As she brings her hands to her face, the battered gold ring on her left ring finger glints again.

"It's hard to love someone as much as you love Sophie and watch people try to hurt her."

"My job, the only job I've ever done well, is to protect her."

"From who?"

She doesn't answer. She is crying too hard. Soon her wracking sobs have turned into a cough. For a moment, I want to leave her there choking on her own tears. She has diabolically tried to scare me away from this story. She was even willing to injure me to do it. And yet I go into the bathroom to get her some tissues and a glass of water.

There is no tumbler at the sink, so I open the medicine cabinet to see if it's inside. But all I find are rows and rows of amber pill bottles.

The names on the prescriptions are all familiar. The first is labeled "Lithium." The next is "Wellbutrin." The Guccis and Pradas of psychopharmacological drugs. It's the patient's name that surprises me: *Helena Rath*. No wonder there were no prescriptions filed in Sophie's name at the drugstore.

"Close that! What are you doing with my pills?" Her voice is as cold as the mirror I'm touching.

"When were you diagnosed?" I ask.

"Years ago."

In the medicine cabinet's mirror Helena and I stare at each other.

Then, I open the lithium bottle—the one with the most recent date—and spill the pills into the toilet. Next I open the bottle of Wellbutrin. And then the bottle of Zoloft. One by one I empty the pills into the bowl and then flush them away, all the while not taking my eyes off Helena, who watches without a single muscle in her face twitching.

Helena is looking at me as if I am insane, but she hasn't reached out or tried to stop me. Not a flicker of fear or panic has flashed in her eyes.

And that's how I know. I saw my father lose his medicine once and it did not make him calm.

"They aren't your pills, are they, Helena? You'd never be able to watch me flush away the medicine that keeps you on this side of sanity. They belong to Sophie. I know they do. You don't even have to tell me."

Helena picks up the trash can and lunges—but not at me—at my image in the mirror. The glass shatters. Hundreds of slivers of reflections of the two of us break apart and fall. Into the sink. Onto the floor. Landing at crazy angles. Sending light reflections onto my face and onto hers. Helena has used broken glass before to try to get rid of me, and she's trying again now, holding a knife of mirror and charging me.

I'm mesmerized by the blood dripping down her cheek like tears, and I move, but a little too slowly. I hear the rip of fabric but don't feel the sting of a cut.

Crossing my arms over my face to avoid her waving arms, I throw myself at her, shoving her. Losing her balance, she falls to the floor, going down fast and landing on her right hand. The shard of mirror she was holding shatters into dozens of even smaller pieces. Broken splashes of light shower the floor.

I back away. Even though I'm fairly certain that now she's only dangerous to herself, I keep a safe distance.

Helena looks up at me. "You can't write about Sophie's illness." Helena's losing spirit: it's leeching out of her, leaving her weak. "We've kept it a secret so long. Please don't ruin it for us," she pleads.

"Why?"

"Because of how Daphne and Stephen tried to use it when she was first diagnosed. And how they are just waiting to use it again. People will judge her because of it. And judge her music. They will read her life in light of the illness."

"Then why did Sophie ask me to come here?"

"So *you* would tell everyone. So she wouldn't have to. But then right before you came, she started getting scared that she'd made a mistake. That maybe it wouldn't be a good thing after all for everyone to know. She couldn't sleep the last few nights. She was moody. Depressed. That's why she took the boat out. That's where she always goes when she's like that. The water helps."

"Has she done this before?" I ask.

"Yes."

"But for this long?"

She shakes her head. "You don't know how bad it can get. I've seen her crawl across a room on her knees only to cry in my arms and beg me to let her die. I've saved her life only to have her stop taking the pills again and again so she could write a new symphony or score and then crash once the burst of creativity was over."

"The pills leveled out the music?" I ask.

"She'd go off the medicine. Write on a high. And I'd just wait and watch for the minute when she crossed over from the manic state to the depressed one. I'd try to get her to go back on the pills, but the depression affected her decision-making. Then the depression would turn dangerous. It was a tightrope walk every time. You aren't supposed to go off the medication. But the doctors couldn't find a cocktail that didn't dull the music. So she'd spend three or four months a year off her medication. One symphony. Or one score.

"And then I'd wait to hear the shrieks in the middle of the night. I'd find her running down to the water screaming that she wanted to drown." She has been talking softly. Now her voice gets louder. "You don't know what it is like!" To make her point, she pounds the floor with her fist. A piece of mirror sticks in the fleshy part of her palm and the blood starts to flow.

I pull a towel off the rack, wrap it around her hand, help her up and out of the bathroom, and sit her down on the couch.

Asking her any more questions right now could be misconstrued as exploiting her pain. But she is not an innocent who de-

serves my sympathy. This is the woman who sent me threats and put me in danger. I have earned the right to do this, even now. "Did Zoë know about the depression?"

Helena shakes her head. "No one knew the extent of it. Certainly not any of her girls. She hid it from them. She needed them to look up to her and see her as their heroine, to worship her. That was what inspired her. You don't worship a flawed, damaged, sick woman. That's why none of them lasted. They could never get close enough. She wouldn't let them. Just me."

"You are special to her, Helena, aren't you? That's why you have to tell Austen what you know. If there's a court case over all this, he's going to be fighting on Charlie's side—to protect him from Daphne. He's going to need your help."

"But I promised her I'd never tell anyone."

She looks like a lost child. She looks the way that I feel when I think about my mother.

"You won't have to break any promises. Austen knows about Sophie's illness."

"No one knows how bad it was," she says emphatically.

"Austen does. Sophie must have told him so he could watch out for the disease in Charlie."

"No, I can't tell anyone," she says. "When Sophie comes back, if she wants to tell, she can."

FORTY-FIVE

AUSTEN SITS BESIDE his son, his arm around Charlie's shoulders. "Thank you for coming over. We would have come up to the house, but he has to stay off his leg for the next twenty-four hours . . ." He nods toward Charlie's cast. "Charlie?" He turns to his son and dips his head, cueing him.

Sheepishly, Charlie starts to speak. "Thank you for what you did. If anything had happened to you, it would have been my fault. I'm sorry."

He glances at his father. Austen nods. Charlie takes a deep breath and continues. "I had no right to take your computer."

I nod. "No you didn't, but I understand why you did."

Charlie bites the inside of his cheek and then looks down. He mumbles the rest of what he has to say without looking at me. "I'm going to get a job for the rest of the summer and I will pay you back what the computer cost."

"Thank you. That would help a lot, but I can't ever get back the work that I lost."

He doesn't know how to respond.

"Charlie told me what he read . . . what was in your notes. And tomorrow we are going to drive into New York and talk to Daphne and Stephen. We're taking a friend of mine with us who is a lawyer."

"You'll need to take Helena with you too. And then take her to a good therapist."

Austen's eyebrows go up—in question. But this isn't the time. I turn to Charlie. I have my own apologies to make.

"I'm sorry," I say to him. "I didn't want you to find out about what your mom and your uncle were doing."

He lowers his head. I can only imagine how hard this is for him. He's not only lost Sophie, but now he has to process this news about his mother and his uncle.

"Dad called the Coast Guard," Charlie says, suddenly brightening. "They said the woman who called in my accident said she was Sophie DeLyon."

I sit down in the chair by the fireplace and look into the empty grate, imagining how big a blaze it must hold in the winter and thinking how much my mother would have loved roasting chestnuts and making popcorn in a fireplace like this.

"No, Charlie," Austen says. "What I said was that a woman who spoke with an accent called and that the operator said she was talking in a rush and he couldn't be sure what she said. It might have been that she said she was Sophie DeLyon or that she was calling for Sophie DeLyon and she wanted to report an accident and that it was an emergency. Exactly what the police told us from the beginning."

Charlie's eyes close. Even though he's heard this before, a fresh tear tracks down his face. When it reaches his chin, he swipes it away.

Austen's hand remains on the boy's shoulder, as if he is afraid to let go of Charlie again for fear of what else might happen. Perhaps he is trying to transfer stamina and strength to him.

I understand this—remember all those afternoons that I sat by my mother's bed holding on to her, to anything connected to her. The blanket, her slipper, the edge of her robe.

With my thumb I touch the round edge of the diamond, hard and cold and unyielding, but there. When I look up, Austen is staring at me. Beside him, Charlie has drifted off to sleep.

I am envious of that sleep, even if it is induced by painkillers. We get up and go out onto the deck.

"I really don't know what to say. If you hadn't gone out there, Charlie might have . . ."

"Don't. He's fine."

"He loves her so much he just couldn't stand the idea that you were going to expose her," says Austen.

"You mean Sophie, not his mother?"

"Yes. And not just because she is his grandmother. It's the musical bond they share. He knows how much she's given up for her music and can't bear to think her reputation will be tarnished. His word. Big word. But he understands the theory clearly. He said that people should judge her only by her music. And not by who she had sex with. *His words.* Or because she has a chemical imbalance. *My words.* He didn't know what to call her manic depression."

"But those things won't threaten her stature as an artist," I say.

"Of course they will. That's what we do to people. Our worst criminals or our most brilliant artists. We expose all their secrets and dilute the power of their work. We talk as much about Judy Garland's drug use as her voice. As much about Richard Burton's drinking as his acting. As much about the women Kennedy slept with as his legacy as president." Austen shakes his head. "You must be exhausted," he says.

"I am past being tired," I say.

And then I tell him about Helena and the threats and everything else I've found out. Austen wants to call the police now, but I convince him that she's not dangerous anymore. "She was trying to scare me away and prevent me from finding out, but I've found out."

"Glass in your bathtub could have done much more than scare you away."

"I know, but I'm no longer a threat to her. I told her I'm leaving."

He doesn't say anything for a moment, and I can't tell what he's thinking from the expression on his face. He shakes his head as if he is saying no to something he is thinking. And then: "It still isn't safe for you to be in the house with her tonight. We have a guest room. You can stay here."

"That's not necessary." Suddenly there is more between us than just the words we are saying.

"Yes, it is."

"Austen, did Charlie mention seeing the video?"

He shakes his head. "He didn't say anything about a video. What video?"

"A few minutes of Sophie and Zoë in bed together."

"Damn it. How did you get that? What were you going to do with it?"

I feel my back stiffen. Perceptions. Assumptions about who we are that damage the chances we have to see each other for what we are. I try to explain it to him with as few words as necessary.

"Did you find the video on Helena's computer too?" he asks.

"No. And I don't think Helena sent it. That was one of the things she didn't want me to know about. I think it came from Stephen to entice me to investigate that area of Sophie's life, so that I'd turn up the affairs and have more to use to prove Sophie's in competence. Helena said Stephen had surveillance cameras hidden in the house at some point."

"The worst thing about all this is that I am not surprised. I know—because I saw it—how much both of them resented their mother."

WE GO INSIDE SO AUSTEN can check on Charlie, and when he comes back to me in the living room he smiles sadly. "It's like he's a little kid again and I have to keep making sure he's okay. When I think about what might have happened, I feel sick. Thank you."

"Stop thanking me."

"Why?"

"Because I was just being a heartless, ruthless writer willing to do anything to get a story."

"For some reason, that is what you want me to believe. But I don't think it's true."

I shrug. "It might as well be, for all that it matters."

"Why would you say that?"

"Austen, would you play?" I tilt my head toward the cello. I am going to leave here tomorrow. I won't see him again. So hearing the music now, watching him play just once, will be all right.

"Something *you wrote*," I add.

He sits down and pulls the instrument into position and begins.

The music is edgy and modern, strong and liquid, and I'm moving on it, riding its waves. His notes take me from lows to midranges to highs. I dip down to touch it and soar up to reach it.

And then he just stops in the middle of a phrase and puts the bow down on the floor. One hand sits on the hip of the instrument, the other on the neck.

"I never wrote the end."

"Why?"

He shrugs.

And then before I can ask him anything else, I see the face in the window: the gardener in the yellow slicker is peering in.

It scares me and I let out a cry.

"What?" Austen asks as he looks toward the window, but the woman is gone.

I run to the kitchen and look out that window just in time to see her walking alongside the house, peeking in the next window, and then the next.

Finally, at Charlie's window, the gardener stands still for a moment. She bows her head, and I can see the peace descend over her. Her posture changes, her energy surges.

My hands are on the window. I want to open it and call out and stop her. But I don't. I stand there, with my fingers frozen on the frame, and watch her walk off into the dark night.

"Justine? What is it?" Austen asks, finding me in the kitchen.

"I thought I saw someone out there. I'm not sure, but I think it's Sophie."

He walks over to me and puts his hand on my shoulder, turning me around to face him.

"Not you too? She's gone, Justine. Don't do this. Don't do it to Charlie. Sometimes you have to let go."

I'm not sure which of us he is talking to.

"I should go home" is the only thing I can think to say.

"Right," he says with a sudden shift of his voice into a lower, colder register. I feel the breeze of a door shutting in my face. I square my shoulders. I shouldn't be here in the first place. Except I can't resist asking him one last question.

"Austen, how did Sophie convince you to stop writing music?"

"Back then all I wanted was to be what she wanted me to be." He shrugs. "She bribed me, in a way, with the cello and a job with the Philharmonic. It was a tradeoff—go it alone as a composer of music no one understood, or have a performing career handed to me on a silver platter."

"And in the bargain she got Charlie?"

"Of course not."

"But she did, didn't she? He's not yours or Daphne's—you told me that yourself. He's hers."

I can feel Sophie now. Smell her. See the burnished hair and the copper clothes. I know her, this seductive, talented woman who slept with people to feel adoration, not love. Who bought loyalty with expensive careers and made sure that those who might threaten what she wanted were thwarted before they had a chance. And the sad, sick woman who crawled across a room on her knees begging Helena to let her die.

Who would take herself off medication to write music. Who renovated this house, who had an outdoor chapel built, and a meditation garden set with shells; who set up scholarships and mentored students, and cast them in the roles that suited her own ambitions, even if it broke their souls.

This woman was completely loved in a healthy way—and of this I am sure—by only one person, and that was Charlie.

Sophie DeLyon conducted people's lives. Often she did what

only a brilliant conductor can do—brought out the real talent from
those under her baton. But because she was also a living, breathing
woman, sometimes she brought out the worst too.

"Good night, Austen."

"Listen, you don't have to talk to me and you can leave in the
morning before I get up, but you are *not* sleeping up there tonight.
No way are you spending the night in that house with the woman
who put glass in your bathtub and sent you voodoo dolls. Wait
here."

I do as he says, and he's back from checking on Charlie in a moment.

"He's fast asleep. Let's go."

"Where?"

"To get your things."

AT THE HOUSE, SEVERAL STUDENTS are playing in
the living room. Practicing for a ghost, according to Austen. The
mournful music accompanies us up the stairs. It sounds as if the instruments are wounded.

Inside my room, in the dark, the box is white enough to appear
to be glowing.

Austen flips on the light, walks over to the table, and looks down
at it.

"What is this?"

And I tell him.

"You still don't know what's in it?" he asks when I'm done explaining.

"I didn't open it."

He doesn't ask why; he seems to know. "You are making the
same mistake with your mother that so many of us made with Sophie. We all gave her power over us. We made her bigger than we
were. People saw her as larger than life—she didn't demand it. But
she just couldn't resist taking it when it was offered. And it destroyed her."

"What does that have to do with my mother?"

"Your father told you . . . You are not seeing her as anything but your mother—one-dimensional, a silhouette—and you are going to have to."

BACK AT THE COTTAGE AUSTEN puts my suitcase on the floor and the box on the dining room table and hands me scissors. I take them but don't do anything with them right away.

He gets up to check on Charlie again, and leaves me alone with the carton. When he comes back, I am still sitting at the table, looking at it.

"You have to open it."

Slowly, I cut the packing tape and pull it off. It comes away in long strips. I lift the flaps and look in at a dozen spiral-bound notebooks with black covers.

"I remember these. She never went anywhere without one. She worked out her recipes in them and took down the things I said when we were cooking."

I run my finger along a silver-ringed spine, and my nail makes a small hollow sound.

"Open one."

I look at him hesitantly. He nods.

"I wasn't allowed to touch them when I was growing up. It was the only rule we had. I wasn't allowed to because Mom said they were work. She would give me notebooks of my own to write in. But I couldn't play with these."

I still haven't pulled out one of the books.

Austen gets up and comes and sits next to me. Shoulder to shoulder. "Justine?" His face is close enough that I feel his breath on my cheek. I think about kissing him now—about leaning over and pressing my lips onto his and getting lost in that kiss.

This is a distraction from the box, I know—but one that would work.

"Justine. Take one out. Get it over with. You were brave enough to get in that boat today. Surely you can look at your mother's notebooks."

Taking in a huge gulp of air, I reach in and pull one out. Nothing happens. I am holding it and still breathing. It's easier to open it and look through it than I had imagined. The words are written in black ink and there are notations of weights and amounts in the margins.

It's not like looking into my mother's eyes or smelling her or feeling her hand on my cheek. It's not like being kissed by her or sleeping on the plane with my head on her shoulder and waking up and staying there just because it feels good to be so close to her.

I take all the books out and stack them on the table. They have no power. There is no magic they can perform, neither good nor bad.

I reach for the box to put it on the floor, and then I see a folder on the bottom. As I lift it out, the diamond I wear glints in the light. Her diamond.

Inside the folder is a sheaf of letters. Different letters on different kinds of paper—none in my mother's handwriting. Words fly off these letters—words that are not about food, but about love and loss and longing.

I read one and then sink down to the floor, my back against the leg of the chair. That wooden dowel is all that is keeping me upright as I read each letter, one after the other. I don't know I am crying until I see the drops pucker the paper.

"Justine?" He crouches beside me.

"They are love letters . . . but not from my father."

"From someone she knew before your father?"

"No . . . the dates . . ." I am double-checking all of the dates, determined to find one from the years before my parents were married.

"No. The letters start the year that the first *Justine Cooks* book came out. And they continue until just before my mother's death." I stop to take a breath and then start quickly again to get it over with—to get the words out of my mouth because they taste bitter. Rancid. Butter gone bad.

"My *mother* had a lover."

I am thinking of my mother at the end, seeing her lying there, paper-thin skin and all bones, and how this man—who loved her so much—could not come and say good-bye. And how she could not say good-bye to him.

"*She* was unfaithful to my father." And even as I say it, I cannot imagine how wrong I have gotten everything.

I AM LYING IN BED in a hotel room in Paris, watching my mother getting dressed to go out for a late supper with her editor, who has flown over to be with us on the book tour. My mother bends down, her hair softly touching my cheek, and her perfume envelops and mesmerizes me. I feel my mother's sticky lipsticked kiss on my cheek.

"If you need me, just call the hotel operator. . . . She'll have me paged . . . but you have to go to sleep now, sweetheart."

But I could not sleep. I never could when my mother left me alone in hotel rooms to go have late suppers or coffee or drinks with her editor.

She often did this. It wasn't that I was scared or even lonely; it was just that I couldn't sleep until I heard the key in the door and the swish of my mother's dress and the click of her high-heel shoes in the bathroom, where she went to undress.

THE NAME ON THE LETTERS was only a first name, but I don't need more. When she left me, she was always having drinks or late suppers with the same man. Paul Enderling. Her editor. Her lover.

For what seems a long time, I do not say anything.

"All these years, I thought it was my father, but it was my *mother* who wanted to leave but wouldn't because of us. It was my mother who was unfaithful," I finally whispered.

What have I done? It's been my mother's failings and my mother's weaknesses I've used as a map of what never to do and what kind of woman never to become. And by trying to be the opposite of who I thought she was, I have turned out to be exactly like her—like her *other*—the woman she kept hidden away.

I don't understand it yet. Except to know that I've had it all backward and that now I will have to reexamine so many things. I'm going to have to talk to my father and listen to my sister.

I get up and go into the bathroom and look in the mirror. Whose eyes are these? My mother's? Or those of the woman I didn't even know? And then behind me, I see Austen.

"Are you all right?"

Strains of a symphony play—has Charlie gotten up? Is he playing? Is it a CD? It is not complete music I hear but rather the idea of music, and in its ephemeral beauty it sounds even more like another language.

"Why is it so hard to describe music?" I ask him, grateful to have something else to talk about, to think about—even for a few minutes—other than what I've discovered. "Does anyone really understand how it works on the brain? How it makes you feel things without a single word? And not just with one person, but how it works across cultures and centuries. The same drumbeat makes us all feel proud. The same violin chord makes us all want to cry."

"What matters isn't that you understand the music, Justine. What matters is that it transports you."

"But how can you stand it—so many people who can't speak your language listening to your words?"

"They understand enough of them."

I shake my head.

Turning from the mirror, I look at him. I feel lost, misplaced— unsure of things about myself that I never questioned before.

"I'm confused. I devoted so much of my life just trying to prevent it from being like hers."

"It doesn't matter anymore."

"Except I've been so very deliberate about some of my choices."

"You think you have, but I wonder. Perhaps you just used her as an excuse to be how you wanted to be."

"I'm tired."

He kisses me sweetly, with no pressure, without intent or question.

"I know. Come, I'm going to put you to bed. And you are going to sleep. And we can talk about it all tomorrow."

Then taking me by the hand, he leads me to the guest room bed and folds down the blanket and the sheets.

"No, tomorrow we have to find the gardener. The one in the slicker."

"Stop!" He's even shocked himself with his harsh tone of voice. But he's not sorry. "I won't let you do this. It's cruel to Charlie. He doesn't need to hear you wondering. He has to stop hoping." His tone is dismissive. He is being a protective father. And while I don't like it, I understand it.

Still dressed, I lie down against the pillows. Just for one minute, I think, and then I'll get up and get undressed. Austen is saying something to me, but I can't keep my eyes open, can't keep focused. I see the box, the voodoo doll, and the boat, and all the while I'm hearing music and wondering how so much has happened in just a few days.

I WAKE IN THE MIDDLE of the night. It's silent in the house, and I lie in bed and try to fall asleep again, but the letters are between me and any kind of peace.

In the living room, I sit on the couch and read through them all one more time. It does not make her a different mother or make me a different daughter. But it does make her another kind of wife and woman. And I don't know what that means. I want there to be a reason my mother kept these letters among our recipes, that she filed them in a place I was sure to find them. Why did she want me to live with her infidelity?

This is what our parents do to us: hold our hands and show us the path, but they no more know that it's safe than they know we will ever reach the end.

When my mother looked into my eyes, she saw herself reflected back: not the truth of who she was but the expurgated *other* she wished she could be.

I make a paper pyre in the hearth and find a box of matches on top of the mantel. In the quiet, while everyone sleeps, I set the fire and watch it jump up and lick the paper. Orange and red and yellow tongues of flame devour the letters. Blackened fragments of paper rise up, float in the hot air, and then drift back down.

Much more quickly than I would have thought, the love letters are gone, and all that is left is a pile of gray, colorless ash.

I stay there until the first rays of the sun start to dawn, and then I get up. There's one letter left behind, and as I reach for it I'm strangely buoyed. But the envelope is empty. Scooping up the ashes I fill the envelope with them and then lick it closed.

FORTY-SIX

AS SOON AS I wake up, I realize how hungry I am. For juice and coffee and for French toast. With melted butter, sugar, and a light dusting of cocoa powder. Searching through the shelves, I have to settle for maple syrup, because while the kitchen is well stocked, I can't find any cocoa.

I break eggs, thinking how fragile they are and yet how hard I have to crack them on the side of the glass bowl. Using a fork, I beat them, watching the yolk and the whites swirl together and become a light yellow froth. A splash of milk, some more mixing, and then I slip the slices of bread into the mixture and let each soak. Quickly, they absorb almost all of the egg batter. I have forgotten this.

The tablespoon of butter sizzles and begins to melt as soon as I drop it into the pan. And just before it browns, I slide in the bread.

The smells, the sounds, the mixing bowl, the spatula, the action—it is like coming home and not realizing how much you missed it until you step over the threshold.

While the French toast browns, I halve oranges and make juice on an old-fashioned squeezer, fitting the orange over the silver cup and then pulling down on the lever and watching the liquid spill out into the glass. I do this eight times, turn over the toast, set the table, and then take the plates out of the cabinet and put them in the oven to warm.

"It smells good." Charlie is standing on his crutches just inside the door, watching.

"French toast," I say, smiling at him.

"Dad—Justine is cooking," Charlie calls out, and then hobbles to the table.

I put a plate of the toast down in front of him, and he starts to pour on the syrup.

"I thought you'd given up your toque?" Austen says from the doorway.

"I did, too. But I woke up starving and had this craving for French toast. I made enough for you. Do you want some?"

WE HAVE FINISHED BREAKFAST. FRENCH toast is better with syrup than the way my mother used to make it. I've had two pieces, but I'm still hungry. I know better than to take more. Instead I sit and wonder how long this truce with Austen will last. Probably until his last cup of coffee of the morning.

"So . . . Are you still planning on leaving today?" he asks.

"Yes. I have to go back to New York and talk to my father. And meet my sister's fiancé."

There is a mess on the table: plates littered with the crumbs of the egg-dipped bread, drops of amber syrup, and glasses, each with just a bit of juice left over. The orange liquid is so bright; it is the only color on the table.

Whenever I think of this morning, which I will many times because it will stand as a marker between the past and the future, I will see those three glasses with what was left of the juice in them—the first juice I had squeezed and the first food I had cooked in four years.

"You saved Charlie's life," Austen says.

"I just came here to write a story," I say.

It is the wrong thing to say—almost cruel—but I want to remind him that he cannot trust me. I want him to remember that I am heartless.

We go back and forth, Austen and I, don't we? Even within the measure of one stanza we go from flat to sharp. Make music and then make something that is less than music. I've played the wrong note. And we should end here.

He frowns, his hands clench. A muscle in his neck twitches.

The phone rings, but Austen ignores it. I look at the phone. I want him to answer it so I can get up and go.

"I used to think it was a problem that you make me think about things other than the cello . . ." he is saying.

The phone rings a second time. He gets up and takes a step toward it and puts out his hand, except he doesn't pick it up yet: he has more to say.

"But maybe it isn't. Maybe I should be thinking about other things," he says.

I nod toward the phone. "You should answer it."

Something in his eyes goes dead. And I breathe a deep breath of relief. It's better not to see anything alive in his eyes. Not to be continually searching his face or listening to his next words for signs of his interest or delight or fervor. It's preferable not to want to feel his damn lips again. I like the disappointment; it cuts me loose and gives me the freedom to leave.

Annoyed, he grabs the phone and holds it up to his ear. "Hello?"

While he is talking, I go outside. The sky today is cloudy, with the sun breaking through for a few minutes at a time and then disappearing again. It's low tide, and up and down the shore, seagulls stand, many of them just placidly looking out at the water. But all the way down the beach, Ludwig is running back and forth in front of the caves and barking.

Suddenly I'm certain that the gardener in the yellow slicker must be Sophie in disguise and she's hiding somewhere in those caves where the police did not know to look. She had to be the one who saw Charlie fall on the sailboat and then called the police. And Ludwig knows it too.

Charlie and Helena are right, she is . . . No . . . how could Sophie—how could anyone—put the people she loved through this symphony of hell?

I'm running now. Feet pounding on the sand, crushing shells.

If she was depressed . . . if her medication needed adjusting . . . or if she stopped taking it again to write, she might have had a psychotic break. That would explain her lack of concern for her family and friends. It would even explain the return to the accent she'd learned to speak without when she first came to America.

Ludwig is panting but wags his tail as I approach.

I bend down and pat his head.

"You know where she is, don't you boy? Show me."

Ludwig takes off and I follow him past the first and the second opening. He stops at the third, waiting for me. Willing me to go in with his sad eyes.

The sand is glistening and the bright green algae growing on the rocks makes the walking treacherous. I tread carefully, stumbling more than once.

Ludwig's incessant barking urges me onward. I take a few tentative steps toward the narrow breach in the rock. At its entrance a miasma of dank air reaches out to envelop me, warning me away. There will be nothing agreeable in this cave. I know that from the odor, from the silence, and from the nervous way Ludwig paces back and forth in front of the opening; his head low, continually sniffing at ground he's already covered.

Sensing my hesitation, his bark becomes even more agitated. As I turn to calm him, I see a flash of light up at the house. A window opening gleams as the sun hits its surface.

And then I see her.

Helena leans out, searching the beach and finding . . . me. A curtain flutters, billows out, concealing her. When the wind dies and the fabric settles, she is gone.

Ludwig's barking has become more plaintive during this delay.

"Okay, boy." I proceed through the entrance and plunge into the gloom.

It takes a few seconds for my eyes to adjust.

This space is no deeper than twenty or thirty feet. The further back I peer, the darker it gets. It must be twenty degrees cooler inside than on the beach. With my first breath, the smell—fetid and briny—assaults me.

I slowly explore the small grotto, prepared for a sight as foul or frightening as the atmosphere. But that is all there is: the dark, the cold, and the stench.

And when I have accepted no one is here, I hear a faint cry.

"Sophie?" I call out.

Silence.

The noise comes from somewhere behind me. Turning slowly, afraid of what I will find, I'm relieved and disappointed to discover it's only Ludwig at the threshold of the cave, producing this almost human cry.

"There's nothing here, boy," I say. But his eyes implore me, and his whine becomes a whimper, echoing in the cave like a melancholy violin lament.

Certain he has my attention now, Ludwig skulks toward an outcropping of rock where three giant boulders form the left interior wall. The way he cautiously creeps forward alarms me. He knows something I can't even guess at. But I follow.

It is not until I get right up to them that I realize one of the rocks is not flush against the wall. There is a space behind this boulder large enough to walk behind.

As I disappear into yet another opening, the stench intensifies. The darkness deepens. I begin to shiver.

Ludwig no longer whines. I wish he would. This silence is worse, even more oppressive. I long to hear something other than my own breathing. I want to leave before my eyes adjust, before I find what lurks beyond this new blackness. But I don't.

I'm surprised when I can see far enough ahead of me to know there is nothing in this second cave either.

Until I glimpse another opening to one more cavern.

And then I hear the labored breathing that I know can only be coming from a human.

"Don't go any further. Leave her alone!"

I spin around. Helena's hair is plastered to her face. Sweat is dripping down her neck; her eyes are wild. Any semblance of pristine gentility is gone.

"Leave her alone. She doesn't need you here," she growls.

Rather than keeping me from taking those last steps, Helena's warning sends me rushing forward.

Yes, here she is. Here in this deeper darkness. In this quietude where I can no longer hear water lapping or birds crying.

There should be music. A solemn cello sonata. The banging of a drum. A bugle playing taps. Anything but dead silence.

I hold my breath, wanting to go. To run. To escape. But all I can do is stare at the corpse of the tall woman laid out on the floor of this black, stinking tomb.

"Leave her alone!" Helena rushes past me to stand in front of the body, shielding it from me. I see the pale soles of Sophie's swollen and rotting feet.

"Helena, how long have you known that Sophie was here?"

"She needed to recuperate after she fell off the boat. She hit her head on the rocks. She has a concussion. She needs peace and quiet so she can get better."

"Helena, Sophie is not—"

"Shhh," she hisses. "Shhh. You'll wake her. She needs to sleep, don't you understand? It's the only thing that will make her better."

Helena moves closer to Sophie's body, crouching at her side. Taking hold of Sophie's stiff, bloated hand, she strokes it. "Go now. Leave us. She needs sleep. She's going to be just fine."

As sickening as the stink is, I can't leave this crazed woman prostrate over her lover's body. I try to reason with her. "Helena, what we need to do is call—"

"Get out!" She rushes me, trying to push me out. Taller than me, and stronger—especially in her hysteria—she manages to throw me off balance.

Once I'm down, she returns to Sophie, whispering to her, "Just sleep . . . just sleep . . ." And then Helena bends down and kisses the lips of the dead woman she still loves so much she cannot bear to let go.

"Helena, we need to call the doctor." I'm trying to keep my voice calm. "He'll give Sophie medicine to make her better."

She looks over at me now as if this hadn't occurred to her, as if it were possible.

A sad, insane smile appears on her pale face. Helena allows me to lead her out of the alcove into the cave, then out to the beach and into the light.

FORTY-SEVEN

WHEN WE GOT back to the house, I called Austen, whispering as I told him the horrible news. He said he would call the police and asked me to stay with Helena until the police came. And then he said one word, his voice cracking on the second syllable of Charlie's name as he realized the terrible task he had ahead of him.

So I waited, sitting with Helena in the kitchen, both of us drinking tall glasses of water while the house full of Sophie's colleagues and students continued their vigil. None of them knew what I already knew and what Austen was telling Charlie.

I did not see Charlie or Austen again before leaving Euphonia.

The police came in the back door, and a silent ambulance drove down onto the beach. After I gave a statement and was free to go, I called a taxi and paid the driver over a hundred dollars to drive me all the way into New York.

I couldn't imagine sitting on a train with other people around me, stopping in all the towns between Greenwich and the city. I couldn't imagine being on a train with my mother's notebooks and the ashes of her love letters.

It is only an envelope of burned paper remains, but I keep it in my pocketbook, and on the ride back to the city, I touch it several times to make sure it is still there . . . not that I expect the envelope to have disappeared . . . but rather because I wish it would. The letters have confused me.

My mind ricochets between the images of Sophie's body and my mother's. Two women, one I saw dying, one I saw dead. One I knew only when she was alive, the other was dead the whole time I was getting to know her.

SWEETHEART. I CAN HEAR HER voice as her hand strokes my cheek. I push her away. But what about the letters? What about the lies?

Her hand comes back, undeterred. *Justine,* she whispers, trying to soothe me.

I want to lean into her, to disappear in the circle her arms make around me. No one has ever loved me the way my mother did. I have never loved anyone back the way I loved her. I was part of her. There was nothing complicated about it.

Have the letters changed that?

I HAVE THE TAXI STOP so I can drop my bags off at the apartment and then go straight to the restaurant. I don't call to check that it will be okay.

Standing in the kitchen doorway, I watch my father and Maddy doing prep. They work in practiced tandem: it is a satisfying partnership. I breathe in all the familiar smells that I know as well as my own face in the mirror. Parsley, sage, thyme, onions, garlic, oregano, wine, bread baking, chocolate, vanilla, saffron . . . all the scents . . . all the scents of my life.

He sees me first, then Maddy follows his glance.

"What did you do with her ashes?" I ask them. It is not what I expected I'd say.

WE DON'T SAY ANYTHING. We don't recite any poetry or offer up prayers. Our act of devotion is that we are here together, finally, to let her go.

She was born near here, on East End Avenue and Eighty-eighth

Street, in a hospital that was then called The Doctor's Hospital. When we were young, she sometimes brought Maddy and me uptown to this park to be with our grandmother—her mother—who still lived in the apartment where she had grown up.

Playing here, having picnics, watching tugboats chug up the river, my grandmother would—at my insistence—tell me stories about what my mother was like when she was my age.

I loved this park more than any other acre of green in New York because she had loved it here. And now she runs alongside us. I have seen enough photographs of her to recognize the six-year-old on roller skates. The ten-year-old on a bike—the wind blowing her hair out behind her. The twenty-year-old young mother walking with her own mother and her newborn baby on this boardwalk.

Specters of her.

I watch my father reach into a small white shopping bag and pull out a clear plastic pouch. A gold urn or a silver box would be fitting, but not a plastic bag. But there she is. Not gleaming white dust, but dull pulverized sand.

My father stands slightly in front of us, close to the iron railing. Maddy and I flank him and hide him from view, blocking him from the possibility of passersby, even though there is no one else here. We do this because it is illegal to throw anything into the river—even someone's ashes, even if she grew up on this shore.

And then before I am ready, as if he is pulling a bandage off quickly to lessen the slow pull of pain, my father empties the pouch over the water.

No.

Have I said this or thought it?

Quickly I lean forward and reach out with my hand cupped against the wind to catch her. A quarter of a teaspoon is all I get. Less than the amount of nutmeg that goes into Apple Humpty Dumplings.

Bone gray dust on my fingers.

Gritty.

Abrasive.

Granular.

Finding the right word does not help.

I lift my fingers toward my mouth to take this small part of her into me, to keep her with me.

Maddy grabs my hand and yanks it away. "You can't."

"Let go." I fight her.

I want to lick the powder off my fingers. Ingest her. Do this last thing to make her more mine, but I don't say any of this. There is no way to give such primitive thoughts words.

"Justine, stop." She won't let go and her grip on my wrist hurts.

If I could take in milk from her breast, why can't I swallow some of her bone?

"She's already in you, Justine. Her blood is flowing in your veins. Her laugh comes out of your throat. You are your mother's daughter, don't you know that? You were her heart," my sister tells me.

My father takes his handkerchief out of his pocket and, without asking me, wipes my fingers clean.

He removes all traces of my mother's remains from my skin.

"Let's go," he says quietly.

We turn, the three of us, and walk away. We have only taken a dozen steps when I stop. There is one thing left to do, back there on the boardwalk above the rushing water.

"I'll catch up with you," I say to them.

I PULL THE ENVELOPE OUT of my bag and shake its contents out over the current. I watch the ashes I brought back from Euphonia blow out in the breeze and drift down.

Her love letters follow her downriver and out to sea. I lean over the railing and look down into the swirling water.

"Good-bye, Mommy," I whisper into the air.

And then I turn my back on the river and walk to where my father and sister are standing.

"Thank you for waiting and not doing this without me."

"You didn't think we had, did you?" my sister asks.

I shake my head.

My sister is crying. And my father takes the same handkerchief he used to wipe my fingers minutes ago and gives it to her. I reach out to touch her arm and the diamond catches the sun. The ring is stone out now, and I stare at it and at my hand.

I somehow had expected to see my mother's hands—but my fingers are not as thin as my mother's. My fingernails are longer than hers. Our hands do not do the same things . . . mine touch keys on a computer, my mother's broke eggs and whipped cream and took baking pans out of the oven.

It's only the ring that is the same. And that is both enough and not too much.

"We should go get something to eat," my father says.

I nod because I am hungry and think that perhaps today, after we eat, I might finally feel satisfied, allowing a pleasure I have avoided until now.

FORTY-EIGHT

I T ' S B E E N S E V E N days but everything about Euphonia feels altered. At the gate, Sam waves me through with a sad smile, but at least the fear and the worry are gone from his face.

"You can park down by the boathouse. It's not far from there to the outdoor chapel," he says.

The trees are in full leaf, and the roses in the front of the house have bloomed. There are no storms on the horizon and no clouds in the sky. I stop the car at the house—leave the motor running, and get out just to throw a quarter in the fountain and touch Pan's flute.

I am here for Sophie's memorial service. Informed not by Charlie or Austen, who I have not talked to since the morning I left, but by Zoë.

Parking the car, I hear only the soft lapping of the water on the shore and the low murmur of hushed voices. Over a hundred people have gathered for the service and spill out past the pews onto the lawn that surrounds the chapel. On the stone altar there are ten musicians, most of whom I recognize as the students and colleagues of Sophie's who were staying at the house. Some are tuning up. Others are just sitting, instruments at their feet or on their lap, staring off into space.

I don't see Charlie. Or Austen.

I make my way over to Zoë and Stephen, Daphne and her husband, and offer condolences. It's uncomfortable, but it's the right thing for me to do. The only one to meet my gaze is Zoë, who gets up and comes over to thank me for coming. Around us I recognize many of the people who'd been here, just a week ago, helping search for Sophie. Except for Helena, who is notably absent. I ask Zoë about her.

"She's at Silver Hills, a treatment center in New Canaan," Zoë says, and then explains what took place after I left Euphonia.

HELENA HAD BEEN HELD ON suspicion of murder while the coroner's office performed a postmortem on Sophie's remains. There had never been any question that Helena was at the house the evening Sophie had taken out the boat—there were dozens of witnesses to attest to her whereabouts. But Helena's story about seeing the boat break apart on the rocks and running down to the shore to help Sophie had suggested the possibility that she and Sophie might have argued on the beach that night and that Helena could have caused her ex-lover's death.

Ultimately, the coroner had determined that the pattern of the bruises on Sophie's body and the placement of her head injury were consistent with slipping off the boat and falling onto the rocks. They were not bruises she could have obtained by being pushed or even falling, had she been standing on land.

After Helena was released and brought back to Euphonia, she attempted suicide with what was left of Sophie's medication. She spent two days in the Greenwich hospital and was then moved to the treatment center.

"She thinks she is Sophie," Zoë says. "And that Helena is the one who's died."

Helena has killed herself off to keep Sophie—her *other*—alive.

It's time to take our seats. Zoë goes back to sit with Sophie's family. And I find a place a few rows back.

"Excuse me." The accent is German.

It is the gardener, the older woman with the short gray hair and dirt under her fingernails.

"I think this is yours." She holds out my mother-of-pearl and silver pen.

For the last week, I couldn't remember where I'd lost it—maybe during my crazy run down to the dock or while I was scrambling from my boat to Charlie's.

I'd gotten over the loss of the computer, but the pen had been much worse.

"Where did you find that?" I ask her.

"You dropped it outside the maze," she says.

And now I remember standing in the rain and pulling the instructions out of my pocket and how the gardener had picked my pen up off the ground.

I SEE CHARLIE FIRST, HOBBLING on crutches toward the altar. He sees me, too, and tries to smile in greeting, but his lips can't quite move that far. Austen is at his side, his cello case in one hand, Charlie's violin case in the other. He doesn't see me at first. His eyes are focused on his son.

The movement of Charlie's head toward me makes Austen look my way, but only for a second. I can't read the expression on his face. I've never been able to.

After Austen helps Charlie take his seat and hands him his violin, he says something to him and then walks off the stone terraced altar and comes over to me.

I stand.

The rest of the orchestra continues to tune up.

"Who invited the press?" Austen asks. It is as if the week has not passed. His voice is as cold as it was that last morning.

"I came because . . ." I'm not sure I know what to say, so instead I hold out my empty hands to him. "Austen, I'm here for Charlie. For Zoë." I take a breath. "And for you."

"What about your story?"

I shake my head. "I can't write it."

"Why?"

"I don't have any objectivity. I'm too involved."

And then, even though I think he's a little reluctant, he gambles a smile. And it fills me up.

I think I have been heading toward him for a long time. I don't know if he's the direction I should be taking or if an emotion I have avoided till now—for so many wrong reasons—might be right. But I want to find out.

He reaches out and strums his fingers against my cheek. That's all. But in this moment, in this place, it is enough.

Austen returns to his son and takes the seat beside him, cello between his legs. There are a few more seconds of tuning. And then the service begins without words. None are necessary.

The panicked notes, wrong and discordant, all I ever heard from these players, are gone, replaced with the musical grace of practiced professionals as they perform one of Sophie's sonatas.

The music curls like a wave, and washes over all of us. The sound is vast and deep as it dips then lifts and rises into the clear sky. I have heard this music before. Austen used to play this when my mother lay dying and I would leave her bed to go to his, trying to find some respite.

I still miss her. But without the aching. As thankful as I am for that, I am also scared—who am I without that ache defining me?

The notes soar and plunge, transporting us all. Charlie is playing effortlessly, perfectly, despite his sadness. Every once in a while, glancing over at his father for reassurance, which Austen bestows with a simple nod. In losing his grandmother, Charlie found his father.

The air is full of the music; it bursts over us like an explosion of firecrackers.

I close my eyes and listen, and when I finally open them again, Austen is looking at me and it seems as if the notes he plays are all around me, drawing me close: it's a connection that lingers even as the requiem comes to its end.

ACKNOWLEDGMENTS

Thanks first and always to Loretta Barrett for being champion and friend—and to her associates Nick Mullendore and Allison Heiny.

Gratitude for exceptional editorial guidance and inspired collaboration to my amazing editors Linda Marrow and Dana Issacson—and to everyone at Ballantine for your hard work on my behalf.

To the unsung heroes who work in bookstores and put books into the hands of the people who matter the most—the dear readers.

Heartfelt appreciation to four tireless and special women I am lucky to know: Carol Fitzgerald of The Bookreporter Network (Bookreporter.com), Suzanne Beecher of ChapterADay.com, Karen Templer of Readerville.com, and Linda Richards of January-Magazine.com—all true patron saints of reading.

To a group of friends whose support and advice I probably depend on too much: Katharine Weber, Douglas Clegg, Mara Nathan, Lisa Ann Tucker, Gretchen Laskas, Anne Ursu, Alma Marceau, John Searles, Angela Hoy, CKCF, and Michael Bergmann.

Thank goodness for Readerville.com, where I've found wonderful, wise, and witty coffee-break buddies and title-testers extraordinaire.

To my family—especially my father—for their unfailing support and to Doug Scofield whose music and love are gifts I am thankful for every day. (Winka)

ABOUT THE AUTHOR

M. J. ROSE is the author of *Flesh Tones,
In Fidelity,* and *Lip Service*. She lives
in Greenwich, Connecticut.

Visit her Web site at www.mjrose.com.